Animalia Indica

Also by Sumana Roy

How I Became A Tree
Missing: A Novel
Out of Syllabus: Poems

Animalia Indica

THE FINEST ANIMAL STORIES IN INDIAN LITERATURE

edited by

Sumana Roy

illustrations by

Rohan Dahotre

ALEPH

ALEPH

ALEPH BOOK COMPANY
An independent publishing firm
promoted by ***Rupa Publications India***

First published in India in 2019
by Aleph Book Company
7/16 Ansari Road, Daryaganj
New Delhi 110 002

ISBN: 978-93-88292-57-3

Printed and bound in India by Replika Press Pvt. Ltd.

1 3 5 7 9 10 8 6 4 2

CONTENTS

SUMANA ROY
An Animal on Animals ix

1. RUDYARD KIPLING 2
Rikki-Tikki-Tavi
2. SARAT CHANDRA CHATTOPADHYAY 18
Mahesh
Translated from the Bengali by Arunava Sinha
3. PREMCHAND 30
A Tale of Two Bullocks
Translated from the Hindi by Rohit Manchanda
4. SHRIPAD NARAYAN PENDSE 44
Jumman
Translated from the Marathi by Shanta Gokhale
5. GEORGE ORWELL 82
Shooting an Elephant
6. THAKAZHI SIVASANKARA PILLAI 90
The Flood
Translated from the Malayalam by O. V. Usha
7. KHUSHWANT SINGH 98
The Mark of Vishnu
8. HABIB KAMRAN 103
Bulbuls
Translated from the Kashmiri by Neerja Mattoo

9. R. K. NARAYAN 131
A Horse and Two Goats
10. MANJULA PADMANABHAN 148
The Copper-tailed Skink
11. RUSKIN BOND 161
The Last Tiger
12. ACHYUTANANDA PATI 185
The Owlet Who Craved the Sun
Translated from the Odia by Shaswat Panda
13. VIKRAM SETH 193
The Crocodile and the Monkey
14. R. R. BORADE 199
Labour
Translated from the Marathi by Anjali Nerlekar
15. PAUL ZACHARIA 204
The Reflections of a Hen in Her Last Hour
Translated from the Malayalam by A. J. Thomas
16. NILANJANA ROY 208
The Summer of the Crows
17. PERUMAL MURUGAN 223
Poonachi
Translated from the Tamil by N. Kalyan Raman
18. MOTI LAL KEMMU 228
A Tale of Animals
Translated from the Hindi by Siddhartha Gigoo and Tej K. Zadoo
19. KANISHK THAROOR 233
Elephant at Sea
20. SUJATHA 247
Snake
Translated from the Tamil by Malini Seshadri

21. SYED MUHAMMAD ASHRAF 257

And Then Laughed the Hyena

Translated from the Urdu by M. Asaduddin

Acknowledgements 268

Notes to the Stories 270

Notes on the Authors 275

Notes on the Translators 280

AN ANIMAL ON ANIMALS

SUMANA ROY

As I write this, more a response than an introduction to a book of delightful stories by Indian writers about animals, I hear my seven-year-old nephew playing in the background. He wants to be an animal—most of his games involve impersonations of his favourite animals. I'm tempted to join him and his friend in the game, and I do, unable to hold myself back after I hear him say, 'Then you'll fall down and die—all dinosaurs died like that, falling down.' His friend attempts to mimic the imagined dinosaur, I come in and pretend to be another dinosaur, but am immediately shooed away: 'You're a human, you can't play with us.'

I want to ask my nephew what makes him want to imagine himself as an animal. It is a question I'd have liked to ask Kafka and the storytellers of the *Panchatantra* and the *Jataka Tales*. On the other side of language is the question I'd have liked to ask those we call animals—do they ever play games or tell stories imagining themselves as humans? It is possible that only the human is aware of being human in a way that an insect or bat isn't.

My nephew is not alone in his desire to become an animal, of course. Cinema, television shows, literature, video games, the automobile industry—all of these attest to man's subconscious desire to experience animal life as if we were not animals at all. There's a bit of forgetfulness involved here, and a little bit of desire—a playfulness and curiosity that works both ways now, in animals being turned into residents of human spaces, of homes and zoos, as well as the human's imagined life as a hybrid, half-human and half-animal.

I write this sitting inside a plane—I'm acutely aware of the animal-like ambition, to be a bird temporarily. So many humans inside a bird, in a way there can't be in the zoological world. The aeroplane is modern man's Trojan horse—man becoming animal, that animal swallowing many, many men temporarily, only to disgorge them later. As I began to collect stories for this anthology, helped by my editors, David Davidar (whose idea this book is, and who has directed me to most of the stories here), Aienla Ozukum and Isha Banerji, I had the sense of the blood of the *Panchatantra* running through the writers of the twentieth century in a way I hadn't anticipated at all.

Animalia Indica: The Finest Animal Stories in Indian Literature is the first anthology of its kind in the Indian subcontinent. While its ancestor might be seen to be the *Panchatantra*, with life and living illustrated through stories of animals, we are never allowed to forget that these animals are stand-ins for human prototypes. Morality is the axis of these ancient animal stories, common to almost all cultures across the world. The stories in *Animalia Indica*, written in the last one hundred years or so, in English and translated from various Indian languages into English, make us aware of how far the modern Indian has come from the moral imagination of the anonymous storytellers and story collectors of the *Panchatantra* and the *Jataka Tales*. Industrialization, journeys to the city, and the city itself led to the marginalization of animals from urban lives not just physically but also in the imagination. These stories by modern Indian writers, about goats and cows, birds and dogs, horses and snakes, and various other animals, give us unexpected pleasure in the discovery of a self within us of whose existence we are mostly unaware or even forgetful. These stories also challenge the centrality of the human figure, an inheritance from the Renaissance that now controls our storytelling impulses. They allow us to live like the best stories do—live another life, becoming a lizard on a window sill, an ant between toes, lice in hair, or zebras in zoos. This book is, however, not a zoo, a show of exhibits—it is a sanctuary, of human-animals with the needle tipping slightly towards the right. A modern European imagined a human turning into an insect about a hundred years ago. It changed Western literature and popular culture.

Has something similar taken place here? The hundred odd years that we chose as chronological bookends for this anthology owe as much to our curiosity to study this, as also our interest in how Homo sapiens from the Indian subcontinent started looking at their relationship with animals after 1859, after Charles Darwin had made us aware that we, too, were *only* animals.

The awareness of these developments, of science annotating the imagination, made us decide that folk tales or children's stories, whose character had remained largely unchanged, did not really belong to this book. The logic of selection that we'd set ourselves, primarily with the time period, meant that we would need to include not just 'Indian' writers but also those like George Orwell and Rudyard Kipling, those who had lived in the country and written about animals—these stories (and I say 'story' even though Orwell's 'story' is bibliographically listed as an essay, because the subject is based on what we now know to be a piece of fiction) allow us an entry into the colonial imagination and its relation with animals. Nearly half of these stories were written originally in English; apart from a few excerpts from long fiction, Motilal Kemmu's Hindi novella, Perumal Murugan's novel about a black goat, Nilanjana Roy's novel about cats and their familiars in Delhi, and Ruskin Bond's novella about a tiger, the rest are short stories. As we looked through translations of stories from the Indian languages, we noticed that many of these stories did not travel well when translated into English. Another word about the selection: this anthology does not aim to be representative—not of India and its languages (this book is not an encyclopaedia); nor is it a version of a natural history museum where all specimens of animal life can be found.

The title is quite self-explanatory: 'Animalia' refers to the animal kingdom, and 'Indica', an older name of India found in Greek and Latin texts, to writers from India. The writers are 'Indian', but is there such a thing as an 'Indian animal' too? A little earlier, I mentioned a European writer imagining a human turning into an insect—one of the transformative moments in modern literature. What is the Indian counterpart to that revolutionary act in European literature? Or, to put it differently, how have 'Indian' animals marked our literature? Do the animals in the *Panchatantra* and *Aesop's Fables* behave similarly or in different ways in similar situations? Is it possible that the birth of our nation, the invasion of technology, and the rise of individualism affected animals as much as they did humans? The Indian cow, to take the easiest example, is quite obviously not the same as the 'non-Indian' cow, and the Indian elephant is not the same as an elephant from other parts of the world. As the scholar Rachel Dwyer reminds us: 'Early Europeans found the animal gods of Hinduism the most distasteful…they were seen as "primitive", or "low class or indigenous". In other words, these deities were seen as too worldly compared to the more abstract, classical deities. Yet, other deities are also animals or part animal, including the avatars of Vishnu; Hanuman; and many mythical creatures, and the Jatakas tell the stories of the Buddha's incarnations in various animal forms.' I am tempted to believe that these aren't just stories by Indian writers about animals; these are stories by Indian writers about Indian animals.

Take the two kinds of animals in R. K. Narayan's story—a horse and two goats, which is, not without reason, the title of the story itself. The goats are alive, not losing an opportunity to eat whatever they find edible; the horse is a statue. The Indian man is interested only in the goats, and how they can keep a poor man like him alive; the American is interested only in the statue of the horse, to the point of being almost blind to the presence of the goats. It is not only that the Indian Tamil speaker and the American man do not understand each other's language—even their animals come from different linguistic spaces, one from life, the other from art. I found myself thinking about the Kala Ghoda statue in Bombay as I read Narayan's story, its history and its life in the present, in the city's art district. The American thinks of the future, he's making plans about how he could carry the statue to his house in America, where he might place the statue. The Indian recounts, in a rehearsed manner but with great belief and passion, the significance of the horse from mythology. It is, thus, not only that the kinds of animals are different—they inspire different kinds of reactions in those who observe and interact with them, particularly how they respond to time.

The Narayan story underlines a trope that one finds in many of the stories here—the Westerner's interest in taming or controlling the 'Indian animal'. In George Orwell's 'Shooting the Elephant', we are made aware of the same urge:

> And it was at this moment, as I stood there with the rifle in my hands, that I first grasped the hollowness, the futility of the white man's dominion in the East. Here was I, the white man with his gun, standing in front of the unarmed native crowd—seemingly the leading actor of the piece; but in reality I was only an absurd puppet pushed to and fro by the will of those yellow faces behind. I perceived in this moment that when the white man turns tyrant it is his own freedom that he destroys. He becomes a sort of hollow, posing dummy, the conventionalized figure of a sahib. For it is the condition of his rule that he shall spend his life in trying to impress the 'natives', and so in every crisis he has got to do what the 'natives' expect of him.

The animal-controlling mission, which is invariably tied to masculinity—a fact that I'm reminded of when I see how few women characters there are in the stories—is reiterated time and again. I'd like to spend a moment comparing the elephant in Orwell's story with the elephant in Kanishk Tharoor's story, 'Elephant at Sea'. In both, the elephant is an 'Indian animal'. Tharoor's title, quite the obverse of Orwell's, acknowledges, even if slyly through metaphor ('at sea'), the endangered life of the elephant—by putting the elephant on a boat and displacing it from its natural habitat. Tharoor makes us recall the culture of cruelty towards circus animals, but the direction of the elephant's journey, from India to Africa, is one that also speaks to the white man in Orwell's story. The two stories, when read together, also force us to look at the politics of migration, and how they apply differently to human and animal life: the white man in India, the controller; the Indian elephant in Morocco, the controlled. It is one of life's coincidences that I came to Tharoor's story a few days after reading Rachel Dwyer's essay on the elephant-god, Ganesha, Siddhivinayak. The cruelty in Orwell's story seems even more disturbing when I read these lines:

> In India, the hit film *Haathi mere Saathi* (The Elephants Are My Friends, dir. M. A. Thirumugham, 1971) features a boy who was raised by elephants who show him more kindness than human beings, their loyalty and self-sacrifice making them seem like humans—or gods—and their empathy and gentleness as well as warm companionship make them even more loveable as they hug the hero with their trunks.

The white man's shooting the elephant is representative of his conquest of a land and all its inhabitants, just as the Moroccan princess's desire for the animal, to ride it, perhaps come from the same space, though it has been feminized. In a telling passage in Tharoor's story, the elephant on the ship confronts a whale—the humans around it immediately presume a kind of tension between the two animals. The reason is primarily taxonomical, and therefore the presumptions are utterly human—the whale, they think, is the 'elephant of the sea'. In moments such as these, in this story and many others, we are brought face to face, on the level of metaphor, with interference by Homo sapiens in the rest of the kingdom; as flies to wanton boys, truly.

The American woman in Manjula Padmanabhan's story, 'The Copper-tailed Skink', who we are never allowed to forget is childless, is guilty of the same. She has come to India on a field trip, and is looking for 'samples'. She registers things that somehow come to be related—the sad irony of being childless in an overpopulated country like India, the discovery of two lizards, both female. Much that happens in the story is about laying eggs in our subconscious: How do animals—and humans—reproduce? how will they continue to do so in a changing time, in a confused world? Eggs, and how they transform into things that fly and climb, seem to fascinate the human mammal, perhaps because evolution has denied it this opportunity. Habib Kamran's 'Bulbuls' documents this fascination and curiosity in a manner that brings in the ethics about human interference in the larger world of animals. Should man save the tiny bulbuls from being killed by a cat? On the surface, that seems to be the most natural thing to do, for birds, because of their size, beauty and vulnerability, inspire kindness in us, in a way larger animals do not. It is one of the truths these stories provide—that our emotions, of awe, fear, beauty, kindness are, in many ways, dependent on the size and shape of the animals. The story by Sujatha (the pseudonym of S. Rangarajan), 'Snake', is a study of this emotion—why does the body of a snake generate fear and aversion in us? How many of us buy soft toys of snakes, for instance?

This is largely a book of stories in prose, but there are a couple of poems, by Rudyard Kipling and Vikram Seth. Reading them aloud—as I suppose rhyming verse is meant to be read—I wondered which form animals might prefer: prose or poetry. The human imagination has liked to put birdcall and the sounds made by animals into what is similar to the refrain in poetry: a kind of repetition (visible in Kipling's name of Rikki-Tikki-Tavi too), best exemplified in the children's-rhyme 'Old MacDonald had a farm', with its moo-moo-here and moo-moo-there, and so on.

Seth takes the familiar story of the crocodile and the monkey but changes the form we have so far received it in. What does that do to the story centuries later, and what does it say about the modern Indian's imagination? Verse, because of the metre Seth uses and the form he employs, takes us back to a time when this rhythm may have originated, closer to the time when this might have been a preferred way of telling such a story. In doing so, Seth unconsciously makes us aware of how far the human has moved away from the animal-world. Verse holds this animal world like amber does dead flies—it seems to be the only way to remind ourselves of what has now been lost to the point of extinction, not just the animals but that world of far greater osmosis between humans and the rest of the animal family.

Seth's story in verse has its axis in a familiar binary—one between land and water. The monkey is an animal of the land, the crocodile of water. One of the central thrills of the story is this—that other animals, besides the amphibians, of course, are usually at home in only one of the elements. Only a human could have written this story, for it is only the human, who, in spite of being a creature of land, has taught themselves to swim like animals in water and invent things that allow them to be a temporary residents of air. That said, in both air and water, man's life is one of fortunate tenancy. Only of land is man a true resident. This awareness marks these stories—in 'The Flood', for instance, the dog's helplessness, at being stranded on a roof while his owner and their neighbours have abandoned the place to escape from the flood, is actually a representation of the human's fear of water, one that goes back to Noah's Ark. This story recalls older ones, as if the stories and animals are connected by a similar arc of evolution. Reading 'The Flood', I thought of a familiar tale that Anand Vivek Taneja recounts in his essay 'Saintly Animals':

> There were four men who were travellers, and the fifth of them was a dog. The dog expired on the bank of water. The men said, 'This poor creature was a companion to us. Let us bury him and leave a sign, so that when we come back we may remember the place where our dog is buried.' Before they left they made a mound of earth that had the appearance of a grave.

The old fears have changed form, and I find it interesting to notice how they have been transformed in literature. The snake, for instance, has had a cursed life there, right from the Bible onwards—in the story by S. Rangarajan, we watch, with pity and fear, the old Aristotelian emotions of tragedy, as the mention of the snake itself seems to compulsorily invite the desire in humans to kill. Fear of the snake is also the animating impulse in Kipling's 'Rikki-Tikki-Tavi' and Khushwant Singh's 'The Mark of Vishnu'. This has caused me the greatest bewilderment while reading the stories—this new world, so completely ensconced in the urban, that the presence of animals, unless domesticated into 'pets', causes fear. Humans and animals co-existed even in residential spaces once, not as pets but 'naturally', as humans do with each other. Like a parent finds it difficult to imagine a life before they became parents, modern man seems to have been inflicted by this amnesia too. Even insects terrify us, as if reminding us of a past life where we were them.

I find myself making comparisons as I read through the stories. I miss something—it is the sound of the animals speaking. Animals in the *Panchatantra*, as in other folktales, speak—their speech is comprehensible to us. I'm tempted to say that they speak in the language of men. But what I actually mean is that at that time in the history of the world, men and animals shared a common language. The animals in these stories rarely speak—they make sounds, scary sounds, imagined sounds, like the chat-chat of the hyena or the shoon-shoon in Moti Lal Kemmu's story. Their voices have been taken away from them, their desires reduced to onomatopoeia, so that we don't know whether they are happy or sad, complaining or content. Sometimes, when they speak, as in Kipling's 'Rikki-Tikki-Tavi', Premchand's 'A Tale of Two Bullocks', Nilanjana Roy's 'The Summer of the Crows', Vikram Seth's 'The Crocodile and the Monkey', Moti Lal Kemmu's 'A Tale of Animals', R. R. Borade's 'Labour', Achyutananda Pati's 'The Owlet Who Craved the Sun' and Paul Zacharia's 'The Reflections of a Hen in Her Last Hour', I find myself comparing their speech patterns, as if I were a student of linguistics. What does their new language tell us about the new world? Sometimes, when an animal gets a speaking part, as in 'The Reflections of a Hen in Her Last Hour', it is just before its death. Which brings us to the unavoidable question—why do so many of the animals in these stories die? And the related footnote—do they die in the folktales? Yes, they do, from some moral vice. But in these stories, the reason for their death is, almost always, man. Whether it's poverty that doesn't allow the cow Mahesh in Sarat Chandra's story any food, not even water in a famine-hit land, or a situation that is the obverse of this one, as in the Marathi story 'Jumman', where the goat is turned into a god and worshipped, an action that bullies the animal and eventually results in its death, or the elephant and tiger shot in Orwell's and Bond's, all of them point to the obvious—what one animal has done to the rest of the animal world.

R. K. Narayan's story also holds in it another recurring motif running through stories about animals from rural India—the sale of animals. Cows and goats, even the baby goat Poonachi, who looks more like a kitten than goat, and of course, a statue of a horse—all of these must be sold to save their owners. And many of these sold animals return to their owners in spite of being sold—there is a great moving moral in this, one still left untouched by our moral consciousness. That is also a subject that is largely foreign to the oldest stories of animals in our subcontinent.

Drawing this unavoidable lineage between the folktales and this anthology also reminds me of something inescapable about our passage into modernity—the *Panchatantra*, for all we know, wasn't meant to be stories for children in the way they've been categorised today, in the same way perhaps that the Gita wasn't just meant to be a 'Holy' book once. That the stories in these folktales were not restricted to a young age group as they are today tell us, too, why the stories in *Animalia Indica* are meant primarily for adults—the animals are a stand-in for humans in the latter's earliest stories in the way they are not in any of the stories in the anthology, except Seth's re-creation of the tale in verse. Does that explain why so many of the human characters in these stories have names beginning with the 'm' sound—manu, manus, man? Animal was both companion and competitor, and it might have been this that made them an easy substitute to the human in their stories. That, sadly, isn't true anymore, and what we have instead, playing as a recurrent theme in these stories, is isolation, both of man and the animal. The animal is alone in a way that they aren't in any of the folktales—the plight of the dog on the roof, killed by starvation and isolation in 'The Flood' is actually the story of the animal now. Even as pets in our households, they are as alone as Robinson Crusoe was on that island, without their own species for company.

I have, just a little while ago, remarked on the emotion of fear that drives many of the stories in this anthology. Man's fear of the animal, interestingly, is largely absent in the folk narratives. The separation between the human and the animal world is, quite obviously, the reason behind this fear—it manifests itself in many ways, whether in man's need to kill the animal in Orwell's story, even though there might not be any real need to, or to kill it because of its lack of resemblance to us, the reason it is easier for us to kill a mosquito than a human. In a story like 'And Then Laughed the Hyena' we see the tremulous fear of the animal as kidnapper, running away with the human child; in 'The Mark of Vishnu' we see a different contour of fear, not just of ignorance of the other but a frustrating lack of control that necessitates violence. Much of the violence in the pages of this book comes from that space—man's urge for power, his attribution of lack of reason to the animal and consequent self-sanctioning of violence to control anything that lives outside the perimeter of reason.

Wendy Doniger, in an essay, 'Cruelty and the Imagination of Animals in India', writes:

> The distinction between (allowed) cruelty to animals and (disallowed) cruelty to people is sanctioned in the Mahabharata story of Mandavya, who is punished, by being impaled alive, for a crime of which he is innocent. When he complains to the god Dharma about this injustice (that is, a-dharma), Dharma says, 'You stuck blades of grass up the tails of little butterflies when you were a child, and this is the fruit of that karma.' Mandavya complains, 'For a rather small offense you have given me an enormous punishment,' and he curses Dharma to be born as a man of low caste. But Mandavya also establishes a moral boundary exculpating children under the age of fourteen of the sin of gratuitous cruelty to animals, which is regarded as 'rather a small offense' compared with the similar treatment of a human. In another famous anecdote in the Mahabharata, Dharma himself takes the form of a dog, to whom Dharma's son, the king, expressly refuses to be cruel.

I'd like to end by saying it seems slightly wrong that a human—an animal that likes to think of itself as much more than animal—should be allowed the privilege of writing an introduction to a book of stories about animals. And a delightful privilege it has been. These stories, that 'instruct and delight', to use Philip Sidney's time-beaten phrase, that move us with tenderness and beauty, while making us aware of the vulnerability of being animal, also, in the end, remind us of the joys of being human—for the pleasure of reading these stories is a uniquely human delight.

RIKKI-TIKKI-TAVI

RUDYARD KIPLING

At the hole where he went in
Red-Eye called to Wrinkle-Skin.
Hear what little Red-Eye saith:
'Nag, come up and dance with death!'

Eye to eye and head to head,
(Keep the measure, Nag.)
This shall end when one is dead;
(At thy pleasure, Nag.)
Turn for turn and twist for twist—(Run and hide thee, Nag.)
Hah! The hooded Death has missed!
(Woe betide thee, Nag!)

This is the story of the great war that Rikki-tikki-tavi fought single-handed, through the bathrooms of the big bungalow in Segowlee cantonment. Darzee, the tailorbird, helped him, and Chuchundra, the muskrat, who never comes out into the middle of the floor, but always creeps round by the wall, gave him advice; but Rikki-tikki did the real fighting.

He was a mongoose, rather like a little cat in his fur and his tail, but quite like a weasel in his head and his habits. His eyes and the end of his restless nose were pink; he could scratch himself anywhere he pleased, with any leg, front or back, that he chose to use; he could fluff up his tail till it looked like a bottle-brush, and his war cry, as he scuttled through the long grass, was: 'Rikk-tikk-tikki-tikki-tchk!'

One day, a high summer flood washed him out of the burrow

where he lived with his father and mother, and carried him, kicking and clucking, down a roadside ditch. He found a little wisp of grass floating there, and clung to it till he lost his senses. When he revived, he was lying in the hot sun on the middle of a garden path, very draggled indeed, and a small boy was saying: 'Here's a dead mongoose. Let's have a funeral.'

'No,' said his mother; 'let's take him in and dry him. Perhaps he isn't really dead.'

They took him into the house, and a big man picked him up between his finger and thumb, and said he was not dead but half choked; so they wrapped him in cotton wool, and warmed him, and he opened his eyes and sneezed.

'Now,' said the big man (he was an Englishman who had just moved into the bungalow); 'don't frighten him, and we'll see what he'll do.'

It is the hardest thing in the world to frighten a mongoose, because he is eaten up from nose to tail with curiosity. The motto of all the mongoose family is 'Run and find out,' and Rikki-tikki was a true mongoose. He looked at the cotton wool, decided that it was not good to eat, ran all around the table, sat up and put his fur in order, scratched himself, and jumped on the small boy's shoulder.

'Don't be frightened, Teddy,' said his father. 'That's his way of making friends.'

'Ouch! He's tickling under my chin,' said Teddy.

Rikki-tikki looked down between the boy's collar and neck, snuffed at his ear, and climbed down to the floor, where he sat rubbing his nose.

'Good gracious,' said Teddy's mother, 'and that's a wild creature! I suppose he's so tame because we've been kind to him.'

'All mongooses are like that,' said her husband. 'If Teddy doesn't pick him up by the tail, or try to put him in a cage, he'll run in and out of the house all day long. Let's give him something to eat.'

They gave him a little piece of raw meat. Rikki-tikki liked it immensely, and when it was finished he went out into the veranda and sat in the sunshine and fluffed up his fur to make it dry to the roots. Then he felt better.

'There are more things to find out about in this house,' he said to himself, 'than all my family could find out in all their lives. I shall certainly stay and find out.'

He spent all that day roaming over the house. He nearly drowned himself in the bathtubs, put his nose into the ink on a writing table, and burnt it on the end of the big man's cigar, for he climbed up in the big man's lap to see how writing was done. At nightfall he ran into Teddy's nursery to watch how kerosene lamps were lighted, and when Teddy went to bed Rikki-tikki climbed up too; but he was a restless companion, because he had to get up and attend to every noise all through the night, and find out what made it. Teddy's mother and father came in, the last thing, to look at their boy, and Rikki-tikki was awake on the pillow. 'I don't like that,' said Teddy's mother; 'he may bite the child.'

'He'll do no such thing,' said the father.

'Teddy's safer with that little beast than if he had a bloodhound to watch him. If a snake came into the nursery now...'

But Teddy's mother wouldn't think of anything so awful.

Early in the morning Rikki-tikki came to early breakfast in the veranda riding on Teddy's shoulder, and they gave him banana and some boiled eggs; and he sat on all their laps one after the other, because every well-brought-up mongoose always hopes to be a house-mongoose some day and have rooms to run about in, and Rikki-tikki's mother (she used to live in the General's house at Segowlee) had carefully told Rikki what to do if ever he came across white men.

Then Rikki-tikki went out into the garden to see what was to be seen. It was a large garden, only half cultivated, with bushes as big as summer houses of Marshal Niel roses, lime and orange trees, clumps of bamboos, and thickets of high grass. Rikki-tikki licked his lips. 'This is a splendid hunting ground,' he said, and his tail grew bottle-brushy at the thought of it, and he scuttled up and down the garden, snuffing here and there till he heard very sorrowful voices in a thorn bush.

It was Darzee, the tailorbird, and his wife. They had made a beautiful nest by pulling two big leaves together and stitching them up the edges with fibres, and had filled the hollow with cotton and downy fluff. The nest swayed to and fro, as they sat on the rim and cried.

'What is the matter?' asked Rikki-tikki.

'We are very miserable,' said Darzee. 'One of our babies fell out of the nest yesterday, and Nag ate him.'

'H'm!' said Rikki-tikki, 'that is very sad—but I am a stranger here. Who is Nag?'

Darzee and his wife only cowered down in the nest without answering, for from the thick grass at the foot of the bush there came a low hiss—a horrid cold sound that made Rikki-tikki jump back two clear feet. Then inch by inch out of the grass rose up the head and spread hood of Nag, the big black cobra, and he was five feet long from tongue to tail. When he had lifted one-third of himself clear of the ground, he stayed balancing to and fro exactly as a dandelion-tuft balances in the wind, and he looked at Rikki-tikki with the wicked snake's eyes that never change their expression, whatever the snake may be thinking of.

'Who is Nag?' said he. '*I* am Nag. The great God Brahm put his mark upon all our people when the first cobra spread his hood to keep the sun off Brahm as he slept. Look, and be afraid!'

He spread out his hood more than ever, and Rikki-tikki saw the spectacle-mark on the back of it that looks exactly like the eye part of a hook-and-eye fastening. He was afraid for the minute; but it is impossible for a mongoose to stay frightened for any length of time, and though Rikki-tikki had never met a live cobra before, his mother had fed him on dead ones, and he knew that all a grown mongoose's business in life was to fight and eat snakes. Nag knew that too, and at the bottom of his cold heart he was afraid.

'Well,' said Rikki-tikki, and his tail began to fluff up again, 'marks or no marks, do you think it is right for you to eat fledglings out of a nest?'

Nag was thinking to himself, and watching the least little movement in the grass behind Rikki-tikki. He knew that mongooses in the garden meant death sooner or later for him and his family, but he wanted to get Rikki-tikki off his guard. So he dropped his head a little, and put it on one side.

'Let us talk,' he said. 'You eat eggs. Why should not I eat birds?'

'Behind you! Look behind you!' sang Darzee.

Rikki-tikki knew better than to waste time in staring. He jumped up in the air as high as he could go, and just under him whizzed by the head of Nagaina, Nag's wicked wife. She had crept up behind him as he was talking, to make an end of him; and he heard her savage hiss as the stroke missed. He came down almost across her back, and if he had been an old mongoose he would have known that then was the time to break her back with one bite; but he was afraid of the terrible lashing return-stroke of the cobra. He bit, indeed, but did not bite long enough, and he jumped clear of the whisking tail, leaving Nagaina torn and angry.

'Wicked, wicked Darzee!' said Nag, lashing up as high as he could reach toward the nest in the thornbush; but Darzee had built it out of reach of snakes, and it only swayed to and fro.

Rikki-tikki felt his eyes growing red and hot (when a mongoose's eyes grow red, he is angry), and he sat back on his tail and hind legs like a little kangaroo, and looked all round him, and chattered with rage. But Nag and Nagaina had disappeared into the grass. When a snake misses its stroke, it never says anything or gives any sign of what it means to do next. Rikki-tikki did not care to follow them, for he did not feel sure that he could manage two snakes at once. So he trotted off to the gravel path near the house, and sat down to think. It was a serious matter for him.

If you read the old books of natural history, you will find they say that when the mongoose fights the snake and happens to get bitten, he runs off and eats some herb that cures him. That is not true. The victory is only a matter of quickness of eye and quickness of foot—snake's blow against mongoose's jump—and as no eye can follow the motion of a snake's head when it strikes, that makes things much more wonderful than any magic herb. Rikki-tikki knew he was a young mongoose, and it made him all the more pleased to think that he had managed to escape a blow from behind. It gave him confidence in himself, and when Teddy came running down the path, Rikki-tikki was ready to be petted.

But just as Teddy was stooping, something flinched a little in the dust, and a tiny voice said: 'Be careful. I am death!' It was Karait, the dusty brown snakeling that lies for choice on the dusty earth; and his bite is as dangerous as the cobra's. But he is so small that nobody thinks of him, and so he does the more harm to people.

Rikki-tikki's eyes grew red again, and he danced up to Karait with the peculiar rocking, swaying motion that he had inherited from his family. It looks very funny, but it is so perfectly balanced a gait that you can fly off from it at any angle you please; and in dealing with snakes this is an advantage. If Rikki-tikki had only known, he was doing a much more dangerous thing than fighting Nag, for Karait is so small, and can turn so quickly, that unless Rikki bit him close to the back of the head, he would get the return-stroke in his eye or lip. But Rikki did not know: his eyes were all red, and he rocked back and forth, looking for a good place to hold. Karait struck out. Rikki jumped sideways and tried to run in, but the wicked little dusty grey head lashed within a fraction of his shoulder, and he had to jump over the body, and the head followed his heels close.

Teddy shouted to the house: 'Oh, look here! Our mongoose is killing a snake'; and Rikki-tikki heard a scream from Teddy's mother. His father ran out with a stick, but by the time he came up, Karait had lunged out once too far, and Rikki-tikki had sprung, jumped on the snake's back, dropped his head far between his forelegs, bitten as high up the back as he could get hold, and rolled away. That bite paralysed Karait, and Rikki-tikki was just going to eat him up from the tail, after the custom of his family at dinner, when he remembered that a full meal makes a slow mongoose, and if wanted all his strength and quickness ready, he must keep himself thin.

He went away for a dust-bath under the castor-oil bushes, while Teddy's father beat the dead Karait. 'What is the use of that?' thought Rikki-tikki. 'I have settled it all'; and then Teddy's mother picked him up from the dust and hugged him, crying that he had saved Teddy from death, and Teddy's father said that he was a providence, and Teddy looked on with big, scared eyes. Rikki-tikki was rather amused at all the fuss, which, of course, he did not understand. Teddy's mother might just as well have petted Teddy for playing in the dust. Rikki was thoroughly enjoying himself.

That night, at dinner, walking to and fro among the wine glasses on the table, he could have stuffed himself three times over with nice things; but he remembered Nag and Nagaina, and though it was very pleasant to be patted and petted by Teddy's mother, and to sit on Teddy's shoulder, his eyes would get red from time to time, and he would go off into his long war-cry of 'Rikk-tikk-tikki-tikki-tchk!'

Teddy carried him off to bed, and insisted on Rikki-tikki sleeping under his chin. Rikki-tikki was too well bred to bite or scratch, but as soon as Teddy was asleep he went off for his nightly walk round the house, and in the dark he ran up against Chuchundra, the muskrat, creeping around by the wall. Chuchundra is a broken-hearted little beast. He whimpers and cheeps all the night, trying to make up his mind to run into the middle of the room, but he never gets there.

'Don't kill me,' said Chuchundra, almost weeping. 'Rikki-tikki, don't kill me.'

'Do you think a snake-killer kills muskrats?' said Rikki-tikki scornfully.

'Those who kill snakes get killed by snakes,' said Chuchundra, more sorrowfully than ever. 'And how am I to be sure that Nag won't mistake me for you some dark night?'

'There's not the least danger,' said Rikki-tikki; 'but Nag is in the garden, and I know you don't go there.'

'My cousin Chua, the rat, told me—' said Chuchundra, and then he stopped.

'Told you what?'

'H'sh! Nag is everywhere, Rikki-tikki. You should have talked to Chua in the garden.'

'I didn't—so you must tell me. Quick Chuchundra, or I'll bite you!'

Chuchundra sat down and cried till the tears rolled off his whiskers. 'I am a very poor man,' he sobbed. 'I never had spirit enough to run out into the middle of the room. H'sh! I mustn't tell you anything. Can't you *hear*, Rikki-tikki?'

Rikki-tikki listened. The house was as still as still, but he thought he could just catch the faintest scratch-scratch in the world—a noise as faint as that of a wasp walking on a windowpane—the dry scratch of a snake's scales on brickwork.

'That's Nag or Nagaina,' he said to himself; 'and he is crawling into the bathroom sluice. You're right, Chuchundra, I should have talked to Chua.'

He stole off to Teddy's bathroom, but there was nothing there, and then to Teddy's mother's bathroom. At the bottom of the smooth plaster wall there was a brick pulled out to make a sluice for the bathwater, and as Rikki-tikki stole in by the masonry curb where the bath is put, he heard Nag and Nagaina whispering together outside in the moonlight.

'When the house is emptied of people,' said Nagaina to her husband, '*he* will have to go away, and then the garden will be our own again. Go in quietly, and remember that the big man who killed Karait is the first one to bite. Then come out and tell me, and we will hunt for Rikki-tikki together.'

'But are you sure that there is anything to be gained by killing the people?' said Nag.

'Everything. When there were no people in the bungalow, did we have any mongoose in the garden? So long as the bungalow is empty, we are king and queen of the garden; and remember that as soon as our eggs in the melon bed hatch (as they may tomorrow), our children will need room and quiet.'

'I had not thought of that,' said Nag. 'I will go, but there is no need that we should hunt for Rikki-tikki afterwards. I will kill the big man and his wife, and the child if I can, and come away quietly. The bungalow will be empty, and Rikki-tikki will go.'

Rikki-tikki tingled all over with rage and hatred at this, and then Nag's head came through the sluice, and his five feet of cold body followed it. Angry as he was, Rikki-tikki was very frightened as he saw the size of the big cobra. Nag coiled himself up, raised his head, and looked into the bathroom in the dark, and Rikki could see his eyes glitter.

'Now, if I kill him here, Nagaina will know; and if I fight him on the open floor, the odds are in his favour. What am I to do?' said Rikki-tikki-tavi.

Nag waved to and fro, and then Rikki-tikki heard him drinking from the biggest water jar that was used to fill the bath. 'That is good,' said the snake. 'Now, when Karait was killed, the big man had a stick. He may have that stick still, but when he comes in to bathe in the morning he will not have a stick. I shall wait here till he comes. Nagaina—do you hear me?—I shall wait here in the cool till daytime.'

There was no answer from outside, so Rikki-tikki knew Nagaina had gone away. Nag coiled himself down, coil by coil, round the bulge at the bottom of the water jar, and Rikki-tikki stayed still as death. After an hour he began to move, muscle by muscle, toward the jar. Nag was asleep, and Rikki-tikki looked at his big back, wondering which would be the best place for a good hold. 'If I don't break his back at the first jump,' said Rikki, 'he can still fight; and if he fights—O Rikki!' He looked at the thickness of the neck below the hood, but that was too much for him; and a bite near the tail would only make Nag savage.

'It must be the head,' he said at last; 'the head above the hood; and when I am once there, I must not let go.'

Then he jumped. The head was lying a little clear of the water jar, under the curve of it; and, as his teeth met, Rikki braced his back against the bulge of the red earthenware to hold down the head. This gave him just one second's purchase, and he made the most of it. Then he was battered to and fro as a rat is shaken by a dog—to and fro on the floor, up and down, and round in great circles; but his eyes were red, and he held on as the body cart-whipped over the floor, upsetting the tin dipper and the soap dish and the flesh brush, and banged against the tin side of the bath. As he held he closed his jaws tighter and tighter, for he made sure he would be banged to death, and, for the honour of his family, he preferred to be found with his teeth locked. He was dizzy, aching, and felt shaken to pieces when something went off like a thunderclap just behind him; a hot wind knocked him senseless, and red fire singed his fur. The big man had been wakened by the noise, and had fired both barrels of a shotgun into Nag just behind the hood.

Rikki-tikki held on with his eyes shut, for now he was quite sure he was dead; but the head did not move, and the big man picked him up and said: 'It's the mongoose again, Alice; the little chap has saved *our* lives now.' Then Teddy's mother came in with a very white face, and saw what was left of Nag, and Rikki-tikki dragged himself to Teddy's bedroom and spent half the rest of the night shaking himself tenderly to find out whether he was really broken into forty pieces, as he fancied.

When morning came he was very stiff, but well pleased with his doings. 'Now I have Nagaina to settle with, and she will be worse than five Nags, and there's no knowing when the eggs she spoke of will hatch. Goodness! I must go and see Darzee,' he said.

Without waiting for breakfast, Rikki-tikki ran to the thorn bush where Darzee was singing a song of triumph at the top of his voice. The news of Nag's death was all over the garden, for the sweeper had thrown the body on the rubbish heap.

'Oh, you stupid tuft of feathers!' said Rikki-tikki angrily. 'Is this the time to sing?'

'Nag is dead—is dead—is dead!' sang Darzee. 'The valiant Rikki-tikki caught him by the head and held fast. The big man brought the bang-stick, and Nag fell in two pieces! He will never eat my babies again.'

'All that's true enough; but where's Nagaina?' said Rikki-tikki, looking carefully round him.

'Nagaina came to the bathroom sluice and called for Nag,' Darzee went on; 'and Nag came out on the end of a stick—the sweeper picked him up on the end of a stick and threw him upon the rubbish heap. Let us sing about the great, the red-eyed Rikki-tikki!' and Darzee filled his throat and sang.

'If I could get up to your nest, I'd roll all your babies out!' said Rikki-tikki. 'You don't know when to do the right thing at the right time. You're safe enough in your nest there, but it's war for me down here. Stop singing a minute, Darzee.'

'For the great, the beautiful Rikki-tikki's sake I will stop,' said

Darzee. 'What is it, O Killer of the terrible Nag?'

'Where is Nagaina, for the third time?'

'On the rubbish heap by the stables, mourning for Nag. Great is Rikki-tikki with the white teeth.'

'Bother my white teeth! Have you ever heard where she keeps her eggs?'

'In the melon bed, on the end nearest the wall, where the sun strikes nearly all day. She hid them there weeks ago.'

'And you never thought it worthwhile to tell me? The end nearest the wall, you said?'

'Rikki-tikki, you are not going to eat her eggs?'

'Not eat exactly; no. Darzee, if you have a grain of sense you will fly off to the stables and pretend that your wing is broken, and let Nagaina chase you away to this bush. I must get to the melon bed, and if I went there now she'd see me.'

Darzee was a feather-brained little fellow who could never hold more than one idea at a time in his head; and just because he knew that Nagaina's children were born in eggs like his own, he didn't think at first that it was fair to kill them. But his wife was a sensible bird, and she knew that cobra's eggs meant young cobras later on; so she flew off from the nest, and left Darzee to keep the babies warm, and continue his song about the death of Nag. Darzee was very like a man in some ways.

She fluttered in front of Nagaina by the rubbish heap, and cried out, 'Oh, my wing is broken! The boy in the house threw a stone at me and broke it.' Then she fluttered more desperately than ever.

Nagaina lifted up her head and hissed, 'You warned Rikki-tikki when I would have killed him. Indeed and truly, you've chosen a bad place to be lame in.' And she moved toward Darzee's wife, slipping along over the dust.

'The boy broke it with a stone!' shrieked Darzee's wife.

'Well! It may be some consolation to you when you're dead to know that I shall settle accounts with the boy. My husband lies on the rubbish heap this morning, but before the night the boy in the house will lie very still. What is the use of running away? I am sure to catch you. Little fool, look at me!'

Darzee's wife knew better than to do *that*, for a bird who looks at a snake's eyes gets so frightened that she cannot move. Darzee's wife fluttered on, piping sorrowfully, and never leaving the ground, and Nagaina quickened her pace.

Rikki-tikki heard them going up the path from the stables, and he raced for the end of the melon patch near the wall. There, in the warm litter about the melons, very cunningly hidden, he found twenty-five eggs, about the size of a bantam's eggs, but with whitish skin instead of shell.

'I was not a day too soon,' he said; for he could see the baby cobras curled up inside the skin, and he knew that the minute they were hatched they could each kill a man or a mongoose. He bit off the tops of the eggs as fast as he could, taking care to crush the young cobras, and turned over the litter from time to time to see whether he had missed any. At last there were only three eggs left, and Rikki-tikki began to chuckle to himself, when he heard Darzee's wife screaming:

'Rikki-tikki, I led Nagaina toward the house, and she has gone into the veranda, and—oh, come quickly—she means killing!'

Rikki-tikki smashed two eggs, and tumbled backward down the melon bed with the third egg in his mouth, and scuttled to the veranda as hard as he could put foot to the ground. Teddy and his mother and father were there at early breakfast; but Rikki-tikki saw that they were not eating anything. They sat stone still, and their faces were white. Nagaina was coiled up on the matting by Teddy's chair, within easy striking-distance of Teddy's bare leg, and she was swaying to and fro singing a song of triumph.

'Son of the big man that killed Nag,' she hissed, 'stay still. I am not ready yet. Wait a little. Keep very still, all you three. If you move I strike, and if you do not move I strike. Oh, foolish people, who killed my Nag!'

Teddy's eyes were fixed on his father, and all his father could do was to whisper, 'Sit still, Teddy. You mustn't move. Teddy, keep still.'

Then Rikki-tikki came up and cried: 'Turn round Nagaina; turn and fight!'

'All in good time,' said she, without moving her eyes. 'I will settle my account with *you* presently. Look at your friends, Rikki-tikki. They are still and white; they are afraid. They dare not move, and if you come a step nearer I strike.'

'Look at your eggs,' said Rikki-tikki, 'in the melon bed near the wall. Go and look, Nagaina.'

The big snake turned half round, and saw the egg on the veranda. 'Ah-h! Give it to me,' she said.

Rikki-tikki put his paws one on each side of the egg, and his eyes were blood red. 'What price for a snake's egg? For a young cobra? For a young king cobra? For the last—the very last of the brood? The ants are eating all the others down by the melon bed.'

Nagaina spun clear round, forgetting everything for the sake of the one egg; and Rikki-tikki saw Teddy's father shoot out a big hand, catch Teddy by the shoulder, and drag him across the little table with the teacups, safe and out of reach of Nagaina.

'Tricked! Tricked! Tricked! Rikk-tchk-tchk!' chuckled Rikki-tikki. 'The boy is safe, and it was I—I—I that caught Nag by the hood last night in the bathroom.' Then he began to jump up and down, all four feet together, his head close to the floor. 'He threw me to and fro, but he could not shake me off. He was dead before the big man blew him in two. I did it. Rikki-tikki-tchk-tchk! Come then, Nagaina, Come and fight with me. You shall not be a widow long.'

Nagaina saw that she had lost her chance of killing Teddy, and the egg lay between Rikki-tikki's paws. 'Give me the egg, Rikki-tikki. Give me the last of my eggs, and I will go away and never come back,' she said, lowering her hood.

'Yes, you will go away, and you will never come back; for you will go to the rubbish heap with Nag. Fight, widow! The big man has gone for his gun! Fight!'

Rikki-tikki was bounding all round Nagaina, keeping just out of reach of her stroke, his little eyes like hot coals. Nagaina gathered herself together, and flung out at him. Rikki-tikki jumped up and backward. Again and again and again she struck, and each time her head came with a whack on the matting of the veranda, and she gathered herself together like a watch-spring. Then Rikki-tikki danced in a circle to get behind her, and Nagaina spun round to keep her head to his head, so that the rustle of her tail on the matting sounded like dry leaves blown along by the wind.

He had forgotten the egg. It still lay on the veranda, and Nagaina came nearer and nearer to it, till at last, while Rikki-tikki was drawing breath, she caught it in her mouth, turned to the veranda steps, and flew like an arrow down the path, with Rikki-tikki behind her. When the cobra runs for her life, she goes like a whiplash flicked across as horse's neck.

Rikki-tikki knew that he must catch her, or all the trouble would begin again. She headed straight for the long grass by the thorn-bush, and as he was running Rikki-tikki heard Darzee still singing his foolish little song of triumph. But Darzee's wife was wiser. She flew off her nest as Nagaina came along, and flapped her wings about Nagaina's head. If Darzee had helped they might have turned her; but Nagaina only lowered her hood and went on. Still, the instant's delay brought Rikki-tikki up to her, and as she plunged into the rat-hole where she and Nag used to live, his little white teeth were clenched on her tail, and he went down with her—and very few mongooses, however wise and old they may be, care to follow a cobra into its hole. It was dark in the hole; and Rikki-tikki never knew when it might open out and give Nagaina room to turn and strike at him. He held on savagely, and struck out his feet to act as brakes on the dark slope of the hot, moist earth.

Then the grass by the mouth of the hole stopped waving, and Darzee said: 'It is all over with Rikki-tikki! We must sing his death song. Valiant Rikki-tikki is dead! For Nagaina will surely kill him underground.'

So he sang a very mournful song that he made up on the spur of the minute, and just as he got to the most touching part the grass quivered again, and Rikki-tikki, covered with dirt, dragged himself out of the hole leg by leg, licking his whiskers. Darzee stopped with a little shout. Rikki-tikki shook some of the dust out of his fur and sneezed. 'It is all over,' he said. 'The widow will never come out again.' And the red ants that live between the grass stems heard him, and began to troop down one after another to see if he had spoken the truth.

Rikki-tikki curled himself up in the grass and slept where he was—slept and slept till it was late in the afternoon, for he had done a hard day's work.

'Now,' he said, when he awoke, 'I will go back to the house. Tell the coppersmith, Darzee, and he will tell the garden that Nagaina is dead.'

The coppersmith is a bird who makes a noise exactly like the beating of a little hammer on a copper pot; and the reason he is always making it is because he is the town-crier to every Indian garden, and tells all the news to everybody who cares to listen. As Rikki-tikki went up the path, he heard his 'attention' notes like a tiny dinner-gong; and then the steady 'Ding-dong-tock! Nag is dead—dong! Nagaina is dead! Ding-dong-tock!' That set all the birds in the garden singing, and frogs croaking; for Nag and Nagaina used to eat frogs as well as little birds.

When Rikki got to the house, Teddy and Teddy's mother (she still looked very white, for she had been fainting) and Teddy's father came out and almost cried over him; and that night he ate all that was given him till he could eat no more, and went to bed on Teddy's shoulder, where Teddy's mother saw him when she came to look late at night.

'He saved our lives and Teddy's life,' she said to her husband. 'Just think, he saved all our lives!'

Rikki-tikki woke up with a jump, for all the mongooses are light sleepers.

'Oh, it's you,' said he. 'What are you bothering for? All the cobras are dead; and if they weren't, I'm here.'

Rikki-tikki had a right to be proud of himself; but he did not grow too proud, and he kept that garden as a mongoose should keep it, with tooth and jump and spring and bit, till never a cobra dared show its head inside the walls.

Darzee's Chant

(Sung in honour of Rikki-tikki-tavi)

Singer and tailor am I—
Doubled the joys that I know—
Proud of my lilt through the sky,
Proud of the house that I sew—
Over and under, so weave I my music—so weave I the house that I sew.

Sing to your fledglings again,
Mother, oh lift up your head!
Evil that plagued us is slain,
Death in the garden lies dead.
Terror that hid in the roses is impotent—flung on the dung-hill and dead!

Who hath delivered us, who?
Tell me his nest and his name.
Rikki, the valiant, the true,
Tikki, with eyeballs of flame,
Rik-tikki-tikki, the ivory-fanged, the hunger with eyeballs of flame.

Give him the Thanks of the birds,
Bowing with tail-feathers spread!
Praise him with nightingale-words—
Nay, I will praise him instead.
Hear! I will sing you the praise of the bottle-tailed
Rikki, with eyeballs of red!

(Here Rikki-tikki interrupted, and the rest of the song is lost.)

MAHESH

SARAT CHANDRA CHATTOPADHYAY

Translated from the Bengali by Arunava Sinha

I

The village was named Kashipur. An insignificant village, with an even more insignificant zamindar, but such was his authority that his subjects went in awe of him.

It was the birthday of the zamindar's youngest son. Having performed the holy rituals, Tarkaratna, the priest, was on his way home in the afternoon. The month of Boishakh was drawing to a close, but there was not even a trace of clouds anywhere, the searing sky seemingly pouring fire on everything below. The field stretching to the horizon before him was parched and cracked, with the blood in the veins of the earth escaping constantly through the crevices in the form of vapour. Gazing at it coiling upwards like flames made the head reel with drunkenness.

Gafoor Jolha lived on the edge of this field. The earthen wall surrounding his house had collapsed, merging his yard with the road. The privacy of the inner chambers had all but surrendered itself to the mercy of the passer-by.

Pausing in the shade of a white teak tree, Tarkaratna called out loudly, 'Are you home, Gafra?'

Gafoor's ten-year-old daughter came to the door. 'What do you need Baba for? He's got a fever.'

'Fever! Call the swine! Monster! Godless creature!'

The screaming and shouting brought Gafoor Mian to the door,

shivering with fever. An ancient acacia stood next to the broken wall, with a bull tethered to it. Pointing to it, Tarkaratna said, 'What's all this? Have you forgotten this is a Hindu village with a Brahmin zamindar?' Red with rage and the heat, his words were fiery, but Gafoor, unable to understand the reason for the outburst, could only stare at him.

'When I passed this way in the morning he was tethered there,' said Tarkaratna, 'and now on my way back he's still tethered the same way. Karta will bury you alive if you kill a bull. He's a devout Brahmin.'

'What can I do, Baba Thakur, I have no choice. I've had this fever for several days now. I collapse every time I try to take him to graze.'

'Then turn him loose, he'll find food on his own.'

'Where can I turn him loose, Baba Thakur? The winnowing isn't done, the grain is still lying in the fields. The hay hasn't been sorted, the earth is burning, there's not a blade of grass anywhere. What if he eats someone's grains or hay—how can I turn him loose, Baba Thakur?'

Softening, Tarkaratna said, 'If you can't let him loose at least give him some straw. Hasn't your daughter made any rice? Give him a bowl of starch and water.'

Gafoor did not answer, only looked at Tarkaratna helplessly and sighed.

Tarkaratna said, 'No rice either? What did you do with the hay? Did you sell your entire share without keeping anything for your beast? You butcher!'

Gafoor seemed to lose his power of speech at this cruel accusation. A little later he said haltingly, 'I did get some hay this year, but Karta Moshai took it away to pay for taxes left over from last year. I fell at his feet, I said, "Babu Moshai, you're the supreme authority, where will I go if I leave your kingdom, give me at least a little hay. There's no straw for the roof, we have just the one room for father and daughter, we can still manage with palm leaves this monsoon, but my Mahesh will die of starvation."'

With a mocking smile, Tarkaratna said, 'Really! What a loving name, Mahesh. I'll die laughing.'

Paying no attention to the taunt, Gafoor continued, 'But the lord had no mercy on me. He allowed me some rice to feed us for two months, but all my hay was confiscated and the poor thing got nothing at all.' His voice grew moist with tears. But this evoked no compassion in Tarkaratna, who said, 'What a man you are. You've eaten up everything but don't want to pay your dues. Do you expect the zamindar to feed you? You people live in a perfect kingdom, still you bad-mouth him, you're such wretches.'

An embarrassed Gafoor said, 'Why should we bad-mouth him, Baba Thakur, we don't do that. But how do I pay my taxes? I sharecrop four bighas, but there's been a famine two years in a row—the grains have all dried up. My daughter and I don't even get two meals a day. Look at the house, when it rains we spend the night in a corner, there's not even enough space to stretch our legs. Look at Mahesh, Thakur Moshai, you can count his ribs. Lend me a little hay, Thakur Moshai, let the creature feed to his heart's content for a few days.' Still speaking, he flung himself to the ground near the Brahmin's feet. Leaping backwards hastily, Tarkaratna exclaimed, 'My god, are you going to touch me?'

'No, Baba Thakur, I'm not going to touch you or anything. But give me some hay. I saw your four huge haystacks the other day, you won't even know if a little of it is gone. I don't care if we starve to death, but this poor creature cannot talk, he only stares and weeps.'

Tarkaratna said, 'And how do you propose to return the loan?'

A hopeful Gafoor said, 'I'll find a way to return it somehow, Baba Thakur, I won't cheat you.'

Snorting, Tarkaratna mimicked Gafoor, 'I won't cheat you! I'll find a way to return it somehow! What a comedian! Get out of my way. I should be getting home, it's late.' Chuckling, he took a step forward only to retreat several steps in fear. Angrily he said, 'Oh god, he's waving his horns, is he going to gore me now?'

Gafoor rose to his feet. Pointing to the bundle of fruit and moistened rice in the priest's hand, he said, 'He's smelt food, he wants to eat...'

'Wants to eat? Of course. Both master and bull are well-matched. Can't get hay to eat, and now you want fruits. Get him out of my way. Those horns, someone will be killed by them.' Tarkaratna hurried away.

Gafoor turned towards Mahesh, gazing at him in silence for a few moments. There was suffering and hunger in the bull's deep black eyes. Gafoor said, 'He wouldn't give you any, would he? They have so much, but still they won't. Never mind.' He choked, and tears began to roll down from his eyes. Going up to the animal, he stroked his back and neck, whispering, 'You are my son, Mahesh, you've grown old looking after us for eight years, I can't even give you enough to eat, but you know how much I love you.'

Mahesh responded by stretching his neck and closing his eyes in pleasure. Wiping his tears off the bull's back, Gafoor murmured, 'The zamindar took away your food, leased out the grazing ground near the crematorium just for money. How will I save your life in this year of starvation? If I turn you loose you'll eat other people's hay, you'll spoil their trees—what do I do with you! You have no strength left, people tell me to sell you off.' No sooner had Gafoor said this in his head than his tears began to roll down again. Wiping them with his hand, he looked around surreptitiously before fetching some discoloured straw from behind his dilapidated house and placing them near Mahesh's mouth, saying, 'Eat up quickly, if not there'll be…'

'Baba?'

'Yes, Ma?'

'Come and eat,' said Amina, appearing at the door. After a glance she said, 'You're giving Mahesh straw from the roof again, Baba?'

This was just what he was afraid of. Reddening, he said, 'Old rotten straw, Ma, it was falling off anyway…'

'I heard you pulling it out, Baba.'

'No, Ma, not exactly pulling it out…'

'But the wall will collapse, Baba…'

Gafoor was silent. The house was all they had left, and no one knew better than him that if he continued this way it wouldn't survive the next monsoon. But how long could they go on?

His daughter said, 'Wash your hands and come, Baba, I've served the food.'

Gafoor said, 'Bring the starch out, Ma, let me feed Mahesh first.'

'No starch left today, Baba, it dried in the pot.'

No starch? Gafoor stood in silence. His ten-year-old daughter knew that when the times were bad even this could not be wasted. He washed his hands and went in. His daughter served him rice and vegetables on a brass plate, taking some for herself on an earthen plate. Gafoor said softly, 'I'm feeling cold again, Amina, is it safe to eat with a fever?'

Amina asked anxiously, 'But didn't you say you were hungry?'

'Maybe I didn't have a fever then, Ma.'

'Then let me put it away, you can have it in the evening.'

Shaking his head, Gafoor said, 'Eating cold food will make things worse.'

'What should I do then?' asked Amina.

Gafoor pretended to think before solving the problem. He said, 'Why don't you give it to Mahesh, Ma? You can make me some fresh rice at night, can't you?'

Amina looked at him in silence for a few moments before lowering her eyes, nodding, and saying, 'Yes, Baba, I can.'

Gafoor reddened. Besides the two actors, only someone up there observed this little charade between father and daughter.

II

Five or six days later, Gafoor was seated outside his front door with an anxious expression on his face. Mahesh had not been home since yesterday morning. He himself was too weak to move, so his daughter Amina had searched high and low for the bull. Returning home in the late afternoon, she said, 'Have you heard, Baba, Manik Ghosh's family has taken our Mahesh to the police station?

'What nonsense,' said Gafoor.

'It's true, Baba. Their servant said, "Tell your father to look for him in the Dariapur pen."'

'What did he do?'

'He got into their garden and destroyed their trees, Baba.'

Gafoor sat in silence. He had imagined all manner of mishaps that might have befallen Mahesh, but had not anticipated this. He was as harmless as he was poor, which was why he had no apprehensions of being punished so severely by any of his neighbours—Manik Ghosh, in particular, for his respect for cows was legendary.

His daughter said, 'It's getting late, Baba, aren't you going to bring Mahesh home?'

'No,' answered Gafoor.

'But they said the police will sell him in the cattle market after three days.'

'Let them sell him,' said Gafoor.

Amina did not know what exactly a cattle market was, but she had noticed her father becoming agitated whenever it was mentioned with reference to Mahesh. She left without another word.

Under cover of the night Gafoor went to Bansi's shop, and said, 'Khuro, I need a rupee,' and deposited his brass plate beneath the raised platform on which Bansi sat. Bansi was familiar with the exact weight and other details of this object. It had been pawned some five times in the past two years, for a rupee each time. So, he did not object this time either.

Mahesh was seen in his usual place the next day. Beneath the same tree, tethered to the same stake with the same rope, the same empty bowl with no food in front of him, the same questioning look in the moist, hungry, black eyes. An elderly Muslim man was examining him closely. Gafoor Mian sat nearby, his knees drawn up to his chin. When the examination was over, the man extracted a ten-rupee note from the knot in his dhoti and, smoothing it repeatedly, went up to Gafoor, saying, 'I don't need change, take the whole thing—here.'

Holding his hand out for the money, Gafoor remained sitting in silence. But just as the old Muslim's companions were about to untie the bull, he suddenly jumped to his feet, saying belligerently, 'Don't you dare touch that rope, I'm warning you.'

They were startled. The old man said in surprise, 'Why not?'

Still furious, Gafoor said, 'What do you mean, why not? It's mine to sell or not. And I'm not selling.' He threw the ten-rupee note on the ground.

They said, 'But you took an advance yesterday.'

'Here's your advance.' Retrieving two rupees from the knot in his dhoti, he flung the coins at them, and they fell with a clatter. Realizing that a quarrel was imminent, the old man said gently with a smile, 'You're putting pressure on us for two rupees more, aren't you? Go on, give his daughter two rupees more. That's what you wanted, isn't it?'

'No.'

'Are you aware that no one will give you a better price?'

'No,' said Gafoor, shaking his head vehemently.

The old man said in annoyance, 'What do you think? Only the skin is worth selling. There's nothing else in there.'

'Tauba! Tauba!' A terrible expletive suddenly escaped Gafoor's lips, and the very next moment he ran into his house threatening to have them thrashed within an inch of their lives by the zamindar's guards unless they left the village at once.

The possibility of trouble made them leave, but soon Gafoor received a summons from the zamindar's court. He realized that word had reached the landowner.

There were people both refined and unrefined in court. Glaring at Gafoor, Shibu Babu said, 'I don't know how to punish you, Gafra. Do you know where you live?'

Bowing, Gafoor said, 'I do. We're starving, or else I would have paid whatever fine you think fit.'

Everyone present was astonished. They had always considered him an obstinate and bad-tempered man. And here he was on the verge of tears, saying, 'I'll never do it again, Karta.' He proceeded to box his own ears, rubbed his nose into the ground from one end of the court to the other, and then stood up.

Shibu Babu said indulgently, 'All right, enough. Don't do all this again.'

Everyone was shocked when they heard the details. They were certain that only the grace of the zamindar and the fear of punishment had prevented the abject sinner from committing worse trangressions. Tarkaratna was present, and provided the scriptural analysis of the word 'go' for cow, enlightening everyone as to why it was forbidden to allow this godless race of heathens to live within village limits.

Gafoor did not respond to any of this, humbly accepting all the humiliation and vilification and returning home cheerfully. Borrowing the starch from the rice pots of neighbours, he gave it to Mahesh to eat, murmuring many endearments as he stroked the bull's back and horns.

III

The month of Joishtho was drawing to a close. The sun was still harsh and severe in the sky. There was no trace of mercy anywhere. People were afraid to even hope for change, hope that the skies could again be moist and pleasurable with the weight of rain-bearing clouds. It seemed that there would be no cessation to the flames burning constantly across the entire fiery earth—that they would not die down till they had consumed everything.

Gafoor returned home on such an afternoon. He was not used to working as a labourer on someone else's fields, and it had been only four or five days since the fever had subsided. He was as weak as he was exhausted. Still, he had gone out in search of work, but all he had got was the unforgiving heat and sun overhead. He could barely see for hunger and thirst. Standing at the door, he called out, 'Amina, is the food ready?'

His daughter emerged slowly and stood grasping the post without an answer.

Gafoor shouted, 'Not ready? Why not?'

'No rice at home, Baba.'

'No rice? Why didn't you tell me in the morning?'

'But I told you last night.'

Contorting his face and mocking her, Gafoor said, 'Told you last night! How can anyone remember if you tell them at night?' The harsh tone he was using stoked his anger. Contorting his face even further, he said, 'How will there be any rice? Whether the sick father gets any or not, the grown-up daughter will eat five times a day. I'm going to lock up the rice from now on. Give me some water, I'm dying of thirst. Now tell me we have no water either.'

Amina remained standing with her eyes downcast. When Gafoor realized after waiting a few moments that there was not even any water to drink at home, he could control himself no longer. Striding up to his daughter, he slapped her resoundingly, saying, 'Haramjaadi, what do you do all day? Why can't you die?'

Without a word his daughter picked up the empty pitcher and went out in the heat, wiping her eyes. Gafoor felt heartbroken as soon as she was out of sight. He alone knew how he had brought up his daughter after her mother's death. He remembered that it was not the dutiful and affectionate girl's fault. Ever since they had run out of the paltry amount of rice he had received for his work in the fields—they had not had two meals a day. On some days, just one—or not even that. His accusation that Amina was eating five times a day was as impossible as it was untrue. Nor was he unaware of the reasons for the lack of water to drink. The two or three tanks in the village were all dry. The little water there was in the pond behind Shibcharan Babu's house was not available to ordinary people. The water that could be collected by digging a hole or two in the middle of the tanks was fought over by a crowd of people.

Being a Muslim, the young girl was not even allowed near that water. She had to wait for hours, pleading for some water, and only if someone took pity on her, and poured her a little could she bring it home. He knew all this. Perhaps there had been no water that day, or no one had had the time to take pity on his daughter during the battle. Realizing that something like this must have taken place, Gafoor found his own eyes filling with tears. At that moment the zamindar's footman appeared like a messenger of death, screaming, 'Gafra, are you home?'

Gafoor answered bitterly, 'I am. Why?'

'Babu Moshai has sent for you. Come along.'

Gafoor said, 'I haven't eaten yet. I'll come later.'

Unable to tolerate such audacity, the footman swore and said, 'The Babu has ordered me to flog you and force you to come.'

Gafoor forgot himself a second time, uttering an unprintable word in retaliation and said, 'No one is a slave in the kingdom of the Empress. I pay my taxes, I won't go.'

But for such a small man to give such a big reason was not just futile but also dangerous. Fortunately, such an insignificant voice would not reach the ears of the important man it was meant for—or else he would have lost both his home and his livelihood. There is no need for an elaborate account of what ensued, but when he returned from the zamindar's court an hour later and lay down in silence, his face and eyes were swollen. The primary cause of such severe punishment was Mahesh. After Gafoor had gone out, Mahesh had broken free from the post, entered the zamindar's yard, eaten his flowers, spoilt the paddy put out in the sun and, when about to be caught, had made his escape after knocking the zamindar's youngest daughter to the ground. This was not the first time it had happened, but Gafoor had been pardoned earlier on the grounds of being poor. He might have been pardoned this time too had he begged and pleaded as in the past, but what he had said—that he paid his taxes and was no one's servant—was the kind of arrogance from a subject that Shibcharan Babu, being a zamindar, could never tolerate. Gafoor had not protested in the slightest against the thrashing and the humiliation, bearing it all in silence. Back home, too, he sat coiled up in silence. He had no awareness of hunger or thirst, but his heart was burning just like the noonday sky outside. However, when he heard his daughter's stricken cry from the yard, he leapt to his feet and ran outside to find Amina lying on the ground and Mahesh lapping up the water trickling out of the shattered pitcher. Gafoor lost his mind. Picking up the plough-head he had brought home yesterday to repair, he smashed Mahesh's head with it repeatedly.

Mahesh tried to lift his head just once, then his starving, skinny body slumped to the ground. A few tears rolled down his eyes, along with a few drops of blood from his ears. His entire body trembled once or twice, after which, stretching out his front and hind legs, Mahesh died.

Amina sobbed, 'What have you done, Baba, our Mahesh is dead.'

Gafoor had turned to stone, neither moving nor speaking, only staring at a pair of unblinking, bottomless dark eyes.

Within an hour or two, a group of cobblers from one end of the village arrived, and slinging Mahesh up on a pole took him to the dumping ground. Gafoor trembled when he saw their shining knives, but closing his eyes, he didn't say a word.

The neighbours said that the zamindar had sent someone to Tarkaratna to find out what should be done next, 'You may have to sell your house as penance.'

Gafoor did not reply to any of this, burying his face in his knees and not moving.

Late that night he woke his daughter up, saying, 'Amina, we must go.'

She had fallen asleep outside the front door. Rubbing her eyes and sitting up, she said, 'Where will we go, Baba?'

Gafoor said, 'To work at the jute mill in Phulbere.'

His daughter looked at him in astonishment. Despite all their troubles her father had never been willing to work at the jute mill. She had often heard him say that it was impossible to maintain one's faith there, that women had neither honour nor protection.

Gafoor said, 'Hurry up, Ma, we have to walk a long way.'

Amina was about to take the tumbler and the brass plate her father ate from, but Gafoor stopped her. 'Leave them here, Ma, they will pay for my penance for Mahesh.'

He left in the dead of night, holding his daughter's hand. He had no family in this village, no one to inform. Crossing the yard, he stopped abruptly beneath the familiar tree and suddenly burst into tears. Raising his eyes to the star-studded black sky, he said, 'Allah! Punish me as you will, but my Mahesh died with a thirst. There was no land he could graze on. Do not forgive the sin of whoever it was who did not let him eat the grass you gave us, or quench his thirst with the water you gave us.'

A TALE OF TWO BULLOCKS

PREMCHAND

Translated from the Hindi by Rohit Manchanda

In the realm of animals, it's the ass that's reckoned the most brainless. When we mean to call someone a dolt of the first order, we say they're an ass. Whether the ass is truly stupid or has been conferred this lofty title on account of its simple-mindedness, its placid forbearance, cannot be resolved. Cows butt you with their horns, and as for the the pregnant cow, she can suddenly assume the avatar of a tigress. The dog, too, is a most pitiful animal, though every now and again it does tip over into a fury. But never has one heard or seen an ass fly into a rage. Thrash the wretched thing to your heart's content, set down before it grass as vile and rotten as you might wish, never will you witness so much as a shadow of discontent pass over its face. While it might in springtime indulge itself in a dash of playsome frolic, we have never seen it wax happy. A pall of gloom always overspreads its face. Joy or sorrow, ruin or fortune, whatever its circumstance, one has never seen its spirits vary. Indeed, the virtues that are celebrated in sages and philosophers have attained their pinnacle in the ass yet man calls him stupid. Such a slur on such exalted virtues!

Quite possibly, simple goodness is not appreciated in this world. Witness, for instance, the travails that Indians are undergoing in Africa. And why are they not permitted to set foot on American soil? The poor souls drink no liquor, lay aside four annas against an evil day, work their hearts out, neither squabble nor brawl with anyone, simply swallow their sorrows when they're vilified, yet stand in disrepute. It's said that they debase the ideals of life. Were they to learn to answer brick with stone, perhaps they'd start being appreciated. The example of Japan is ready to hand. Just a single triumph has secured them a place in the league of the refined races.

But the ass has a younger brother, too, one which is less of an ass than itself. And this is the bullock. Somewhat akin to the sense in which we employ the word 'ass' do we employ the phrase 'the calf's uncle'. Some even regard the bullock as peerless in stupidity. But we do not concur. Every now and again the bullock will lash out, every now and again one will come across a bullock that digs its heels in. It makes known its discontent by sundry other means as well, and it doesn't rank alongside the ass in foolishness.

Jhoori possessed two bullocks, Hira and Moti. They both came of western stock. Comely to behold, sedulous at their work, lofty of stature. Having long stayed together, a sense of brotherhood had grown between them. The two would sit side by side and trade thoughts and views. Just how they contrived to read one another's minds, one cannot say. To be sure, they possessed that occult power which, notwithstanding its claims to be sovereign amongst creatures, humankind has been diddled out of. They expressed their love by licking and sniffing at each other. From time to time, they'd even lock horns, not out of a feeling of antagonism, only from a spirit of sportiveness, from a spirit of intimacy, the way intimacy between friends leads immediately to mutual clouting and thumping. In want of this, friendship remains somewhat brittle, somewhat lightweight. And then trust cannot be reposed. On those occasions when this brace of bullocks were yoked to the plough or to the cart and walked with their necks swaying and swinging, it was the endeavour of each that the greatest possible burden should fall on its own neck. When in the afternoon or evening, after a full day's work, the two were set loose, they'd dissolve their fatigue by licking each other down; once the hay and oil-cake had been placed in the trough, together they'd lower their mouths into it and together seat themselves beside it. Should one remove his mouth, the other would follow suit.

It so came to pass that Jhoori once sent his draught bullocks off to his in-laws. What would the bullocks know of where they were being sent; they merely thought, our master has sold us. Whether they took to being sold off in this manner or took against it, who knows, but Jhoori's brother-in-law's very teeth broke sweat in taking them home. If he urged them on from their rear, they'd skitter to right and left, if he caught hold of their tethers and tugged from up front, they'd strain rearwards. Should he strike them, they'd lower their horns and bellow. Had the Lord favoured them with the faculty of speech they'd have asked Jhoori: why are you banishing us poor souls? We spared no pains in serving you. If the amount of toil we put in didn't do for you, you could have worked us even harder. It was fine with us to perish in your service. Never did we grouse in the matter of grain or fodder. Whatever you fed us, we accepted with bowed heads, why then did you sell us into the hands of this tyrant?

At the hour of dusk the two bullocks reached their destination. They'd stayed hungry all day, but when they were hitched to the trough neither of the two lowered his mouth into it. Their hearts were heavy. That which they'd looked upon as their home had been cut off from them. This new dwelling, this new village, these new folk, was alien to them.

The two of them conferred in their mute tongue, cast sidelong glances at each other and lay down. When sleep fell upon the village they both wrenched themselves free of their tethers and started out for home. Those ropes were pretty sturdy. One couldn't have fancied any bullock to have it in him to break them, but strength had multiplied twofold in this pair at this moment. Just one yank from each, and the ropes had been ripped apart.

When Jhoori awoke in the morning he saw the two bullocks standing in the manger. From the neck of each of them hung one half of a halter. Their legs were muddied up to their knees and in the eyes of both shone the gleam of rebellious love.

Jhoori, on seeing the bullocks, felt a lump rise in his throat. He ran up to them and hugged them close. That vision, of the bullocks being lovingly embraced, was a poignant one indeed.

The boys of the house and the village gathered round and with ringing claps welcomed the bullocks back. Although in the history of the village this incident wasn't without precedent, it was nonetheless important for them. The assembled children settled that due honour ought to be accorded to these noble animals. Some brought rotis for them from their homes, some jaggery, some bran, some chaff.

Said one boy: 'Nobody else will have bullocks such as these.'

A second concurred: 'Made their way back from so far away all on their own.'

Said a third: 'They aren't bullocks. They are men in a prior birth.'

No one had the courage to refute this.

Jhoori's wife, on seeing the bullocks at her doorstep, was incensed. She said: 'Such traitorous bullocks! They had scarcely worked a day there before they bolted.'

Jhoori couldn't stomach this slur on his bullocks. 'How are they traitors? They were probably not given fodder or grain, what could they have done?'

Imperiously, his wife said, 'But, of course. It's only you who knows how to feed bullocks, all the others sustain them on water and water alone.'

Jhoori retorted: 'If they had been given fodder, why would they have fled?'

The woman was peeved. 'They fled because those people do not, unlike nitwits of your sort, eulogise their bullocks. If they feed them, they work them hard at the plough, too. These two, inveterate shirkers, scooted off. I'd like to see where they get their oil-cake and their bran now. I shall give them nothing but dry straw, whether they eat or die.'

And so it played out. The labourer was sternly enjoined to feed the bullocks dry straw.

When the bullocks dipped their mouths into the trough, they found tasteless straw in it. It had neither flavour nor succulence.

What to eat? With hope-filled eyes they fixed their gaze upon the door.

Jhoori said to the labourer—'Why not give them a bit of oil-cake, bey?'

'The mistress will kill me.'

'Well, do it by stealth.'

'No, dada, afterwards you too will sing her tune.'

Next day, Jhoori's brother-in-law came over again and took the bullocks away. This time he yoked them to his cart.

On two occasions or four, Moti sought to tumble the cart into a wayside ditch, but Hira steadied it. He was the more forbearing of the two.

Once they'd arrived at Gaya's home in the evening, he tied both up with thick ropes and, to punish them for yesterday's mischief, gave them dry straw to eat. His own bullocks got oil-cake, ground pulses, the works.

Never previously had our two bullocks experienced such abasement. Jhoori hadn't taken so much as a flowery sprig to them. At the clicks of his urging tongue they'd as good as taken wing. Here they were chastised. Here they suffered the distress of wounded esteem and, to crown it all, they were expected to eat dry straw!

Towards the trough they didn't so much as raise their eyes.

On the second day Gaya yoked the bullocks to the plough, but it was as though the two had vowed not to lift a foot. He thrashed them over and over until he grew weary, but not a foot did the two raise. Once when the lusty blows of his stave fell upon Hira's nose, Moti's anger overflowed its bounds. He took off with the plough. The plough, the rope, the bridle, snapping and splintering, became all as one. Had there not been those thick ropes about their necks, the two would've escaped.

Hira in their mute tongue said—'It's futile to flee.'

Moti returned—'He'd as good as taken your life.'

'This time we're in for a really sound thrashing.'

'So be it, when we've taken birth as bullocks how far can we avoid being thrashed?'

'Gaya's running towards us with two men in tow, both with sticks in their hands.'

Said Moti—'Say the word and I, too, could have some sport with them. Coming at us with sticks indeed.'

'No, brother,' counselled Hira, 'Just stand still.'

'Should he hit me I'll take one or two down.'

'No. That goes against the creed of our race.'

Moti contented himself with rampaging around in his heart. Gaya seized them and hauled them off. It was a blessing he didn't at this moment smite them, else Moti would have turned on him. On seeing the mood he was in, Gaya and his lackeys could make out that, for now, it was expedient to let things be.

Today, again, the same dry straw was put in front of them. The two stood stock still, utterly silent. Within the house people began on their meal. Just then, a smallish girl with two rotis in hand came out, placed these in their mouths, and went back inside. What could a single roti do to assuage their hunger? Yet you might say their hearts had found nourishment. Here, too, lives a gentle soul. The girl was Bhairon's daughter. Her mother was no more. Her stepmother beat her frequently, and so she'd developed species of kinship with these oppressed bullocks.

They'd both be worked under the yoke all day long, they'd get flailed, they'd baulk. Evenings they'd be tethered at the stall and at night, the girl would feed them two rotis. Such was the plenitude of this offering that even their diet of a couple of cheekfuls of dry straw didn't enfeeble them, though in the eyes of both, in their heart and soul, there brimmed the blaze of mutiny.

One day Moti said in their voiceless tongue—'I can't bear it any more, Hira.'

'What do you wish to do?'

'One or two of them I'll hoist on my horns and hurl down.'

'But don't you know, that lovely girl, the one who feeds us rotis, is the daughter of none other than the householder here. The poor child will be orphaned.'

'Shouldn't I then bring down the lady of the house? She's the one who beats that girl.'

'But you forget that it's forbidden to gore women.'

'You don't let us do anything. Well, come on then, let's at least break the ropes and run away.'

'Yes, this I accept, but how is such a thick rope to be broken?'

'There's a way out. First chew upon the rope. It then gives way at one yank.'

When at night the girl had fed them their rotis and left, they tried to chew at the ropes, but the ropes were so fat they couldn't get their mouths around them. They tried time and again, to no avail.

Of a sudden the door to the house opened and the girl emerged. The two of them lowered their heads and set to licking her hands. Their tails stood upright. She caressed their brows and said—'I'll release you. Run away quietly, else these people will kill you. They were talking today about having rope passed through your noses'.

She undid their halters, but both remained silent and still.

Moti asked in their lingo—'Well, why don't you start walking now?'

Hira said—'We could do that. But calamity will descend on this orphan tomorrow. Everyone's suspicion will fall on her.

All at once the girl cried out—'Both uncle's bullocks are escaping, O Dada! Dada! Both the bullocks are making off, hurry up, run!'

A flustered Gaya emerged from within and set off to catch the bullocks. The two of them dashed away. Gaya gave chase. They sped up. Gaya set up a clamour. He then returned in order to enlist a few more men. The two friends got a chance to flee. They just ran on and on, to the point that they no longer knew the path they were on. There was no trace here of the accustomed track that they'd started on. New villages came and went and finally, the pair came to a halt at the edge of a field. They thought: What's to be done now?

Hira said—'It seems we've lost our way.'

'How impetuously you ran. We ought to have felled him there and then.'

'Had we knocked him down what would the world have said? He might abandon his faith, why should we abandon ours?'

The two were getting distracted by hunger. In the field close by stood a crop of pea. They set to grazing. Every now and again, they'd look around watchfully for any signs of pursuit.

When they'd had their fill they began to savour their freedom to the fullest. They started to jump and cavort about exhilaratedly. Then they treated themselves to a satisfying belch. Next, they locked horns and started shoving at each other. Moti rocked Hira back a few paces, so much so that the latter fell into the ditch. Then Hira, too, grew irate, pulled himself together, rose, and tore into Moti. When Moti sensed that play was turning into a scrap, he edged out of it.

But behold! What was this? A bull was bearing down upon them, snorting away. Oh yes, a bull, to be sure. As it charged up to them the two friends began looking around for a way to escape this new threat. The bull was a veritable elephant. To take him on would be to give up one's life. But they wouldn't be spared even if they chose not to fight. What a monster!

Moti said in his speechless tongue—'We're in deep trouble. If we're going to escape with our lives, you'll have to come up with a plan.'

'Hira said in troubled tones—'He's all puffed up with pride. If we plead with him to spare us, it will only fall on deaf ears.'

'Why don't we just run?'

'It is cowardice to flee.'

'Well then, let this spot mark your death. Yours truly is getting out of here.'

'And should he come after you?'

'Well then think up a ploy. Quickly now!'

'There is only one thing that might work and that is for both of us to fight him together. I'll attack him from the front, you do so from the rear. When he's assaulted on two flanks he'll make himself scarce. The moment he strikes at me, you gore him in his belly. It's risky but there's nothing else for it.'

Havind decided upon this plan of action, the two friends went for the bull. Now, the bull had no experience of tackling a concerted assault. Here, the instant he flew at Hira, Moti would attack him from the rear. When the bull turned towards him, Hira would sail into him. No matter how much he tried to isolate the two and knock them to the ground one by one, they were maestros. They gave him no chance. Once, during the battle, in a great fury, the monster bull tried to take Hira out, but Moti gored him in the belly. When, incensed, the bull turned about, Hira pierced him from the other side. At length, much wounded, the bull turned tail and the two friends chased him off over a considerable distance. Finally, winded, the bull fell down.

Giddy with triumph, the friends wondered what to do next.

Moti in their sign language said—'My heart says, just kill the rascal.'

Hira reproached him—'One ought not to use one's horns against a fallen enemy.'

'All this is bunkum. The foe should be so beaten that he cannot rise again.'

'How we are to return home, turn your thoughts to that.'

'Let's first have something to eat, we'll then be able to think.'

Well, right before them lay that field of pea so Moti waded into it. Hira told him not to, but Moti wouldn't listen. They'd scarcely had two or four mouthfuls before a couple of men armed with lathis ran up to attack them. Hira was at the field's edge, and made his getaway. But Moti was right in the middle of the heavily watered field. His hooves started to sink into the slush. Couldn't take flight. Hira on seeing his companion in trouble doubled back. If getting nabbed was inevitable then we both suffer that fate. The watchmen seized hold of him as well. Come morning, and both friends found themselves interned in the municipal pound.

For the first time in their lives the two friends made the acquaintance of a day during which they didn't have a strand of straw to eat. They simply couldn't fathom what manner of master this was. Beside him, Gaya came off as the better of the two. Here there were many buffaloes, many goats, many horses, many asses, but before none was there any fodder; all lay on the ground fading rapidly away. Several had grown so enfeebled that they couldn't get to their feet. All day long the friends fixed unblinking eyes upon the gate, but no one brought them any fodder. At this the duo took to licking the salty mud of the walls, but how could this have allayed their hunger pangs?

When at night, too, no food was forthcoming there leapt up in

Hira's heart the flame of rebellion. He said to Moti, 'Can't stand this any more, Moti!'

Moti, head bowed, replied—'To me, it seems my life's at an end.'

'Come then, let's tear the wall down.'

'Oh, I'm not up to anything now.'

'And this the strength you used to strut and preen over!'

'Oh, all that strutting about has drained out of me.'

The stockade's walls were made of clay. When the sturdy Hira dug his sharp horns into the wall and gave a mighty thrust, big chunk of the wall came right off. This buoyed up his spirits, and he started assaulting the wall at a run; with each stab he would dislodge another piece of the wall.

Just then the watchman of Kanji House came along bearing a lantern, to inventory the animals. On seeing Hira's insolence, he began beating him with a stick and then tied him up with a thick rope. From where he lay Moti said: 'In the end you got a thrashing. And what was accomplished?'

'At least I tried my best, with all my strength.'

'Of what use is this trying-one's-best if it merely deepens our bondage.'

'I'll keep giving it all I have, never mind how much more bondage comes our way.'

'We'll have to bid our lives goodbye.'

'I care for nothing now. We're to die in any case. Just think, if that wall had been breached how many lives would've been saved. So many brethren imprisoned here. No strength in any of them. Another few days of this and they'll die.'

'Yes, that's for sure. Well then, make room and I, too, shall have a go at it.'

Moti, too, dug his horns into the wall. A little mud fell off and again their spirits got a fillip. Then with his horns stuck into the wall he set about applying such force, it was as if he were dueling with an enemy. At length, after some two hours' worth of trying his best, about a cubit's height of wall tumbled down off the top. And when he shoved at it with redoubled vigour, half the wall toppled over.

No sooner had the wall fallen than all the animals, strewn about on the floor half-dead, were roused to action. The three mares charged out headlong. Then the goats scampered away followed by the buffaloes. Only the asses remained where they were. Hira asked, 'Why don't the two of you run away?'

One of the asses said—'What if we're caught again?'

'What's the harm in that? For now at least you have the chance to be free.'

'Oh, but we are scared. We'll stay right here.'

It had gone past midnight. The two asses were still debating on whether to flee or not to flee. And Moti was doing his best to free his friend by breaking the rope he was secured with. Eventually, at length he gave up, and Hira said, 'Save yourself. Leave me here. Perhaps we'll meet elsewhere.'

Mournfully, Moti said: 'Do you really think I'm so self-serving, Hira? You and I have been together so long. Today, when you're in such trouble, how can I leave you?'

Hira said—'You'll get royally thrashed. People will figure out that this was your mischief.'

Moti rejoined, with pride: 'If the offence that led to this rope about your neck leads to me being beaten, it's no matter. At least this much came of it—the lives of nine or ten creatures got saved. They'll all bless us.'

So saying Moti drove the asses out, prodding and shoving them with his horns, then laid himself down to sleep near his friend.

Soon, as dawn broke, such a tumult broke loose over the clerk and the watchman and the other employees as is needless to relate. Suffice it to say that Moti was beaten mercilessly then he, too, was tied up with a stout rope.

For a week, the two friends languished there in captivity. No one placed before them so much as a blade of fodder. Yes, once a day they were allowed a little water. This was their sustenance. Otherwise, all they did was lie there, night and day, under the open sky. Both became so frail that they couldn't so much as rise to their feet. Their ribs were showing through the skin.

One day a drum began to sound outside the stockade. Around noon, some fifty or sixty men assembled there. Then the friends were led out and the men one after another sized them up and, disenchanted, walked away.

Who'd have bought such bullocks, animals that seemed on the verge of dying?

Suddenly a bearded man, with red eyes and a hard expression on his face, began prodding the loins of the bullocks and speaking to the clerk. On seeing his face, intuition set the bullocks' hearts quaking. On the matter of who he was and why he was probing their bodies, they had no doubt at all. Each looked at the other with terror-struck eyes and bowed his head.

Hira said—'We had no right to flee Gaya's home, now there's no saving our lives.'

Moti said irreverently—'They say God is merciful to all, why doesn't He spare some mercy for us?'

'In the eyes of God whether we live or die makes no difference. It's all right, we'll stay with this bearded one for some days. Once God saved us in the form of that girl, why wouldn't He save us now?'

'This man will pull a knife on us, just you see.'

'So what's the worry? Flesh, hide, horn, bone, will all come in handy for someone or the other.'

After they were auctioned off, the two friends left with the bearded one. They trembled with every fibre of their being. They weren't able to lift so much as their feet. But out of terror they ran on stumbling and falling, since if they let up their pace they would be beaten by their new owner.

En route they caught sight of a flock of cattle grazing in a green, luscious pasture. All the animals there were joyous, glossy, spry. One was leaping about, one, pleasurably settled,was chewing the cud. What a happy life was theirs; but how self-centred they were. Not one fretted over the sorry fate of their fellows in the hands of their captor.

All at once the duo sensed that the path they were on was a familiar one. Yes, it was on this same road that Gaya had taken them away. They came upon the same fields, the same gardens, the same villages. They picked up pace. All their fatigue, all their frailness, was swept away. And ah! Here it was! Their very own home was now at hand. It was from this well that we used to draw those leather containers of water, this very well.

Moti spoke up—'Our home's drawing near now.'

Said Hira—'It's the Lord's mercy.'

'I shall now gallop home.'

'Will this one let you?'

'I'll knock him down.'

'Oh, no. Let's just run up to the stall. I shan't step beyond that.'

Wildly, inebriatedly, the two of them dashed towards the house, cavorting and frisking like calves. Just ahead lay their stall. They sprinted to it and came to a standstill. The bearded one, too, was running along, hot on their heels.

Jhoori was sitting at his door, soaking up the sun. On seeing the bullocks, he rushed up to them, started hugging them one after another. Tears of joy started to flow from the eyes of the bullocks. One of them began licking Jhoori's hand.

The bearded one came up and grabbed hold of the bullocks' ropes.

Jhoori said—'They're my bullocks.'

'How are they yours? I've just bought them from the cattle-pound.'

'To my mind, you are stealing them! Leave quietly. They're my bullocks. They'll be bought only when I sell them. Who has any authority to auction my bullocks?'

'I shall go lodge a report at the police station.'

'They're my bullocks. The proof of which is that they're standing at my doorstep.'

Seething, the bearded one advanced, and tried to catch hold of the bullocks. Then and there Moti slashed at him with his horns. The bearded one jumped back. Moti thundered after him. The bearded one took to his heels. Moti gave chase. Once they had left the village behind he halted, though he kept an eye on the bearded one, who from afar was threatening divine vengeance, spewing abuse, hurling stones. And there Moti stood, like a triumphant warrior, barring his way. The village folk looked on at the entertainment, laughing. When the bearded one, vanquished, went away, Moti returned, preening. Hira said—'I was terrified that you might get carried away in your rage and kill him.'

'Had he caught hold of me, I wouldn't have left him alive.'

'He won't come this way again.'

'Should he come I'll make him regret it well before he gets here. I'd like to see how he'll snatch us away.'

'What if he puts a bullet through you?'

'I'd sooner die than be of use to him.'

'No one reckons our lives as lives.'

'For the reason that we're so guileless.'

In a little while the troughs were filled with oil-cake, hay, bran and grain, and the two friends set about eating. Jhoori standing at their side was caressing them as scores of boys looked on. He embraced them. A wave of something like elation swept over the whole village.

Jhoori's wife, too, came running out from within and planted a kiss on the brows of both bullocks.

JUMMAN

SHRIPAD NARAYAN PENDSE

Translated from the Marathi by Shanta Gokhale

Just behind the temple of Mhasoba lies an extensive bit of flat land which they call 'Jotya's backyard'. In the old days, this place was known as 'Dankhni's backyard'. Dankhni is the Devil. There is another place in the village connected to Jotya. As you come to the end of Maharwada you notice a ramshackle porch to your right. This is where Jotya's house stood. The bit of land behind the porch was where Jotya grew his coconuts and vegetables. Pointing to the left of the porch villagers say, 'That was the frontyard. That is where Jotya used to tie Jumman.'

Even today, innumerable legends cling to Jotya's name. Challenges are thrown out, 'Let's see you enter Mhasoba's temple on new moon night,' the villagers say. 'We'll eat our heads, if Jotya doesn't come up to you, all sweaty and wild-eyed, demanding his Jumman back.' So vehement are their voices that no one feels inclined to take up the challenge. Instead, they grow absorbed in the fascinating story of Jumman.

Jotya drew his last breath crying out for Jumman; yet he had never been destined to love a human being. It wasn't that he didn't have family. He did have kids, and a wife, and he earned enough for all of them to eat well and live happily. But such are the quirks of fate, that all the love and devotion he was capable of were lavished on an animal.

If truth be told, it was only after Jumman entered Jotya's life, that it acquired some purpose and meaning. Otherwise nobody would have known or cared even if Jotya had suddenly fallen dead one day.

What was his earlier life like? It had been one long procession of carcasses that had to be skinned and a wife who had to be beaten. Mhasoba had actually been kind to him. He had given him many children. But Jotya never once caressed them. The word 'love' didn't figure in his vocabulary.

His was a life of unremitting toil, but he never stopped to ask himself why. He worked himself to the bone, but nobody had a kind word for him. How could they, when he had never said a polite word to anybody in his life?

When he came home tired from the day's work, his wife and children would look fearful. Others waited impatiently for their men to return, but in Jotya's house it was different, like everything else. As soon as he stepped inside the house, all hell would break loose. He was destined never to hear words of solicitude from members of his family. It was not even as if he drank too much. No. The fault lay in his nature.

If he found there was no curry with his bhakri, he would begin to fling obscenities at his wife. It didn't matter if his children had no curry with their bhakri, as long as he got it. As for his wife and kids, a satisfied belch from him was enough to half-fill their stomachs.

The same story was repeated outside the house. At village meetings, Jotya would sit in a corner. All of a sudden he'd start talking loudly and belligerently. Of course people never paid any attention to him. On the contrary, such was the ill will they bore him on account of his strange and eccentric ways, that a word from him was considered a universal signal for hostilities to begin. Whatever he said, whether it was right or wrong, was promptly squashed. It was generally assumed that he never said anything remotely acceptable.

Perhaps it was his profession that lay at the root of his peculiarities. His work was skinning dead cattle. He had a hereditary right over all the cattle that died in his village and in the neighbouring villages. He had a bit of land, too, but he never tended it. That was women's work according to him. Had he worked on the land, perhaps some of its softness might have entered his heart. But that was not to be!

Jotya was approaching his fifties when death touched his house. He never quite understood what took his wife. The poor wretch would scream about a lump in her stomach. Jotya decided that this was a pretext to avoid work. So the minute she started screaming he would beat her. 'Are you the only one who feels pain?' he would shout. 'How is it that we never feel any?' Because of this, even when she could barely stand, she would still come out into the yard to clean the skins. Flies would be buzzing around. She would begin to retch. When the retching began, Jotya would yell, 'So that's the new trick eh? You think you can fool me by vomiting, do you? But you can't.'

He could not be fooled. So she died. She dropped dead in the midst of the skins and vomit. At first Jotya thought she was faking her own death. 'She's putting it on,' he said. It was only when the villagers had got all the funeral things ready that he seemed to wake up to reality. Jotya cremated her and came home to find his children weeping disconsolately. For the first time in his life something moved inside his guts, and he wept. But that was that. The children, however, went on and on with their grief. At this, his anger blazed forth. According to him, there was a limit to grief. Two days was enough.

Cholera broke out in the village the following year. Though the entire village suffered, no one was as crushed by the disease as Jotya's family. By the end of the epidemic, the only one alive in that entire house, which had once hummed with human voices, was a spectral Jotya.

At night Jotya would hear the sounds of crying. He would get up, search the house and then return to his bed, disappointed. There was a gaping void in his life which he struggled to fill.

It wasn't an easy thing to do. When he woke up in the morning he would sit still for a long time. There was nobody he could shout at and curse now. He would sit there, then slowly lift the palm of his hand up to his eyes, with the vacant gaze of one demented. His hand seemed to tell him long-forgotten tales. It told of fingers that had slapped and fingers that had pinched. And even now, he could feel those fingers tingle with the memory. Remember, said the hand, remember how you pinched your children's ears between this very thumb and forefinger? Remember their screams? Look at us. We are the five Pandavas. We beat your wife with sticks. The hand seemed to sprout teeth and grin mockingly at him. The fingers seemed to push hard at his pupils. He saw his wife once again as she had been, limping and moaning in agony.

If he went near the hearth, the pots, pans and ladles would start talking to him. Their voices were quiet, but Jotya felt they were hurling themselves at him in fury.

His work came to a halt. What was he to do with the skins he brought home? Who was there to be bullied into scraping off the gobs of flesh that clung to them? And whose maw was he going to fill with the money he made breaking his back over these skins?

Life was a void into which came old memories, crowding and jostling. Jotya had never asked himself the meaning of life, but he was now convinced that his life had lost all meaning. He wouldn't eat for two days at a time, and then, when his head swam with hunger pangs, he would scrape the ashes out of the hearth and light a fire. He would sit over the dough, brooding, and then return to kneading it. As he bit into his bhakri, he would ask himself, 'What does it all mean? This eating and drinking and walking and laughing and talking?' He found all his actions incomprehensible. When he walked he would mutter to himself, 'Now, what is this I'm doing? I'm walking. What exactly does that mean? I place one foot forward, like this. Then? Then I put the other one forward. Really? How fascinating. But why be so fascinating? Why not just stand in one place?' He would open his mouth to yawn and immediately mutter to himself, 'Now why did I do that?'

For days he hovered on the brink of insanity.

Strangely enough, even in this state, there was one thing which hurt him deeply. There he was, the lone survivor of the holocaust, and yet not a soul from the village had come to enquire after him. Yet every time one of his family had died, he had plied his neighbours with liquor, and done everything else that custom required of him.

He felt disproportionately dejected over this show of callousness. But actually, Maharwada was behaving with him exactly as it had always done. It was he who had changed. He had now begun to think about things which had never occured to him before. In the old days, he had never had the time for such thoughts. All his time had been taken up by cursing and beating. Now there was nothing to do. So he began noticing all kinds of trivial matters.

At last, tired of being alone, he started visiting people himself. If people don't talk to me, he thought, there's no reason why I can't talk to them. People responded immediately. He discovered later that they had felt very deeply sorry for him in his misfortune. The more he saw of them, the more he blamed himself for having doubted them.

He began spending a great deal of his time away from home. At the end of the day's work, he would drop in at some neighbour's house, and sit chewing tobacco and lime and exchanging news. People said, 'Jotya has changed. But too late. His wife and kids weren't meant to enjoy this happiness.'

Jotya had really changed. Babies were no longer afraid of cuddling up to him. When they learned to stand by holding on to his shoulders, he would ache with remorse and guilt. 'Were my kids hungry for this kind of love? Did Mhasoba take them away from me because I wouldn't give it to them?' He trembled with fear at this thought. He mustn't spurn these little ones now, or Mhasoba might take them away too. Then he would hold the babies close and kiss them. Once in a while, an infant would smile at him, and he would feel exhilarated. God must have created babies to bring some happiness into human life, he thought. Children began to play happily around the old man and with him too. Jotya had certainly changed.

It was around this time that Jumman entered his life. How they met would seem an irrelevant question in the light of what happened. The important thing is that they met.

Jotya's transformation received its finishing touch with Jumman. Jumman turned him into a ball of butter, ready to melt at the slightest hint of heat. He continued to go out for work as he had always done. But now with Jumman in tow. Many were the occasions when Jotya would plead with him, 'My pet, why do you come after me? I am out till the sun comes overhead. You are too young. How can you possibly bear the heat? Won't you feel hungry, thirsty?' But Jumman paid no heed to him. The minute Jotya stepped out of the house Jumman would be right behind. Sometimes Jotya would play around with him. He would push him back onto the porch and scold him with mock severity, 'Now stop being naughty.' And when Jumman popped right out again, he would laugh and say, 'You were never one for obeying. Come on, then.' As he passed through Maharwada with Jumman on his shoulders, the entire neighbourhood would come out to watch the pair. They would say, 'Jotya, you had children, but you didn't want them. And now you pamper Jumman.' Once in a while Jotya would hear these remarks, and pain would tear through his heart. He would imagine his children running ahead of him crying, 'Baba, let us come with you. If you can take Jumman, why not us?' There was a time when such thoughts would have driven him berserk. But now he had Jumman to give him courage and fortitude.

When such thoughts assailed him, he would lower Jumman to the ground and rub his grizzled face against the little goat's over and over again. This chased all inauspicious thoughts out of his mind, and he would resume his journey with his usual energy. As soon as he came to his place of work, he would set Jumman down. Jumman would gambol away while Jotya got down to work. He would call out to Jumman when it was time to go home; Jumman would come frisking back and rub himself against Jotya's legs. Jotya would once again hoist him on to his shoulders, and thus father and son…

Often Jotya would trick Jumman and leave the hut without being noticed. People would ask, 'Where's the little one today, Jotya?' and he would reply, 'He is a real pest. I've left him behind.' Their reunion after three or four hours of separation was a touching sight. Jumman would rub himself against Jotya again and again. Then Jotya would lift him onto his lap and caress him. Ever since Jumman had come into his house, Jotya had not eaten alone. At dinner, he would make Jumman sit beside him. He would feed him a piece of bhakri first and then have some himself. That is the way all their meals went.

Jumman was growing up. He began to figure out how things worked. He grew horns. He began to find his way around alone. He began visiting the neighbours' houses. The children loved him. As soon as they saw him, they would start chasing him, shouting, 'Jumman, Jumman.' Right away, a game of catch-catch would begin. Jumman would dodge away and disappear. The whole of Maharwada would then ring with shouts. The children would set up a chant:

There goes the thief, catch him quick
Silly old Jumman, we know your trick.

Jumman would run helter-skelter. With the greatest effort, the children would surround him. They would then tie him up and drag him around the village. Jumman bore the rough handling without any complaint; in fact he rather enjoyed it.

When these games were being played, a worried looking Jotya would suddenly appear. He would scold the children and take Jumman away by the ear. On the way home, Jumman too would come in for his share of scolding. Jotya would say, 'It's no use looking at me like that. You're just as bad as they are.'

There was something about Jumman which won the people over. The kids adored him, and so did the grown-ups. He had managed to soften their hearts too. When the kids became rough with Jumman, Jotya wasn't the only one to give them a scolding. Whoever happened to be nearby would run to Jumman's aid. The women would give him leftovers. If they had put papads and other stuff out to dry, he would come and sniff at the food; but nobody minded him. Instead, they would playfully pinch him and say, 'Aren't you going to leave anything for us to eat, you little rascal?'

With all this pampering, Jumman grew fat and sleek. His body began to attract many glances. He now possessed a pair of haughty horns.

And then one day, he suddenly began to behave in the strangest manner. Never before had he disobeyed Jotya. His word had always been the law. But now he paid no heed to Jotya. When Jotya caressed him and tried to kiss him as usual, Jumman butted him with all his might.

Then he set off at great speed. The children chanted:

There goes the thief, catch him quick

But Jumman was in a strange mood. When the children tried to stop him, he butted them too and slipped away. The children knew at once that this was not his usual playful butting. They ran back to Maharwada and told their amazing tale to everybody.

The villagers joined Jotya in the chase. They could see Jumman in the distance. He had bleated himself hoarse. Jotya ran towards him, and as soon as he was within earshot, he called out, 'Jumman, Jumman! Aren't you tired? Come back.'

Jumman turned around. As soon as he saw the exhausted Jotya coming up behind him, he broke into a run again. He was too tired now either to run or bleat, but he kept on running. The villagers were right behind Jotya. The chase continued. Jumman dodged all of them. If anyone came too near, he would rise up on his haunches, fix him with surly eyes and go full tilt for him.

Finally they managed, somehow, to hem him in. He was exhausted after all the running. Jumman, who had so far stood firmly on his hind legs at every assault, now lost his balance and came crashing down. He lay on the ground, helpless. Panting like a pair of bellows, Jotya threw himself upon Jumman. He called out in a piteous voice, 'What came over you, Jumman? Why did you run away like that? I shall not let you go anywhere now.' Jotya began to hoist him on to his shoulders. Somebody shouted, 'Jotya, he's not a kid any more. Give him a couple of hard slaps, and let him walk. He's given you enough trouble today.'

'Oh please, don't say that. Look at the state he's in. Yes, he's been wicked today, but has he ever been like this before?' So saying, Jotya picked him up. His knees quaked under the weight of that huge body. He looked as if he would collapse any moment but he somehow made it home.

Everybody gathered at Jotya's house, curious to know what had come over Jumman. They examined him thoroughly, but found nothing wrong. Only his eyes looked bloodshot. Somebody fetched an onion from the woods. It was cut in two and the pieces placed on Jumman's eyes. There was nothing wrong with his eyes, of course, but some old man had suggested an onion be pressed into service, and someone had run off to find one. Somebody else suggested that it was all due to the evil eye. The idea was so appealing that everyone agreed with it. There was nothing more natural than that someone should have cast an evil eye on Jumman. You just had to see his sleek body, and his haughty carriage to know he was a rare beast. Someone said just then that he had seen Jumman going towards Black Madhwa's house a couple of days ago. Madhwa had noticed him. He must have cast an evil eye on him. There was no doubt in anybody's mind. Curd and rice were brought out. Jotya waved the mixture in circles around Jumman's head. Jumman watched with stupid eyes.

Jumman now lay motionless. His stomach was hollow with hunger. Jotya brought him something to eat and drink. Soon Jumman fell asleep.

But Jotya didn't sleep at all that night. He remembered how his children had suddenly left him one day. He would start up from his mat, go to Jumman and stroke him all over. Jumman slept peacefully till the morning.

No sooner did the cock crow than he began once again to bleat loudly. It was the same wild call of the previous day. It drove Jotya crazy with worry. He called out to Jumman from where he lay, 'Jumman, my pet, what has happened to you? Why are you doing this? All these days you've been a companion to me. Are you now going to betray me?' There were tears in Jotya's eyes.

Jotya got up and went to Jumman who was straining at the rope that held him, while he continued to scream and cry. The neighbours woke up. They called out, 'Are you awake, Jotya? Jumman is crying.' Jotya answered from his house, 'Please come, somebody. I need your help, Jumman is acting strange.' Jotya tried to cover Jumman's mouth with his hand. Jumman lowered his head menacingly. Jotya mustered his courage and caught hold of Jumman's proud horns in his tight fists. Fortunately, he was on his guard, for the next moment Jumman charged. Jotya kept his grip on his horns, and, in the scuffle that followed, Jumman lost his balance. Before Jotya could do anything, Jumman had crashed to the ground. On the verge of tears, Jotya shouted, 'Oh, why don't you listen? You've fallen now, and you've hurt yourself badly, haven't you?' He bent over to check if Jumman was hurt, but the goat was already up and ready to charge.

Jotya gave up then. 'To hell with you,' he muttered and lay down on his rough mat. But that did not solve the problem. Jumman continued his weird bleating. A little while later, a thought flashed into Jotya's mind. 'Maybe he's hungry, that's all.' He got up instantly, went out and plucked a basketful of green leaves. He called out soothingly to Jumman. 'Jumma, Jumma,' he said, holding the basket before him. Jumman had just been waiting for something to butt. He flung himself at the basket, making it fly in the air like straw. Jotya sat with his hand pressed against his head. Then he got up again. He drew fresh water from the well and placed it before Jumman. Jumman might have butted that too, but this time Jotya was ready. Guessing his mood from his stance, he removed the bucket before the goat could overturn it.

Jotya didn't know what to do now. He hadn't eaten a morsel since the previous evening. Jumman had killed any interest he might have had in food and drink.

By this time dawn had brightened into day. Jotya left the house. Everybody enquired after Jumman. Jotya merely shook his head, unable to speak. People wanted to help. They made various suggestions. Someone said, 'Maybe, he is rabid.'

'What do you mean he is rabid?' Jotya asked.

'Rabid, like a dog goes rabid.'

Jotya was incensed by the idea. He felt that if this kind of talk spread, they wouldn't think twice before killing Jumman.

'Dogs go rabid. But whoever heard of a goat going rabid? Don't talk like a fool.' Jumman had not gone rabid, but Jotya was certainly on the verge of doing so. He consulted the village elders. None of them knew what to make of Jumman's malady. Jotya asked them in despair, 'Please tell me. What should I be doing?'

'Jotya, why have you left Jumman alone at home and come away? He'll strain at the rope too hard and break his neck, or something. Run home this minute...'

'I am scared to go home alone. Will someone come with me?'

Jotya returned home, accompanied by a few people, Jumman was still struggling and screaming.

'This is how it's been since morning. What shall I do? Tell me, please?'

'Jotya, let him go,' an old man said.

'How will that help? He'll run away.'

'Let him.'

'Let him?'

'Yes. Let him run away. Let him go where he wants to. We'll know what he wants then.'

'And if he falls down and breaks his bones?'

'We'll be right behind. Only we won't try to stop him.'

As soon as he was released, Jumman set off at tremendous speed. There was nobody to hold him now. Jotya and the villagers followed at a distance. Jumman twisted and turned. After some time, his followers realized where he was going. He was off to Black Madhwa's place. As soon as he got there, he walked into the midst of the herd of she-goats, his head held high, and his pulse back to normal. There was no sign of the frenzy that had been driving him crazy.

'Jotya, oh Jotya, your Jumman's come of age, that's all. He needs a wife. Nothing we can do for him. Let's go home.'

Jumman became a permanent guest at Black Madhwa's place. Jotya would make a daily trip to Madhwa's and return home with a crestfallen face. Trying to bring Jumman home was futile.

One day he forcibly brought him home. The children began to dance around him singing, 'Jumman's back. Jumman's back.' Jumman too seemed happy. All the villagers came to see him. Jotya felt as if a stone had been lifted off his chest. But the relief didn't last long. Within a few days, Jumman suffered a relapse of the old malady. Quietly, Jotya set him free. Jumman pranced away to his new home. Jotya sat forlornly, muttering, 'Jumman, how can you be so ungrateful? I saved you from the knife when you were but two months old. I felt sorry for you then. I knew those scoundrels were feeding you and looking after you only to make a good bit of mutton two years later. You endeared yourself to me, and now, suddenly you've become independent. You've grown horns. It's not right to run after women so much; to forsake the man who saved you, reared you like a child, often gave you his food when there wasn't enough for two. Does a wife mean so much? Who do I have now to care for in my old age? My children left me; maybe that was my fault. But where did I go wrong with you? I never let you suffer, did I?'

He couldn't sleep, food had lost its savour. The only thing he could see was a vision of Jumman standing before him. 'The little idiot is at Madhwa's. They'll torture him there, I know,' he would say to himself. He knew Madhwa only too well. There wasn't much to choose between him and the butcher, though he might not wield the knife himself. His way of life had always shocked Jotya. To be able to rear little lambs, feed them till they grew nice and fat, and then sell them off for slaughter was incomprehensible to him. It was sheer barbarity. Madhwa was a shrewd man whose fields and spacious house had all received sustenance from the blood of countless goats. Others could have made their pile too in similar fashion. All you needed was four she-goats. Within a year they would breed you a decent herd. But people didn't want such tainted money. The very idea used to repel Jotya. Whenever he met Madhwa on the road, he would remember this about him and avert his eyes.

Jotya was in a dreadful state now. All these days the villagers had been sympathetic, but now even they had given up. How long could they continue to show concern? They were slowly forgetting Jumman. They said, 'There's no need to worry about Jumman now. He's done well for himself.' The cause of the malady had been discovered, the cure found, the patient had recovered, and so people forgot him. They thought Jotya's love for Jumman exaggerated. Whenever Jotya visited them now, they grew nervous. Jotya would always ask the same question, 'How long do you think Jumman will be like this?'

'Till he dies,' they would answer, annoyed. Jotya would gape at them and say, 'Please don't say that. I've seen too much death. I'm tired now. I'd rather you killed me…' When Jotya talked like this, the speaker would feel sorry. He would remember what Jotya had been through. Then he would hasten to reassure Jotya, 'He'll be back one of these days. He's not been away too long. Why are you in such a hurry?'

'He won't come. If I go there, he doesn't even look at me. He's grown so strange. Wine and women, they are equally bad. He has become an addict. He'll never come back.'

What could anybody say to this? The listener would escape under the pretext of having to drive away a cow from his yard.

Jotya would return home. He was alone in that deserted house. He could not concentrate on his work. Then, to add to his troubles, he quarreled with Madhwa. Jotya would go to Madhwa's place at all hours. If the goats were out grazing, he would run after them. He would start cleaning Jumman. Jumman would run away. Then the she-goats would become restive. This would make the goatherd angry. He would shout at Jotya. Jotya would plead with him, try to pacify him. One day the goatherd blew up. If Jumman was such a wonderful creature, let him be admired in his own village, the goatherd didn't give a damn. At last he complained to Madhwa. Madhwa said, 'Don't ever come here again.'

'Give me back my Jumman. Then I won't.'

'Give you back what I didn't take? I've got two dozen Jummans like yours.'

'You have taken my Jumman from me.'

'I took him? Am I on the streets begging to want your Jumman?'

Jotya stood with his head bowed. He realized how foolishly he had spoken. After some time Madhwa said to him, 'If you take Jumman away within two days, well and good. If not, he's mine by the law of trespass. If you ever come this way after that, I'll break your leg. Just remember that. There he comes. Now take him away, and keep him…'

Jotya tried all sorts of tricks, but Jumman would not go with him. He tried to lift him, but Jumman was stronger and heavier than before and he had grown weak. Even then he managed to lift up Jumman. He lowered Jumman's belly across his shoulders and grasped hold of the goat's legs. As Jotya staggered off with the goat his legs trembled under the strain, and out of sheer fear. If Jumman didn't go with him he would have to give up his right on him. The thought petrified him. Jumman was bleating harshly. Jotya blubbered, 'Jumma, please don't cry. My legs are trembling.'

He hadn't gone more than ten paces when he collapsed under Jumman's weight, bringing Jumman down with him. Jumman promptly shook himself free and made off.

'Jumman, Jumman, Jumman,' Jotya called after him, but the arrogant lecher was nowhere in sight. Jotya stood up with a great effort. His knees were bruised. He rubbed some mud on them, and went back to Madhwa's house.

The goats were tied in the yard. He spotted Jumman in the corner. He went to him, stroked his back, made sure he wasn't hurt, and then settled down to wait for Madhwa.

Madhwa came out to the yard. Jotya's state made him laugh.

'Have you gone mad, Jotya?' he asked.

'Not yet, but I shall very soon. What did you say a while ago? That I could take Jumman in the next two days, didn't you?'

'Yes. By day after tomorrow. I'll give you two more days if you like. I don't want your goat. But I can't have you nosing around here every day. That's why I made up my mind. Otherwise he doesn't bother me. I've got forty. One more makes no difference. But you'd better take him. I'll give you four days. Or make it eight. But I don't want to see you here after that.'

Jotya felt weighed down with gratitude. He wouldn't have imagined Madhwa could be so soft. Eight days! Enough time to tie Jumman up and take him home if need be. He went home happy.

And...

On the ninth day Jumman became Madhwa's property.

The terrible news spread throughout the village the minute Madhwa claimed Jumman. Many had predicted this would happen. And yet, though they'd been fully prepared for the dreadful eventuality, they were shocked when it actually came about. People whispered in subdued voices. Someone said, 'Is the news true in the first place? I don't want to waste my tears.' The speaker's untimely wit was not appreciated. But he had expressed a valid doubt. So a few elders left hurriedly to make sure.

They discovered that every bit of the news was true.

How was Jotya to be told of this ghastly development? The villagers sat brooding over the problem. Jotya would start weeping the minute he heard the news. But there was no time to waste. If they acted quickly, there was still some chance that Jumman might be saved.

Four village elders got together and started for Jotya's house. Jotya was lying on his mat. He had lost his grip on himself since Jumman had become Madhwa's. He spent most of his time lying flat on his mat. He got up, or slept, as his mood took him. There was nothing left to eat in the house now, except for a measure of flour.

Jotya saw the elders approaching while they were still some distance away. When he saw them turning towards his house, he was surprised. People had gradually stopped coming to see him after Jumman had left. It had been different when Jumman…

Whenever he thought of this, he felt sad. He was sad now. When Jumman had been with him, there had been joy in the house. Children used to turn up, morning, noon and night. They would tease Jumman. They would complain to Jotya about him. Then Jotya would scold him. He would explain to the children, 'He's still young. That's why he's naughty. I'll scold him, don't worry. We'll punish him.'

The children would protest, 'No, no. Don't punish him. We don't mind if he plays pranks on us. We'll do the same to him. Please don't worry.'

When the adults passed by his house they would say, 'Jotya, how is Jumman today? Is he at home, or is he out visiting?'

Jotya would say, 'Oh, I've given up. He's too much for me.'

Then they would say, 'That's because you've spoilt him. What he needs is a good spanking.'

That was the way it used to be all through the day. And now, not a soul came his way. They were too scared to come. They weren't prepared to listen to Jotya talk about Jumman. It was always the same. Old stories, memories, and then inevitably, the tears. It was the same with the children as with the grown-ups. Nobody had the patience to console him every day. There's not much you can say to console people, and once all that could be said was said, people stopped coming.

The house now looked sepulchral. It was the second time Jotya was going through this kind of experience. The first time, he hadn't known what was happening. It took him many days to understand. But in those days he had been strong, not old and frail as he was now. This time he had known what was coming. And yet, when the expected happened, it took half his life from him.

Jotya cheered up when he saw that people were still concerned about him. And right on the heels of this thought came another, sweeter thought. 'Perhaps they have come with some good news about Jumman.' So far all news had been bad. Who knows...

But a single glance at their faces dashed all his hopes, and now he trembled with fear.

The elders sat down beside him and said, 'How are you feeling, Jotya?'

Jotya remained silent. 'Why don't you speak, Jotya?' they asked again.

By now Jotya, observing their long, solemn faces, was making the most ghastly conjectures about the object of their visit. He said angrily, 'Look here. Why don't you just tell me what you've come to tell me? I don't like the way you look. I know it's something terrible...'

'Where's Jumman?'

'Dead. Didn't you know? Or at least he's at Madhwa's. But that's as good as dead to me. It's two days since he died...'

'He's really going to die. If you hurry, you might save him.'

'H...he's...w...w...w...' However hard he tried, not a single word would form.

'Jotya, Jotya, don't worry. Jumman isn't dead...yet.'

Jotya gaped at them without understanding. He slapped his forehead with his hand, meaning to say that he was suffering the results of his own doings. He was born to bring sorrow upon me... But not a single word emerged from his mouth. He couldn't speak. The visitors tried to reassure him. They had decided to break the news to him gently to lessen the shock of it. But Jotya had got into such a bad state merely imagining what had happened that they were baffled. They didn't know how to deal with him. The end that faced Jumman was not unavoidable. It was true that he was on the road to death, but he could still be saved. Yet what could they do if Jotya suddenly fainted when they finally told him the news? Looking at him now they realized one thing for sure. If Jumman died, whenever that happened, Jotya would be his companion on the funeral pyre.

'Jotya, Jumman is not dead. But if you insist on behaving as though he his, then he might have to die. So don't waste any more time. Put on your shirt and come with us.'

'He's at Madhwa's, isn't he?'

'Don't ask questions. Just come.'

'I can't go alone…'

'You're not going alone. We're going with you.'

'But Jumman won't come with me.'

'We'll see about that. Just come with us.'

'Please don't shout at me. I said that only because he's grown woman-mad these days.'

'That madness has got him into bad trouble. The butcher isn't going to spare him for his women.'

'And then...'

'And then nothing. Are you coming with us or not? Or, do you just want to go and die with your Jumman?'

'Please don't be like that.'

'Be like what? You've become impossible. Things were better without Jumman around here.'

'But you care all the same, don't you?' Jotya said, putting on his shirt.

'That's the whole trouble. Ready? Got your money?'

'Will we need money?'

'Won't we? Or do you think the butcher values your tears the way we do? You can cry as much as you like and nobody there will even notice. Now hurry up. Get your money, and come.'

'How much?'

'At least ten rupees.'

'Ten?' said Jotya, and promptly sat down.

'How much do you have?'

'I might be able to scrape together a couple of rupees...'

'That's just great. Then you might as well keep sitting here. Bloody pauper.'

Jotya remained sitting, his hand pressed to his forehead.

'Aren't you coming?'

'But the money? Where can I get that much from? You'd better go.'

'Go? And what about Jumman?'

'Let him die.'

'Let Jumman die?'

'What else? Why did he have to choose a pauper for a master? He'll die out there and I'll die here. Will my hide help?'

'Human hide fetches nothing. And yours isn't even healthy, with all those scars and wrinkles…'

Jotya didn't respond. The visitors left, and Jotya lay down once again, thinking… Something had got hold of Jumman. They were dragging him off somewhere. He couldn't even walk, they were dragging him so mercilessly. He was casting pathetic glances at Jotya. Jotya was in despair. Jumman was saying, 'I'll never do it again. It was all my fault. Take me back. Please take me back. These people are going to slaughter me. Please take me home...'

Jotya hurriedly looked through all his pockets. There wasn't a paisa in them. Jumman's cries asking to be taken back grew fainter and fainter, and then faded away. Soon after he heard a 'baaaaaa'. That was the last bleat Jumman was destined to utter. Then there was a sound of gulping and Jotya saw a struggling body…

Crazy with fear, Jotya flung himself down on his mat. He remained that way for a long time, listening to Jumman's heart-rending bleating.

An hour later, the elders of the village returned. One of them said roughly, 'Come on, get up. We're going.'

'Where?' asked Jotya, starting up.

'Now stop being a fool, just come.'

'But the money?'

'We've seen to that.'

'Which good person did you meet?'

'The whole village. We went begging to every house, collecting twenty-five paise here and fifty paise there. Your Jumman is a nuisance…'

'And yet you love him.'

'That's why he's a nuisance. He's made everybody mad.'

But Jotya remained sitting where he was. When he seemed to be making no signs of moving, someone said, 'What are you thinking of now, Jotya?'

'How can I return the money? I don't even remember to eat these days. I've grown weak. I can't work the way I used to.'

'You don't have to return the money.'

'But then…' Jotya wasn't sure at all whether he should say what was in his mind. They might not like it. He was trying to make up his mind…

'What's the "but" now for? Here we are, running around for you, and you decide to act like a bashful bridegroom.'

'I'll tell you if you promise not to get annoyed…'

'We've had enough of that, Jotya, goodbye.' The villagers rose to go.

'Please don't go,' Jotya pleaded, on the verge of tears. 'I'm coming.'

The place reeked with a stench that even Jotya found difficult to endure. Ten of twelve fattened goats stood in a corner. Among them was Jumman, cowering against the wall. His once proud head was now lowered. Every minute brought to his ears the screams of his brethren. He had finally understood where he had been brought. His milk-white body now bore a red mark. His eyes brimmed with fear. Every sound, every human voice, made him look around fearfully. His eyes met Jotya's and he let out a terrified bleat of appeal to him. Jotya's heart melted to water.

'Oh, Jumman. Is this what you were destined for?'

Tears flowed from Jotya's eyes. He rushed to Jumman's side. Jumman instantly recognized his love-filled caress, so familiar to him from infancy. He allowed his head to rest on Jotya's hand.

When Jotya arrived on the outskirts of the village with Jumman, the whole village turned out to welcome this unlikely pair of father and son. It was the return of the runaway son. Children hung garlands around his neck, and stuck nosegays in his graceful horns. The red footprints of Death had been washed off his body. The villagers followed the pair into the village crying, 'Jumman's back, Jumman's back.'

The village collected another fund and handed it over to Jotya.

'Jotya, you must use this for a Satyanarayan puja. With bhajans.'

This puja became a much talked about event, even in the surrounding villages.

Jotya's house came alive once again. The children began to flock there. Once again there was shouting, noisy games, quarrels and scoldings. Jotya began working again and earning money. When he had saved ten rupees, he went from house to house; but no one wanted their money back. People told him not to be a fool.

'Jotya, do you think you're the only one who loves Jumman? We love him too. He has brought us joy. If we take your money, our children will be ashamed of us.'

Till then Jumman was known only within the village. But soon he began to be talked of in all the neighbouring villages. There was obviously something very unusual about an animal for whose redemption a whole village had raised money. The way the villagers had bought him from the butcher, welcomed him with garlands and nosegays, performed a Satyanarayan puja in celebration—these strange events gripped people's imagination. Every man had his own opinion to express on the Jumman episode. One said, 'The whole village must be mad. Whoever heard of a goat being given a name! Jumman! And the fund. And the puja. The whole thing is crazy.' They silenced the man saying, 'People don't go around wasting time on a goat unless there's a very special reason!' The man immediately realized his mistake.

Of course the surrounding villages made these events out to be much more astonishing and miraculous than they had actually been. What was this Jumman actually like, for whose salvation an entire village had pooled its resources and for whom a Satyanarayan puja had been performed? How did he walk? How did he talk? What did he eat? What did he drink?

Someone started the rumour that he only ate food which was

generally eaten on fast days; that he never touched leftovers; that he granted boons; that he licked the ailing, and believe it or not, cured them of their ailments.

Another man made an unexpected discovery. Since Jumman's arrival in the area, the annual scourge of cholera had not made an appearance. The discovery was verified. It was quite true. There hadn't been an outbreak of cholera in the last two years. It didn't take long after this for Jumman, the goat to become Jumman, the local deity.

Jotya knew nothing about these developments. One fine morning somebody came to visit Jotya's child. Then a second came, and a third. There seemed to be no end to the visitors that morning. Jotya was completely baffled. Everybody who came would stand before Jumman reverently, inspect him from head to foot and then go away with the sublime conviction that they had been in the presence of some kind of divine phenomenon. They swore that Jumman was different from other goats as earth is from sky. Each person would return saying, 'When I went in I was sure this was some tall story that some joker had put about. But, God help me; it's not so at all. You've got to see it to believe it. He's obviously got something in him. Did you notice his eyes? Oh you didn't? You must observe the shape. They are like conchshells. And the pupils are like whorls. Yes. Both the pupils. That is what I found so strange. Forgive my doubts, Lord Jumman. I never meant to doubt you.' Saying this, the speaker would slap himself across the face and bow reverently before Lord Jumman.

The number of devotes increased from day to day. The yard where Jumman was tied up was spruced up. The corner where Jumman actually sat was plastered smooth with cowdung. Framed pictures of gods and saints were hung up. The roof was covered with bundles of grass to prevent the sun from troubling Jumman.

To begin with, nobody actually folded their hands before Jumman. They didn't have the courage to. They would worship him without any outward sign. Then they began doing furtive namaskars. One devotee noticed these surreptitious signs of worship; he folded his hands openly, in full view of the people. This made namaskars an accepted ritual in Jumman worship. This was followed by the burning of camphor and incense sticks, and the offering of fruits and flowers. The devotees would begin to crowd in even before the sun rose. Some of them would come to ask for boons, some to offer thanks for boons granted. There seemed to be no end to those asking Jumman for boons. He was adorned every day with garlands and nosegays. Bright new clothes were made for him. Jumman no longer needed to go searching for succulent green leaves in the hot sun. His devotees came to him with flowers in one hand and a branch of foliage in the other.

Jumman now took to blessing his devotees with divine revelations. He appeared to one man in a dream. The man broadcast the news. Another felt, 'It might happen to me too.' And it did, regularly. Every small movement that Jumman made now acquired portentous significance. When he shook his head sideways, it meant 'No'. When he moved it up and down, it meant 'Yes'. Everybody came to recognize these signs. They would ask him a question and then sit staring at his head for an answer. Even his ears, feet, and body revealed important answers to people. The hopes, ambitions, and desires of many depended on the movements of these organs. 'Our boy says he wants to work on daily wages in Bombay. Should he go or not?' A young man's parents would ask Jumman. And so it went.

Jotya no longer needed to worry about food, or anything else. In fact, he found it difficult to cope with all the rice, fruits, garlands, money and coconuts that had to be collected at the end of the day. The village children came to help him. He would distribute the offerings amongst them. In the old days they had gone to Jotya's place to visit Jumman. Now the offerings became an added attraction, and one which was, perhaps, stronger than Jumman. By nine o'clock at night, the devotees would disperse and the children would come hurrying in. The slower ones were encouraged, with clouts from their parents, to go and collect their share from Jotya. Of course, what the parents said was, 'You little wretch. Do you want poor Jotya to die of all that work? Go help him. Go.' When the child returned there was always the satisfying clink of coins in his pocket, and some rice and a couple of coconuts in his hands. Jumman had become a sort of cornucopia for the entire village.

When the whole place had been put back into order, Jotya would drag Jumman indoors, tear the garlands and clothes off his body, and demand angrily, 'Look here, you bastard, what tricks are you up to? Where's this god of yours, just show me. A few lunkheads decide to start worshipping you, and you sit back and take it, do you? All you had to do was to butt that first dimwit good and proper, and he would have chased all the others away. But you're just lapping it all up. Aren't you? Go on, own up. I'm asking you a question like one of those foolish devotees. Tell me, yes or no?'

Jumman shook his head sideways. Jotya roared, 'No? No? Then why don't you butt them? All your show of might is reserved for your old man? Isn't that right? Don't gape at me like a halfwit. Just tell me if I'm right or wrong...'

Jumman moved his head up and down. Jotya laughed and said, 'Then why don't you show them how you feel about it? Did I save you from the slaughterhouse so you could start these monkey tricks? You know Jumma, this is really strange. I twist your ears, I curse you, but your god doesn't seem to mind. Where's he run off to? Doesn't he want to punish me? Oh the fools, the dolts...' Then Jotya would pinch Jumman's cheeks, fondle him and make him sleep beside him.

The first crowing of the cock would give Jotya nervous palpitations. Now the monsters will start pouring in. They will torture Jumman in a hundred ways. I won't get a minute with him till nightfall. What is to be done with these fools...

At last Jotya decided he had had enough. 'This foolishness must end. Here's an ordinary goat, and they make him into a god. If he was god, why did I have to run around so much to save him from the knife? I've just about had enough. From tomorrow nobody comes here. We'll live on anything, Jumman and I—even on air. That's our problem.'

The next day Jotya got up and left the house with Jumman in tow as in the old days. The whole village was stunned. They said, 'Where are you off to?'

'Where do you think? To work.'

'But why do you want to take god with you?'

'God? What god are you talking about? This is my Jumman, and I'm taking him out to graze.'

'Jotya, you've got too smart for your boots. Watch out.'

'What did I do?'

'You are offending god.'

Jotya went on without heeding them. Further on, Jotya began to meet Jumman's devotees. Jotya was dragging Jumman along. That terrible sight rent their hearts. Such an outrage was not to be allowed to continue. The devotees stopped Jotya.

'Where are you going, Jotya?'

'Where? To work, of course. Get out of my way.'

'Why do you need to work?'

'Why do *you*?'

'You've not been starving all these days have you, you ungrateful man?'

'Watch what you are saying. I can't help it if people choose to pour stuff into my house.'

'So, what did we say? It was just a remark... Look. You brought up Jumman with such love. Do you know how much merit that has brought you? You have every right to sit back and be fed.'

'I don't want to sit back and be fed. I don't want dead food.'

'How could you call offerings to Jumman dead food? You are blaspheming.'

'Offerings for a goat! You've all gone mad and you're trying to make a fool of me.'

'We're mad, are we? We'll forgive you only on account of that one merit of yours. What do you take Jumman for?'

'A goat with the usual horns, beard and four legs.'

'Dear god, block our ears against such evil. Jotya will bring disaster upon us if he talks this way. The cholera will return. Jotya, you're asking for a beating.'

'Do garlands and flowers make a god out of goat? How can you be so foolish? Some idiot started talking nonsense and you started running after a goat. I can't even fondle him when I want to with you people around. I won't stand for it. Get out of my way.'

'Let Jumman go, then we'll let you go wherever you want to.'

'What do you mean? Do you think Jumman belongs to you?'

'If you don't hand him over quietly, we'll have to take him by force.'

'You will not get Jumman. And you will stop coming to my house from now on. I don't want your money or anything else. I'll work as I've always done, and earn my bit of bhakri. My Jumman will graze and fill his stomach.'

'Your Jumman? Who gave him to you?'

'Who gave him to me? It's a very old story. I'll tell you if you want to know.'

'But who saved Jumman? Who paid the money?'

'I offered it to you. You wouldn't take it. That's not my fault.'

'Just tell us whether we paid the money or not.'

Jotya did not answer. Somebody repeated in a louder voice, 'Jotya, is it true or false that we paid the money?'

'False. Absolutely false.'

'False? Say that again.'

'Of course, it's false. Why didn't you take the money when I offered to return it to you? I had a suspicion then that you might stake a claim on Jumman. I should have made things clearer... I was a fool not to.'

'Then you must bear the consequences. But why are you behaving like this, Jotya? There's nothing you don't have!'

'Oh, no? I can't even get near Jumman. The yard is always choked with people. He's just a common goat, but you have made him into a god. What do I have left then to call my own? You'll get your Jumman on one condition.'

'Just say it. We can't do a thing unless you tell us what you want.'

'Give me a poison which will kill me in five minutes. You can then have Jumman. Nothing will matter once I'm dead.'

'Jotya, you were never one to talk straight. Come on folks. Get hold of Jumman.'

'Hey, don't. What are you...'

'There's no "hey don't" now.'

'Don't treat him roughly. No. I won't let him go. You watch it. I will...the bastards...'

A short struggle and then Jumman was in the hands of the villagers. Jotya stood looking at the fools for some time. Then he retraced his steps sadly homewards. He felt forsaken once again just as he had been that first time that his life had been ruined. He came home reluctantly. Seeing him, somebody shouted, 'Jotya has come.' But Jotya paid no attention to him. He went inside the house with his head bent. Jumman was already looking ugly. That night was as disturbed as the previous night. Jotya twisted and turned, thinking. He had heard whispered remarks that Jumman would be removed from his yard. He made up his mind that he would never let that happen.

He woke up early the next morning and went to Jumman. Jumman was already awake. Jotya stroked him and said, 'Jumma, we'll have to leave, don't you agree? Don't look so sad. Come. Where? Silly Billy. Wherever the road takes us. We'll first go to Dankhni's yard, and do our namaskar to Mhasoba. Then we'll go into the hills. The Katkaris live there. They are an illiterate tribe, but not half as illiterate as these fools. Let us spend the rest of our lives there. If I die first, you must kill yourself. If you die first, I'll kill myself.'

So saying, he untied Jumman, and the two of them started off. They emerged from Maharwada and entered Dankhni's yard. Jotya did a namaskar to Mhasoba, and they took the hill road.

The morning had grown bright by the time they reached the jungle path. Just then...Jotya thought he heard a kind of buzzing sound. He pricked up his ears but couldn't identify it. He walked a few paces more, and soon there was no doubt left at all. The buzzing sound was quite clear now.

From far away a black cloud seemed to be moving over the sea shorewards, at great speed. Jotya's legs gave way. He pulled Jumman towards him and pointed out the weird phenomenon to him. At one point Jotya was convinced that the cloud was coming straight at him.

But when he looked closer he thought otherwise. The buzzing was continuous. Jotya tried to gauge the dimensions of this quivering cloud but soon gave up the attempt. Seeing its immensity, Jotya trembled with fear. Where was this cloud, stretching across the entire horizon, travelling to? It swung from side to side making it difficult to tell where it was going. Jotya forgot all about going to live with the Katkaris in the hills as he sat watching the apparition. Jumman gradually moved away in search of leaves.

The buzzing continued. Jotya realized that the cloud was unmistakably moving towards him. Suddenly he remembered the words of the villagers, 'You will bring disaster upon the village.'

Could this be that disaster? The thought struck fear into his heart. He began to sweat profusely. The strength drained out of his limbs. He sank to the ground. He held his head between his hands to stop the hammering inside, he looked around for Jumman. The buzzing was growing louder.

He stood up, petrified, calling out, 'Jumman, Jumman.' But Jumman was nowhere around. The terrifying buzzing that continued to come from across the sea, the villagers' words, Jumman's disappearance were the three fears that chased Jotya with malevolent ferocity. He wondered, 'Was I wrong to bring Jumman away? Suppose some calamity does strike the village?'

Bzz, bzz. The sound grew louder and louder. Jotya racked his brains. 'What shall I do, what shall I do?'

Bzz, bzz, bzzzzz...

'Oh my god! I don't want to live in this jungle! What a terrible prediction!!! Where's Jumman?'

Bzzzz, bzzzz, bzzzz...

Jotya was drowning in a whirlpool of turbulent thoughts.

'Jumman, Jumman, Jumman.' Jotya called out in a voice cracked with fear. Jotya began to run. He couldn't afford to stop, as the buzzing grew louder, and yet louder.

Were the villagers' words going to come true after all?

It was true then that Jumman *was* a divine animal.

He still couldn't believe it.

The sound grew louder, it was on the verge of swallowing him up. There was still no sign of Jumman.

Jotya mustered all his strength, pressed his hands against his stomach and screamed, 'Jumman. Don't try my patience. Please come. As you are. We'll go home. I can't bear this, really I can't.'

From somewhere far away came the sound of Jumman's bleating. Soon he was by Jotya's side. 'Thank god, you've come. Let's go. We will go home. Forget what I told you. I don't like what I'm seeing. Do you see that, in the west?'

Jotya glanced in the direction he was pointing out to Jumman. The cloud, which had been black all this while, was now glowing bright red. It was like witchcraft. Had god sent a cloud of fire upon the village for Jotya's sin?

Jotya couldn't bear to look at it. He took hold of Jumman, and beating his head with his hand, he hastened home.

They reached Dankhni's yard once again, and Jotya couldn't believe what he saw. Every tree within sight was glowing bright red like live ember. Whole plantations of coconut and betel were alight with the same red glow.

He set off for the village at tremendous speed, but had to stop soon to call out to Jumman, 'Jumma, Jumma, hurry. What is happening? Do you really have divine powers? Do you belong to god? Not to me? I was wrong. Forgive me.' He bowed before Jumman with profound devotion. 'I'm a fool. I'm a villain. I'm a swine. Please forgive me. Will you? I give up my claim on you. But we'll have to hurry. The day's no longer ours. It belongs to the enemy.' Jotya walked faster.

Every tree in the village had turned red. All of a sudden Jotya shouted, 'Locusts! A locust invasion. That's the end of the village. We're ruined.'

Whatever courage Jotya had left, now drained away. Something within him seemed to be heaving up in waves, and, with every wave, his mouth began to taste rancid. He felt feverish. It seemed as though his eyes were being sucked into his body. His old body seemed to be getting smaller every moment. But there was one thing he had to do before his body caved in. He must tie Jumman in the yard, garland him and do a namaskar to him. But if he collapsed before that, where would Jumman go? And what would happen to the village? He was sure that what he intended doing was the only way of saving the village from this awful visitation.

The locusts were everywhere. They were ahead of him, behind him, and all around him. Masses of locusts. Not a single tree had been spared. Many trees were already ruined. They looked like beautiful women shaved of their luxuriant locks. It was a terrifying sight.

Jotya reached his house. Someone from a neighbouring house shouted, 'Jotya, where have you been? Run in, and don't kill a single locust.'

Jotya pulled Jumman in, and stared out with dead eyes. He didn't have the courage to go into the backyard. Everything was bright red, and the obscene sound of nibbling echoed through the air. Everything was being destroyed. Palm fronds were turning in an instant into bare ribs. Jotya couldn't bear to sit indoors. He came out into the backyard. Jumman came after him, but he pushed him back in.

'What do you want? Are you hungry? There's not a single green leaf for you. You'll have to make do with dry grass now, if you can get it.'

He locked Jumman in, and came out. The ground was covered with a thick layer of something black. Now what was this? Jotya bent down. Showers of something that was red and black came pelting down from above. He picked up a bit of the substance from the ground, and shouted, 'Shit, it's shit. That's right, you bastards. Eat, and shit, and spread havoc.' He picked up a stone. He was about to fling it into the air when he remembered the warning, 'Don't kill the locusts.'

'And why not?' Jotya demanded enraged. 'Are these locusts also creatures of god like Jumman?' The thought sapped him of all his strength. The stone fell from his hand. His trees were being rapidly shaved.

Tick, tick, tick, they nibbled.

Zzzzzzzzzz, they buzzed.

Pitter patter, they shat.

Jotya couldn't bear to stand there. He turned into the house with his hand pressed to his head. How was it all going to end? Why doesn't anybody stop these creatures? What's happened to the village? What kind of spell is it under? And who had cast that spell? How could the village calmly watch death approaching it?

But that was the way it was. Not a single person was willing to come out of his house. Jotya was sure that if everybody made a din, if they beat drums and old tins, hurled stones, and made fires, the locusts would go back the way they had come. But some of them would die, and the villagers had said that they must not be killed. Why? Nobody had the answer to that. And what if the entire village became destitute? What if? It already was.

All that was left in the gardens and plantations were stumps and shit. The place was one big graveyard. The entire coastal strip had been reduced to ashes by the locusts.

Soon after this, a meeting was held in Jotya's village. The villagers pondered the problem deeply. How were they to recover from such a loss? With whose help? It was obviously not possible for man alone to solve the problem so they prostrated themselves before Mhasoba. They asked for a boon in return for which they made a promise. They prayed to Mhasoba to help them make up this year's losses within the coming year. Jotya vehemently opposed the idea. But he stood alone against the entire village. All he could hope for now was that Mhasoba would not let him down, and it was on the strength of this hope that he finally consented to this inhuman solution.

His feet dragged heavily as he returned home. As soon as he stepped into the yard, Jumman came racing towards him. Jumman always eased Jotya's sorrow during times of trial. So he pulled Jumman towards him and kissed him over and over again.

He was ravenously hungry, yet he did not feel like eating. Every now and again he would glance at Jumman and suddenly hug him.

Then he'd console himself, saying Mhasoba will never grant them the boon. It was simply not possible to make good the loss of an entire year's crop within a year. He felt he was worrying unnecessarily about something which would never take place. He would smile confidently and stroke Jumman's back, then take him out.

The villagers began, once again, to shower Jumman with love. True, there were no more flowers and garlands, but Jumman knew again that he was something special. He carried himself with the hauteur of a bull who was dedicated to the gods. He could go where he liked, graze where he liked, and return home only when he was full. Jumman, who had grown thin for a while, now fattened up again. He wandered around with his head held high while children followed him, calling out, 'Jumman, Jumman.'

Jotya, however, was being corroded with doubt from within. What if the villagers were granted the boon they had asked of Mhasoba? He had no desire to eat, or sleep or live.

He lived merely because he breathed.

He stopped visiting people. He stopped talking to people. People asked him, 'Jotya, what's come over you all of a sudden? Why do you let the famine get you down so much? You've neither wife nor kids. The famine hardly affects you.' Jotya would look at them uncomprehendingly.

He would hang around the house for hours on end. And when Jumman came near him he would burn with shame. After all he had raised him like a son...

The village had now begun to feel the effects of the locust invasion. Because people had reserve stocks of rice, they didn't actually starve but money became scarce. There were no betel nuts, and no coconuts. There was no money to buy spices. Falling ill became a luxury, because nobody could afford medicines. People went around with pinched faces.

And yet they didn't give way to despair.

As soon as the first showers came, they got down to work with every ounce of energy they could muster. Every yard was cleared of the layers of excreta that had gathered there and then thoroughly cleaned.

The palm trees, shorn of their foliage, were cut down. It was a terrible sight. Trees which had pulsated with the sap of life but a few days ago were now being torn down and stacked up for firewood. The village performed the last rites of the dead yards with tears in their eyes; the womenfolk worked with tears in their eyes; and when children brought out bhakris to their parents, they too were weeping.

The tasks were done, all the same, with the heartlessness of butchers. The heaps of excreta that had been collected were flung into the fields. The yards were clean. Now the rains would come, and planting would begin.

Everybody had the greatest faith in Mhasoba. How could he not grant them the boon they had asked for? Their faith was indestructible, their hope strong. This saw them through the famine.

Jotya was watching everything.

The fields were ploughed.

They were sown.

And, exactly on the expected day, the rains came.

There was jubilation all around.

The rains did not let them down a single time throughout the season.

The incessant showers made Jotya fearful.

He sent up a silent prayer to Mhasoba.

But the rains continued unabated. Never before had Jotya seen such a perfect monsoon.

Navratra ended. Dussehra came.

Jotya said to Jumman, 'Jumman, Jumman, what have I done? What will I do if something dreadful happens? Nothing will wash away my sins.'

The reaping began.

A weight descended on Jotya's heart with every sheaf of corn he saw, bursting with ripened grain.

The whole village danced in ecstatic joy.

Even the palms planted in the backyards came thrusting out of the soil to welcome this splendid harvest. People were stunned to see the height and grace of the saplings. Such things had never before occurred in the memory of even the oldest inhabitants of the village.

The day for measuring the paddy came. People called out to Jotya on their way to the threshing floor.

'Jotya, Jotya, god has been merciful. Mhasoba has blessed us. Come out to the threshing floor. We bring the paddy home today.'

Jotya neither moved nor spoke.

They shook him. He said after a time, 'Go on without me.'

'And have you complain later on? No thanks.'

'I can't make it. I've lost all my strength. You go along.'

'How can you lose your strength in one day? You managed to walk by yourself to the threshing floor yesterday all right.'

So they brought a cart and tried to lift Jotya into it. Jotya protested, 'You monsters, what are you doing? I don't want to come.'

Nobody paid any attention to his blabbering. One took hold of his head, another supported his back, a third turned to his legs, and a fourth cried, 'Heave ho!' And the next minute Jotya found himself being gently placed inside the cart.

The cart moved.

Jotya could see neither houses nor people. When he was being put in the cart, Jumman had looked on curiously. Jotya glanced at Jumman once and he could no longer control his tears.

The measuring began.

'One, two...'

The pile of grain grew rapidly higher. The measuring ended. The villagers danced. The pile stood before them, and yet they could not believe their eyes. The harvest had increased threefold. Whose doing was it?

Mhasoba's.

Who else?

Nobody knew where Jotya found the strength to do it, but he jumped out of the cart shouting, 'That's not true. Not true. Mhasoba has not granted the boon.'

'Jotya, stop drivelling.'

'I am not drivelling. Mhasoba had nothing to do with it.'

'Then maybe it was your father who gave us this harvest.'

'I don't know about that, but Mhasoba didn't.'

'Jotya's being too clever for his own good. He needs to be thrashed so he stops this foolishness. Else, we'll have the locusts back again.'

'Let him have his say. Now, Jotya, you say that this isn't Mhasoba's doing.'

'It isn't.'

'Then how do you account for this bumper harvest? None of the other villages have had one.'

'You worked hard. You threw the excreta into the fields...'

People guffawed loudly at this.

'Jotya, being old doesn't give you the right to talk nonsense.'

'I'm not talking nonsense. Just use your heads. If you ask the people in the other villages, they'll tell you that they threw the excreta into the sea. That's why they lost their crop. Our fields got readymade manure; it's simply a question of coincidence.'

'You're right. It is a coincidence. And why was this coincidence beneficial to us and not to others? Why are you silent now? Don't you understand, you fool, that it is the boon that has worked for us. Not shit manure!'

Jotya found no answer to this.

The next day a meeting was held. When was the promise made to Mhasoba to be fulfilled? Jotya had decided not to attend the meeting, but as on the previous day, people went to his house. They carried him bodily to the meeting. Their behaviour seemed to make Jumman nervous and he bleated in a strange voice.

When Jotya returned after the meeting, Jumman was even more astonished. Jotya was actually sobbing as he walked home. As he entered the house, the sound of his helpless sobbing filled the air.

'Jumman, Jumman,' Jotya cried, flinging his arms around him, and laying his trembling head on his shoulders. 'Jumman, what have I done!'

This continued all through the night. And, as usual, the night hurried on to make way for a new day. But it seemed to Jotya that people were walking on their heads instead of their legs, that birds were sobbing in agony instead of singing, that the village was on fire, that a disaster worse than the locust invasion had struck the village, and that the flames from this immense conflagration were leaping up towards the sky.

The villagers came to Jotya's house even before the sun had risen. They came with flowers and garlands and incense.

They called out, 'Jotya, it's time to go.'

Jotya did not say a word.

They entered the house.

Jotya was nowhere to be seen.

They searched the whole house.

Then they began looking for Jumman.

Even Jumman seemed to have disappeared.

The house was empty.

Where were they?

The villagers hurried out.

The auspicious time must not be missed. What if they couldn't find them before sunrise?

The thought put fear into them, and they ran around looking for the man and his goat. Their suspicions were right.

Jotya and Jumman were running as fast as they could through Dankhni's yard.

Jotya glanced around, and shouted, 'Jumman, we're done for. Run faster. Run.'

Jumman loitered on the way. He found the green leaves too tempting. Jotya shouted, 'What kind of a famine have you come out of? Don't you understand how important every second is?'

Saying this, Jotya picked up Jumman and tried running carrying him. But a few paces later, he put him down again, panting heavily. He couldn't understand why his strength had suddenly deserted him. Beside himself with fury, he whacked Jumman hard and shouted, 'Trot. Run. Walking's not going to get us anywhere.'

Jumman started running with Jotya following. Not far behind them were the pursuing villagers.

As the pair was trying to cut through Dankhni's yard someone should have told them how futile it was to flee. But who was to tell them? They were frothing at the mouth, and dripping with sweat, but they continued to run, foolishly.

The distance between them and the villagers had closed to almost nothing. The villagers were shouting again and again, 'Jotya, you can't get away. How far will you run? Look at the state you're in!'

Jotya ran past the Mhasoba temple and began climbing the hill.

And then, the villagers were upon him. 'Jotya, why are you being such a fool?'

'Who's being a fool, you swine? You're the fools. You worshipped Jumman first as a god and now...' He couldn't bear to complete the sentence. Mhasoba was just behind. He silently called upon his help. But even before his prayer was out, the villagers had got hold of Jumman. It wasn't very long now to sunrise. They tied Jumman's limbs. Jotya winced to see how roughly they handled him. 'Please be gentle, at least,' he pleaded.

'We're being gentle, Jotya. You are not the only one who loved Jumman.'

'Oh, you bastards. Is this your love?'

They began to take Jumman away. Jotya's legs were barely holding him up. Jumman was somewhere in the middle of the crowd of villagers. Jotya followed the crowd. The distance between Jumman and Jotya was growing wider. Jotya could not bear to see the way Jumman was being handled. 'Don't drag him like that. He's tired. Can't you understand? How can I make you understand?'

The villagers crowded around Mhasoba's temple. Jotya stood a great distance away. They worshipped Jumman, adorning him with flowers and garlands. Then somebody shouted, 'Call Jotya. Otherwise he'll complain that he wasn't allowed to see him before the end.'

Some people went to call Jotya. His eyes were alight with flames of fire. He stood there without a word. His lips were dry, his body drenched with sweat; his tongue felt as if it was being pulled inwards and the ground below his feet seemed to be shifting.

The scent of burning incense wafted through the air.

A moment later...

As Jotya watched from a distance...

Somebody pressed Jumman's chest. The jet of blood that spurted out of his body drenched the idol of Mhasoba.

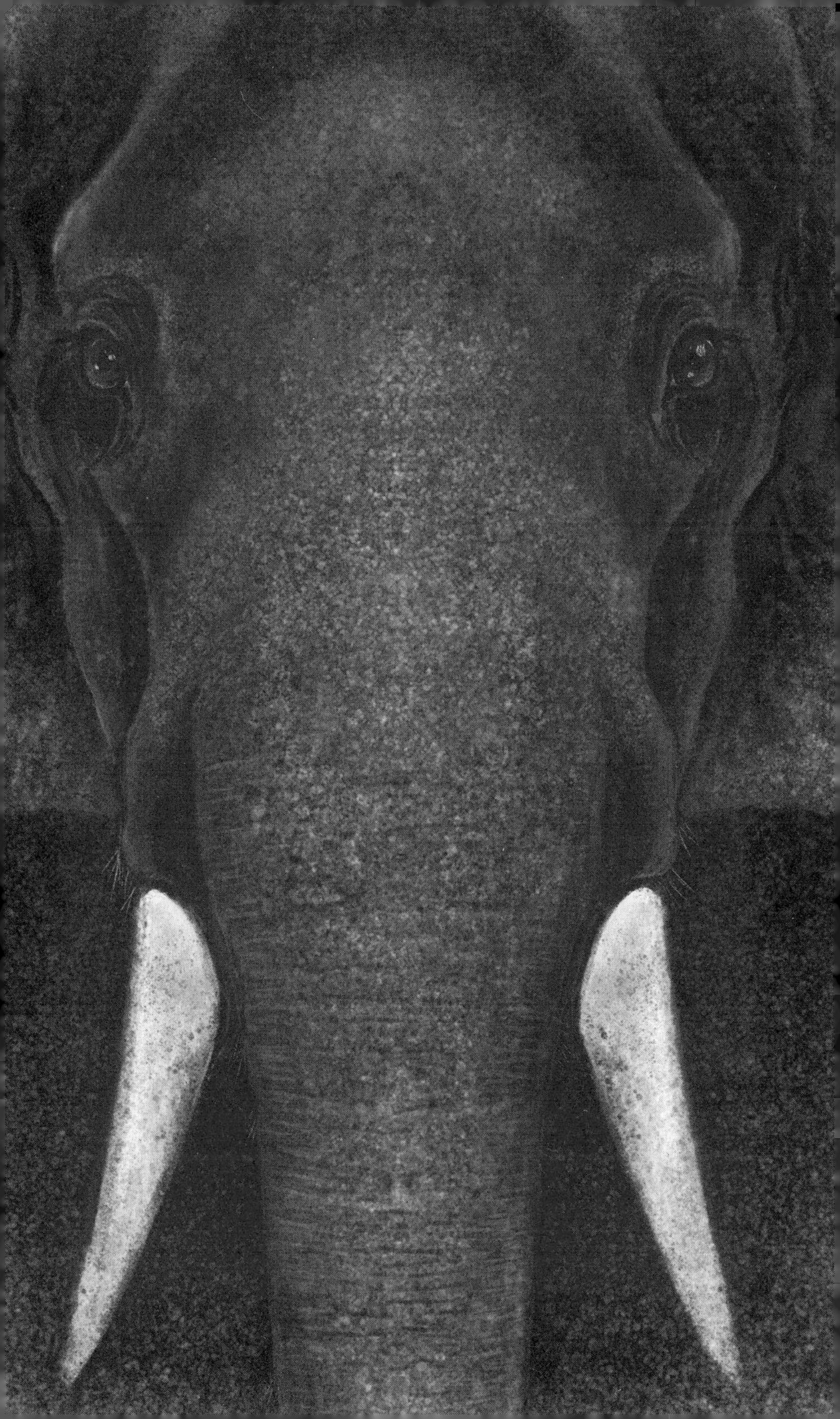

SHOOTING AN ELEPHANT

GEORGE ORWELL

In Moulmein, in Lower Burma, I was hated by large numbers of people—the only time in my life that I have been important enough for this to happen to me. I was sub-divisional police officer of the town, and in an aimless, petty kind of way anti-European feeling was very bitter. No one had the guts to raise a riot, but if a European woman went through the bazaars alone somebody would probably spit betel juice over her dress. As a police officer I was an obvious target and was baited whenever it seemed safe to do so. When a nimble Burman tripped me up on the football field and the referee (another Burman) looked the other way, the crowd yelled with hideous laughter. This happened more than once. In the end the sneering yellow faces of young men that met me everywhere, the insults hooted after me when I was at a safe distance, got badly on my nerves. The young Buddhist priests were the worst of all. There were several thousands of them in the town and none of them seemed to have anything to do except stand on street corners and jeer at Europeans.

All this was perplexing and upsetting. For at that time I had already made up my mind that imperialism was an evil thing and the sooner I chucked up my job and got out of it the better. Theoretically—and secretly, of course—I was all for the Burmese and all against their oppressors, the British. As for the job I was doing, I hated it more bitterly than I can perhaps make clear. In a job like that you see the dirty work of Empire at close quarters. The wretched prisoners huddling in the stinking cages of the lock-ups, the grey, cowed faces of the long-term convicts, the scarred buttocks of the men who had been flogged with bamboos—all these oppressed me with an intolerable sense of guilt. But I could get nothing into perspective. I was young and ill-educated and I had had to think out my problems in the utter silence that is imposed on every Englishman in the East. I did not even know that the British Empire is dying, still less did I know that it is a great deal better than the younger empires that are going to supplant it. All I knew was that I was stuck between my hatred of the empire I served and my rage against the evil-spirited little beasts who tried to make my job impossible. With one part of my mind I thought of the British Raj as an unbreakable tyranny, as something clamped down, in saecula saeculorum, upon the will of prostrate peoples; with another part I thought that the greatest joy in the world would be to drive a bayonet into a Buddhist priest's guts. Feelings like these are the normal by-products of imperialism; ask any Anglo-Indian official, if you can catch him off duty.

One day something happened which in a roundabout way was enlightening. It was a tiny incident in itself, but it gave me a better glimpse than I had had before of the real nature of imperialism—the real motives for which despotic governments act. Early one morning the sub-inspector at a police station the other end of the town rang me up on the phone and said that an elephant was ravaging the bazaar. Would I please come and do something about it? I did not know what I could do, but I wanted to see what was happening and I got on to a pony and started out. I took my rifle, an old .44 Winchester and much too small to kill an elephant, but I thought the noise might be useful in terrorem. Various Burmans stopped me on the way and told me about the elephant's doings. It was not, of course, a wild elephant, but a tame one which had gone 'must'. It had been chained up, as tame elephants always are when their attack of 'must' is due, but on the previous night it had broken its chain and escaped. Its mahout, the only person who could manage it when it was in that state, had set out in pursuit, but had taken the wrong direction and was now twelve hours' journey away, and in the morning the elephant had suddenly reappeared in the town. The Burmese population had no weapons and were quite helpless against it. It had already destroyed somebody's bamboo hut, killed a cow and raided some fruit stalls and devoured the stock; also it had met the municipal rubbish van and, when the driver jumped out and took to his heels, had turned the van over and inflicted violences upon it.

The Burmese sub-inspector and some Indian constables were waiting for me in the quarter where the elephant had been seen. It was a very poor quarter, a labyrinth of squalid bamboo huts, thatched with palm leaf, winding all over a steep hillside. I remember that it was a cloudy, stuffy morning at the beginning of the rains. We began questioning the people as to where the elephant had gone and, as usual, failed to get any definite information. That is invariably the case in the East; a story always sounds clear enough at a distance, but the nearer you get to the scene of events the vaguer it becomes. Some of the people said that the elephant had gone in one direction, some said that he had gone in another, some professed not even to have heard of any elephant. I had almost made up my mind that the whole story was a pack of lies, when we heard yells a little distance away. There was a loud, scandalized cry of 'Go away, child! Go away this instant!' and an old woman with a switch in her hand came round the corner of a hut, violently shooing away a crowd of naked children. Some more women followed, clicking their tongues and exclaiming; evidently there was something that the children ought not to have seen. I rounded the hut and saw a man's dead body sprawling in the mud. He was an Indian, a black Dravidian coolie, almost naked, and he could not have been dead many minutes. The people said that the elephant had come suddenly upon him round the corner of the hut, caught him with its trunk, put its foot on his back and ground him into the earth. This was the rainy season and the ground was soft, and his face had scored a trench a foot deep and a couple of yards long. He was lying on his belly with arms crucified and head sharply twisted to one side. His face was coated with mud, the eyes wide open, the teeth bared and grinning with an expression of unendurable agony. (Never tell me, by the way, that the dead look peaceful. Most of the corpses I have seen looked devilish.) The friction of the great beast's foot had stripped the skin from his back as neatly as one skins a rabbit. As soon as I saw the dead man I sent an orderly to a friend's house nearby to borrow an elephant rifle. I had already sent back the pony, not wanting it to go mad with fright and throw me if it smelt the elephant.

The orderly came back in a few minutes with a rifle and five cartridges, and meanwhile some Burmans had arrived and told us that the elephant was in the paddy fields below, only a few hundred yards away. As I started forward practically the whole population of the quarter flocked out of the houses and followed me. They had seen the rifle and were all shouting excitedly that I was going to shoot the elephant. They had not shown much interest in the elephant when he was merely ravaging their homes, but it was different now that he was going to be shot. It was a bit of fun to them, as it would be to an English crowd; besides they wanted the meat. It made me vaguely uneasy. I had no intention of shooting the elephant—I had merely sent for the rifle to defend myself if necessary—and it is always unnerving to have a crowd following you. I marched down the hill, looking and feeling a fool, with the rifle over my shoulder and an ever-growing army of people jostling at my heels. At the bottom, when you got away from the huts, there was a metalled road and beyond that a miry waste of paddy fields a thousand yards across, not yet ploughed but soggy from the first rains and dotted with coarse grass. The elephant was standing eight yards from the road, his left side towards us. He took not the slightest notice of the crowd's approach. He was tearing up bunches of grass, beating them against his knees to clean them and stuffing them into his mouth.

I had halted on the road. As soon as I saw the elephant I knew with perfect certainty that I ought not to shoot him. It is a serious matter to shoot a working elephant—it is comparable to destroying a huge and costly piece of machinery—and obviously one ought not to do it if it can possibly be avoided. And at that distance, peacefully eating, the elephant looked no more dangerous than a cow. I thought then and I think now that his attack of 'must' was already passing off; in which case he would merely wander harmlessly about until the mahout came back and caught him. Moreover, I did not in the least want to shoot him. I decided that I would watch him for a little while to make sure that he did not turn savage again, and then go home.

But at that moment I glanced round at the crowd that had followed me. It was an immense crowd, two thousand at the least and growing every minute. It blocked the road for a long distance on either side. I looked at the sea of yellow faces above the garish clothes-faces all happy and excited over this bit of fun, all certain that the elephant was going to be shot. They were watching me as they would watch a conjurer about to perform a trick. They did not like me, but with the magical rifle in my hands I was momentarily worth watching. And suddenly I realized that I should have to shoot the elephant after all. The people expected it of me and I had got to do it; I could feel their two thousand wills pressing me forward, irresistibly. And it was at this moment, as I stood there with the rifle in my hands, that I first grasped the hollowness, the futility of the white man's dominion in the East. Here was I, the white man with his gun, standing in front of the unarmed native crowd—seemingly the leading actor of the piece; but in reality I was only an absurd puppet pushed to and fro by the will of those yellow faces behind. I perceived in this moment that when the white man turns tyrant it is his own freedom that he destroys. He becomes a sort of hollow, posing dummy, the conventionalized figure of a sahib. For it is the condition of his rule that he shall spend his life in trying to impress the 'natives', and so in every crisis he has got to do what the 'natives' expect of him. He wears a mask, and his face grows to fit it. I had got to shoot the elephant. I had committed myself to doing it when I sent for the rifle. A sahib has got to act like a sahib; he has got to appear resolute, to know his own mind and do definite things. To come all that way, rifle in hand, with two thousand people marching at my heels, and then to trail feebly away, having done nothing—no, that was impossible. The crowd would laugh at me. And my whole life, every white man's life in the East, was one long struggle not to be laughed at.

But I did not want to shoot the elephant. I watched him beating his bunch of grass against his knees, with that preoccupied grandmotherly air that elephants have. It seemed to me that it would be murder to shoot him. At that age I was not squeamish about killing animals, but I had never shot an elephant and never wanted to. (Somehow it always seems worse to kill a large animal.) Besides, there was the beast's owner to be considered. Alive, the elephant was worth at least a hundred pounds; dead, he would only be worth the value of his tusks, five pounds, possibly. But I had got to act quickly. I turned to some experienced-looking Burmans who had been there when we arrived, and asked them how the elephant had been behaving. They all said the same thing: he took no notice of you if you left him alone, but he might charge if you went too close to him.

It was perfectly clear to me what I ought to do. I ought to walk up to within, say, twenty-five yards of the elephant and test his behaviour. If he charged, I could shoot; if he took no notice of me, it would be safe to leave him until the mahout came back. But also I knew that I was going to do no such thing. I was a poor shot with a rifle and the ground was soft mud into which one would sink at every step. If the elephant charged and I missed him, I should have about as much chance as a toad under a steamroller. But even then I was not thinking particularly of my own skin, only of the watchful yellow faces behind. For at that moment, with the crowd watching me, I was not afraid in the ordinary sense, as I would have been if I had been alone. A white man mustn't be frightened in front of 'natives'; and so, in general, he isn't frightened. The sole thought in my mind was that if anything went wrong those two thousand Burmans would see me pursued, caught, trampled on and reduced to a grinning corpse like that Indian up the hill. And if that happened it was quite probable that some of them would laugh. That would never do.

There was only one alternative. I shoved the cartridges into the magazine and lay down on the road to get a better aim. The crowd grew very still, and a deep, low, happy sigh, as of people who see the theatre curtain go up at last, breathed from innumerable throats. They were going to have their bit of fun after all. The rifle was a beautiful German thing with cross-hair sights. I did not then know that in shooting an elephant one would shoot to cut an imaginary bar running from ear-hole to ear-hole. I ought, therefore, as the elephant was sideways on, to have aimed straight at his ear-hole, actually I aimed several inches in front of this, thinking the brain would be further forward.

When I pulled the trigger I did not hear the bang or feel the kick—one never does when a shot goes home—but I heard the devilish roar of glee that went up from the crowd. In that instant, in too short a time, one would have thought, even for the bullet to get there, a mysterious, terrible change had come over the elephant. He neither stirred nor fell, but every line of his body had altered. He looked suddenly stricken, shrunken, immensely old, as though the frightful impact of the bullet had paralysed him without knocking him down. At last, after what seemed a long time—it might have been five seconds, I dare say—he sagged flabbily to his knees. His mouth slobbered. An enormous senility seemed to have settled upon him. One could have imagined him thousands of years old. I fired again into the same spot. At the second shot he did not collapse but climbed with desperate slowness to his feet and stood weakly upright, with legs sagging and head drooping. I fired a third time. That was the shot that did for him. You could see the agony of it jolt his whole body and knock the last remnant of strength from his legs. But in falling he seemed for a moment to rise, for as his hind legs collapsed beneath him he seemed to tower upward like a huge rock toppling, his trunk reaching skyward like a tree. He trumpeted, for the first and only time. And then down he came, his belly towards me, with a crash that seemed to shake the ground even where I lay.

I got up. The Burmans were already racing past me across the mud. It was obvious that the elephant would never rise again, but he was not dead. He was breathing very rhythmically with long rattling gasps, his great mound of a side painfully rising and falling. His mouth was wide open—I could see far down into caverns of pale pink throat. I waited a long time for him to die, but his breathing did not weaken. Finally I fired my two remaining shots into the spot where I thought his heart must be. The thick blood welled out of him like red velvet, but still he did not die. His body did not even jerk when the shots hit him, the tortured breathing continued without a pause. He was dying, very slowly and in great agony, but in some world remote from me where not even a bullet could damage him further. I felt that I had got to put an end to that dreadful noise. It seemed dreadful to see the great beast lying there, powerless to move and yet powerless to die, and not even to be able to finish him. I sent back for my small rifle and poured shot after shot into his heart and down his throat. They seemed to make no impression. The tortured gasps continued as steadily as the ticking of a clock.

In the end I could not stand it any longer and went away. I heard later that it took him half an hour to die. Burmans were bringing das and baskets even before I left, and I was told they had stripped his body almost to the bones by the afternoon.

Afterwards, of course, there were endless discussions about the shooting of the elephant. The owner was furious, but he was only an Indian and could do nothing. Besides, legally I had done the right thing, for a mad elephant has to be killed, like a mad dog, if its owner fails to control it. Among the Europeans opinion was divided. The older men said I was right, the younger men said it was a damn shame to shoot an elephant for killing a coolie, because an elephant was worth more than any damn Coringhee coolie. And afterwards I was very glad that the coolie had been killed; it put me legally in the right and it gave me a sufficient pretext for shooting the elephant. I often wondered whether any of the others grasped that I had done it solely to avoid looking a fool.

THE FLOOD

THAKAZHI SIVASANKARA PILLAI

Translated from the Malayalam by O. V. Usha

The temple stood on a rise, the highest ground for miles around. Despite this, its deity was submerged in water up to its neck. There was water everywhere you looked. In the three-roomed uppermost storey of the building, sixty-seven children, three hundred and fifty-seven adults and assorted dogs, cats, goats and fowl had taken refuge from the floodwaters.

Most of the locals had fled their homes, and made their way to dry land. If the family owned a boat, one of them would remain behind to guard their house and their possessions.

Chennan, the pariah, had been standing in water an entire night and day. It had been three days since his master had escaped to safety. Chennan did not own a row boat so inside his hut he had built an elevated platform out of coconut fronds and twigs that jutted above the level of the floodwaters. The family spent two days in this primitive loft, hoping the floodwaters would recede soon. Chennan was concerned that if they left the hut, his five banana trees that were heavy with fruit and his hayrick would be stolen. The waters continued to rise. Chennan was now knee-deep in water as he stood on his platform. A couple of rows of thatch on the roof slipped under water. Chennan shouted for help, but who was there to hear him? He was convinced that he and his dependents—his pregnant wife, four children, a cat and a dog—would die within the next twelve hours, as, by then, the waters would have risen above the roof. The downpour, which had started three days ago, showed no signs of abating.

Undoing a portion of the thatch from inside the hut, Chennan somehow scrambled on to the roof and looked around. He saw a big boat moving north. He yelled to the men in the boat for help. They heard him, and began rowing towards his hut. Chennan pulled out his children, his wife, the dog and the cat through the opening he had made in the roof. When the boat came alongside the hut, the children began climbing into it. Just then they heard a voice.

'Chennacho… Poohay…!'

It was Matiyathara Kunheippan, calling out from the roof of his house.

Chennan hastily helped his wife into the boat. The cat also jumped in. No one remembered the dog. It was sniffing at something on the western edge of the roof when the boat began to move away from the house.

When the dog eventually returned to the spot on the roof from which the family had made its escape, the boat was far away. The animal began to run around frantically on the roof, sniffing here and there, whining all the while. A frog which had been sitting on the roof was alarmed by the commotion the dog was creating and jumped into the flood as the dog drew close. The movement frightened the dog; it reared back, then stared intently at the ripples caused by the frog when it had dived into the water.

The dog was hungry now, and began sniffing around for food. It disturbed another frog, which urinated on its nose, before jumping into the water. The dog sneezed and snorted, shook its head violently, began cleaning its face with its forepaws.

The rain, which had stopped for a while, began lashing down again, and the dog crouched down miserably under its onslaught. Meanwhile, its master and family had got to safety in Ambalappuzha.

Night fell. An enormous crocodile, half-submerged in the water, drifted by the hut. The dog put its tail between its legs in terror, and howled, but the crocodile paid no attention to it and was soon out of sight.

Starving, terrified, tired, and without any protection from the driving rain, the dog crouched on the roof of the hut. It howled piteously and the gusting wind carried its cries of distress across great distances. The few people who remained in that flooded wilderness guarding their huts probably felt sorry for the dog when they heard its anguished howls.

Its master was probably eating his dinner. He was probably rolling a ball of rice for the dog between his fingers, as was his practice at the end of a meal. The dog's howls began to weaken, then died away. It pricked up its ears when it heard a man reciting the Ramayana. It remained silent for a while, almost as if it was listening to the chanting of the verse, and then began barking again as loudly as it could manage. The melodious chanting of the Ramayana rose clear and strong into the still night. The rain had stopped. The dog listened intently to the sound of that human voice. The voice died away into the cold air. Now there was no sound except that of the gusting of the wind, and the lapping of waves against the hut.

The dog lay down on the roof. It snuffled miserably. A fish splashed in the dark water. A frog jumped. The dog barked once or twice, then fell quiet.

When the sun came up, the dog began a low howling, almost as if it were keening. Rows of frogs, lined up on the roof of the house, would eye the dog, and if it made a move, would jump into the water. The dog looked at the thatched roofs poking out of the floodwater in the vicinity, hoping that they would contain food; but there was no food to be had. It began nuzzling at its fur, feeding on the fleas it found there; it scratched the flea bites with its hind legs, and then it briefly fell asleep in the feeble warmth of the sun.

Dark clouds enveloped the sun. The wind rose, and with it the waves. The carcasses of drowned animals floated past the hut. The dog looked longingly at them, and barked once or twice.

Every now and again small row boats would come into view and the dog would look at them hopefully. One of them went past in the distance and disappeared behind a thick clump of ketaki shrubs. It began to drizzle again. Sitting on the roof, the dog presented a picture of utter helplessness.

The rain stopped. A small boat appeared in the distance and steadily drew closer. It moored under a coconut tree close to the hut. The dog wagged its tail, stretched, yawned, growled under its breath. The man in the boat climbed the tree, lopped off a coconut, sliced it open, drank its contents and then rowed away.

A crow flew down and landed on the huge rotting carcass of a dead buffalo that was floating by, and began to rip and tear at the flesh. Chennan's dog barked longingly at the prospect of a meal. The crow ate its fill and flew away. A green bird landed on a banana trunk and chirped. An ant's nest that had become dislodged from somewhere upriver snagged on the eaves of the hut. Thinking that it was something it could eat, the dog nosed at the nest, and got bitten for its pains. It jumped away, snorting and sneezing, its tender nose flushed and swollen.

That afternoon, a small row boat drifted by, with two men in it. The dog began barking joyfully, jumping up and down in its happiness. Its demeanour, the way it was trying to express itself, seemed almost human. It went down to the water's edge, ready to jump into the boat.

'Look, a dog,' one of the men said. The dog began to whimper in a peculiar key—it was almost as though it was responding to the compassion in the man's voice.

'Let it be,' said the second man.

The dog whimpered, opened and closed its mouth, it seemed as though it was praying to the men to rescue it. It tried twice to jump into the boat, and was rebuffed both times. The boat began to move away from the house. The dog howled. It was heart-rending. One of the men looked back.

'Ayyooo…' The sound wasn't from either of the men but the dog. 'Ayyooo…' It was an exhausted, pitiful sound. It was almost as if the animal was bidding goodbye to the world.

The men did not look back again. The boat drew steadily away, and the dog remained where it was on the roof, watching it go. Its moaning and the expression on its face seemed to say that it would love human beings no more. The boat disappeared from sight.

The dog lapped up some water, looked at some birds flying overhead. A water snake was borne along by the flood at great speed towards the hut. Startled, the dog retreated along the roof. The snake slipped into the opening in the thatch through which Chennan and his family had made their escape. The dog peered into the opening and began to bark furiously.

The barking gradually tapered away into a whimpering. It was a sound of lament, full of the hunger the animal hadn't been able to sate, its despair at the hopelessness of its situation, and its fear that it might not survive. What it was trying to express would have been clear to anyone—even to a man from Mars.

With nightfall, a storm picked up. The roof of the hut began to shake as waves battered against it. The dog nearly fell off—twice. A long, sinister head rose out of the dark water. The dog began to bark frantically when it saw the crocodile. From somewhere close by came the sound of chickens squawking.

Another boat came into view, heavily loaded with coconuts and bunches of bananas. It stopped beside a banana tree close to the hut.

'Where is that barking coming from? Hasn't the hut been vacated?' one of the men in the boat asked.

The dog turned towards the sound of the men's voices and began barking. As one of the men began to climb the banana tree, the dog's barking grew in fury and menace.

'Better watch out, that dog sounds really angry, it might bite you,' the man who had remained in the boat warned his companion who had climbed the tree. No sooner had he spoken than the dog leapt at the thief who was trying to steal Chennan's bananas. The man tumbled down into the water, the dog with him. The thief's companion pulled him into the boat, while the dog swam back to its rooftop. It clambered back on, and shook the water off its coat, barking furiously all the while. The thieves lopped all the bananas off the trees, and loaded them on to the boat.

The men goaded the angry animal on to even greater rage. 'Just you wait, we've got something to show you,' they said grimly.

They transferred as much hay as they could from Chennan's hayrick on to their boat. Then one of the men got on to the roof and advanced threateningly towards the dog. It attacked him immediately, and sank its teeth into his leg. Howling in agony, the man jumped back into the boat, while his companion took hold of an oar and brought it crashing down on the dog's head. The animal yelped, and retreated.

The man who had been bitten lay in the bottom of the boat, tossing and turning in agony. As the boat receded into the distance, the dog sent it on its way with a volley of barks. It was close to midnight by then. An enormous bloated carcass of a cow drifted up to the house, and snagged on the roof. The dog kept an eye on the carcass. After a while, pushed by the current, the carcass began to move away slowly. Galvanized into activity, its tail wagging, grunting, the dog rushed down the roof to where the carcass was still within reach, and began tearing at the flesh, sating its terrible hunger. Just then, with a loud cracking noise, the entire carcass was dislodged from the roof, and the dog, which was eating from it, went with it. The carcass rolled over in the current, and the dog disappeared from view. Now one could only hear the sound of the gushing wind, the cacophony of frogs, and the sibilant whisper of the waves. There was no other sound.

Those who still stood guard in some of the flooded homes could no longer hear the dog's piteous whining, or heart-rending moaning. Every so often, another bloated carcass of some drowned animal would float by on the flood. Crows fed on some of them. Everywhere you looked there was nothing but desolation. And the only people who thrived in this wilderness of water and destruction were thieves and looters.

The hut collapsed after a while, and sank out of sight. And the loyal animal, which had stood guard over its master's property for as long as it could, was gone as well. The crocodiles had it now. It was all over, the waters covered everything.

The flood receded slowly. One day, Chennan swam across to the spot where his hut had once stood, looking for his dog. Under one of the coconut trees, he saw the corpse of a dog, gently rocking in the eddies of the shallow water. Chennan turned it over with his foot to check if it was his dog, he thought it might be. One of the animal's ears was missing. You couldn't even tell what colour the dog was, for its skin had rotted and sloughed away.

THE MARK OF VISHNU

KHUSHWANT SINGH

'This is for Kala Nag,' said Gunga Ram, pouring the milk into the saucer. 'Every night I leave it outside the hole near the wall and it's gone by the morning.' 'Perhaps it is the cat,' we youngsters suggested.

'Cat!' said Gunga Ram with contempt. 'No cat goes near that hole. Kala Nag lives there. As long as I give him milk, he will not bite anyone in this house. You can all go about with bare feet and play where you like.'

We were not having any patronage from Gunga Ram.

'You're a stupid old Brahmin,' I said. 'Don't you know snakes don't drink milk? At least one couldn't drink a saucerful every day. The teacher told us that a snake eats only once in several days. We saw a grass snake which had just swallowed a frog. It stuck like a blob in its throat and took several days to dissolve and go down its tail. We've got dozens of them in the lab, in methylated spirit. Why, last month the teacher bought one from a snake charmer which could run both ways. It had another head with a pair of eyes at the tail. You should have seen the fun when it was put in the jar.

There wasn't an empty one in the lab. So the teacher put it in one which had a Russels viper. He caught its two ends with a pair of forceps, dropped it in the jar, and quickly put the lid on. There was an absolute storm as it went round and round in the glass, tearing the decayed viper into shreds.

Gunga Ram shut his eyes in pious horror.

'You will pay for it one day. Yes, you will.'

It was no use arguing with Gunga Ram. He, like all good Hindus, believed in the Trinity of Brahma, Vishnu, and Shiva, the creator, preserver, and destroyer. Of these he was most devoted to Vishnu. Every morning he smeared his forehead with a V mark in sandalwood paste to honour the deity. Although a Brahmin, he was illiterate and full of superstition. To him, all life was sacred, even if it was of a serpent or scorpion or centipede. Whenever he saw one he quickly shoved it away lest we kill it. He picked up wasps we battered with our badminton rackets and tended their damaged wings. Sometimes he got stung. It never seemed to shake his faith. More dangerous the animal, the more devoted Gunga Ram was to its existence. Hence the regard for snakes; and above all, for the cobra, who was the Kala Nag.

'We will kill your Kala Nag if we see him.'

'I won't let you. It's laid a hundred eggs and if you kill it all the eggs will become cobras and the house will be full of them. Then what will you do?'

'We'll catch them alive and send them to Bombay. They milk them there for anti-snakebite serum. They pay two rupees for a live cobra. That makes two hundred rupees straightway.'

'Your doctors must have udders. I never saw a snake have any. But don't you dare touch this one. It is a phannyar—it is hooded. I've seen it. It's three hands long. As for its hood!' Gunga Ram opened the palms of his hands and his head swayed from side to side. 'You should see it basking on the lawn in the sunlight.'

'That just proves what a liar you are. The phannyar is the male, so it couldn't have laid the hundred eggs. You must have laid the eggs yourself.'

The party burst into peals of laughter.

'Must be Gunga Ram's eggs. We'll soon have a hundred Gunga Rams.'

Gunga Ram was squashed. It was the lot of a servant to be constantly squashed. But having the children of the household make fun of him was too much even for Gunga Ram. They were constantly belittling him with their new-fangled ideas. They never read their scriptures.

Not even what the Mahatma said about non-violence. It was

just shotguns to kill birds and the jars of methylated spirit to drown snakes. Gunga Ram would stick to his faith in the sanctity of life, he would feed and protect snakes because snakes were the most vile of God's creatures on earth. If you could love them, instead of killing them, you proved your point.

What the point was which Gunga Ram wanted to prove was not clear. He just proved it by leaving the saucerful of milk by the snake hole every night and finding it gone in the mornings.

One day we saw Kala Nag. The monsoons had burst with all their fury and it had rained in the night. The earth which had lain parched and dry under the withering heat of the summer sun was teeming with life. In little pools frogs croaked. The muddy ground was littered with crawling worms, centipedes and velvety ladybirds.

Grass had begun to show and the banana leaves glistened bright and glossy green. The rain had flooded Kala Nag's hole. He sat in an open patch on the lawn. His shiny black hood glistened in the sunlight. He was big—almost six feet in length, and rounded and fleshy, like my wrist.

'Looks like a King Cobra. Let's get him.'

Kala Nag did not have much of a chance. The ground was slippery and all the holes and gutters were full of water. Gunga Ram was not at home to help.

Armed with long bamboo sticks, we surrounded Kala Nag before he even scented danger. When he saw us his eyes turned a fiery red and he hissed and spat on all sides. Then, like lightning Kala Nag made for the banana grove. The ground was too muddy and he slithered. He had hardly gone five yards when a stick caught him in the middle and broke his back. A volley of blows reduced him to a squishy-squashy pulp of black-and-white jelly, spattered with blood and mud. His head was still undamaged.

'Don't damage the hood,' yelled one of us. 'We'll take Kala Nag to school.'

So we slid a bamboo stick under the cobra's belly and lifted him on the end of the pole. We put him in a large biscuit tin and tied it up with string. We hid the tin under a bed.

At night I hung around Gunga Ram waiting for him to get his saucer of milk. 'Aren't you going to take any milk for Kala Nag tonight?'

'Yes,' answered Gunga Ram irritably. 'You go to bed.'

He did not want any more argument on the subject.

'He won't need the milk any more.'

Gunga Ram paused.

'Oh, nothing. There are so many frogs about. They must taste better than your milk. You never put any sugar in it anyway.'

The next morning Gunga Ram brought back the saucer with the milk still in it. He looked sullen and suspicious.

'I told you snakes like frogs better than milk.'

Whilst we changed and had breakfast Gunga Ram hung around us. The school bus came and we clambered into it with the tin. As the bus started we held out the tin to Gunga Ram.

'Here's your Kala Nag. Safe in this box. We are going to put him in spirit.'

We left him standing speechless, staring at the departing bus.

There was great excitement in the school. We were a set of four brothers known for our toughness. We had proved it again.

'A King Cobra.'

'Six feet long.'

'Phannyar.'

The tin was presented to the science teacher.

It was on the teacher's table, and we waited for him to open it and admire our kill. The teacher pretended to be indifferent and set us some problems to work on. With studied matter-of-factness he fetched his forceps and a jar with a banded Krait lying curled in muddy methylated spirit. He began to hum and untie the cord around the box.

As soon as the cord was loosened the lid flew into the air, just missing the teacher's nose. There was Kala Nag. His eyes burnt like embers and his hood was taut and undamaged. With a loud hiss he went for the teacher's face. The teacher pushed himself back on the chair and toppled over. He fell on the floor and stared at the cobra, petrified with fear. The boys stood up on their desks and yelled hysterically.

Kala Nag surveyed the scene with his bloodshot eyes.

His forked tongue darted in and out excitedly. He spat furiously and then made a bid for freedom. He fell out of the tin on to the floor with a loud plop. His back was broken in several places and he dragged himself painfully to the door. When he got to the threshold he drew himself up once again with his hood outspread to face another danger.

Outside the classroom stood Gunga Ram with a saucer and a jug of milk. As soon as he saw Kala Nag come up he went down on his knees. He poured the milk into the saucer and placed it near the threshold. With hands folded in prayer he bowed his head to the ground craving forgiveness. In desperate fury, the cobra hissed and spat and bit Gunga Ram all over the head—then with great effort dragged himself into a gutter and wriggled out of view.

Gunga Ram collapsed with his hands covering his face. He groaned in agony. The poison blinded him instantly. Within a few minutes he turned pale and blue and froth appeared in his mouth. On his forehead were little drops of blood. These the teacher wiped with his handkerchief. Underneath was the V mark where Kala Nag had dug his fangs.

BULBULS

HABIB KAMRAN

Translated from the Kashmiri by Neerja Mattoo

1

It was the last fortnight of April, that time of year when one loves to sit in the sun. That is what I was doing, sitting in my garden right opposite the rose bush which is entangled with the branches of another tree next to the wall. I was just a few metres away from the wall and saw a bulbul fly right into its centre. Another bulbul kept watch on the wall. The first one came out and the second went in. For the rest of the day, I saw the pair taking turns bringing twigs, blades of grass, bits of string, some long, some thick, in their beaks and taking them into the rose bush.

One day I peeped into the bush and saw that the bulbuls had woven a nest. It had been fashioned with twigs on the outside, secured tightly with the inner branches of the rose bush. The inside of the nest was soft, woven with linen-like fibres of god-knows-what tree. It looked so downy inside, smooth and tender. It was the size of a large china cup on the outside, while the inside was smaller. What surprised me, however, was that it had room to accommodate just one bulbul. I had always imagined that, like human beings, birds too had homes in which the adult pair and their children could live. In the case of bulbuls, at least, I was proved wrong. It was obvious that only one, the female, could stay in the nest, while the male spent the night outside.

A few days later, I peeped into the nest and found three tiny eggs in it. They were the size of little marbles, but not perfectly round. They were oval in shape. So far, I had only seen white eggs, but these had black spots and streaks over the white surface. I picked one up. It felt warm. I kept looking at it. It really was a pretty little thing. Suddenly, there was a loud twittering. I looked up and saw the pair of bulbuls in a highly disturbed state, making a commotion from where they were perched on the wall. They appeared to be glaring at me. I felt like someone who had been caught trespassing. It was almost as if I had put my hand into someone's pocket and had my wrist gripped hard by him. The egg had been in my palm for barely a few seconds, yet the agitation of the bulbuls was extreme. I hastily put back the egg in the nest.

The next morning I was again drawn to the rose bush and took a look inside. The eggs were hidden, under the bulbul's protective warmth. Whenever I looked into the nest afterwards, I always found the bulbul in it. I wondered when it went out to find food. So far the only eggs I had seen being hatched were pigeon's eggs. And there, both the male and female took turns sitting on them. But here it was not possible for me to tell whether a similar practice was being followed or only the mother bird at the job. As far as I could see, there was this one bulbul, always there, on duty, steadfast and constant.

A few days later when I went to take a look, I found the bulbul not in the nest, but perched on its edge, looking intently at something in the nest. After a while it flew away, giving me an opportunity to look inside. There were tiny baby bulbuls in place of the eggs. They were very small, each hardly the size of a tiny tadpole. Two little twigs for wings, two more thin ones for legs, no sign of a beak. Two small dots suggested the eyes. Now I understood the meaning of the Kashmiri phrase used to describe someone of very tender age as 'one whose very eyes are not yet fashioned!' They were extremely delicate looking things even more fragile than a newborn baby, just little lumps of frail flesh, with not even a trace of down on them. The neck was just a bit of thick thread; one of them stretched its neck and something like a beak opened at the end of it, as if begging for food. But the next moment it fell back among its siblings, and once again all three lay huddled together, resting on one another, necks intertwined. The tiny faces of the chicks were still undefined by any features. All three birds put together were no longer than the yolk of a hen's egg. I must have observed them for hardly ten or fifteen seconds—it is taking longer to describe it—when I was startled by loud twittering. Once again the pair of bulbuls were highly agitated, fluttering their wings restlessly, perched on the wall, their eyes on me and the nest. Somewhat nervous, I withdrew quickly. Instantly, one of the adult birds flew into the nest and sheltered the chicks. It was afternoon at that time. Till the light faded, I kept peeping into the nest through the tracery of the rose branches, and always found the babies hidden under the mother's wings.

The next morning I went out again, curious to see what the bulbuls were feeding their young ones. For most of the day, I noticed one bulbul constantly in the nest, the babies under its wing. Its mate came in with something in its beak. It looked like a slender bit of peel. God knows whether it was plant matter or perhaps the wing of a dead moth, but it was certainly something soft. The bulbul bringing the food would land on a rose branch near the nest and the one in the nest would fly away, as if to give the other one room to feed the chicks what it had fetched. After the babies were fed, it too would fly away. From then onwards, the two would take turns foraging for food, bringing in something or the other in their beaks and feeding the babies. I noticed, however, that the interval between meal times seemed to progressively lengthen. Perhaps they did not want to overfeed those delicate stomachs.

As a matter of routine, I would leave grains of rice or crumbs of bread for the bulbuls on my veranda. As soon as the bulbuls saw them, they would fly down from wherever they were—swinging from an electric cable or the branch of a tree—and begin pecking at the food. On the day I observed the babies being fed for the first time, I scattered some rice as usual. The adult bulbuls arrived and began to eat. I wondered why they did not pick any for their babies, perhaps it was too hard and not the right kind of food for the tiny ones.

Two days later, clouds began to gather in the afternoon and by evening it was raining. During the night it turned into a regular downpour. I couldn't keep my thoughts away from the bulbuls and their little ones in the nest in the rose bush, unprotected from the pelting rain. The next morning I went out very early to take a look and found one of the bulbuls in the nest, guarding its treasure under its wing. Meanwhile, the cloud cover thickened further and soon there was thunder and lightning. The fury of the storm increased very quickly and the rain came down in a deluge. The wind was so powerful that it bent the tallest willow, forcing it to touch the earth. The rose bush shook violently. Suddenly it was so cold that people were forced to hug their kangris in the month of May! Even through the raging storm, I stepped out from time to time and always found the bulbul at its post, sheltering the babies from the onslaught of the elements. Drenched to the bone, and seemingly shrunk by the intense cold it held on, bearing the brunt of the piercing wind and water, while shielding the fledglings, and giving them the warmth of its own body.

That day I never saw the bulbul leave its nest to look for food. Apparently, what was necessary was to save the babies from the rain and cold, the question of satisfying its own hunger did not arise.

By afternoon the rain had stopped and the bulbul emerged, quickly foraged for food and, putting a few grains in its mouth, picked up something for the babies and fed them. Soon it was joined by the other bulbul and the two fed them as fast as they could, obviously the famished babies needed quick nourishment.

Today, the fourth day, was bright and sunny and warmer. Now it was continuous hard work for the bulbuls; they took it in turns to find food for the babies and to shelter them under their wings.

The next day, I threw some rice on the veranda floor. The bulbuls came and pecked at the food as usual. But today they carried some grains in their beaks to the nest and fed them to the little ones. Within four days then, the fledglings graduated to what had been deemed too tough for them to eat at birth. But I also noticed that for the adult bulbuls, rice was not as important as worms. They would forage among branches of trees and plants intently, their quick, sharp eyes searching for insects and other tiny living things that they would grab at with lightning speed. The main focus of their search was flowering plants, because these were the haunts of bees, butterflies and other insects. Throughout the day, with no rest at all, they would flit from plant to nest and back again.

Suddenly I wanted to see how much the little birds had grown. I waited for both the bulbuls to fly away to a distance, before taking a peep into the nest. The baby birds had grown beyond my expectations. They even had tiny, soft feathers covering their heads and backs. I had hardly looked at them for a few seconds when I was startled by a loud flapping of wings above my head. It was one of the adult bulbuls, trying to frighten me away from the nest.

I retreated obediently.

For the next three or four days, I would sit in the sunny garden, reading the newspaper or a book, keeping an eye on the comings and goings of the bulbuls, but not approaching the nest too often.

The baby bulbuls had hatched eight days ago. Now the parents were busy throughout the day, gathering caterpillars and other tiny creatures to feed the babies. They did not seem to rest at all. They no longer hid their young under their wings. Their main preoccupation was to feed them as much as possible. The babies seemed to have become insatiable. One of the parents just had to approach the nest for them to stretch their necks and start twittering, trying to push each other away to snatch every morsel.

Again I was seized by the desire to take a look inside the nest to see how much they had grown since I had last checked on them. I waited for the parents to leave on their mission and peeped in. How they had grown in eight days! The feathers on their head and neck were quite thick. They even had little wings now. The beaks looked bigger and they could open their eyes too. The pace at which they had grown quite justified the amount of food they seemed to need. No wonder they were always hungry! This time too I was startled by one of the parents agitatedly flapping its wings next to my ear. I did not know how it had rushed back so quickly, barely a few seconds after I had peered into the nest. Its flight, so close to me was no ordinary flight, it rushed at me like a bullet and if I had been hit I would certainly have been injured, even knocked unconscious. It was not the fear of me that had kept it from striking me, it was fear for its own safety. Its life and safety were precious for the sake of its offspring. Hence the bulbul's explosive flight, so close to my ear, had missed me on purpose; its intention had been to move me away from the nest by startling me.

The next afternoon, as I was sitting in the sun as usual, a cat appeared and climbed the wall against which the rose bush containing the bulbul nest leaned. The cat leapt down and began to pace the yard, sniffing as she went. Then she saw the nest in the bush. Eyes riveted on the nest, she advanced slowly towards it. I could see that the cat posed grave danger to the nest so I got up and shooed her away. But now I began to worry, I could not guard the nest all the time, who knew when the cat might strike again? What would happen to the vulnerable nest? I wondered how I could keep the fledglings safe. Supposing I lifted the nest, along with the baby bulbuls, and settled it in a wooden crate, leaving just a small hole for the parent bulbul to enter? But would it be wise to shift the nest? I wondered. They say that birds are suspicious by nature, they might refuse to go into the crate. What would happen then? Wouldn't it do the babies even greater harm? The only thing to do was to pull the portion of the bush that we had trained to climb the wall away from it and wrap it, thorns and all, around the branches on which the nest had been constructed. Soon enough, I was able to make a thorny fortification around it. I was satisfied that no cat could penetrate the defensive wall I had built, the long, pointed thorns would be excellent deterrents.

As the wall itself might give the predator a foothold, I fortified the nest on that side of the wall by barricading it with thorny robinia branches and brambles. Now I was satisfied that the nest was secure from the cat.

One outcome of my elaborate security arrangements was that I myself could no longer reach the nest to peek inside. All I could see from a distance was the baby bulbuls, stretching out their necks with beaks open, begging for food. Their growth never ceased to amaze me. Each passing day saw more and more of their bodies covered with thicker and ever thicker feathers. But whenever I lingered near the nest for a while, I would find the parent bulbuls flying in agitatedly, setting off a loud clamour, hovering uncomfortably close to my head, as if warning me to stay off their territory, causing me to move back hastily.

I noticed something odd in the way they fed their babies. Whenever they flew in with something in their beaks—a worm, or insect, they would not rush to the nest straightaway. First, they would perch for a while on a robinia or willow branch, then fly to the flower bush adjacent to the rose bush with the nest in it and wait for a few minutes more. Only then would they go into the nest and feed the babies. Leaving the nest for more food, they would go through the same motions: the flowering tree, the wall, the wire, the robinia. I cannot tell whether they behaved this way always or only when they found me watching them. Perhaps they did not want to be followed to the nest by the watchful eyes of a stranger, man or animal.

One day when I was, as usual, deeply absorbed in their activity, I thought I could hear one of the bulbuls, 'Do you have nothing else to do? Why are you so fascinated by us that you cannot keep your eyes off us, following all our movements like a spy? Do you think we are some kind of performers or jugglers, putting on a show to entertain you? We are just feeding and bringing up our young ones, don't you humans do the same with your children? Does someone watch you like this too? Or was it a mistake to build our nest under your eye, hatch our eggs within your sight? Is that why you are constantly bothering us?'

Had the bulbuls been really endowed with the power of speech, they would certainly have spoken like this. We humans dislike being watched by others. That a stranger should be spying on us all the time would certainly be a torment.

It was the twenty-first of May, exactly two weeks since the hatching. The rose bush was in full bloom, laden from top to bottom with flowers, with hardly a leaf in sight. They were blazing red roses, as though the whole bush was a burning brand. Or perhaps a bride in crimson robes. The nest could no longer be seen.

But still the bulbuls and their family continued to be the focus of my attention. I saw the male bulbul fly in with a caterpillar dangling from his beak. As usual he flew around for a while, perched on a branch of a tree, a wire, the wall and finally the rose bush. But strangely enough, I did not see him go into the nest, nor did I see the caterpillar in his beak a little later.

Did he eat it all by himself or lose it in flight? I wondered. I bowed my head low and tried to look inside the nest, but I could not see it, hidden as it was behind the blooming roses. What I did see, however, were two baby bulbuls, perched on a branch of the flowering tree adjacent to the rose bush. 'Oh, so they have come out for their first stroll,' I said aloud to myself. I had not imagined at all that within such a short time they would be strong enough to leave the security of the nest. That explains why the bulbul did not need to go inside the nest to feed them.

The little bulbuls were perched contentedly on the branch of the tree. They were now completely covered with little feathers and the wings too could be seen, tiny, of course. But the feathers were short, not having grown to their full length yet. The tail too was still short, though the beak had acquired respectable dimensions. There was just a hint of a plume on the heads. But there were only two baby bulbuls.

What happened to their sibling? I wondered. My query was soon answered when I saw the other bulbul fly in and rush into the bush with something in its beak. After a while it emerged, and following its movements, I looked in and saw the third little bulbul, not in the nest, but nicely esconced on a branch of the rose bush. The bulbuls kept coming in and leaving after feeding all three baby bulbuls.

The tiny bulbuls sat still on the branch, eyes closed, heads joined together. Their stillness was almost like that of a yogi in meditation or a Sufi brooding on eternal truths. Only when a parent came with something for them would they open their eyes briefly, flutter their wings, stretch their necks and open their mouths to receive nourishment, twittering loudly, competing with the others. The feeding session over, they would again close their eyes, as if to get back to meditating upon issues of grave concern. From time to time, one of them would plunge its beak into its feathers, scratching its chest and abdomen, or pecking under its wings. They would do this to each other too, opening their eyes briefly for the purpose.

The baby bulbuls looked as pretty and cute as little boys decked out for a ceremony. I could well imagine the satisfaction and pride a mother feels when she takes her children for an outing, all washed, groomed and dressed up for the occasion. The bulbul couple were perhaps experiencing a similar sense of elation and satisfaction, at a job well done. What an effort it had taken to make it possible for their babies to not only be able to leave the nest but also to swing so confidently from the branch of a tree! I could not take my eyes off the scene for quite some time. Then I went up the steps of the veranda to go in for tea, but suddenly retraced my steps and went back to my chair in the garden and began to watch the baby bulbuls again. The thought that had brought me back, foregoing my tea, was that the branch occupied by the little bulbuls was barely a foot or so from the cat's take-off point. In a single leap they would become a morsel in her mouth. The perch they had chosen had no thorny branch or bramble to protect it. In my mind, I went over the whole painful process of how the bulbuls had woven their nest, laid eggs in it, hatched them, shielded the young ones from thunder and lightning, kept them warm under their wings and spared no effort to feed and to nurture them, day and night, until they were capable of leaving the nest and perching on the branch of a flowering tree all by themselves. Did they go through all these travails only to have the cat finish them off in a couple of minutes? I had to prevent it. I decided to stay on and keep watch. In the evening they might go back to the nest and then I would be free from my vigil.

It was almost sunset and I was still at my self-appointed post. Once I went very close to the little ones. I brought my head almost next to them. I noticed that their eyes were open, but they did not stir. I should say that, in fact, they took no notice of me at all, it was as if they did not see me. Maybe they did see me but had not yet acquired the sense to distinguish friend from foe, or to know fear. I remembered that a couple of years ago I had found a baby mynah under a tree in my own garden and waited to see if any adult mynah would come looking for it, but none came. I thought it was some child's doing, throwing it here after plucking it out of its nest. The little thing could only flutter its wings; it could not fly. When I held my hand out to it, it stretched its neck and opened its beak wide as though hoping to be fed. I put a few grains of rice into it and the nestling quickly swallowed them. This led me to believe—wrongly, as it turned out—that baby birds do not recognize their parents, any approaching shadow will make them stretch their necks out and open their beaks for food.

The memory of that incident with the baby mynah gave rise to an unusual desire in me—I wanted to put something with my own fingers into mouths of the baby bulbuls. This wave of desire rose with such a compelling surge that I was swept along and found myself standing right next to the baby bulbuls. But still they took no notice of me. I held out my hand with a few grains of rice in it in the belief that as soon as the shadow fell upon their field of vision, their beaks would open to receive my offering. But that did not happen, in fact quite the opposite—the approaching shadow made one little bird hop away to the other side of the wall, towards the alley. This was most unexpected. I had never thought the nestling was capable of proper flight. In fact only a short while ago I had found it stretching its little wings and there were not even regular feathers on them yet. I panicked, almost certain that the nestling must have fallen into the alley to be consumed within moments by a street dog or an alley cat, or picked up by a child, to get crushed in his fist. I rushed out into the street to save it and put it back in the nest, but it was nowhere to be seen. I scanned the whole street, even went into my neighbouring compound to look, with no luck. Then I happened to glance at my neighbour's wall and found the baby bulbul comfortably perched there. I went into my house and climbed the stairs to the next floor, from where I could get a better view of what the baby bulbul would do next. I was still a bit apprehensive of it losing its way. The little bird took flight again and landed on a branch of a willow tree in a corner of my compound. After a while, another flight, and it was almost on the top of a tree outside. Now it was no longer possible to see this creature, hardly the size of a walnut, through the thick foliage. I saw a bulbul approaching with something in its beak, sitting for a while under the tree on which the baby bulbuls had been perched earlier. Then it suddenly flew directly to the tree to which the baby bulbul had flown. How could the parent see its offspring through that thick screen of leaves? I was amazed that the parent could so easily spot the tiny thing. No, it could not be their eyesight, the little birds certainly had an innate sense that enabled them to locate their young ones, I was sure.

Meanwhile, the fledgling from the interior of the rose bush emerged and flew to the ground. It did not fly high but hopped around a bit, keeping low. There were a number of flowering shrubs and plants close to where I was seated in my chair, their branches all entangled together. They grew all haphazardy, a dense growth rather than a wild plantation. So there was a huge heap of leaves underneath, almost a metre in height and equally wide. It was so densely packed that it was almost impenetrable. The little bird from the rose bush went towards this very leaf dump and before I knew it, it had disappeared into the dump. I went close to the dump, tried to probe it, but could see nothing. The other parent flew in with food. It, too, went to the same dump, flying around it. It seemed as if it had spotted the little bulbul going into the dump. After a while it too disappeared from view. God knows how it had found its way through the tightly packed mound of dead leaves. Soon it was out again, perched on the wall.

Shortly after, the little bird followed. I did not move from my chair—I did not want to frighten it back into the dump and lose it. The other parent flew in and joined its mate on the wall, both watching their baby. It seemed to me that they were trying to suggest something to it. The baby apparently took the hint and began to try to fly up with the aid of its tiny wings to where the parents were. It rose to half the height of the wall, wavered a little and then clung to it, frozen, unable to fly either up or down, watched agitatedly by its parents from above. But they made no move to come to its aid. I was again driven by the desire to do something for the baby in distress—why should I not help it? I could easily pick it up and put it back into its nest in the rose bush. That seemed to be the only way to rescue it. Otherwise it might be forced to fall back and seek refuge in the leaf dump. I rose and rushed to it. The baby made no movement at all, which confirmed my belief that these baby bulbuls had not yet learnt to fly properly. I picked it up and it set up a huge clamour, a loud twitter. As I moved away, both parents threw themselves on the ground near my feet. I took one step and they too moved and again they were before my feet, on the ground. This was no pleading and falling on my feet—they were trying to block my way, afraid that I was trying to snatch the baby away from them. But I managed to somehow place the nestling on the rose bush and came away. But what surprised me now was that instead of going to the baby now back in the rose bush, they both went to the crown of the tree, where the first baby had flown to. Why did they not go to the rescued baby? I looked into the rose bush again, but I could not see the baby anywhere, I had no idea where it could have gone. And what happened to the third baby whom I had not seen leaving the rose bush? Why were the parents not worried about him being fed? Why were they not going to him? I wanted to find answers to all these questions. The biggest mystery was why the parents were not going to the rose bush at all. After all, their nest was still there and so were two of their nestlings. I just could not accept that the parents would not carry food for them—it was impossible. I inspected the bush again but neither baby bulbul was visible. I went around the whole clump, the flowering tree and all around, I even turned the branches and shoots this way and that way, scanning the whole area, stood on my toes and looked behind the wall, crawled under the bush and searched through the tangle of branches, but there was no sign of a bird. Obviously they were no longer there. The only thing there was the nest, now empty. I had been there all the time, not moved away even for a second, how did they give me the slip? Now I knew why the parents did not go to the rose bush—there was no need. But what I still did not know was how they knew the babies were not there without going to the nest. I sat down in my chair, despondent. I was deeply remorseful, holding myself responsible for breaking up this family of bulbuls.

Suddenly, from the leaf dump emerged a bulbul, advancing slowly, with a strange gait, its wings spread out, as if wanting to fly but unable to do so. Is that what is meant by 'broken knees', or rather 'broken wings', I wondered. The bulbul hopped and went into another grassy growth opposite the rose bush. I consoled myself that this was one of the two babies that had disappeared earlier and waited for it to re-emerge from the dump—I no longer dared to go close. After a while the bulbul did re-emerge and I saw it from close quarters: it had a tall crest, long tail, it was the size of a full grown adult bulbul—it was not a baby bulbul but one of the parents. Again it advanced with slow, hesitant steps, wings spread out, as if dragging its dead weight along. It came very close to me and began to do something which I have no words to describe. It was a dance of agony, a painful writhing, an attempt to annihilate itself. Before my very eyes the bulbul seemed to assume a human face. It was sorrow in an excruciating form, a mourning and an appeal. But it was not a loud human wail, it was a silent weeping. Birds of the air can only be articulate in joy, sorrow makes them dumb. To anyone who can read it, the message in the eyes of all creatures in pain is loud and clear. I saw its mate arrive and come close to it, as if offering solace and support. The bulbul seemed to somewhat compose itself. Then they both flew to the tree to where the first baby had flown.

For a long time after, I could not bring myself to leave the place. I waited for as long as there was light, for any member of the family to return to the nest. But my hope was in vain—none of them came back.

I spent a restless night, worrying about the fate of the bulbuls and their young ones. Where could they have spent the night? In what plight? I had never wished them any harm, and now my guilt was overpowering, the thought that it was my hand that was responsible for this state. It was I who had destroyed their home and hearth, how could I forgive myself? Man considers himself wise and capable and tries to intervene, hoping to do good to creatures so much smaller than him, forgetting that the wisdom and ability required for their good is inherent in the very nature of these creatures, big and small. An intervening human hand ultimately only does damage.

As soon as it was light, I went to the nest. It was still empty. No bird had returned to it. I stood there for a long time, looking around, hoping. After a couple of hours I saw a bulbul foraging among the branches of a tree. Finally, finding something, I saw it flying with its laden beak to the same tree to which that first baby bulbul had flown the previous day. I did not see either the parents or a baby bulbul for the next few days. It was the last day of May when I saw one of the bulbuls flying to a tree in my yard with food in its beak. I looked hard and noticed two baby bulbuls perched on a branch of the tree. I did not see the third sibling. The babies I saw were now quite capable of flying from one branch of a tree to another with their parents.

I would still glance occasionally at the empty nest. I was hoping that the bulbuls would hatch two batches of eggs in a season. Something that I had understood very well by now was that as parents, the birds were extremely responsible, not leaving their offspring till the time they were capable of finding their food. They continued to feed them till a certain time and after that, they forced them to find their own nourishment. I thought that sooner or later it would be time for the bulbuls to lay eggs again and then they would need this nest in the rose bush. That is why I was determined to keep it safe, so that one day the pair would return to it.

One day when I went to the bush as usual, the nest had disappeared. Where was it? Could the bulbuls have taken it away? But that was unbelievable. So what had happened? The mystery was solved when I found it ensconced in a showcase in my own home. It contained two white pigeon-egg-like forms. Someone from the household had torn the nest from the bush, put two white elliptical objects in it to turn it into a decoration piece, and put it on display in the showcase. I lifted it out and threw away the two pebbles. Carefully, I attached it to the branch from where it had been plucked, securing it with wires. I believed that the bulbuls would certainly need it again.

But that never happened—the bulbuls did not return to their old nest, which they had left that day when the rose bush was rich with blooms. They did not come back because their offspring had left it for some unknown place.

2

It's now been a year since the incident I've narrated earlier. The windows of my bedroom face the Anchar Lake, which lies to the west of my house. It is spring, time to get the rooms painted, for which my room was stripped bare. Since it would take a day or two, I shifted to the room above, which faced my own yard. It was that season of the year when the days are warm but the nights cold. So the windows were kept closed at night. When I woke up the next morning, it was almost dawn. In fact, something had woken me up. It was the loud and clear chirruping of a bulbul, coming from somewhere very close, perhaps just outside the closed window. I got out of bed, threw the windows open and went downstairs.

The same thing happened the next morning. I was woken up by birdsong—the loud, clear, persistent chirruping of a bulbul. I sat up in my bed and listened to the regular, intermittent chirp. It was so close, but how could the bulbul be here, in this room with the windows still shut? I looked around and was amazed to see a bulbul on the floor, almost next to my pillow. I couldn't tell out how it had come in through the closed windows. The door was still bolted. Obviously the bird had come in the previous evening and spent the night in my bedroom. But why did it give no hint of its presence last evening or throughout the night? It was only when it felt the need to go out in the morning that it had actually called out to me so that I would get up and open the window for it. I got up, and threw the window open and it flew away.

That day, as my daughter came out of the room after making my bed, she said that, every day, just before dusk, a bulbul had been flying into the room and apparently spending the night perched on the base of the electric light on the wall. I went up to look and saw it there. My entry into the room or even the fact that I went so close to it did not seem to disturb it at all. Perhaps it had accepted that there was someone else to share the comfort of the room with it. The next morning I got up before the bulbul called me and opened the window for it.

The bulbul was alone. My belief that a bulbul builds a nest only to lay eggs, hatch them and nurture its fledgings was now confirmed. The nest is not a home in the human sense. Since it was early spring, this bird had not yet thought of building a nest, perhaps it didn't even have a mate yet.

A few days later, a TV set was set up in the room and in the evening the whole family gathered there to watch television. The set had been placed opposite the light fixture where the bulbul would perch. At sunset, the bulbul came in as usual and sat on a windowsill for a while, shifted to another, and finally to the light fixture on the ceiling. Here, its perch was precarious, so it moved again and went towards its own perch, but seeing figures moving on the TV screen and people sitting before it, it was distracted and moved back to a windowsill. Then it flew away, god knows where. It never came back to the room to spend the night.

3

Another year had passed.

There is a willow tree in a corner of my yard towards the west. It is a young tree, not full grown yet, its trunk just about the size of a large pestle. We had pruned it drastically last winter, and left it standing barely two metres tall. The adjacent wall is only about a metre high. The pruning had left three thick horns at the base where the branches had been. When spring came, they burst into tiny shoots which began to grow into branches. By early May, there was a luxuriant coppice of willow branches on the crest. As was my habit, I was sitting in the chair in my garden, basking in the spring sunshine. There was still a nip in the air. Towards afternoon I caught sight of a bulbul carrying a blade of grass in its beak and flying into the dense thicket of the willow. It was followed by its mate, which also carried a bit of grass in its beak. It was obvious that they were building their nest, but this time I did not interest myself in their activity. The experience of the past two years had taught me that I should not interfere in the affairs of birds or other animals, neither try to help nor harm them through any of my actions. I would go nowhere near their nest. What it contained was none of my business. There is a bathroom near the willow in the yard, infrequently used. One day when I went to the tree, I saw a nest. There was a bulbul, brooding in it. About a week later, I saw the pair taking turns foraging for insects and worms, bringing them in their beaks and disappearing into the willow branches. From my seat neither the nest nor its inhabitants were visible, but their purposeful comings and goings left no doubt that they had their little ones in the interior of the thick willow branches.

A couple of days later, I was at my usual place basking in the sun when I happened to glance at the ground under my feet and my heart missed a beat—there was a dead bird lying there, a very small bird. I shuddered at the sight. It wasn't easy to identify it—though in size and colouring it looked like a bulbul, its head was hidden. I picked up a twig and began to turn the body over. I was horror struck to see that it had no head, it had apparently been chopped off. I gave it another turn and saw the yellow of its bottom. It was a bulbul. I had to know whether it was one of the pair from the nest in the willow. I went to take a look at the nestlings and noticed bulbul feathers scattered all around the tree. There were some feathers near the nest too. There was no doubt now that the dead bulbul was one from the nest.

From a distance, I kept watch to see if someone would come to feed the babies. Soon a bulbul flew in, a caterpillar in its beak, fed it to its babies and flew away. It made similar trips with something or the other as grub, one after the other. Now it was alone at the job. At noon, I saw a cat striding across the wall, and I understood the whole scenario: the bulbul shielding its young under its wings, and the cat pouncing upon it so easily in one leap from the wall. After all, there was just a metre between the top of the wall and the nest. But why had the predator consumed only the bird's head? A closer examination of the location of the nest revealed that the willow branches must have facilitated the cat's job, providing convenient footholds. The sight got rid of my vows of non-interference, how could I watch and not do anything to help? I tore away the branches from the side of the wall, but then realized that I had made a mistake by removing a screen from that side and laid the nest bare for everyone to see. But the screen when still standing had provided no protection from a predator either, I thought. Would the bulbul have met this fate, its head eaten and the body cast to the ground, if it had been effective?

Now there was only one bulbul trying to do the job of two, so the nestlings had to wait longer for their feed. Earlier, taking turns had resulted in shorter sorties. Another thought that bothered me now was whether the dead bird was male or female. It is not easy to determine the sex of bulbuls as in the case of poultry or sparrows, because the male and female bulbuls are the same in colour and appearance. Perhaps, one way to distinguish gender was the size. I think that, like in all species, the female is slightly smaller in frame. But there was a problem here—there was no other bulbul to compare it with. I gave the problem much thought. I remembered that two years ago I would see one of the pair go into the nest from time to time and give the warmth of its body to the babies. This bulbul was not doing that, it could barely manage to feed them, the question of brooding did not arise. Perhaps that was a female's job. Maybe when the cat climbed the tree, the bulbul was aware of what was coming—birds and animals are supposed to have a sharper sense of danger. It would have had the option of flying away to save itself. But this bulbul must not have done so for that would have left the babies unprotected; it had chosen to sacrifice itself to the cat rather than let harm come to the little ones. Such sacrifice only a mother can make, generally. All this made me feel that the dead one must have been female, though nothing could be said with a degree of certainty.

Now I began to worry about the safety of the babies. I noticed two sheets of galvanized iron lying in the yard. I lifted them one by one and placed them near the wall against the willow. They stood a good metre above the top of the willow. Now there was no way the cat could get at the nest from the wall. I took my seat and watched out for the bulbul to come with food for its young ones. It came and occupied its place on a branch; after a while it flew to the wall, where it stayed for a while. But when it tried to approach the nest, the metal sheets blocked its way. Every time it tried to fly into the nest, the sight of black rusted sheets seemed to frighten it, making it turn back. Defeated, it went back to its perch on the branch with the food still in its beak. I could see that it was feeling quite disoriented with the altered position of the nest, no longer sure whether it was safe to go in. Assessing the situation, I got up and flung away the sheets. The bulbul flew to the wall, then into the nest. It came out after a while, the worm in its beak gone—the babies had been fed.

My observation two years ago had shown that as dusk began to fall, the bulbul would come and cover the babies in the nest under its breast. Throughout the night it would maintain its position, its underbelly serving as an incubator to give the fragile ones warmth, its wings spread over them as a protective umbrella. Once, out of curiosity, I had shone a torch inside, but the beam of light shining on its head did not make the bulbul shift its position. It calmly sat on, shielding its young. So I waited for this bulbul too to come to its post before night fell. But it did not come. I waited till it was quite dark. By this time all the feathered creatures had returned to their nests. The bulbul still did not come. I was in a dilemma—should I put up the sheets or not? Supposing the bulbul returned at some time in the night and the sheets held it back? But even if it went to its duty in the nest, without the protection of the sheets, it would only suffer the same fate as its mate. My mind was made up—I would put up the sheets, I must, if the bulbul family was to be saved from the cat. I went ahead and put the sheets back in place. After some time I took a look at the nest, but the bulbul was not back. God knows where it had decided to spend the night. Now I was even more sure that the dead bird was a female. I prodded the nest with a stick and a little bird stretched its neck to see. I thought there must be a couple of other babies in it.

The next morning I was up at dawn. I went out and dragged a stool to the willow. This would be my first close look at the nest. I had to check on the babies to see whether they had weathered the cold of the night or were frozen to death. I saw that there were three of them, covered with fine, tiny feathers. The wings had just begun to grow. But they seemed to be stuck to one another, almost bundled together; their heads seemed to have fallen upon each others' backs, as if their necks had been broken. I could hear a painful wheeze emanating from the little ones rather like a death rattle. I prodded one with a pencil, but there was no response. The same with another. No lifting of the head or any other movement to suggest that they were alive except for the fact that they were breathing. I waited for the parent bird to come. How would it deal with the situation? Whom would he feed the morsels he brought? These ones were certainly not in any position to accept them. When the adult bulbul arrived, it peered into the nest, as if to examine its contents. There was no food in its beak. Then it just flew away.

About half an hour later, when the sun shone upon the nest directly, the bulbul was back. This time he had something in his beak. He flew in and dropped what he had brought into the nest. He made another trip and again almost threw the food in. Apparently the babies were accepting the food, because the bulbul continued to make one sortie after another. Why the bulbul had waited to feed them only after the sun had been hitting the nest for quite some time became clear to me. The cold had rendered the babies nearly unconscious and quite unable to feed. It was only when the warmth of the sun breathed new life into them that the bulbul understood that now was the time to feed them, and proceeded to do so, making regular sorties thereafter. It seemed to me that the trips were occurring with greater frequency, as though the whole purpose of his life was to feed his babies.

Something new appeared on the scene now—something quite unexpected which lent a totally different dimension to the situation: as the bulbul flew in with food, it was accompanied by another bulbul. When he perched on a branch, the other one did the same. If he landed on a wire, sure enough the other one followed. The same pattern was followed as the bulbul went to the wall, but when he went to the nest to his babies, the other one would hold back, finding a perch on another branch. It just wouldn't go anywhere near the nest itself, but kept its eyes on the bulbul in the nest all the time. As soon as the babies had been fed and the bulbul flew down searching for grains on the ground, the other bulbul would take its place next to him, either doing the same or waiting for it to finish. Wherever the bulbul from the nest went, he was trailed by the other. I wondered where the newcomer had come from. There had been no sign of another bulbul yesterday, so where had it sprung from? Why was it clinging to the other like a shadow?

There could be only one explanation—the other one was probably a loner too, it had no mate, hence its decision to attach itself to the former. I still wanted to know who, between the two, was the female. I had already decided that the dead bird was the babies' mother. Besides, I knew that birds are not homosexual and their mate is always of the opposite sex. This was the season for the female of the species to build a nest and lay eggs, hence her need to find a mate. That is why she was constantly at his side, trying to woo him. However, he seemed completely uninterested, showing no inclination at all for building a relationship with her. The question of raising another family until the nestlings were ready to fend for themselves did not arise.

One attribute of the feathered species is that they move in pairs, with no room for a third. Neither of the couple can be wooed away by an interloper of another sex. In fact, no bird tries to do so. If at all an attempt is made, the intruder is soon driven away, pecked at mercilessly by the others, till it disappears from the scene. But here the case was slightly different. Though the male was paying no heed to the new female's overtures he was not trying to chase or push her away either. Apparently, while burdened with the responsibility of the babies, he had to stay aloof, but was not keen to antagonize her by an aggressively hostile stance. After all, he was mateless and would soon need one. Strangely enough, even while she was so enamoured of him, the female made no attempt to associate herself with the nest and its inmates.

I watched the whole drama till noon. It was time for my tea—a cup of tea is all I have for lunch. I rose to go in, but not before carefully scanning the surrounding area to satisfy myself that no predator lay in wait. I came back immediately after finishing my tea, hardly taking ten minutes or so. I dragged a stool to the willow and climbed on it to take a look inside the nest. The earth seemed to fall from under my feet when I saw that there were just two fledglings in the nest. Where was the third sibling? It was impossible that it could have flown away from the nest, or fallen from it. The babies had no wings at all, just some tiny feathers, so how could it fly. I looked in every direction, but there was no sign of a cat anywhere. I should not have moved, I should have kept watch, I blamed myself, but what was the use?

The bulbul flew in with food, trailed by the female. Once he had fed the young ones, he perched on a branch. The female, who had kept her gaze on him all the time while he was feeding his brood, flew very close to him, almost sticking to him. By now the male seemed to have softened towards her; he allowed her to touch him and sit so close that the two bodies seemed to be one. They stayed like that for a while and then flew away together. It was quite some time before he returned with food. Now the intervals between feeds grew longer and longer and with each departure, it was a longer wait for the babies, even though with their rapid growth, the need for food was more pressing. At one time, when the food-bearing male came, accompanied as usual by the female, the babies had had to wait a really long time. After feeding them, he flew down and sat on the lawn. The female followed, and drew very close to him and began to flutter her wings provocatively. Then she flew around him in progressively smaller circles till her body touched his again. Finally she gave him a caress with her beak, planting what looked like a kiss on his neck and the two flew away together in a different direction.

Suddenly an idea struck me. Why not check my watch for the time he would take to come back this time, I thought. Ten minutes passed, then fifteen, half an hour, an hour and a quarter, but there was still no sign of his coming. Finally, after about an hour and a half, they both turned up, the male sat on the wall and the female on a stretched rope. I glanced up and found that the male bulbul's beak was empty—no worm, insect or grain of food for the nestlings. He went to the nest and sat on a willow branch, and then he seemed to examine the nest and the babies in it carefully. But he did not go into the nest, nor did he drop any morsel of food into it. Then he went to the same branch where the female was and perched on it. He had arrived after such a long interval of time but with nothing for the babies, made no attempt to feed them, in fact suddenly he had become distant—had he lost all interest in them? Consumed by this anxiety, and in order to check, again I drew the stool to the willow and looked into the nest, holding out my hand. The female was unconcerned, but the male raised a huge clamour, displaying tremendous unease. He seemed to be in agony, flitting from one branch to another in a panic until I withdrew. Only then did the two of them fly away, while it was now my turn to wait restlessly for his return, glancing at my watch every minute. When would he bring food for the little ones—I couldn't rid myself of this worry. I looked in every direction—somehow I did not want to believe that he would abandon them thus. Half an hour or so later, the pair returned and the first thing I looked at was the male's beak, and my dismay was deep to see it empty. This time, too, he had brought no food for them. Even though this was not the first time that he had come empty-beaked, yet he would go to the nest and seemed to be keen to ascertain the welfare of his brood, but this time there was no such gesture. Now he was as unconcerned and untouched by feeling towards the nest and its contents as his new mate was. And I was plagued by the worry of who would care for the little ones or feed them now.

Meanwhile, a visitor arrived. Since I was in the garden he let himself in. I had no choice but to get up, greet him and take him inside the house. I did ask for tea to be brought to my guest, but apart from some formal small talk I had no desire to really converse with him. I was afraid that the conversation might drag on, and my thoughts were actually on the bulbul babies. I did not want them to come to any harm. My lack of conversation soon bored the guest and he rose to leave. Seeing him off, I returned to my usual place in the garden. I had been away for slightly over twenty minutes. Once again I stood on the stool, peeping into the nest. My breath stopped when I saw that there was only one baby bulbul in it. There was no sign of the second one anywhere, neither was there any evidence of the presence of a cat in the vicinity. So who could have taken the little thing away from its nest? It did not seem likely that the cat had made its appearance in my brief absence from the scene, killed the baby bulbul and made such a clean getaway. I had never seen it trying to approach the nest from my side or withdraw at my sight. The fact, however, was that now there was only one baby bulbul left. I no longer nourished any hope that he would be fed by anyone, he would certainly die of hunger or the cold at night, I was sure. I was also convinced, more than ever before, that the dead bulbul had been a female. If the male had died instead of her, would she have abandoned her babies, no matter how hard another male might have tried to woo her? Even if she did build another relationship, I was sure the babies would have been her first priority. In fact she would have made the new male in her life join in and help her raise them. All this was my feeling, there was no way that I could prove this with a scientific experiment. But my observation of human behaviour told me that I was right. Of course it could well be said that no judgement on birds could be based on a study of the behaviour of humans—but how am I to explain?

I plunged into gloom over the fate of the poor lone bulbul baby. Even though I had lost all hope, something kept me glued to my place in the garden, hoping against hope that a glimmer of paternal love might grow into a blazing light and bring the bulbul back to his offspring. It was almost evening by now, but there was still enough light. Suddenly my heart leapt to see the pair of bulbuls swim into my field of vision. Again I looked at the bulbul's beak, but it was empty. He flew to the willow and took his place on a branch, making no attempt to go and look inside the nest. Then he went back to the other tree, where his new mate was. The two then went into an elaborate courtship ritual beak to beak. The female buried her beak in the male's feathers and began to stroke his head, neck, breast, belly and back. The male who seemed to have surrendered himself completely to her attentions, appeared to relax, totally at peace with everything, content. The female flew down to the ground, picked up a blade of grass in her beak and threw it away. Perhaps the preparations for a new home were afoot, I told myself.

The two flew away, leaving me to worry about the lone baby bulbul in the nest. It was nearly dark and again I stood on my stool. The baby did not seem to be doing too badly, considering it had had nothing to eat for almost three hours. It held its head high and peered this way and that. I climbed down from the stool and picked up a few grains from the ground, held them out on my palm to its beak. My plan was to see if it would accept food from me. In that case, I could take it inside the house, nest and all and save it from hunger and cold. But no matter how hard I tried, it would not open its mouth. Nothing could persuade it to budge. I just could not offer it any nourishment. Defeated, I climbed down. Soon it would be time for me to go in, have my cup of evening kahwa, what was the use of lingering here, I thought. But I had one problem to solve before I retired for the night—I had to decide whether to put up the shield of sheets against the wall or not. Would it be all right to continue to protect this baby from the cat or not? Supposing I did nothing, the cat would finish it off in no time at all. It might thus find a quick death and be released from the agony of a sure but slow death by starvation. Last night, the three of them had been hugging each other for warmth; they had been in a pathetic state in the morning, but at least they had been alive. Tonight, the baby bulbul was all by itself. How cruelly the cold would put an end to its life. Even if it survived it somehow, what torture it would be to wait for food that would never come. No one to pay heed to its open beak and a creeping death… I would be abominably cruel to leave it to such a fate. I just could not make up my mind.

Which way would it be best for the bulbul chick to die—to be devoured by the cat or a slow, lingering, more painful death caused by the chill and starvation? That was the question I kept asking myself.

As I took sips of my kahwa, hope began to rise in my heart. I thought the sun might breathe new life into it. The male bulbul might show affection again by coming back and feeding it… The tender thing might be saved after all… So many possibilities pressed upon my mind. I decided to go and look into the nest first. I stood on the stool and peered in. The little birdling was gone and the nest was empty.

It remained empty, but the bulbul did not bring his new bride into it. Perhaps she did not want to lay her eggs or hatch them in someone else's home. As winter approached, we again pruned the willow. Along with the cut branches, down came the nest and, mingling with the heap of rubbish, it vanished.

A HORSE AND TWO GOATS

R. K. NARAYAN

Of the seven hundred thousand villages dotting the map of India, in which the majority of India's five hundred million live, flourish, and die, Kritam was probably the tiniest, indicated on the district survey map by a microscopic dot, the map being meant more for the revenue official out to collect tax than for the guidance of the motorist, who in any case could not hope to reach it since it sprawled far from the highway at the end of a rough track furrowed up by the iron-hooped wheels of bullock carts. But its size did not prevent its giving itself the grandiose name Kritam, which meant in Tamil 'coronet' or 'crown' on the brow of this subcontinent. The village consisted of less than thirty houses, only one of them built with brick and cement. Painted a brilliant yellow and blue all over with gorgeous carvings of gods and gargoyles on its balustrade, it was known as the Big House. The other houses, distributed in four streets, were generally of bamboo thatch, straw, mud, and other unspecified material. Muni's was the last house in the fourth street, beyond which stretched the fields. In his prosperous days Muni had owned a flock of forty sheep and goats and sallied forth every morning, driving the flock to the highway a couple of miles away. There he would sit on the pedestal of a clay statue of a horse while his cattle grazed around. He carried a crook at the end of a bamboo pole and snapped foliage from the avenue trees to feed his flock; he also gathered faggots and dry sticks, bundled them, and carried them home for fuel at sunset.

His wife lit the domestic fire at dawn, boiled water in a mud pot, threw into it a handful of millet flour, added salt, and gave him his first nourishment for the day. When he started out, she would put in his hand a packed lunch, once again the same millet cooked into a little ball, which he could swallow with a raw onion at midday. She was old, but he was older and needed all the attention she could give him in order to be kept alive.

His fortunes had declined gradually, unnoticed. From a flock of forty, which he drove into a pen at night, his stock had now come down to two goats, which were not worth the rent of a half-rupee a month the Big House charged for the use of the pen in their backyard. And so the two goats were tethered to the trunk of a drumstick tree which grew in front of his hut and from which, occasionally, Muni could shake down drumsticks. This morning he got six. He carried them in with a sense of triumph. Although no one could say precisely who owned the tree, it was his because he lived in its shadow.

She said, 'If you were content with the drumstick leaves alone, I could boil and salt some for you.'

'Oh, I am tired of eating those leaves. I have a craving to chew the drumstick out of sauce, I tell you.'

'You have only four teeth in your jaw, but your craving is for big things. All right, get the stuff for the sauce, and I will prepare it for you. After all, next year you may not be alive to ask for anything. But first get me all the stuff, including a measure of rice or millet, and I will satisfy your unholy craving. Our store is empty today. Dal, chilli, curry leaves, mustard, coriander, gingelly oil and one large potato. Go out and get all this.' He repeated the list after her in order not to miss any item and walked off to the shop in the third street.

He sat on an upturned packing case below the platform of the shop. The shopman paid no attention to him. Muni kept clearing his throat, coughing and sneezing until the shopman could not stand it anymore and demanded, 'What ails you? You will fly off that seat into the gutter if you sneeze so hard, young man.' Muni laughed inordinately, in order to please the shopman, at being called 'young man'. The shopman softened and said, 'You have enough of the imp inside to keep a second wife busy, but for the fact the old lady is still alive.' Muni laughed appropriately again at this joke. It completely won the shopman over; he liked his sense of humour to be appreciated.

Muni engaged his attention in local gossip for a few minutes, which always ended with a reference to the postman's wife who had eloped to the city some months before.

The shopman felt most pleased to hear the worst of the postman, who had cheated him. Being an itinerant postman, he returned home to Kritam only once in ten days and every time managed to slip away again without passing the shop in the third street. By thus humouring the shopman, Muni could always ask for one or two items of food, promising repayment later. Some days the shopman was in a good mood and gave in, and sometimes he would lose his temper suddenly and bark at Muni for daring to ask for credit. This was such a day, and Muni could not progress beyond two items listed as essential components. The shopman was also displaying a remarkable memory for old facts and figures and took out an oblong ledger to support his observations. Muni felt impelled to rise and flee but his self-respect kept him in his seat and made him listen to the worst things about himself. The shopman concluded, 'If you could find five rupees and a quarter, you would pay off an ancient debt and then could apply for admission to swarga. How much have you got now?'

'I will pay you everything on the first of the next month.'

'As always, and whom do you expect to rob by then?'

Muni felt caught and mumbled, 'My daughter has sent word that she will be sending me money.'

'Have you a daughter?' sneered the shopman. 'And she is sending you money! For what purpose, may I know?'

'Birthday, fiftieth birthday,' said Muni quietly.

'Birthday! How old are you?'

Muni repeated weakly, not being sure of it himself, 'Fifty.' He always calculated his age from the time of the great famine when he stood as high as the parapet around the village well, but who could calculate such things accurately nowadays with so many famines occurring? The shopman felt encouraged when other customers stood around to watch and comment. Muni thought helplessly, my poverty is exposed to everybody. But what can I do?

'More likely you are seventy,' said the shopman. 'You also forget that you mentioned a birthday five weeks ago when you wanted castor oil for your holy bath.'

'Bath! Who can dream of a bath when you have to scratch the tank-bed for a bowl of water? We would all be parched and dead but for the Big House, where they let us take a pot of water from their well.' After saying this Muni unobtrusively rose and moved off.

He told his wife, 'That scoundrel would not give me anything.'

'So go out and sell the drumsticks for what they are worth.'

He flung himself down in a corner to recoup from the fatigue of his visit to the shop. His wife said, 'You are getting no sauce today, nor anything else. I can't find anything to give you to eat. Fast till the evening, it'll do you good. Take the goats and be gone now,' she cried and added, 'Don't come back before the sun is down.' He knew that if he obeyed her she would somehow conjure up some food for him in the evening. Only he must be careful not to argue and irritate her. Her temper was undependable in the morning but improved by evening time. She was sure to go out and work—grind corn in the Big House, sweep or scrub somewhere, and earn enough to buy foodstuff and keep a dinner ready for him in the evening.

Unleashing the goats from the drumstick tree, Muni started out, driving them ahead and uttering weird cries from time to time in order to urge them on. He passed through the village with his head bowed in thought. He did not want to look at anyone or be accosted. A couple of his cronies lounging in the temple corridor hailed him, but he ignored their call. They had known him in the days of affluence when he lorded over a flock of fleecy sheep, not the miserable gawky goats that he had today. Of course he also used to have a few goats for those who fancied them, but real wealth lay in sheep; they bred fast and people came and bought the fleece in the shearing season; and then that famous butcher from the town came over on the weekly market days bringing him betel leaves, tobacco, and often enough some bhang, which they smoked in a hut in the coconut grove, undisturbed by wives and well-wishers. After a smoke one felt light and elated and inclined to forgive everyone including that brother-in-law of his who had once tried to set fire to his home. But all this seemed like the memoirs of a previous birth. Some pestilence afflicted his cattle (he could, of course, guess who had laid his animals under a curse) and even the friendly butcher would not touch one at half the price... and now here he was left with the two scraggy creatures. He wished someone would rid him of their company too. The shopman had said that he was seventy. At seventy, one only waited to be summoned by God. When he was dead what would his wife do? They had lived in each other's company since they were children. He was told on the day of their wedding that he was ten years old and she was eight. During the wedding ceremony they had had to recite their respective ages and names. He had thrashed her only a few times in their marriage, and later she had the upper hand. Progeny, none. Perhaps numerous progeny would have brought him the blessing of the gods. Fertility brought merit. People with fourteen sons were always so prosperous and at peace with the world and themselves. He recollected the thrill he had felt when he mentioned a daughter to that shopman; although it was not believed, what if he did not have a daughter?—his cousin in the next village had many daughters, and any one of them was as good as his; he was fond of them all and would buy them sweets if he could afford it. Still, everyone in the village whispered behind their backs that Muni and his wife were a barren couple. He avoided looking at anyone; they all professed to be so high up, and everyone else in the village had more money than him. 'I am the poorest fellow in our caste and no wonder that they spurn me, but I won't look at them either,' and so he passed on with his eyes downcast along the edge of the street, and people left him also very much alone, commenting only to the extent, 'Ah, there he goes with his two great goats; if he slits their throats, he may have more peace of mind.' 'What has he to worry about anyway? They live on nothing and have nobody to worry about.' Thus people commented when he passed through the village. Only on the outskirts did he lift his head and look up. He urged and bullied the goats until they meandered along to the foot of the horse statue on the edge of the village. He sat on its pedestal for the rest of the day. The advantage of this was that he could watch the highway and see the lorries and buses pass through to the hills, and it gave him a sense of belonging to a larger world. The pedestal of the statue was broad enough for him to move around as the sun travelled up and westwards; or he could also crouch under the belly of the horse, for shade.

The horse was nearly life-size, moulded out of clay, baked, burnt and brightly coloured, and reared its head proudly, prancing with its forelegs in the air and flourishing its tail in a loop. Beside the horse stood a warrior with scythe-like mustachios, bulging eyes and aquiline nose. The old image-makers believed in indicating a man of strength by bulging out his eyes and sharpening his moustache tips. They had also decorated the man's chest with beads which looked today like blobs of mud through the ravages of sun and wind and rain (when it came), but Muni would insist that he had known the beads to sparkle like the nine gems at one time in his life. The horse itself was said to have been as white as a dhobi-washed sheet, and had had on its back a cover of pure brocade of red-and-black lace, matching the multi-coloured sash around the waist of the warrior. But none in the village remembered the splendour as no one noticed its existence. Even Muni, who spent all his waking hours at its foot, never bothered to look up. It was untouched by the young vandals of the village who gashed tree trunks with knives and tried to topple off milestones and inscribed lewd designs on all the walls. This statue had been closer to the population of the village at one time, when this spot bordered the village; but when the highway was laid through (or perhaps when the tank and wells dried up completely here) the village moved a couple of miles inland.

Muni sat at the foot of the statue, watching his two goats graze in the arid soil among the cactus and lantana bushes. He looked at the sun; it had tilted westwards no doubt, but it was not the time yet to go back home; if he went too early, his wife would have no food for him. Also he must give her time to cool off her temper and feel sympathetic, and then she would scrounge and manage to get some food. He watched the mountain road for a time signal. When the green bus appeared around the bend he could leave, and his wife would feel pleased that he had let the goats feed long enough.

He noticed now a new sort of vehicle coming down at full speed. It looked both like a motor car and a bus. He used to be intrigued by the novelty of such spectacles, but of late, work was going on at the source of the river on the mountain and an assortment of people and traffic went past him, and he took it all casually and described to his wife, later in the day, not everything as he once did, but only some things, only if he noticed anything special. Today, while he observed the yellow vehicle coming down, he was wondering how to describe it later when it sputtered and stopped in front of him. A red-faced foreigner who had been driving it got down and went round it, stooping, looking, and poking under the vehicle; then he straightened himself up, looked at the dashboard, stared in Muni's direction, and approached him. 'Excuse me, is there a gas station nearby, or do I have to wait until another car comes—' He suddenly looked up at the clay horse and cried, 'Marvellous!' without completing his sentence. Muni felt he should get up and run away, and cursed his age. He could not readily put his limbs into action; some years ago he could outrun a cheetah, as happened once when he went to the forest to cut fuel and it was then that two of his sheep were mauled—a sign that bad times were coming. Though he tried, he could not easily extricate himself from his seat, and then there was also the problem of the goats. He could not leave them behind.

The red-faced man wore khaki clothes—evidently a policeman or a soldier. Muni said to himself, 'He will chase or shoot if I start running. Sometimes dogs chase only those who run—O Shiva, protect me. I don't know why this man should be after me.' Meanwhile the foreigner cried, 'Marvellous!' again, nodding his head. He paced around the statue with his eyes fixed on it. Muni sat frozen for a while, and then fidgeted and tried to edge away. Now the other man suddenly pressed his palms together in a salute, smiled, and said, 'Namaste! How do you do?'

At which Muni spoke the only English expressions he had learnt, 'Yes, no.' Having exhausted his English vocabulary, he started in Tamil: 'My name is Muni. These two goats are mine, and no one can gainsay it—though our village is full of slanderers these days who will not hesitate to say that what belongs to a man doesn't belong to him.' He rolled his eyes and shuddered at the thought of evil-minded men and women peopling his village.

The foreigner faithfully looked in the direction indicated by Muni's fingers, gazed for a while at the two goats and the rocks, and with a puzzled expression took out his silver cigarette-case and lit a cigarette. Suddenly remembering the courtesies of the season, he asked, 'Do you smoke?' Muni answered, 'Yes, no.' Whereupon the red-faced man took a cigarette and gave it to Muni, who received it with surprise, having had no offer of a smoke from anyone for years now. Those days when he smoked bhang were gone with his sheep and the large-hearted butcher. Nowadays he was not able to find even matches, let alone bhang. (His wife went across and borrowed a fire at dawn from a neighbour.) He had always wanted to smoke a cigarette; only once had the shopman given him one on credit, and he remembered how good it had tasted. The other flicked the lighter open and offered a light to Muni. Muni felt so confused about how to act that he blew on it and put it out. The other, puzzled but undaunted, flourished his lighter, presented it again, and lit Muni's cigarette. Muni drew a deep puff and started coughing; it was racking, no doubt, but extremely pleasant. When his cough subsided he wiped his eyes and took stock of the situation, understanding that the other man was not an inquisitor of any kind. Yet, in order to make sure, he remained wary. No need to run away from a man who gave him such a potent smoke. His head was reeling from the effect of one of those strong American cigarettes made with roasted tobacco. The man said, 'I come from New York,' took out a wallet from his hip pocket, and presented his card.

Muni shrank away from the card. Perhaps he was trying to present a warrant and arrest him. Beware of khaki, one part of his mind warned. Take all the cigarettes or bhang or whatever is offered, but don't get caught. Beware of khaki. He wished he weren't seventy as the shopman had said. At seventy one didn't run, but surrendered to whatever came. He could only ward off trouble by talk. So he went on, all in the chaste Tamil for which Kritam was famous. (Even the worst detractors could not deny that the famous poetess Avvaiyar was born in this area, although no one could say whether it was in Kritam or Kuppam, the adjoining village.) Out of this heritage the Tamil language gushed through Muni in an unimpeded flow. He said, 'Before God, sir, Bhagwan, who sees everything, I tell you, sir, that we know nothing of the case. If the murder was committed, whoever did it will not escape. Bhagwan is all-seeing. Don't ask me about it. I know nothing.' A body had been found mutilated and thrown under a tamarind tree at the border between Kritam and Kuppam a few weeks before, giving rise to much gossip and speculation. Muni added an explanation, 'Anything is possible there. People over there will stop at nothing.' The foreigner nodded his head and listened courteously though he understood nothing.

'I am sure you know when this horse was made,' said the red man and smiled ingratiatingly.

Muni reacted to the relaxed atmosphere by smiling himself, and pleaded, 'Please go away, sir, I know nothing. I promise we will hold him for you if we see any bad character around, and we will bury him up to his neck in a coconut pit if he tries to escape; but our village has always had a clean record. Must definitely be the other village.'

Now the red man implored, 'Please, please, I will speak slowly, please try to understand me. Can't you understand even a simple word of English? Everyone in this country seems to know English. I have got along with English everywhere in this country, but you don't speak it. Have you any religious or spiritual scruples for avoiding the English speech?'

Muni made some indistinct sounds in his throat and shook his head. Encouraged, the other went on to explain at length, uttering each syllable with care and deliberation. Presently he sidled over and took a seat beside the old man, explaining, 'You see, last August, we probably had the hottest summer in history, and I was working in shirt-sleeves in my office on the fortieth floor of the Empire State Building. You must have heard of the power failure, and there I was stuck for four hours, no elevator, no air conditioning. All the way in the train I kept thinking, and the minute I reached home in Connecticut, I told my wife Ruth, "We will visit India this winter, it's time to look at other civilizations." Next day she called the travel agent first thing and told him to fix it, and so here I am. Ruth came with me but is staying back at Srinagar, and I am the one doing the rounds and joining her later.'

Muni looked reflective at the end of this long peroration and said, rather feebly, 'Yes, no,' as a concession to the other's language, and went on in Tamil, 'When I was this high,' he indicated a foot high, 'I heard my uncle say…'

No one can tell what he was planning to say as the other interrupted him at this stage to ask, 'Boy, what is the secret of your teeth? How old are you?'

The old man forgot what he had started to say and remarked, 'Sometimes we too lose our cattle. Jackals or cheetahs may carry them off, but sometimes it is just theft from over in the next village, and then we will know who has done it. Our priest at the temple can see in the camphor flame the face of the thief, and when he is caught…' He gestured with his hands a perfect mincing of meat.

The American watched his hands intently and said, 'I know what you mean. Chop something? Maybe I am holding you up and you want to chop wood? Where is your axe? Hand it to me and show me what to chop. I do enjoy it, you know, just a hobby. We get a lot of driftwood along the backwater near my house, and on Sundays I do nothing but chop wood for the fireplace. I really feel different when I watch the fire in the fireplace, although it may take all the sections of the Sunday *New York Times* to get a fire started,' and he smiled at this reference.

Muni felt totally confused but decided the best thing would be to make an attempt to get away from this place. He tried to edge out, saying, 'Must go home,' and turned to go. The other seized his shoulder and said desperately, 'Is there no one, absolutely no one here, to translate for me?' He looked up and down the road, which was deserted in this hot afternoon; a sudden gust of wind churned up the dust and dead leaves on the roadside into a ghostly column and propelled it towards the mountain road. The stranger almost pinioned Muni's back to the statue and asked, 'Isn't this statue yours? Why don't you sell it to me?'

The old man now understood the reference to the horse, thought for a second, and said in his own language, 'I was an urchin this high when I heard my grandfather explain this horse and warrior, and my grandfather himself was this high when he heard his grandfather, whose grandfather…'

The other man interrupted him with, 'I don't want to seem to have stopped here for nothing. I will offer you a good price for this,' he said, indicating the horse. He had concluded without the least doubt that Muni owned this mud horse. Perhaps he guessed by the way he sat at its pedestal, like other souvenir-sellers in this country presiding over their wares.

Muni followed the man's eyes and pointing fingers and dimly understood the subject matter and, feeling relieved that the theme of the mutilated body had been abandoned at least for the time being, said again, enthusiastically, 'I was this high when my grandfather told me about this horse and the warrior, and my grandfather was this high when he himself…' and he was getting into a deeper bog of reminiscence each time he tried to indicate the antiquity of the statue.

The Tamil that Muni spoke was stimulating even as pure sound, and the foreigner listened with fascination. 'I wish I had my tape recorder here,' he said, assuming the pleasantest expression. 'Your language sounds wonderful. I get a kick out of every word you utter, here'—he indicated his ears—'but you don't have to waste your breath in sales talk. I appreciate the article. You don't have to explain its points.'

'I never went to a school, in those days only Brahmins went to schools, but we had to go out and work in the fields morning till night, from sowing to harvest time…and when Pongal came and we had cut the harvest, my father allowed me to go out and play with others at the tank, and so I don't know the Parangi language you speak, even little fellows in your country probably speak the Parangi language, but here only learned men and officers know it. We had a postman in our village who could speak to you boldly in your language, but his wife ran away with someone and he does not speak to anyone at all nowadays. Who would if a wife did what she did? Women must be watched; otherwise they will sell themselves and the home,' and he laughed at his own quip.

The foreigner laughed heartily, took out another cigarette, and offered it to Muni, who now smoked with ease, deciding to stay on if the fellow was going to be so good as to keep up his cigarette supply. The American now stood up on the pedestal in the attitude of a demonstrative lecturer and said, running his finger along some of the carved decorations around the horse's neck, speaking slowly and uttering his words syllable by syllable, 'I could give a sales talk for this better than anyone else... This is a marvellous combination of yellow and indigo, though faded now... How do you people of this country achieve these flaming colours?'

Muni, now assured that the subject was still the horse and not the dead body, said, 'This is our guardian, it means death to our adversaries. At the end of Kali Yuga, this world and all other worlds will be destroyed, and the Redeemer will come in the shape of a horse called Kalki; this horse will come to life and gallop and trample down all bad men.' As he spoke of bad men the figures of his shopman and his brother-in-law assumed concrete forms in his mind, and he revelled for a moment in the predicament of the fellow under the horse's hoof: served him right for trying to set fire to his home...

While he was brooding on this pleasant vision, the foreigner utilized the pause to say, 'I assure you that this will have the best home in the USA. I'll push away the bookcase, you know I love books and am a member of five book clubs, and the choice and bonus volumes really mount up to a pile in our living room, as high as this horse itself. But they'll have to go. Ruth may disapprove, but I will convince her. The TV may have to be shifted too. We can't have everything in the living room. Ruth will probably say, "What about when we have a party?" I'm going to keep him right in the middle of the room. I don't see how that can interfere with the party—we'll stand around him and have our drinks.'

Muni continued his description of the end of the world. 'Our pandit discoursed at the temple once how the oceans are going to close over the earth in a huge wave and swallow us—this horse will grow bigger than the biggest wave and carry on its back only the good people and kick into the floods the evil ones—plenty of them about,' he said reflectively. 'Do you know when it is going to happen?' he asked.

The foreigner now understood by the tone of the other that a question was being asked and said, 'How am I transporting it? I can push the seat back and make room in the rear. That van can take in an elephant'—waving precisely at the back of the seat.

Muni was still hovering on visions of avatars and said again, 'I never missed our pandit's discourses at the temple in those days during every bright half of the month, although he'd go on all night, and he told us that Vishnu is the highest god. Whenever evil men trouble us, he comes down to save us. He has come many times. The first time he incarnated as a great fish, and lifted the scriptures on his back when the floods and sea waves...'

'I am not a millionaire, but a modest businessman. My trade is coffee.'

Amidst all this wilderness of obscure sound Muni caught the word 'coffee' and said, 'If you want to drink "kapi", drive further up, in the next town, they have Friday market, and there they open "kapi-otels"—so I learn from passers-by. Don't think I wander about. I go nowhere and look for nothing.' His thoughts went back to the avatars. 'The first avatar was in the shape of a little fish in a bowl of water, but every hour it grew bigger and bigger and became in the end a huge whale which the seas could not contain, and on the back of the whale the holy books were supported, saved, and carried.' Having launched on the first avatar it was inevitable that he should go on to the next, a wild boar on whose tusk the earth was lifted when a vicious conqueror of the earth carried it off and hid it at the bottom of the sea. After describing this avatar Muni concluded, 'God will always save us whenever we are troubled by evil beings. When we were young we staged at full moon the story of the avatars. That's how I know the stories; we played them all night until the sun rose, and sometimes the European collector would come to watch, bringing his own chair. I had a good voice and so they always taught me songs and gave me the women's roles. I was always Goddess Lakshmi, and they dressed me in a brocade sari, loaned from the Big House...'

The foreigner said, 'I repeat, I am not a millionaire. Ours is a modest business; after all, we can't afford to buy more than sixty minutes' TV time in a month, which works out to two minutes a day, that's all, although in the course of time we'll maybe sponsor a one-hour show regularly if our sales graph continues to go up...'

Muni was intoxicated by the memory of his theatrical days and was about to explain how he had painted his face and worn a wig and diamond earrings when the visitor, feeling that he had spent too much time already, said, 'Tell me, will you accept a hundred rupees or not for the horse? I'd love to take the whiskered soldier also but I've no space for him this year. I'll have to cancel my air ticket and take a boat home, I suppose. Ruth can go by air if she likes, but I will go with the horse and keep him in my cabin all the way if necessary,' and he smiled at the picture of himself voyaging across the seas hugging this horse. He added, 'I will have to pad it with straw so that it doesn't break...'

'When we played Ramayana, they dressed me as Sita,' added Muni. 'A teacher came and taught us the songs for the drama and we gave him fifty rupees. He incarnated himself as Rama, and he alone could destroy Ravana, the demon with ten heads who shook all the worlds; do you know the story of Ramayana?'

'I have my station wagon as you see. I can push the seat back and take the horse in if you will just lend me a hand with it.'

'Do you know Mahabharata? Krishna was the eighth avatar of Vishnu, incarnated to help the Five Brothers regain their kingdom. When Krishna was a baby he danced on the thousand-hooded giant serpent and trampled it to death; and then he suckled the breasts of the demoness and left them flat as a disc though when she came to him her bosoms were large, like mounds of earth on the banks of a dug-up canal.' He indicated two mounds with his hands. The stranger was completely mystified by the gesture. For the first time he said, 'I really wonder what you are saying because your answer is crucial. We have come to the point when we should be ready to talk business.'

'When the tenth avatar comes, do you know where you and I

will be?' asked the old man.

'Lend me a hand and I can lift off the horse from its pedestal after picking out the cement at the joints. We can do anything if we have a basis of understanding.'

At this stage the mutual mystification was complete, and there was no need even to carry on a guessing game at the meaning of words. The old man chattered away in a spirit of balancing off the credits and debits of conversational exchange, and said in order to be on the credit side, 'O honourable one, I hope God has blessed you with numerous progeny. I say this because you seem to be a good man, willing to stay beside an old man and talk to him, while all day I have none to talk to except when somebody stops by to ask for a piece of tobacco. But I seldom have it, tobacco is not what it used to be at one time, and I have given up chewing. I cannot afford it nowadays.' Noting the other's interest in his speech, Muni felt encouraged to ask, 'How many children have you?' with appropriate gestures with his hands. Realizing that a question was being asked, the red man replied, 'I said a hundred,' which encouraged Muni to go into details, 'How many of your children are boys and how many girls? Where are they? Is your daughter married? Is it difficult to find a son-in-law in your country also?'

In answer to these questions the red man dashed his hand into his pocket and brought forth his wallet in order to take immediate advantage of the bearish trend in the market. He flourished a hundred-rupee currency note and asked, 'Well, this is what I meant.'

The old man now realized that some financial element was entering their talk. He peered closely at the currency note, the like of which he had never seen in his life; he knew the five and ten by their colours although always in other people's hands, while his own earning at any time was in coppers and nickels. What was this man flourishing the note for? Perhaps asking for change. He laughed to himself at the notion of anyone coming to him for changing a thousand or ten-thousand-rupee note. He said with a grin, 'Ask our village headman, who is also a moneylender; he can change even a lakh of rupees in gold sovereigns if you prefer it that way; he thinks nobody knows, but dig the floor of his puja room and your head will reel at the sight of the hoard. The man disguises himself in rags just to mislead the public. Talk to the headman yourself because he goes mad at the sight of me. Someone took away his pumpkins with the creeper and he, for some reason, thinks it was me and my goats…that's why I never let my goats be seen anywhere near the farms.' His eyes travelled to his goats nosing about, attempting to wrest nutrition from minute greenery peeping out of rock and dry earth.

The foreigner followed his look and decided that it would be a sound policy to show an interest in the old man's pets. He went up casually to them and stroked their backs with every show of courteous attention. Now the truth dawned on the old man. His dream of a lifetime was about to be realized. He understood that the red man was actually making an offer for the goats. He had reared them up in the hope of selling them some day and, with the capital, opening a small shop on this very spot. Sitting here, watching the hills, he had often dreamt how he would put up a thatched roof here, spread a gunny sack out on the ground, and display on it fried nuts, coloured sweets, and green coconut for the thirsty and famished wayfarers on the highway, which was sometimes very busy. The animals were not prize ones for a cattle show, but he had spent his occasional savings to provide them some fancy diet now and then, and they did not look too bad. While he was reflecting thus, the red man shook his hand and left on his palm one hundred rupees in tens now. 'It is all for you or you may share it if you have a partner.'

The old man pointed at the station wagon and asked, 'Are you carrying them off in that?'

'Yes, of course,' said the other, understanding the transportation part of it.

The old man said, 'This will be their first ride in a motor car. Carry them off after I get out of sight, otherwise they will never follow you, but only me even if I am travelling on the path to Yama Loka.' He laughed at his own joke, brought his palms together in a salute, turned round and went off, and was soon out of sight beyond a clump of thicket.

The red man looked at the goats grazing peacefully. Perched on the pedestal of the horse, as the westerly sun touched the ancient faded colours of the statue with a fresh splendour, he ruminated, 'He must be gone to fetch some help, I suppose!' and settled down to wait. When a truck came downhill, he stopped it and got the help of a couple of men to detach the horse from its pedestal and place it in his station wagon. He gave them five rupees each, and for a further payment they siphoned off gas from the truck and helped him to start his engine.

Muni hurried homewards with the cash securely tucked away at his waist in his dhoti. He shut the street door and stole up softly to his wife as she squatted before the lit oven wondering if by a miracle food would drop from the sky. Muni displayed his fortune for the day. She snatched the notes from him, counted them by the glow of the fire, and cried, 'One hundred rupees! How did you come by it? Have you been stealing?'

'I have sold our goats to a red-faced man. He was absolutely crazy to have them, gave me all this money and carried them off in his motor car!'

Hardly had these words left his lips when they heard bleating outside. She opened the door and saw the two goats at her door. 'Here they are!' she said. 'What's the meaning of all this?'

He muttered a great curse and seized one of the goats by its ears and shouted, 'Where is that man? Don't you know you are his? Why did you come back?' The goat only wriggled in his grip. He asked the same question of the other too. The goat shook itself off. His wife glared at him and declared, 'If you have thieved, the police will come tonight and break your bones. Don't involve me. I will go away to my parents…'

THE COPPER-TAILED SKINK

MANJULA PADMANABHAN

Devanahalli, 3 October

Dearest Jem—wrote Madeleine—From where I sit, I can see little Mrs Rao walking across the yard with her tummy sticking out, looking like a *cartoon* of a pregnant woman… Madeleine looked up from her letter again, just to confirm that this was really true—Oh dear—it doesn't sound very polite to say that, does it? Well, she'll never know; I don't think she reads English, so…

She stopped again and looked out. The light was blinding outside. The pale earth might have been a mirror, from the way it reflected the blazing overturned bowl of the sky.

In five minutes Rao will be here, she thought. Eight hundred and fifty million Indians in India, and I have to be working with the only one who is always on time. Like a precision chronometer, she thought, as if he doesn't exercise any choice in his punctuality, as if it's hardwired into his system. Negating the virtue of it, really, when you stop to think of it. After all, the point of having a quality is when you can choose not to have it. She smiled to herself, faintly. Such a European idea, that! Not Indian at all.

In India—or so it seemed, given her three-month acquaintance—the aim appeared to be to make automata of everyone, eradicate the whole tiresome issue of choice altogether. She looked out of the window. There was Mrs Rao, waddling back across the yard, her belly like—but no, there is nothing that a pregnant woman's belly is like, except itself. Other things could be compared to pregnant bellies, but not the thing itself. It was just too gross, too grotesque to be in any way metaphorized. And there she was, Mrs Rao: three small children wriggling about in the little hut in which she and Rao—Dr Rao, Madeleine corrected herself—lived. And now a fourth one on its imminent way... Had she planned her life that way? Thought about it? Dreamt of something else?

Madeleine sighed to herself and shut her eyes. It didn't seem likely. The subcontinent seemed to tick away according to a schedule set by a handful of naked sages in some bygone era. And whenever you asked any questions about why something was done in a particular way or why it couldn't be done in some other way, the answer, through howsoever roundabout a route, always came back to: 'But...it is our *tradition*! Our *custom*. Our *habit*.' Or whatever else. No effort at thought or change. Just beetling on, like...*animals* she thought angrily to herself—angry because she hated to admit such thoughts to her mind, because she wanted to believe that such abjectly racist notions could not find a lodging place in her person. And yet—they did. They had. That's what India's done to me, she thought, suddenly in a spasm of the same anger, that's what…

There was a knock on the door. And: 'Dr Whitely?' came Rao's thick-accented voice. And: it was precisely ten after three.

'Coming!' called Madeleine, trying to add a smile to her voice. *He* was always smiling. Always. Like the punctuality... She sighed, then hurriedly found her straw hat, her sunglasses, the specimen box and an expiring packet of Marie biscuits to take along with her kit for the afternoon's expedition. A quick check to ensure that her bottle of Bisleri for the day was still in her knapsack, then she went out on to the veranda, and into the glare of the yard, where Dr Rao now stood, smiling.

'Not too early, I hope? he said.

She posted the letter to Jeremy the next morning—or rather, she gave it to Rao, who would give it to the caretaker of the PWD guest house compound in which she and Rao lived, who would then saunter down to the post office to actually post it. As luck would have it, a letter came from Jeremy that very afternoon, telling her of his travel plans. It arrived along with Rao at the hour appointed for the afternoon excursion to the 'field' and she was so delighted that she insisted on sitting right down and reading the whole thing before they left. It took her all of fifteen minutes, during which time she forgot about Rao and his ridiculous grin so entirely that when she finally did look up from the letter, it took her a few seconds to remember who he was, this dark-skinned, little man, much too tubby for his thirty-two years, staring out at nothing, with a busy-looking frown on his forehead and his hands behind his back, the fingers automatically popping knuckles as he waited.

In penance for that wait, all the way to the search-areas she allowed herself to be cross-examined about the letter.

'Madam is very happy today, I think!' said Rao, as an opening device. 'Is letter coming with good news, must be!' Despite his PhD, his English was atrocious.

'Yes,' said Madeleine, 'it *is* good news! Jeremy's...' a pause to recall: had she called Jem a husband before this? Or had she left things vague?'... my—uh—friend Jeremy's coming—next month!' It was wonderful. It meant that they would actually manage to have two whole weeks together, at last, after so long.

'I see...' said Rao, frowning and smiling at once.

'She is...'

'*He*!—' said Madeleine in irritation, '*He*! Jeremy's a man!' A little rude, her tone, but she couldn't bear it, not even for an instant, to have that misunderstanding of the name to contend with.

'He,' continued Rao, 'is taking train? Plane?'

'Train, I think,' said Madeleine, making a mental note to look into his bookings right away. It was hellish, getting that sort of thing done. But they would *have* to get the timing exactly right. It was really now or never.

'He is...family friend?' asked Rao, in what she had come to recognize was his 'delicate' voice. He used this voice whenever he wanted to satisfy his insatiable curiosity about her personal life. It was in this voice that he asked her about her age (forty-one), family (mother, divorcee); father (living, though unseen for many years); siblings (none); financial status (by Indian standards, very wealthy; by Western, comfortable) and so on and on. Whatever else they discussed, these issues of family and social typecasting seemed to be what he really cared about.

'Well, yes, in a way,' she said, thinking, I'll have to make up some story to explain why he sleeps in my bed! Or—what the hell, it can't matter, no one can possibly object. Then the sort of thought that she didn't like to acknowledge the existence of asserted itself: they wouldn't *dare* to object. As a Western woman, a visiting scholar attached to the University of Mysore, she had a racial, hierarchical immunity.

And, in order to dispel the shadow of this thought, she said, aloud, 'I mean, I've known him for eleven years...he's also a biologist.'

By the time they reached the vast stony plain in which they were working, Jeremy was pretty thoroughly described: a molecular biologist, working with rat enzymes, exciting research, many international seminars and assignments...

Madeleine and Rao usually spent a little over three hours carefully screening designated areas of the field. Rao, an entomologist, found an endless supply of beetles to forage and there was a good-natured bantering between the two of them about her relative paucity of 'finds'. In the three weeks that she had been searching in the district, she had found only ten specimens. But among those ten, was one of the kind that biologists thrill to discover: a hitherto unnamed, undiscovered species.

She had found it on the third day after her arrival in Devanahalli. Rao had been assigned to her as he was conveniently working in the locality in which she had an interest and he had taken her to the huge barren property, over forty acres of almost wholly uncultivable land over which they were now slowly and methodically searching. The understanding was that he would assist her in bagging specimens while conducting his own research. And in the bargain, of course, he would serve as a convenient interpreter, guide and chaperon.

The skink had been basking on a rock when she first sighted it. Right off, even at a distance, she had recognized that it was unfamiliar, with that prescience which field researchers develop over the years, waiting for just such an experience to come their way. A prickling of the nerves, a heightening of every faculty. She caught the cocky little creature easily enough, perhaps it had been a little dazzled by the sun. It practically fell into her fine-meshed long-handled net though it had had several avenues of escape. And then it had lain there thrashing a few moments before accepting its fate with the same calm dignity of countless small captives before it.

Madeleine had seen this stoic reaction often in her career and always admired it; for them, these diminutive entities, there was none of that screaming, cursing and railing against fate of larger beings! Instead, the stillness, the bright, alert eyes, the fragile limbs, the tiny claws held tense for the slightest opportunity of escape; and only the painfully rapid pumping of the narrow chest betraying the panic which must surely be overwhelming its smallness.

What had caught her attention in her first glimpse was confirmed: her specimen was a true skink and its tail was a bright copper pink, delicately metallic. The colour was probably a diversionary tactic to attract potential predators to the relatively expendable tail. Like that well-documented blue-tailed skink whose cerulean blue appendage would break off and wriggle delectably while its owner scampered away to freedom. But copper? No copper-tailed skink had been recorded or described so far as Madeleine was aware!

And her heart had raced. So foolish, at her age, with her experience behind her, her standing in academic circles, to be so wildly excited! But her mind had already started composing its Latin name: *Mabuya... Mabuya cupranus* perhaps. Followed by, in discrete parentheses, and only in textbooks read by other scholars like herself, her surname: (Whitely). Such a small thing, so trivial an achievement, yet it seemed to make everything worthwhile. The years of study, the travelling, the hours in the hot and pitiless sun and yes, even the time away from Jeremy.

The specimen she had caught had been a female, of medium size. She hoped now to consolidate her find with one more individual, preferably, of course, a male. Not much was known about the genus of skinks, even the better known species. Local people tended to regard them with fear, perhaps because of their resemblance to snakes—it was easy, with the shiny scales, the quicksilver, pouring movements, and the pigmy limbs, to be mistaken.

But they were harmless, like so many creatures which excited fear in humans. Madeleine had encountered her first skink as an undergraduate in the modest reptile garden maintained by a handful of enthusiasts in her college in Scotland. She had been charmed by it, and in later years built her career around others of its kind.

Which was what had brought her to India and thence to her personal discovery.

Ever since that first heady afternoon, however, she had drawn a blank. Whatever companions her captive skink had sported with, they had all, apparently, vanished into the solid rock. She had caught a pair of common skinks and then a rarely sighted snake skink, but she already had specimens of these. Every night, as she did the rounds of her ten specimen-boxes, with fresh water and a newly caught cache of insects to dole out, she would come to the copper-tail last of all and gaze at it fondly as it gulped and swallowed its dinner with undignified gusto.

Lizzie, she would think, I just *have* to find a mate for you! Or else—wry smile, here—you might end up like me! Childless, that is. Though, of course it was quite possible that Lizzie was already a matron, several clutches of successfully hatched and dispatched eggs behind her. But something tells me not, thought Madeleine, looking at the slender graceful body. Definitely nubile, I'd say, maybe even a virgin—!

After ten days of captivity this theory seemed to suffer a setback, with the discovery, in Lizzie's cage, of one small white egg. Naughty girl! thought Madeleine reprovingly at first, getting preggers then running off to bask in the sun, only to be caught!

But some days later, when she held the egg up against a light to check for signs of development inside, she saw that it wasn't viable. It happened sometimes with reptiles, as with domesticated chickens, this issuing forth of 'vegetarian' eggs. It seemed in Madeleine's eyes to make Lizzie's celibacy all the more poignant. Like me and my monthly ovum, thought Madeleine, every twenty-eight days, wandering hopefully down all the long lonesome length of a fallopian tube, pining in its mute, hormonal way for the company of a couple of thousand suitors, whip-tailed and frantic...

She and Jeremy had been 'trying'—that dreadful word—for some years to have a child. They had started out casually, with a light-hearted abandonment of contraceptives. Then, gradually, as the months bled by, a vague urgency crept in, a sense of time running out and opportunities to 'fecundate', as Jeremy put it, growing scarcer. It was now five years since they had abandoned altogether any pretence of spontaneity in sexual matters. They plotted the time they could spend together, on ovulation charts instead of ordinary calendars.

Finally, they had even been to a fertility clinic. But they gave up after seven months of enduring the white-walled, tube-lit squalor of it all. As Jeremy had said, 'masturbating into a red plastic flask five times a week, with an adjoining roomful of healthy young lab-technicians waiting impatiently to process the "sample"—if that isn't a perversion of all that is sacred in the temple of the body, what is?'

They reverted to ovulation dates and taking diurnal temperatures. But by then there was a different kind of problem. The schedules of the global community of bioscientists seemed to preclude procreation. Either they were together at the wrong moment in Madeleine's ovulation cycle or even if they got that part right, their commitments immediately afterwards made it seem madness to plan a baby. Madeleine could swear that there had been two occasions at least when she had felt the glow of a microscopic consciousness forming in the depths of her being, only to feel it fade away and die at the prospect of her professional agenda in the months ahead.

They had finally agreed upon a cut-off date: if she hadn't got pregnant by her forty-second birthday, they would close shop on the whole circus. Adopt a Vietnamese, breed terriers, grow bonsai. Or whatever.

The India trip had come about in such a way that it had seemed, initially, that Jeremy might have been able to take a sabbatical in time to spend the entire four months with her. But by the time she reached India that hope had been pared back, until now, it was clear that the last fertile two weeks left to them before her birthday were going to be on the dates he mentioned, in October.

Oh, Lizzie, whispered Madeleine to the specimen box, late that night, after she had reread her letter for the nth time, Oh, Lizzie, hope for me that he *will* be able to come! But the skink, gorging itself on a succulent moth, merely blinked its delicate eyelids and paid no heed at all.

The Rao's child, their second boy, was born three days before Jem was due to arrive. Madeleine went to the clinic unwillingly, on the afternoon of the birth, just to be polite. She had feared that the arrangements would be unbearably primitive. But when she got there she was relieved to find a small, reasonably clean building, with dazzlingly white lime-washed walls.

The baby was wee, red-faced and hirsute: a surprise for Madeleine who was used to the bald newborns of her country. She felt out of place in the clinic, with her blondness and her height, towering over the nurses, over Rao and the couple of nameless female hangers-on who crowded the cubicle in which Mrs Rao lay, big-eyed and smiling weakly. There were four other recent mothers in the clinic. There was a smell of damp warm cloth, warm bodies, hair oil and flowers: not bouquets, but the small chaplets that the women wore in their hair.

But Madeleine stayed only just long enough to observe the civilities. She walked along the quiet lane back to the guest house, feeling disturbed. She knew from past experience that the pills she had taken to stimulate ovulation made her feel slightly weepy. But that knowledge did not make it easier to dispel the vague horror she had felt in the clinic.

It had come from facing, suddenly and without anticipation, the reproductory behemoth that is India. Suddenly, there, in the humble village clinic it had sprung into view, this awesome organic factory. Fuelled with blood and semen, its employees working around the clock, ceaselessly cranking out new lives, one for every thirty seconds. Amidst all the squalor, the chaos, the endless queues, the bungling and the waste, the forge of reproduction was burning bright. Its primordial technology was intact, its efficiency unchallenged.

And then, Rao. Normally, she saw him as the mildly comic figure, decent in the main, with whom she had spent the better part of each day for the last four weeks. I've never really thought of him as a man, she acknowledged to herself, not merely in the sense of not being attracted to him—rather, as if I hadn't noticed his masculinity at all. He had been one more detail in the landscape, neutral, neither male nor female. When they were together in the field she often stripped down to a T-shirt and shorts for the sake of comfort, and had not thought twice about it, not for an instant, what his opinion of her or of her body might be.

But there, in the clinic, he had suddenly been revealed as an Active Male, busily passing on his genetic data in the honoured and time-tested fashion. Was he a thoughtful and considerate lover?... But, no, she told herself, there are some avenues of thought not worth pursuing, and the speculation was forced out of her mind.

On the last day of October, on the day that Jem arrived in India, in Delhi, the Indian Prime Minister Mrs Gandhi was assassinated. There were riots in the capital. Buses were burnt, trains were cancelled. Madeleine got a message by telegram from Jeremy telling her to delay her departure for Mysore, where she had planned to meet him.

And then, for four days of agonized waiting, no news. The local paper and the radio were awash with the tide of shock, grief and blood which attended the shooting. Even the little hamlet of Devanahalli seemed to stiffen in the grip of the tension which spread quickly to all parts of the nation. But of passengers arriving from Helsinki, no news. Then a second telegram arrived: STUCK IN DELHI STOP STOMACH INFECTION STOP AM WRITING LETTER LOVE JEM—and no indication whatsoever of how she could be in touch with him!

Rao and she had ventured out to the field on the morning of the day the telegram was delivered. But when he came to fetch her for the afternoon's expedition, he found her sitting in front of the copper-tail's box, holding the telegram and crying silently. He said nothing and left on his own for the field.

Later, of course, it all came out: the first telegram had included the address of Jem's hotel but that vital information had been deleted from the version she received. His third telegram with a little more detail arrived after he did and the letter, written from the clinic recommended by the British High Commission, never arrived at all.

It seemed that he had acquired the infection from the sandwiches he had eaten at the airport while waiting with all the other stranded passengers for the situation to normalize in the city. He had required immediate hospitalization and was semiconscious for almost two days. He had had to remain in a fearsomely expensive private clinic for a week before he was strong enough to travel again. By that time, of course, all his train bookings had been rendered meaningless. In the bureaucratic mayhem which followed the assassination, new bookings were almost impossible to confirm and being in touch with Devanahalli by telephone was out of the question.

All in all, by the time Madeleine collected Jem from the railway station it was three weeks from the anticipated date of his arrival. Much, much too late. Madeleine had already started bleeding. They held hands all the way from Mysore to Devanahalli in the taxi, saying very little. Rao was surprisingly circumspect when they finally got back to the guest house. He left them alone even to the extent of suggesting to Madeleine that she take her 'good friend' on the afternoon's field visit instead of 'himself'.

They had walked about that rock-studden, barren plain, the two of them, tall, pale-skinned, fair-haired, alien. The sun was still scorching where it touched the napes of their necks, but there was a wind twitching in the grasses and gusting the crows out of the sky. The weather was turning in its sudden way and there was a freshness, a sharpness. It rained that night.

Jem stayed for ten days. While he was there, they found another copper-tail, but it was also female.

'Never mind,' said Jem, back at the guest house that night, sitting out on the veranda. 'Bring them both back with you, no harm done.'

The lights were off to discourage the squadrons of moths and beetles which otherwise served as an excellent air-borne supermarket for the captive lizards in the boxes.

'Would it be quite right, do you think?' said Madeleine after a slight silence. 'Without a male, l mean.'

'You'll want living proof of your new species, surely,' Jem said.

But in the darkness Madeleine was shaking her head. 'It seems wrong, it seems unfair...'

There was another slight pause. She could almost hear Jem's eyebrows being raised in mild consternation. 'Biologists can't afford to be sentimental, you know,' was all he said.

'I'll have enough slides,' she said, 'and measurements—and in any case, they could easily die en route. They're notoriously delicate——'

Jeremy shrugged, causing the cane settee they were sharing to wobble slightly. 'Come on! It won't destroy the planet's equilibrium if two miserable lizards don't get their chance to mate and reproduce!'

Madeleine tucked in the corners of her mouth; for a moment she felt as if she might burst into tears, there and then. But she was no longer taking her pills and her eyes were dry. 'You're right,' she said, evenly. 'It's silly to think of them as...' But she didn't end her sentence.

They parted company in Mysore and made plans to meet again in England at Christmas. Madeleine extended her stay in India by another month, which she could choose to spend in Devanahalli, but decided against. There were two other locations, one in Orissa and another in Bengal, to which she had open invitations.

Rao and his family bade her a sweet-laden farewell, more festive than solemn. I guess they'll move back into the main building now, from the hut, was how she rationalized it, as she waved from the taxi which was hired to take her to Mysore. I wonder what they really think of me, she thought. Of course I'll never know.

The taxi took a route which followed the outer boundary of the field area of her survey. When they had gone far enough for her to be reasonably sure that Rao could no longer see her even if he had tried, Madeleine put out a hand and signed to the driver that she wanted him to stop.

Hopping quickly out of the car and careless of the goggle-eyed interest of the driver, she strode out to a shallow dip in the rock. From her shoulder bag she brought out a pouch in which the two lizards lay, coiled and attentive. She shook them loose from the bag, half-kneeling on the rock. Then straightened up and smoothed the wrinkles out from her skirt as she watched them dart away immediately. She watched them till they had vanished from sight, then turned back to the car, the breeze lifting her fine hair off her shoulders and tugging her skirt around her knees.

THE LAST TIGER

RUSKIN BOND

On the left bank of the Ganga, where it emerges from the Himalayan foothills, there is a long stretch of heavy forest. There are villages on the fringe of the forest, inhabited by bamboo cutters and farmers, but there are few signs of commerce or religion. Hunters, however, have found it an ideal hunting ground over the last seventy years, and as a result the animals are not as numerous as they used to be. The trees, too, have been disappearing slowly; and, as the forest recedes, the animals lose their food and shelter and move on, further into the foothills. Slowly, they are being denied the right to live.

Only the elephants could cross the river. And two years ago, when a large area of forest was cleared to make way for a refugee resettlement camp, a herd of elephants—finding their favourite food, the green shoots of the bamboo, in short supply—waded across the river. They crashed through the suburbs of Haridwar, knocked down a factory wall, plucked away several tin roofs, held up a train, and left a trail of devastation in their wake until they reached a new forest, still untouched, where they settled down to a new life—but an unsettled, wary life. Because, they did not know when men would appear again, with tractors and bulldozers and dynamite.

There was a time when this forest provided food and shelter for some thirty or forty tigers; but men in search of trophies shot them all, and today there remains only one old tiger in the jungle. Many hunters have tried to get him. But he is a wise and crafty old tiger who knows the ways of men, and he has so far survived all attempts on his life.

This is his story. It is also the story of the jungle.

Although the tiger has passed the prime of his life, he has lost none of his majesty; his muscles ripple beneath the golden yellow of his coat, and he walks through the long grass with the confidence of one who knows that he is still king, even though his subjects are fewer. His great head pushes through the foliage, and it is only his tail, swinging high, that shows occasionally above the sea of grass.

He is heading for water, the only water in the forest (if you don't count the river, which is several miles away)—the water of a large jheel, which is almost a lake during the rainy season, but just a muddy marsh at this time of the year, in the late spring.

Here, at different times of the day and night, all the animals come to drink—the long-horned sambar deer, the delicate spotted chital, the swamp deer, the wolves and jackals, the wild boar, the panthers—and the tiger. Since the elephants have gone, the water is usually clear except when buffaloes from the nearest village come to wallow, and then it is very muddy. These buffaloes, though they are not wild, are not afraid of the panther or even of the tiger. They know the panther is afraid of their long horns and they know the tiger prefers the flesh of the deer.

Today, there are several sambar at the water's edge, but they do not stay long. The tiger is coming with the breeze, and there is no mistaking its strong feline odour. The deer hold their heads high for a few moments, their nostrils twitching, and then scatter into the forest, disappearing behind screens of leaf and bamboo.

When the tiger arrives, there is no other animal near the water. But the birds are still there. The egrets continue to wade in the shallows, and a kingfisher darts low over the water, dives suddenly, a flash of blue and gold, and makes off with a slim silver fish, which glistens in the sun like a polished gem. A long brown snake glides in amongst the water lilies and disappears beneath a fallen tree which lies rotting in the shallows.

The tiger waits in the shelter of a rock, his ears pricked up for the least unfamiliar sound; for he knows that it is often at this place that men lie up for him with guns; for they covet his beauty—they covet his stripes, and the gold of his body, and his fine teeth and his whiskers and his noble head. They would like to hang his pelt on a wall, and stick glass eyes in his head, and boast of their conquest over the king of the jungle.

The old tiger has been hunted before, and he does not usually show himself in the open during the day, but of late he has heard no guns, and if there were hunters around, you would have heard their guns (for a man with a gun cannot resist letting it off, even if it is only at a rabbit—or at another man). And, besides, the tiger is thirsty.

He is also feeling quite hot. It is March, and the shimmering dust-haze of summer has come early this year. Tigers—unlike other cats—are fond of water, and on a hot day will wallow for hours.

He walks into the water, in amongst the water lilies, and drinks slowly. He is seldom in a hurry when he eats or drinks. Other animals might bolt their food, but they are only other animals. A tiger has his dignity to preserve!

He raises his head and listens. One paw remains suspended in the air. A strange sound has come to him on the breeze, and he is wary of strange sounds. So he moves swiftly through the grass that borders the jheel, and climbs a hillock until he reaches his favourite rock. This rock is big enough to hide him and to give him shade. Anyone looking up from the jheel might think it strange that the rock has a round bump on the top. The bump is the tiger's head. He keeps it very still.

The sound he has heard is only the sound of a flute, sounding thin and reedy in the forest. It belongs to a boy, a slim brown boy who rides a buffalo. The boy blows vigorously on the flute, while another, slightly smaller boy, riding another buffalo, brings up the rear of the herd.

There are about eight buffaloes in the herd, and they belong to the families of Ramu and Shyam, the two Gujjar boys who are friends. The Gujjars are a caste who possess herds of buffaloes and earn their livelihood from the sale of milk and butter. The boys are about twelve years old, but they cannot tell you how many months past twelve, because in their village nobody thinks birthdays are important. They are almost the same age as the tiger, but he is old and experienced while they are still cubs.

The tiger has often seen them at the tank, and he is not worried. He knows the village people will bring him no harm as long as he leaves their buffaloes alone. Once, when he was younger and full of bravado, he had killed a buffalo—not because he was hungry but because he was young and wanted to test his strength—and after that the villagers had hunted him for days, with spears, bows and arrows, and an old muzzle-loader. Now he left the buffaloes alone, even though the deer in the forest were not as numerous as before.

The boys know that a tiger lives in the jungle, for they have often heard him roar, but they do not know that today he is so near to them.

The tiger gazes down from his rock, and the sight of eight fat black buffaloes does make him give a low, throaty moan. But the boys are there, and besides—a buffalo is not easy to kill.

He decides to move on and find a cool shady place in the heart of the jungle, where he can rest during the warm afternoon and be free of the flies and mosquitoes that swarm around in the vicinity of the tank. At night he will hunt.

With a lazy, half-humorous roar—'A—oonh!'—he gets up from his haunches and saunters off into the jungle.

Even the gentlest of a tiger's roars can be heard half a mile away, and the boys, who are barely fifty yards off, look up immediately.

'There he goes!' calls Ramu, taking the flute from his lips and pointing with it towards the hillock. He is not afraid, for he knows that an un-hunted and uninjured tiger is not aggressive. 'Did you see him?'

'I saw his tail, just before he disappeared. He's a big tiger!'

'Do not call him tiger. Call him Uncle, or Maharaj.'

'Oh, why?'

'Don't you know that it's unlucky to call a tiger a tiger? My father always told me so. But if you meet a tiger, and call him Uncle, he will leave you alone.'

'I'll try and remember that,' says Shyam.

The buffaloes are now well into the water, and some of them are lying down in the mud. Buffaloes love soft, wet mud and will wallow in it for hours. The more mud the better. Ramu, to avoid being dragged down into the mud with his buffalo, slips off its back and plunges into the water. Using an easy breaststroke, he swims across to a small islet covered with reeds and water lilies. Shyam is close behind him.

They lie down on their hard, flat stomachs, on a patch of grass, and allow the warm sun to beat down on their bare brown bodies. Ramu is the more knowledgeable boy, because he has been to Haridwar several times with his father. Shyam has never been out of the village.

Shyam says, 'The pool is not so deep this year.'

'We have had no rain since January,' says Ramu. 'If we do not get rain soon, the tank may dry up altogether.'

'And then what will we do?'

'We? There is a well in the village. But even that may dry up. My father told me that it failed once, just about the time I was born, and everyone had to walk ten miles to the river for water.'

'And what about the animals?'

'Some will stay here and die. Others will go to the river.

But there are too many people near the river now—not only temples, but houses and factories—and the animals stay away. And the trees have been cut, so that between the jungle and the river there is no place to hide. Animals are afraid of the open—they are afraid of men with guns.'

'Even at night?'

'At night men come in jeeps, with searchlights. They kill the deer for meat, and sell the skins of tigers and panthers.'

'I didn't know a tiger's skin was worth anything.'

'It is worth more than our skins,' says Ramu knowingly. 'It will fetch six hundred rupees. Who would pay that much for our skins?'

'Our fathers would.'

'True—if they had the money.'

'If my father sold his fields, he would get more than six hundred rupees.'

'True—but if he sold his fields, none of you would have anything to eat. A man needs land as much as a tiger needs a jungle.'

'True,' says Shyam. 'And that reminds me—my mother asked me to take some roots home.'

'I will help you.'

They wade into the jheel until the water is up to their waists, and begin pulling up water lilies by the root. The flower is beautiful but the villagers value the root more. When it is cooked, it makes a delicious and nourishing dish. The plant multiplies rapidly and is always in good supply. In the year when famine hit the village, it was only the root of the water lily that saved many from starvation.

When Shyam and Ramu have finished gathering roots, they emerge from the water and pass the time in wrestling with each other, slipping about in the soft mud which soon covers them from head to toe.

To get rid of the mud, they dive into the water again and swim across to their buffaloes. Then, digging their heels into the thick hides of the buffaloes, the boys race them across the jheel, shouting and hollering so much that all the birds fly away in disgust, and the monkeys set up a shrill chattering of their own in the dhak trees.

In March, the twisted, leafless flame of the forest or dhak trees are ablaze with flaming scarlet and orange flowers.

It is evening, and the twilight is fading fast, when the buffalo herd finally wends its way homewards, to be greeted outside the village by the barking of dogs, the gurgle of hookah pipes, and the homely smell of cowdung smoke.

The tiger makes a kill that night. He approaches with the wind against him, and the unsuspecting spotted deer does not see him until it is too late. A blow on the deer's haunches from the tiger's paw brings it down, and then the great beast fastens onto the struggling deer's throat. It is all over in a few minutes. The tiger is too quick and strong, and the deer does not struggle for long.

The deer's life is over, but he has not lived in fear of death. It is only man's imagination and fear of the hereafter that makes him afraid of meeting death. In the jungle, sudden death appears at intervals. Wild creatures do not have to think about it, and so the sudden passing of one of their number due to the arrival of some flesh-eating animal is only a fleeting incident soon forgotten by the survivors.

The tiger feasts well, growling with pleasure as he eats, and then leaves the carcass in the jungle for the vultures and jackals. The old tiger never returns to the same deer's carcass, even if there is still some flesh on it. In the past, when he has done that, he has often found a man sitting in a tree over the kill, waiting for him with a rifle.

His belly full, the tiger comes to the edge of the forest, looks out across the wasteland out over the deep, singing river, at the twinkling lights of Haridwar on the opposite bank, and raises his head and roars his defiance at the world.

He is a lonesome bachelor. It is five or six years since he had a mate. She was shot by trophy-hunters, and the cubs, two of them, were trapped by men who trade in wild animals: one went to a circus, where it had to learn undignified tricks and respond to the flick of a whip, the other, more fortunate, went first to a zoo in Delhi and was later transferred to a zoo in America.

Sometimes, when the old tiger is very lonely, he gives a great roar, which can be heard throughout the forest. The villagers think he is roaring in anger, but the animals know that he is really roaring out of loneliness. When the sound of his roar has died away, he pauses, standing still, waiting for an answering roar, but it never comes. It is taken up instead by the shrill scream of a barbet high up in a sal tree.

It is dawn now, dew-fresh and cool, and the jungle dwellers are on the move. The black, beady little eyes of a jungle rat were fixed on a small brown hen who was returning cautiously to her nest. He had a large family to feed, and he knew that in the hen's nest was a clutch of delicious fawn-coloured eggs. He waited patiently for nearly an hour before he had the satisfaction of seeing the hen leave her nest and go off in search of food.

As soon as she had gone, the rat lost no time in making his raid. Slipping quietly out of his hole, he slithered along among the leaves, but, clever as he was, he did not realize that his own movements were being watched.

A pair of grey mongooses were scouting about in the dry grass. They, too, were hungry, and eggs usually figured large on their menu. Now, lying still on an outcrop of rock, they watched the rat sneaking along, occasionally sniffing at the air, and finally vanishing behind a boulder. When he reappeared, he was struggling to roll an egg uphill towards his hole.

The rat was in difficulties, pushing the egg sometimes with his paws, sometimes with his nose. The ground was rough, and the egg wouldn't go straight. Deciding that he must have help, he scuttled off to call his spouse. Even now the mongoose did not descend on that tantalizing egg. He waited until the rat returned with his wife, and then watched as the male rat took the egg firmly between his forepaws and rolled over on to his back. The female rat then grabbed her mate's tail and began to drag him along.

Totally absorbed in their struggle with the egg, the rats did not hear the approach of the mongooses. When these two large furry visitors suddenly bobbed up from behind a stone, the rats squealed with fright, abandoned the egg, and fled for their lives.

The mongooses wasted no time in breaking open the egg and making a meal of it. But just as a few minutes ago, the rat had not noticed their approach, so now they did not notice the village boy, carrying a small, bright axe and a net bag in his hands, creeping along.

Ramu too was searching for eggs, and when he saw the mongooses busy with one, he stood still to watch them, his eyes roving in search of the nest. He was hoping the mongooses would lead him to the nest, but, when they had finished their meal, the breeze took them in another direction, and Ramu had to do his own searching. He failed to find the nest, and moved further into the forest. The rat's hopes were just reviving when, to his disgust, the mother hen returned.

Ramu now made his way to a mahua tree.

The flowers of the mahua tree can be eaten by animals as well as men. Bears are particularly fond of them and will eat large quantities of its flowers which gradually start fermenting in their stomachs with the result that the animals get quite drunk. Ramu had often seen a couple of bears stumbling home to their cave, bumping into each other or into the trunks of trees—they are short-sighted to begin with, and when drunk can hardly see at all—but their sense of smell and hearing are so good that they finally find their way home.

Ramu decided he would gather some mahua flowers, and climbed swiftly into the tree, which is leafless when it blossoms. He began breaking the white flowers and throwing them to the ground. He had been in the tree for about five minutes when he heard the whining grumble of a bear, and presently a young sloth bear ambled into the clearing beneath the tree.

He was a small bear, little more than a cub, and Ramu was not frightened, but, because he thought the mother might be in the vicinity, he decided to take no chances, and sat very still, waiting to see what the bear would do. He hoped it wouldn't choose the same mahua tree for a meal.

At first the young bear put his nose to the ground and sniffed his way along until he came to a large white anthill. Here he began huffing and puffing, blowing rapidly in and out of his nostrils, so that the dust from the anthill flew in all directions. But he was a disappointed bear, because the anthill had been deserted long ago. And so, grumbling, he made his way across to a wild plum—a tall tree, the wild plum—and shinning rapidly up the smooth trunk, was soon perched in its topmost branches. It was only then that he saw Ramu.

The bear at once scrambled several feet higher up the tree, and laid himself out flat on a branch. It wasn't a very thick branch and left a large expanse of bear showing on either side of it. The bear tucked his head away behind another branch, and, so long as he could not see Ramu, seemed quite satisfied that he was well hidden, though he couldn't help grumbling with anxiety, for a bear, like most animals, is afraid of man—until he discovers that man is afraid of him.

Bears, however, are also very curious—and curiosity has often led them into trouble. Slowly, inch by inch, the young bear's black snout appeared over the edge of the branch, but, immediately, the eyes came into view and met Ramu's. He drew back with a jerk and the head was once more hidden. The bear did this two or three times, and Ramu, highly amused, waited until it wasn't looking, then moved some way down the tree. When the bear looked up again and saw that the boy was missing, he was so pleased with himself that he stretched right across to the next branch, to get at a plum. Ramu chose this moment to burst into loud laughter. The startled bear tumbled out of the tree, dropped through the branches for a distance of some fifteen feet, and landed with a thud in a heap of dry leaves.

And then several things happened almost at the same time.

The mother bear came charging into the clearing. Spotting Ramu in the tree, she reared up on her hind legs, grunting fiercely. It was Ramu's turn to be startled. There are few animals as dangerous as a rampaging mother bear, and the boy knew that one blow from her clawed forepaws could rip his skull open.

But before the bear could approach the tree, there was a tremendous roar, and the tiger bounded into the clearing. He had been asleep in the bushes not far away—he liked a good sleep after a heavy meal—and the noise in the clearing had woken him.

He was in a very bad temper, and his loud 'A—oonh!' made his displeasure quite clear. The bears turned and ran from the clearing, the youngster squealing with fright.

The tiger then came into the centre of the clearing, looked up at the trembling boy, and roared again.

Ramu nearly fell out of the tree.

'Good day to you, Uncle,' he stammered, showing his teeth in a nervous grin.

Perhaps this was too much for the tiger. With a low growl, he turned his back on the mahua tree and padded off into the jungle, his tail twitching in disgust.

That night, when Ramu told his parents and grandfather about the tiger and how it had saved him from a female bear, a number of stories were told about tigers, some of whom had been gentlemen, others rogues. Sooner or later the conversation came round to man-eaters, and Grandfather told two stories, which he swore were true, though the others only half believed him.

The first story concerned the belief that a man-eating tiger is guided towards his next victim by the spirit of a human being previously killed and eaten by the tiger. Grandfather said that he actually knew three hunters who sat up in a machan over a human kill, and when the tiger came, the corpse sat up and pointed with his right hand at the men in the tree. The tiger then went away. But the hunters knew he would return, and one man was brave enough to get down from the tree and tie the right arm of the corpse to the body. Later, when the tiger returned, the corpse sat up and pointed out the men with his left hand. The enraged tiger sprang into the tree and killed his enemies in the machan.

'And then there was a bania,' said Grandfather, beginning another story, 'who lived in a village in the jungle. He wanted to visit a neighbouring village to collect some money that was owed him, but as the road lay through heavy forest, in which lived a terrible man-eating tiger, he did not know what to do. Finally, he went to a sadhu who gave him two powders. By eating the first powder, he could turn into a huge tiger, capable of dealing with any other tiger in the jungle, and by eating the second he could become a bania again.

'Armed with his two powders, and accompanied by his pretty, young wife, the bania set out on his journey. They had not gone far into the forest when they came upon the man-eater sitting in the middle of the road. Before swallowing the first powder, the bania told his wife to stay where she was, so that when he returned after killing the tiger, she could at once give him the second powder and enable him to resume his old shape.

'Well, the bania's plan worked, but only up to a point. He swallowed the first powder and immediately became a magnificent tiger. With a great roar, he bounded towards the man-eater, and after a brief, furious fight, killed his opponent. Then, with his jaws still dripping blood, he returned to his wife.

'The poor girl was terrified and spilt the second powder on the ground. The bania was so angry that he pounced on his wife and killed and ate her. And afterwards, this terrible tiger was so enraged at not being able to become a human again that he killed and ate hundreds of people all over the country.'

'The only people he spared,' said Grandfather, with a twinkle in his eye, 'were those who owed him money. A bania never gives up a loan as lost, and the tiger still hoped that one day he might become a human again and be able to collect his dues.'

Next morning, when Ramu came back from the well which was used to irrigate his father's fields, he found a crowd of curious children surrounding a jeep and three strangers with guns. Each of the strangers had a gun, and they were accompanied by two bearers and a vast amount of provisions.

They had heard that there was a tiger in the area, and they wanted to shoot it.

One of the hunters, who looked even stranger than the others, had come all the way to India for tiger, and he had vowed that he would not leave the country without a tiger's skin in his baggage. One of his companions had said that he could buy a tiger's skin in Delhi, but the hunter did not like the idea and said he'd have nothing to do with a tiger that he hadn't shot.

These men had money to spend, and, as most of the villagers needed money badly, they were only too willing to construct a machan for the hunters. The platform, big enough to take the three men, was put up in the branches of a tall toon, or mahogany tree.

It was the only night the hunters used the machan. At the end of March, though the days are warm, the nights are still cold. The hunters had neglected to bring blankets, and by midnight their teeth were chattering. Ramu, having tied up a goat for them at the foot of the tree, made as if to go home but instead circled the area, hanging up bits and pieces of old clothing on small trees and bushes. He thought he owed that much to the tiger. He knew the wily old king of the jungle would keep well away from the goat if he thought there were humans in the vicinity. And where there are men's clothes, there will be men.

As soon as it was dark, the goat began bleating, loud enough for any self-respecting tiger to hear it, but perhaps the ruse was too obvious, or perhaps the clothes Ramu had hung out were warning enough, because the tiger did not come near the toon tree. In any case, the men in the tree soon gave themselves away.

The cold was really too much for them. A flask of brandy was produced, and passed round, and it was not long before there was more purpose to finishing the brandy than to finishing off a tiger. Silent at first, the men soon began talking in whispers, and to jungle creatures a human whisper is as telling as a trumpet call. Soon the men were quite merry, talking in loud voices. And when the first morning light crept over the forest, and Ramu and his friends came by to see if the goat still lived, they found the hunters fast asleep in the machan.

The shikaris looked surly and embarrassed when they trudged back to the village.

'No game left in these parts,' said one.

'The wrong time of the year for tiger,' said another.

'I don't know what the country's coming to,' said the third.

And complaining about the weather, the quality of cartridges, the quality of rum, and the perversity of tigers, they drove away in disgust.

It was not until the onset of summer that an event occurred which altered the hunting habits of the tiger and brought him into conflict with the villagers.

There had been no rain for almost two months, and the grass had become a dry yellow. Some refugee settlers, living in an area where the forest had been cleared, were careless in putting out a fire. The tiger sniffed at the acrid smell of smoke in the air, and, wandering to the edge of the jungle, saw in the distance the dancing lights of a forest fire. As night came on, the flames grew more vivid, the smell stronger. The tiger turned and made for the jheel, where he knew he would be safe, provided he swam across to the little island in the centre.

Next morning he was on the island, which was untouched by the fire. But his surroundings had changed. The slopes of the hills were black with burnt grass, and most of the tall bamboo had disappeared. The deer and the wild pig, finding that their natural cover had gone, fled further east.

The tiger prowled throughout the smoking forest but he found no game. Once he came across the body of a burnt rabbit, but he could not eat it. He drank at the jheel and settled down in a shady spot to sleep the day away. Perhaps, by evening, some of the animals would return. If not, he too would have to look for new hunting grounds—or new game.

The tiger had not eaten for five days and he was so hungry that he had been forced to scratch about in the grass and leaves for worms and beetles. This was a sad comedown for the king of the jungle. But even now he hesitated to leave the area, for he had a deep suspicion and fear of the forests further south and east—forests that were fast being swallowed up by human habitation. He could have gone north, into the hills, but they did not provide him with the long grass he needed. A panther could manage quite well in the hills, but not a tiger who loved the natural privacy of heavy jungle. In the hills, he would have to hide all the time.

At break of day, the tiger came to the jheel. The water was now shallow and muddy, and a green scum had spread over the top. But the water was still drinkable, and the tiger had quenched his thirst.

He lay down across his favourite rock, hoping for a deer, but none approached. He was about to get up and go away when he heard the warning chatter of a lone langur. Some animal was definitely approaching.

The tiger at once dropped flat on the ground, his tawny skin merging with the dry grass. A heavy animal was moving through the bushes, and the tiger waited patiently until a buffalo emerged and came to the water. The buffalo was alone.

He was a big male buffalo, and his long, curved horns lay right back across his shoulders. He moved leisurely towards the water, completely unaware of the tiger's presence.

The tiger hesitated before making his charge. It was a long time—

many years—since he had killed a buffalo, and he knew the villagers would not like it. But hunger helped him overcome his caution. There was no morning breeze, everything was still, and the smell of the tiger did not carry to the buffalo. The monkey still chattered in a nearby tree, but his warning went unheeded.

Moving at a crouch, the tiger skirted the edge of the jheel and approached the buffalo from the rear. The water birds, who were used to the presence of both animals, did not raise an alarm.

Getting closer, the tiger glanced around to see if there were men, or other buffaloes, in the vicinity. Then, satisfied that he was alone, he crept forward. The buffalo was drinking, standing in shallow water at the edge of the tank, when the tiger charged from the side and bit deep into the animal's thigh.

The buffalo turned to fight, but the tendons of his right hind leg had been snapped, and he could only stagger forward a few paces. But he was not afraid. He bellowed, and lowered his horns at the tiger, but the great cat was too fast and, circling the buffalo, bit into the other hind leg.

The buffalo crashed to the ground, both hind legs crippled, and then the tiger dashed in, using both tooth and claw, biting deep into the buffalo's throat until the blood gushed out from the jugular vein.

The buffalo gave one long last bellow before dying.

The tiger, having rested, now began to gorge himself, but, even though he had been starving for days, he could not finish the buffalo. At least one good meal still remained when, satisfied and feeling his strength return, he quenched his thirst at the jheel. Then he dragged the remains of the buffalo into the bushes and went off to find a place to sleep. He would return to the kill when he was hungry.

The villagers were upset when they discovered that a buffalo was missing, and next day, when Ramu and Shyam came running home to say that they had found the carcass near the jheel, half-eaten by the tiger, the men were disturbed and angry. They felt that the tiger had tricked and deceived them. And they knew that once he found he could kill buffaloes quite easily, he would make a habit of it.

Kundan Singh, Shyam's father, and the owner of the dead buffalo, said he would go after the tiger himself.

'It is all very well to talk about what you will do to the tiger,' said his wife, 'but you should never have let the buffalo go off on its own.'

'He had been out on his own before,' said Kundan. 'This is the first time the tiger has attacked one of our beasts. A shaitan—a devil—has entered the Maharaj.'

'He must have been very hungry,' said Shyam.

'Well, we are hungry too,' said Kundan. 'Our best buffalo—the only male in our herd—'

'The tiger will kill again,' said Ramu's father.

'If we let him,' said Kundan. 'Should we send for the shikaris?'

'No. They were not clever. The tiger will escape them easily. And, besides, there is no time. The tiger will return for another meal tonight. We must finish him off ourselves!'

'But how?'

Kundan Singh smiled secretively, played with the ends of his moustache for a few moments, and then, with great pride, produced from under his cot a double-barrelled gun of ancient vintage.

'My father bought it from an Englishman,' he said.

'How long ago was that?'

'At the time I was born.'

'And have you ever used it?' asked Ramu's father, who was not sure that the gun would work.

'Well, some years back, I let it off at some bandits. You remember the time when those dacoits raided our village? They chose the wrong village, and were severely beaten for their pains. As they left, I fired my gun off at them, and as a result they didn't stop running until they had crossed the Ganga!'

'Yes, but did you hit anyone?'

'I would have, if someone's goat hadn't got in the way at the last moment. But we had roast mutton that night! Don't worry, brother, I know how the thing works. It takes a fistful of powder and bullets the size of pigeon's eggs!'

Accompanied by Ramu's father and some others, Kundan set out for the jheel, where, without shifting the buffalo's carcass—for they knew the tiger would not come near them if it suspected a trap—they made another machan in a tall tree some thirty feet from the kill.

Later that evening—at the 'hour of cow-dust', Kundan Singh and Ramu's father settled down for the night on their crude tree platform.

Several hours passed, and nothing but a jackal was seen by the watchers. And then, just as the moon came up over the distant hills, Kundan and his companion were startled by a low 'A—oonh', followed by a suppressed, rumbling growl.

Kundan grasped his old gun, while his friend drew closer to him for comfort. There was complete silence for a minute or two—a time that was an agony of suspense for the watchers—and then there was the sound of a stealthy footfall on some dead leaves under the tree.

A moment later the tiger walked out into the moonlight and stood over his kill.

At first Kundan could do nothing. He was completely overawed by the size of this magnificent tiger. Ramu's father had to nudge him, and then Kundan quickly put the gun to his shoulder, aimed at the tiger's head, and pressed the trigger.

The gun went off with a flash and a tremendous roar, but the bullet only singed the tiger's shoulder.

The enraged animal rushed at the tree and tried to leap into its branches. Fortunately the machan had been built at a safe height, and the tiger, unable to reach it, roared twice, and then bounded off into the forest.

'What a tiger!' exclaimed Kundan, half in fear and half in admiration. 'I feel as though my liver has turned to water.'

'You missed him completely,' said Ramu's father. 'Your gun makes a big noise, but an arrow would have been more accurate.'

'I did not miss him,' said Kundan, feeling offended. 'You heard him roar, didn't you? He would not have been so angry if he had not been hit. If I have wounded him badly, he will die.'

'And if you have wounded him slightly, he may turn into a man-eater, and then where will we be?'

'I don't think he will come back,' said Kundan. 'He will leave these forests.'

They waited until the sun was up before coming down from the tree. They found a few drops of blood on the dry grass, but no trail led into the forest, and Ramu's father was convinced that the wound was only a slight one.

The bullet, missing the fatal spot behind the ear, had only grazed the back of the skull and cut a deep groove at its base.

It took a few days to heal, and during this time the tiger lay low and did not go near the jheel except when it was very dark and he was very thirsty. The villagers thought the tiger had gone away, and Ramu and Shyam—accompanied by some other youths, and always carrying sticks and axes—began bringing the buffaloes to the tank again during the day; but they were careful not to let any of them stray far from the herd, and they returned home while it was still daylight.

While the buffaloes wallowed in the muddy water, and the boys wrestled on their grassy islet, a tawny eagle circled high above them, looking for a meal—a sure sign that some of the animals were beginning to return to the forest. It was not long before his keen eyes detected a movement in the glade below.

What the eagle saw was a baby hare, a small, fluffy thing, its long, pink-tinted ears laid flat along its sides. Had it not been creeping along between two large stones, it would have escaped notice. The eagle waited to see if the mother was about, and even as he waited he realized that he was not the only one who coveted this juicy hare. From the bushes there had appeared a sinuous yellow creature, pressed low to the ground and moving rapidly towards the hare. It was a yellow jungle cat, hardly noticeable in the scorched grass. With great stealth and artistry the jungle cat stalked the baby hare.

He pounced. The hare's squeal was cut short by the cat's cruel claws, but it had been heard by the mother hare, who now bounded into the glade and without the slightest hesitation attacked the surprised cat.

There was nothing haphazard about the hare's attack. She flashed around behind the cat and jumped clean over it. As she landed, she kicked back, sending a stinging jet of dust shooting into the cat's face. She did this again and again.

The bewildered cat, crouching and snarling, picked up the kill and tried to run away with it. But the hare would not permit this. She continued her leaping and buffeting till eventually the cat, out of sheer frustration, dropped the kill and attacked the mother.

The cat sprang at the hare a score of times lashing out with its claws, but the mother hare was both clever and agile enough to keep just out of reach of those terrible claws, and drew the cat further and further away from her baby—for she did not as yet know that it was dead.

The tawny eagle saw his chance. Swift and true, he swooped.

For a brief moment, as his wings overspread the furry little hare and his talons sank deep into it, he caught a glimpse of the cat racing towards him and the mother hare fleeing into the bushes. And then, with a shrill 'kee-ee-ee' of triumph, he rose and whirled away with his dinner.

The boys had heard this shrill cry and looked up just in time to see the eagle flying over the jheel with the small hare held firmly in its talons.

'Poor hare,' said Shyam. 'Its life was short.'

'That's the law of the jungle,' said Ramu. 'The eagle has a family too, and must feed it.'

'I wonder if we are any better than animals,' said Shyam.

'Perhaps we are a little better,' said Ramu. 'Grandfather always says, "To be able to laugh and to be merciful are the only things that make man better than the beast".'

The next day, while the boys were taking the herd home, one of the buffaloes lagged behind. Ramu did not know the animal was missing until he heard her agonized bellow. He glanced over his shoulder just in time to see the big striped tiger dragging the buffalo into a clump of young bamboo. At the same time the herd became aware of the danger, and the buffaloes snorted with fear as they hurried along the forest path. To urge them forward, and to warn his friends, Ramu cupped his hands to his mouth and gave vent to a yodelling call.

The buffaloes bellowed, the boys shouted, and the birds flew shrieking from the trees. It was almost a stampede by the time the herd emerged from the forest. The villagers heard the thunder of hoofs, and saw the herd coming home in dust and confusion, and knew that something was wrong. 'The tiger!' shouted Ramu. 'He is here! He has killed one of the buffaloes.'

'He is afraid of us no longer,' said Shyam.

'Did you see where he went?' asked Kundan Singh, hurrying up to them.

'I remember the place,' said Ramu. 'He dragged the buffalo in amongst the bamboo.'

'Then there is no time to lose,' said his father.

'Kundan, you take your gun and two men, and wait near the suspension bridge, where the Garur stream joins the Ganga. The jungle narrows there. We will beat the jungle from our side, and drive the tiger towards you. He will not escape us, unless he swims the river!'

'Good!' said Kundan, running into his house for his gun, with Shyam close at his heels. 'Was it one of our buffaloes again?' he asked.

'It was Ramu's buffalo this time,' said Shyam, 'A good milk buffalo.'

'Then Ramu's father will beat the jungle thoroughly. You boys had better come with me. It will not be safe for you to accompany the beaters.'

And so, Kundan Singh carrying his gun and accompanied by Ramu, Shyam and two men, headed for the river junction, while Ramu's father collected about twenty men from the village and, guided by one of the boys who had been with Ramu, made for the spot where the tiger had killed the buffalo.

The tiger was still eating when he heard the men coming. He had not expected to be disturbed so soon. With an angry 'Whoof!' he bounded into the bamboo thicket and watched the men through a screen of leaves and tall grass.

The men did not seem to take much notice of the dead buffalo, but gathered round their leader and held a consultation. Most of them carried hand drums which hung down to their waists by shoulder-straps. They also carried sticks, spears and axes.

After a hurried conversation, they turned to face the jungle and began beating their drums with the palms of their hands.

Some of the men banged empty kerosene tins. These made even more noise than the drums.

The tiger did not like the noise and retreated further into the jungle. But he was surprised to find that the men, instead of going away, came after him into the jungle, banging away on their drums and tins, and shouting at the top of their voices. They had separated now, and advanced singly or in pairs, but nowhere were they more than fifteen yards apart. The tiger could easily have broken through this slowly advancing semicircle of men—one swift blow from his paw would have felled the strongest of them—but his main aim was to get away from the noise. He hated and feared the noise made by men.

He was not a man-eater and he would not attack a man unless he was very angry or very frightened or very desperate; and he was none of these things as yet. He had eaten well, and he would like to rest in peace—but there would be no rest for any animal until the men had gone with their tremendous clatter and din.

For an hour Ramu's father and the others beat the jungle, calling, drumming and trampling the undergrowth. The tiger had no rest. Whenever he was able to put some distance between himself and the men, he would sink down in some shady spot to rest, but, within five or ten minutes, the trampling and drumming would sound nearer, and the tiger, with an angry snarl, would get up and pad silently north along the narrowing strip of jungle, towards the junction of the Garur stream and the Ganga. Ten years back, he would have had jungle on his right in which to hide; but the trees had been felled long ago, to make way for more humans, and now he could only move to the left, towards the river.

It was about noon when the tiger finally appeared in the open. He longed for the darkness and security of the night, for the sun was his enemy. Kundan and the boys had a clear view of him as he stalked slowly along, now in the open with the sun glinting on his glossy side, now in the shade, or passing through the shorter reeds.

He was still out of range of Kundan's gun, but there was no fear of his getting out of the beat, as the 'stops' were all picked men from the village. He disappeared among some bushes but soon reappeared to retrace his steps, the beaters having done their work well. He was now only one hundred and fifty yards from the rocks where Kundan Singh waited, and he looked very big.

The beat had closed in, and his exit along the bank downstream was completely blocked; so the tiger turned into a belt of reeds, and Kundan Singh expected that his head would soon peer out of the cover a few yards away. The beaters were now making a great noise, shouting and beating their drums, but nothing moved, and Ramu, watching from a distance, wondered, 'Has he slipped through the beaters?' And hoped he had.

Tins clashed, drums beat, and some of the men poked into the reeds with their spears or long bamboos. Perhaps one of these thrusts found a mark, because at last the tiger was roused, and with an angry, desperate snarl he charged out of the reeds, splashing his way through an inlet of mud and water.

Kundan Singh fired, and his bullet struck the tiger on the thigh.

The mighty animal stumbled; but he was up in a minute, and, rushing through a gap in the narrowing line of beaters, he made straight for the only way across the river—the suspension bridge that passed over the Ganga here, providing a route into the high hills beyond.

'We'll get him now,' said Kundan, priming his gun again. 'He's right in the open!'

The suspension bridge swayed and trembled as the wounded tiger lurched across it. Kundan fired, and this time the bullet hit the tiger on the shoulder. The animal bounded forward, lost his footing on the unfamiliar, slippery planks of the swaying bridge, and went over the side, falling headlong into the strong, swirling waters of the river.

He rose to the surface once, but the current took him under and away, and only a thin streak of blood remained on the river's surface.

Kundan and the others hurried downstream to see if the dead

tiger had been washed up on the river's banks; but though they searched the riverside for several miles, they did not find the tiger. The river had taken him to its bosom. He had not provided anyone with a trophy. His skin would not be spread on a couch, nor would his head be hung upon a wall. No claw of his would be hung as a charm around the neck of a child. No villager would use his fat as a cure for rheumatism.

At first the villagers were glad because they felt their buffaloes were safe. Then the men began to feel that something had gone out of their lives, out of the life of the forest; they began to feel that the forest was no longer a forest. It had been shrinking year after year, but, as long as the tiger had been there and the villagers had heard it roar at night, they had known that they were still secure from the intruders and newcomers who came to fell the trees and eat up the land and let the floodwaters into the village. But, now that the tiger had gone, it was as though a protector had gone, leaving the forest open and vulnerable, easily destroyable. And, once the forest was destroyed, they too would be in danger...

There was another thing that had gone with the tiger, another thing that had been lost, a thing that was being lost everywhere—something called 'nobility'.

Ramu remembered something that his grandfather had once said, 'The tiger is the very soul of India, and when the last tiger has gone, so will the soul of the country.'

The boys lay flat on their stomachs on their little mud island and watched the monsoon clouds gathering overhead.

'The king of our forest is dead,' said Shyam. 'There are no more tigers.'

'There must be tigers,' said Ramu. 'How can there be an India without tigers?'

The river had carried the tiger many miles away from its home, from the forest it had always known, and brought it ashore on a strip of warm yellow sand, where it lay in the sun, quite still but breathing.

Vultures gathered and waited at a distance, some of them perching on the branches of nearby trees.

But the tiger was more drowned than hurt, and as the river water oozed out of his mouth, and the warm sun made new life throb through his body, he stirred and stretched, and his glazed eyes came into focus. Raising his head, he saw trees and tall grass.

Slowly he heaved himself off the ground and moved at a crouch to where the grass waved in the afternoon breeze. Would he be harried again, and shot at? There was no smell of Man. The tiger moved forward with greater confidence.

There was, however, another smell in the air—a smell that reached back to the time when he was young and fresh and full of vigour—a smell that he had almost forgotten but could never quite forget—the smell of a tigress!

He raised his head high, and new life surged through his tired limbs. He gave a full-throated roar and moved purposefully through the tall grass. And the roar came back to him, calling him, calling him forward—a roar that meant there would be more tigers in the land.

THE OWLET WHO CRAVED THE SUN

ACHYUTANANDA PATI

Translated from the Odia by Shaswat Panda

The owlet slowly opened his eyes. For the first time. Inside the tree-hollow, everything was pitch dark. The little fellow was sheltered by the warm protective wings of his mother. A sudden storm of cawing from the upper branches of the tree startled his mother. Her wings trembled with fear for a moment; then she shook her feathers, and rearranged them protectively around the owlet. He relaxed in the warmth of her embrace. She gently rubbed her beak on his, and asked him to stay quiet. Mother's behaviour intrigued him. Nevertheless, he obeyed. After a while, he grew restless. His body felt so light that he thought he could stand upright. He tried stretching his legs. His mother gave him room. She nudged his feet apart with her beak, trying to help him straighten his tiny limbs. He looked outside. It seemed less dark now. He immediately squeezed his eyes shut. He opened them again, glanced briefly at his mother, and looked up at the sky. It was clear that he was restless.

His mother's intuition kicked in. She drew him close. She touched his tiny beak with her own and said, 'My love, how smart have you become! But be a little more patient. Let your wings grow feathers and I myself will teach you how to fly. I will show you how to flap your wings. You will then be able to discover the world for yourself. You might be surrounded by darkness here, but the world outside, when you explore it, will not appear so dark. You will see the bright moonlight streaming down from the sky. Tiny stars will kiss you with their twinkling eyes. I will show you all the beautiful things that are there to see. Just wait till you grow up and you become strong enough, my son.' Saying so, she fetched a tiny slice of guava and stuffed it into his beak. As he swallowed it, he exclaimed, 'Ah! It's so sweet.' He assumed the world must be sweet, too, and he couldn't wait to explore it.

Some creature howled beneath the tree. Tucked comfortably under his mother's belly, the little owlet began to drowse, dreaming of the world outside. It seemed as though there were tiny pieces of ripe and delicious guava scattered everywhere. The moon was slowly descending from the heavens. The darkness had disappeared completely. As he dreamt, a smile forced its way through his beak. Abruptly, a piercing noise roused him from his dreams. It was very dark outside; his mood soured. His mother was sitting outside the hole, stretching her wings. The owlet cried out: 'Ma, I want to see the world, right now. I shall go and play with the moon.' No sooner had he spoken than his mother came back into their roost and enveloped him in the warmth of her embrace. He slid out of her grasp. He hated the darkness and wanted to get out. His mother said: 'You have been brought into this world, why would anyone stop you from seeing it! But if you venture out before you have grown up and become strong, you will get easily fooled and harmed. Just be patient, son! It's just a matter of time before I myself show you around. Lie down now, I'm going to get you something to eat. You must be very quiet when I'm gone, not the slightest sound from you.' She gave him an affectionate peck and made her way out of the hollow. Just before she flew off, she turned and gave him a long, long look. The owlet closed his eyes and his mother left. He was soon back in the world of dreams. The whole world looked bright and cheerful. It was inviting, tempting him with delicious guavas. He had grown more feathers on his wings than even his mother had on her own. He was flying high, brushing his feathers against the moon, and laughing.

Time passed. The owlet's legs grew strong and he could stand up. More feathers had started appearing on his wings. He had been getting more and more restless to explore the world outside. The world in his dreams was lit up by moonlight and there were ripe guavas everywhere. He kept badgering his mother to let him fly. Unable to curb his impatience, the mother owl brought him to the opening of the roost for the first time. She pointed her beak in the direction of the moon and showed it to him. His eyes shone with joy as he looked at it. How beautiful it was! Quite unlike the dark hole he had been rotting in for so long.

He clung to his mother's wings as he made his first attempts to fly, hopping from one branch to another. His wings started to ache. Gathering all his strength, he soared to the topmost branch of the tree. He sat there with his gaze fixed on the moon. The ache in his wings slowly ebbed away. The sky was lit with a soft and gentle light. He had the urge to open his beak and gulp down that stream of moonlight. Just as his fantasies were scaling new heights, his mother flew up and nudged him to go back to their roost in the dark hole of the tree.

One day, the mother owl had dozed off. The owlet gingerly moved out of the roost. 'It is so bright outside; there is so much light. The moon looks much bigger and brighter than the other day,' he said to himself. The radiance of this moon made his eyes burn. Two young mynahs on the branch above his head sang along in tune with their mother as they went hopping from one branch to another. He felt let down by his mother. Why didn't she teach him to sing under the big moon, just as the mynah did for her chicks! He approached the two birds and began to hoot a song. The mynah chicks began screaming in fear and their mother immediately flew at him and tried to peck him. Attracted by the noise, a crow flew overhead, cawing loudly. The caw of the crow disturbed his mother's sleep. She quickly flew out and pulled him back into the cavity of the tree. Infuriated by the way in which his mother was spoiling his fun, the owlet began pecking and clawing at her. Once again, he tried to fly out. His distraught mother tried to put some sense into him. 'Calm down, son! Shut your mouth! That big moon that you are looking at is the sun. The sun is not meant for us. We are creatures of the dark. We do not even get to see the moon every day. We are destined for darkness. We can either choose darkness or death.'

His mother's words angered the owlet. Why should he not go into the world of the sun? Why should he not wander freely in daylight? Who had made such laws? Laws that seemed designed to destroy his dreams? Angrily, he tried to flounce out again. His mother pulled him back. In his rage at being thwarted, he pulled a few feathers from his mother's body with his beak. In frustration and pain, she cried out. Suddenly remorseful, he calmed down and came back to her. He couldn't bear to see his mother crying. Outside, the crows continued to caw. She felt annoyed with herself for mentioning that cursed sun to her son. 'We are denizens of darkness. We are an inauspicious species. We are a cursed lot, son. The sons of light are waiting to hunt us down.' Her grief refused to subside. Trying to console her, the owlet said, 'Calm down Ma, just wait and watch. Let me grow up. I will take you to the world of light…it's a promise. I will destroy all our enemies.'

It was the night of the new moon. The owlet and his mother were sitting on the branch of a mango tree. The little one seemed rather grumpy. Suddenly, a piercing ray of light from the house next door filled his sight. This made him very happy and he started tooting. A voice from the house began to yell at him, 'Wretched bird, get the hell out of here or else I will brand you with a hot spatula. May you die of cholera!' Mother clamped his mouth shut with her beak. The owlet was furious. 'They are acting as if light is their property, and they can't stand the little joy I get from it,' he muttered angrily. He decided that he was not going to let his desire be thwarted. He would sneak into the house through a window and grab some light. However, his mother's frantic pleas prevailed and he was dissuaded from that impetuous course of action.

He carefully examined his wings before shuffling out of the roost that evening. All his feathers were fully grown. He started moving his feet as if he were dancing to some tune. The legs were strong. He pecked at the bark of the tree; his beak had gained considerable strength. And now here he was, flying. He spent the night inside the hollow of another tree. For him, there was no going back home that night. He had made up his mind to wander in the world of the sun. He would conquer light, he had resolved. He was ready to face his enemies.

With the coming of the dawn, red streaks of light spread across the horizon. He had never before seen the glorious spectacle of light entering and illuminating every corner of the kingdom of the sun. He watched this ceremony of light unblinkingly, as if he were in a trance. Flocks of birds tapped their wings to the beat of their song and began to soar into the sky. He thought it ridiculous that hundreds of other birds could traverse the kingdom of light and savour the taste of life whereas he was expected to fearfully rot in the darkness. As he thought about this, his spirits began to rise. As the sun rose its glow grew brighter. Would it really be impossible for him to find a place in the beautiful world of light? He refused to give in to that thought. He was determined to have his share of fun, stake his claim to the kingdom of light.

He took wing, and began to fly aimlessly through the sky, looking at everything that came into view. Suddenly something ambushed him from behind. He turned around and saw that the bird which had attacked him looked like the ones his mother had warned him about when he was little. Enraged, he turned on the crow. The crow cried out for help. Soon, a mighty swarm of his brethren rushed to the crow's rescue. The owlet realized it would be impossible to fight so many of them. He fled to the nearest house he could see, beating his wings strongly in the air. He managed to sneak in through the skylight on top of the wall. Once inside, he made his way deeper into the house. Perched on a rafter he tried to regain his breath. Meanwhile, the crows circled in the sky, cawing. He was waiting for the large group to disperse, so that he could single out his target and avenge himself. He was determined to claim his due from the world. He wouldn't be consigned to the darkness; he was a child of the light, his heart told him. He would enjoy light to the fullest, he thought.

Dhanbir and Dhirmallu were lying ill in bed in the room that the owlet had crept into. They shivered from the fever that made their temperatures soar. Dhirmallu tossed and turned in bed, and occasionally, he would shout in his delirium. 'Ensure that agacha is mixed well in mustard oil in the proportion of eighty to one. Make sure you file a case against Madana Barik. Bloody scoundrel! His sister Chandrama is acting like some sati-savitri. Just because I put my hand on her shoulder affectionately, she tried to hit me!' He called out to his wife, 'That Priya Mishra has no intention of paying back the debt, it seems. Ask our men to go and collect paddy from his field. Bloody rascal, just because he has learnt a few letters of the alphabet, he wouldn't wish me! That Bengali fellow has promised to deliver one quintal of smuggled opium. Keep an eye on him,' he instructed her.

These are the mighty lords of the world of light. The sun illuminates their land every day, the owlet thought. He kept staring at them with his eyes wide open.

Suddenly, one of Dhirmallu's devoted men saw the bird. 'This is an ominous, inauspicious sign! Great danger will befall this house. There is an owl here when the lord of this house is ill!' he shouted. The owlet was shooed away with a long bamboo stick. Both his wings were injured in the attack; he barely managed to crawl on to the roof. Crows flew from the trees to attack him. A servant managed to hit him with a stick. He fell from the roof. Turmeric water was sprinkled all over and around the house and a pile of hay was burnt to purify the place. Everybody became calmer, now that the evil had been mitigated.

But the owlet's troubles were far from over. The crows continued their onslaught. Blood began oozing from his body. He looked up; the sun was shining brightly. With great difficulty he flapped away in the direction of his roost but his strength gave out before he could reach the cavity where he and his mother nested. He crashed to the ground at the bottom of the tree. His anxious mother had been waiting helplessly for him. Hearing her son's desperate cries she flew down to him. She was speechless when she saw her son lying in a pool of blood. He looked up. The young mynahs were hopping and singing on the branches of the tree. The sun continued to shower its radiance on the scene.

He called out to his mother. As she sat disconsolately beside him, he pressed his weakening body against her warmth and said softly; 'Ma, do not cry. If you give birth to my brothers, tell them that their elder brother became a martyr, trying to conquer the world of light.'

And then the little owlet who craved the sun died. Above him, the object of his desire continued to shine—even more brightly than before.

THE CROCODILE AND THE MONKEY

VIKRAM SETH

On the Ganga's greenest isle
Lived Kuroop the crocodile:
Greeny-brown with gentle grin,
Stubby legs and scaly skin,
He would view with tepid eyes
Prey below a certain size—
But when a substantial dish
—Dolphin, turtle, fatter fish—

Swam across his field of view,
He would test the water too.
Out he'd glide, a floating log,
Silent as a polliwog—
Nearer, nearer, till his prey
Swam a single length away;
Then he'd lunge with smiling head,
Grab, and snap, and rip it dead—
Then (prime pleasure of his life)
Drag the carcass to his wife,
Lay it humbly at her feet,
Eat a bit, and watch her eat.

All along the river-bank
Mango trees stood rank on rank,
And his monkey friend would throw
To him as he swam below

Mangoes gold and ripe and sweet
As a special summer treat.
'Crocodile, your wife, I know
Hungers after mangoes so
That she'd pine and weep and swoon,
Mango-less in burning June.'
Then Kuroop the crocodile,
Gazing upwards with a smile,
Thus addressed his monkey friend:
'Dearest monkey, in the end,
Not the fruit, but your sweet love,
Showered on us from above,
Constant through the changing years,
Slakes her griefs and dries her tears.'
(This was only partly true.
She liked love, and mangoes too.)

One day, Mrs Crocodile,
Gorged on mangoes, with a smile
—Sad, yet tender—turned and said:
'Scalykins, since we've been wed,
You've fulfilled my every wish
—Dolphins, turtles, mangoes, fish—
But I now desire to eat,
As an anniversary treat,
Something sweeter still than fruit,
Sugar-cane or sugar-root:
I must eat that monkey's heart.
'What?' 'Well, darling, for a start,
He has been so kind to me;
Think how sweet his heart must be.
Then, the mango pulp he's eaten
Year on year must serve to sweeten
Further yet each pore and part,
Concentrating in his heart.'

'Darling, he's my friend.' 'I know;
And he trusts you. Therefore go—
Oh, my breath grows faint, I fear…'
'Let me fan you—it's the heat—'
'No—I long for something sweet.
Every fruit tastes bitter now.
I must eat his heart somehow.
Get him here, my love, or I,
Filled with bitterness, will die.'

When the monkey saw Kuroop
He let out a joyful whoop,
Jumped from branch to branch with pleasure,
Flinging down the golden treasure:
'Eat, my friend, and take your wife
Nectar from the tree of life—
Mangoes ripe and mangoes rare,
Mangoes, mangoes everywhere.'
Then Kuroop the crocodile
Gazed up with a gentle smile:
'Monkey, you are far too kind,
But today, if you don't mind,
Dine with both of us, and meet
Her whose life you've made so sweet.
When you meet her you will see
Why she means so much to me.
When she takes you by the paw
Something at your heart will gnaw.
When you gaze into her eyes
You will enter Paradise.
Let us show our gratitude:
Share our friendship and our food.'

'Dear Kuroop, dear crocodile,
You can swim from isle to isle.

I can leap from limb to limb,
But, my friend, I cannot swim.
And your island's far away.
If I get a boat some day ...'
'Nonsense; jump upon my back.
You're no heavier than my sack
Filled with mangoes to the crown.'
So the monkey clambered down,
Bearing mangoes, and delighted
With such warmth to be invited.

Thcy were just halfway across
When the crocodile said: 'Toss
All those mangoes in the water.'
'But these fruit are all I've brought her.'
'You yourself are gift enough,'
Said Kuroop in accents gruff.
'Ah, my friend, that's very gracious.'
'Well, my wife's not so voracious—
And I'm certain that today
She won't eat fruit. By the way,
Tell me what your breast contains.
Mango nectar fills your veins.
Does it also fill your heart?'
Said the monkey with a start:
'What a very curious question.'
'Well, she might get indigestion
If it's too rich, I suspect.'
'What?' 'Your heart.' 'My heart?' 'Correct.'

'Now,' Kuroop said with a frown,
'Which would you prefer—to drown
In the Ganga or to be
Gutted by my wife and me?
I will let you choose your end.

After all, you are my friend.'
Then he slowly started sinking.
'Wait—' the monkey said, 'I'm thinking.
Death by drowning, death by slaughter
—Death by land or death by water—
I'd face either with a smile
For your sake, O crocodile!
But your wife's felicity—
That's what means the most to me.
Noble lady! How she'll freeze,
Dumb with sorrow, when she sees,
Having prised my ribs apart,
That my breast contains no heart.
If you had not rushed me so,
I'd have found the time to go
To the hollow where I keep
Heart and liver when I sleep,
Half my brain, a fingernail,
Cufflinks, chutney, and spare tail.
I had scarcely woken up
When you asked me here to sup.
Why did you not speak before?
I'd have fetched them from the shore.'

Now Kuroop the crocodile
Lost, then quickly found, his smile.
'How my sweetheart will upbraid me!
Monkey, monkey—you must aid me.'
'Well...'—the monkey placed his paw
Thoughtfully upon his jaw—
Well, although the day is hot
And I'd really rather not—
We could go back, fetch my heart,
Check its sweetness, and depart.'

So the crocodile once more
Swam the monkey back to shore,
And, with tears of thankfulness
Mingled with concern and stress,
Worried what his wife would say
With regard to his delay,
Begged his friend: 'Come back at once.
'I'm not such a double-dunce,'
Yelled the monkey from on high;
'Tell your scaly wife to try
Eating her own wicked heart
—If she has one—for a start.
Mine's been beating in my breast
Night and day without a rest.
Tell her that—and as for you,
Here's my parting gift—'He threw
Mangoes—squishy, rotten, dead—
Down upon the reptile's head,
Who, with a regretful smile,
Sat and eyed him for a while.

LABOUR

R. R. BORADE

Translated from the Marathi by Anjali Nerlekar

The season of steady rains had receded and now, an unreasonable rain started from clouds that seemed untimely pregnant. The sky would fill up once in ten to fifteen days. Occasionally it would sprinkle the hot, steaming yard with water. Seeming to winnow the woods, the rain would splash down in a circle for a while and then the sky would grow quiet again. And then there were times when the rain would pull no punches. The sky would fill up everywhere you looked. It would become dark as night. And it would rain uncontrollably, for hours at a stretch. The rain would then retreat after having stung the doggedly ripening crops.

From where she lay, Putali kept an eye on the eastern horizon where the clouds were gathered together like guests invited to an event. Slowly, the sun hid behind the clouds and it felt as if someone was holding a shade over one's head. It looked as though it was going to rain soon. Putali shook her head vigorously to dislodge the flies from her tired eyes and wet nostrils. She stood up, just barely. Her entire body was trembling and her legs were about to collapse. Putali dug her hooves into the ground. She was scarcely able to carry the weight of her heavy belly on her shaky legs. But she felt better for having stood up.

She lifted her exhausted gaze and tried looking around. At first, everything was blurry. She felt as if someone had placed a sheer curtain in front of her eyes. But gradually her gaze settled and she was able to focus. She looked at the expanse in front of her. The other cattle had started walking briskly in the direction of the village. The dust flying from their hooves floated in the air. Putali looked around her. This wasteland that stretched in front of her was covered with thorny weeds and thistle. A little distance away, there was a stubby and thorny acacia tree. Other than that, there was no other shelter anywhere in sight. Putali glanced again at the cattle walking in the direction of home and she began to low intensely. She bellowed as if her voice were being squeezed out of her and she suddenly felt nauseous because of that effort. Lowing a second time became too difficult for her. She opened her mouth and then shut it again. She looked at the cattle disappearing into the distance again. As she stared desperately at them, her eyes filled with tears. Helplessly, she looked to her left at the stunted tree. Gauging the intervening expanse between it and her present location in her mind, she turned towards it and began walking.

Lifting one foot after the other, she started her journey. She had barely walked a few steps when she felt a sudden movement in her stomach. The bulge inside her was moving continuously now. With pleading eyes she looked up at the sky. Each cloud seemed to be hugging the next as if a carpenter had trimmed the edges and joined them together like pieces of wood. It was getting darker and the rains looked like they were approaching fast. With an effort, she picked up her pace. She had barely walked a short distance when she felt a piercing pain in her stomach. The pain made her body go limp and every hair on her body stood up in agony. She spread her hind legs, and crouching her body, urinated profusely. She straightened up. Just then a drop of rain splashed on her back. She shivered. She raised her head and watched the darkening sky. Then, with determination, she started walking again. Again, she felt an intense pain in her stomach. The waves of pain kept coming, one after another. It was as if a mill-wheel was churning in her stomach. Putali slumped to the ground. Then she hoisted herself up again with an effort. But the stomach pains were unstoppable. She lay down, got up again. After several such attempts to sit down and stand up again, she felt a new and soft sensation within her belly. Gentler, even pleasurable, this feeling; she stood there with eyes closed, experiencing this inexplicably enjoyable sensation.

Just then a balloon the colour of a shiny pebble emerged from her belly and started filling up with air fast. She felt as if a heavy burden had been tied to her. She began walking slowly. She lifted her head and looked at the tree in front of her. The balloon began to swell until it was almost as big as a large water container and then as if overfull with air, it burst. Putali was relieved. It felt like her burden had lightened.

She looked up at the sky. The black clouds were ranged in shells one atop the other. It looked like the sky had been plastered with black ink. She looked again at the acacia tree that tood a little way ahead. Again, she gauged the distance between herself and the tree and began walking. Step by step, the mill-wheel in her stomach that had temporarily stopped started churning again. The bulge in her belly started moving. Pain lanced continuously through her. Putali lowered her head and let the labour pangs come.

Then she felt as if someone had touched an axe to the inside of her underbelly. She shuddered deeply. The waves of pain crashed through her one after another. As they kept coming, the hooves made an appearance, just about four fingers long, and then they stopped there. She kept heaving with pain but the hooves would not move. There was a firestorm in her belly now. Everything seemed to be tossing around wildly within her. Putali clenched the muscles of her face. She tried looking ahead but she was unable to see the tree that had seemed to be so close. It felt like a curtain of darkness was falling in front of her eyes. Putali sank to the ground and, holding her breath, she heaved again. The hooves, stuck inside her all this while, started moving out again. It seemed she would be released from this agony in a little while. She closed her eyes and kept pushing. The hooves were emerging rapidly.

Just then the sky thundered, signalling the coming rain. Putali was terrified. She stood up with a jerk and tried to start walking towards the tree. But she could not lift a foot. A strong gust of wind swirled around her. With the wind came rain. At first it was just a few drops but it soon turned into a steady downpour of heavy and large raindrops. The heavy drops started ringing on the half-emerging hooves and that sound resounded within her stomach. It was like the sound of drum sticks on a drum.

Putali felt helpless. She tossed her head and made an attempt to low. But no sound came from her throat. Just as abruptly as it had begun, the heavy downpour stopped. Putali was relieved. She looked again at the tree. She attempted to walk towards it once more. Just as she lifted one foot, she felt a big convulsion within her belly. Planting her feet determinedly on the ground, she stopped right there, shuddering again. The inner jolts kept coming after that first one. The face of the calf was emerging little by little.

Just then it thundered again. The rain came down in streams as thick as one's fingers, making a loud sound as it hit the ground. The thunder sounded like gunshots. Lightning whiplashed across the sky, so bright it shocked the eyes. Putali looked up. She tried to focus and see as far as she possibly could but visibility was down to a few feet. She could not see the tree in front of her. The pains in her stomach kept on coming. She kept feeling the convulsions in her belly. The calf was slowly moving out of her.

The rain refused to stop cascading down and the calf was struggling to come out. Putali started trying to contract her body, to hold her breath in order to try and suck the hooves inside of her again. But the hooves would not go in, and the calf would not put its face back in. The breath, which she had been trying to hold, started escaping into the atmosphere like steam. Her body loosened up and the calf began to emerge, inch by inch, even as the rain, as if stoked with some demented energy, kept pelting down. There was water wherever the eyes could see. Putali tried to contract her body again but the calf would not heed her. Instead, Putali's pangs grew stronger and faster and more of the calf began to emerge. Desperate and helpless, Putali looked all around her. Just then an enormous bolt of pain surged through her. The calf put its face completely out. Putali realized this and was confused. She began turning round and round, as if in a circus ring. Trying to suck the calf's face and body into her body, she started screaming loudly. Putali kept circling round and round as if mesmerized and the rain, as if crazed, kept falling…

THE REFLECTIONS OF A HEN IN HER LAST HOUR

PAUL ZACHARIA

Translated from the Malayalam by A. J. Thomas

Oh, my jackal! Please don't look at me like this. Thrills run up and down my body. My eyes are glazing over. In this darkness infused with the fragrance of coffee blossoms, I am already feeling intoxicated. I can't bear this gaze of yours. Although I am afraid to look at you, I know that you are looking at me. I know that from the darkness at the base of this coffee tree your eyes are fixed on me, flaming with a light that none of the lamps of this world can match. When I think of that, I am desperate to look into your glowing eyes. But, because of my fear, it is to the sky that I look instead, as I sit on the branch of this coffee tree. When I see the stars blazing in the sky like clusters of coffee blooms, I'm reminded of your fiery eyes and my head bends to look downwards, thinking about your hypnotic gaze. Please don't confuse me like this. Can you see me in this darkness? What am I to you? A heart-throb from the bough up above? A rustle of feathers? Doesn't my form get away from your eyes and vanish into the foliage and dark clouds?

Don't trouble me like this. Am I not just a mere hen, a female? Where do I get the strength from, to suppress so much excitement? Look, my feathers are standing up as I thrill to your presence! Why do you bother me so much, my stealthy suitor? You are a frightening presence in the dark, but thrilling all the same. Isn't that the reason I began to like you although I am afraid of you? Oh, voyeur, do you know how desperate I am to see you? Still, I can't gather enough courage to look at you! What is this fear that has lodged deep inside me and threatens to pull me down? It is not the kind of fear that I felt when the dog of the household rushed at me from behind the pepper-vine-covered tree. I fled, scattering dry leaves everywhere but the dog is a fool, an idiot! Will I let him touch me? That slave who spends half his life on a chain. I found his springing at me meaningless, I couldn't care less. With you, it's different. Your pursuit of me, braving sticks, stones, gun and crackers comes across as hot, smart, and compelling. Even if you catch hold of me, there will be pleasure in it.

What will you do to me if you get hold of me? What will you do with me before you eat me? Is it merely to eat me that you keep looking at me like this, even at the risk of forsaking your own life? Is a hen so very tasty? I wish I could look into your eyes and ask you all these questions. But what to do, I am afraid.

Today, you didn't howl at all. I was straining my ears since dusk. When you howl from your lair, which I have never been able to look at or walk into, I am plunged into an amazing reverie. How dark and remote your world! It is your amazing howls that rise at odd hours from the land of the night, more than the crowing at the beginning of light, that makes me want to dream, gives my mind a boost. More than the crowing of roosters cuddling me, your howls exhilarate me. Will you take me to your lair? When I sit at its entrance, awaiting your pleasure, will you howl just once for me? Let the moon rise early, to give your howl a skyward-rising tang; let the moon climb into the sky. As you take me along, I'll look at your face and eyes. I will no longer be fearful. I know that my fear will fade away the moment you catch me.

Weren't you the rustle and movement I sometimes detected at dusk through the darkening vistas of the coffee plantation? Weren't you the commotion that sometimes came towards this courtyard, climbing stone-walls, rubbing against the trunks of the trees, shaking thickets? I remember once when I was in the coop, we suddenly sensed something in the wind, in the dark, and started shuddering and huddled together. Wasn't it you who came flowing in the wind?

On moonlit nights, I have seen, sitting on this bough, a figure prowling through the thickets of water hyacinths on the banks of the pond in the southern compound. Where were you going? Why didn't you come and stand at the base of this coffee tree of mine, in those days? And look at me with your blazing eyes?

Did you know that every day I would hide so I wouldn't be shooed into the coop at night? When the others had been shut up, I would perch alone on this coffee bough. It is not suffocating here, as it is in the coop. And no roosters to force themselves on me. And there isn't that long wait in the morning, for the coop to be opened. I enjoy myself sitting here, listening to the rhythmic whispers of dewdrops falling on the leaves and the rumble of rain as it draws near. Lightning flickers and fades in the far limits of the sky.

I also enjoy the excitement and shock your impending arrival evokes in me. When your howls sound through the silent trees, thrills course through my body. I peck at the branch I am sitting on, clutch it firmly. My head reels when I think that you are actually sitting in the grass at the base of this coffee tree, looking up at me. I feel as if the stars are clustering together and blazing even brighter. The treetops shimmer and separate right in front of my eyes. Will I fall down even before getting your invitation? If so, will you accept me?

Weren't you looking at me as you lay hidden in the tall grass of the plantation, when I was raking the tilled soil in the western field of the farm? I could feel the sharp pin pricks of your gaze at the base of every feather. I stood there, my head lowered, still and quiet, without the strength to look back at you. In my imagination, your form grew and grew until it covered the entire expanse of grass and trees. I stood there for a long time, waiting for you to come to me. It was only when I heard the scream of the kites in the sky that I was jolted out of my trance and ran away from there. Did you feel that I was not beautiful when you saw me in the sunlight? Didn't you like me in daylight?

How many days have I hidden my eggs in heaps of dry leaves in the banana grove for your pleasure! Haven't you seen the people of the family coming in search of them? Wasn't it you who ate all of them? Or was it that damned dog or that rat snake which hisses from the hole in the stone-wall? They were eggs I laid only for you, most gladly and contentedly. They were eggs I gave you, even forgetting my desire to brood over them.

Yesterday and the day before, I had let fall through the dusk a feather to inform you of my vigil on this coffee bough. You know I can't help flying up to this branch and sitting here on account of my uncontrollable fear. It's only when I am perched at this height that I can meditate on you. I can't do it any other way. And I can't help waiting for you. And I can't help experiencing your gaze. Here's another feather as a sign of my presence. Although I had hoped to look into your eyes, my gaze following the path of the feather as it drifted down towards you, I wasn't able to do so. So here's yet another feather as a sign of my love, yearning and fear. Let me lower my eyes together with it. Oh, my jackal, here I come. Here I come, stoned with the fragrance of coffee blossoms and love. I fall into your eyes. Do not go away thinking that it's a bunch of flowers that has broken off and fallen down. It's your hen. Here I am, coming down. Please support me. Please hold me.

THE SUMMER OF THE CROWS*

NILANJANA ROY

All through that winter, Tigris saw dark visions. She dreamed of black clouds coming down from the sky until they became shrouds for the wildings. She was anxious—first she asked the wildings to consider leaving Nizamuddin, and then she grew more insistent. But who would make a clan shift because of the dreams of a young cat just over a year old? Even her mother, Neferkitty, who was the clan's most fierce queen, refused to take Tigris's demands seriously.

In spring, the dreams that haunted Tigris grew more vivid; but it was one of the most beautiful springs we had seen. One of those rare ones, where the nights were jasmine-drenched, the prey thick on the ground, and the Bigfeet left us alone for a change. If it was a perfect spring, the following season was anything but, for that summer was the summer of the crows.

First there was just one flock, and then two, and then more and more, settling raucously in the hedges and trees of Nizamuddin. We wildings were indifferent—crows had always been part of the colony—and then, as more and more of them came in, wary. You know what crows are like, Tooth: loud and bustling and given to throwing parties every evening with brawls between the younger lot. And they can be mean, and some of them are very clever thieves—they'll wait for a cat or a cheel to make the kill, and then sneak in and swipe the lot.

But they're also fun: look at Blackwing and Brightbeak and their brood, and the way they keep watch for all of us here. These crows, though, were different. They came in like the gathering monsoon

---

*Extracted from *The Wildings*.

clouds, masses of them, shrouding the trees in black and grey, filling the skies with their relentless cawing and squabbling. And then the clan remembered Tigris's visions, and in our hearts and whiskers we were afraid. At first, Stoop paid them no mind. She went on her daily patrols as always and stayed far away, on the highest gables, roosting in the trees in the wild, unclaimed lot. Conquer wasn't happy when she issued an order that all cheels were to leave Nizamuddin and make their homes as far away from the crows as possible, in Humayun's Tomb and across the canal in Jangpura, but he obeyed her, coming back himself for flying visits.

I was puzzled too, it wasn't like Stoop to cede territory—she was always one for a good fight, your mother. But she told me one day when our paths crossed, 'I don't understand this, Miao, there's something behind the crows' behaviour. It's not your normal invasion—they've run away, they don't have real leaders or tribes and that makes them dangerous. I need to think about how to get them out of here.'

She tried to speak to their leaders, but Bitterbite and Bakbuk flapped out of their nests at her and cawed their threats furiously, refusing to answer questions. Stoop parried their darts at her easily, rising into the feathery embrace of the nimbus clouds, and didn't try to engage them again.

We missed the cheels. Your family sometimes preys on kittens, or old cats, or ones that are sick, and we raid your nests if we find them on lower ground, and we've killed fledglings too, but there's no real enmity between us. Moreover, the tradition you grew up in, Tooth, where we leave part of the kill for you and you for us in lean hunting weather—it goes back to the first cats and cheels who settled in the old alleys of Nizamuddin.

I sometimes looked up at the sky, and I'd see a tiny, faraway speck against the sun—Stoop, gliding above us, looking down at Nizamuddin, quartering her turf. I often wondered what she saw, and when her shadow floated over me, darkening the ground for a fleeting second, I missed her.

The crows were becoming bolder. They stole from us, attacked our kittens until we had to keep all of them, nine-weekers and younger, carefully corralled in the tiny park at the back, with the toms guarding them, and even so we lost quite a few. They harried the lizards and the mice, the rats and the bandicoots, and then they began to attack the Bigfeet's homes and their pets—and this was dangerous for all of us, Tooth.

Six of the crows got into one of the homes, opened up the cage of these guinea pigs who were kept as pets, and killed them all. Poor things. They were silly little creatures with no conversation at all: 'I gots food! I not gots food! I gots more food than you gots!' was about as much as they could manage. But they didn't deserve that ending, and there was no need for it—the crows who did it weren't even looking for food. They were just bored.

After a pair of hutch rabbits went the same way, and the crows attacked a Bigfoot child, we saw that the Bigfeet were getting restless, and angry. And we were fearful, because we didn't know what they would do, but we were sure it wouldn't be anything that was good.

I would have gone to Stoop then, but she had disappeared. Oh, her patrol was there all right, but they flew further and further away, only circling Nizamuddin once during the day, and Stoop was nowhere to be seen.

I had too many troubles of my own to worry about Stoop for long, anyway. Nizamuddin has always been rich in hunting, and the Bigfeet leave wonderful things out for all of us in their garbage heaps, but there were too many crows, and more crowding in every day. Bitterbite and Bakbuk led several murders of crows out foraging most days and they were becoming more vicious, stalking us cats and stealing our kills whenever they could. One murder of crows left suddenly, led by Breakbone, and we heard they'd settled in the Jangpura market, across the canal.

Then one day Stoop flew back with worrying news. 'The Bigfeet are setting out poison,' she said. She tried to tell Breakbone, because she believed it was her duty to warn all other creatures, even the hostiles.

'Get away with you, you bag of bones,' was what Breakbonesaid, 'you're just trying to keep us away from good feeding so that you and your flea-ridden friends can hunt without competition.' So Stoop said no more, but a week later, she came back to tell us that all the garbage heaps in the market were covered with black feathers.

Breakbone and his gang had fallen victim to the poison.

After that, not a single crow tried to leave Nizamuddin, even though more and more crows came flooding in by the day. Living became a desperate struggle; we keep our eyes on the sky, never knowing when their sharp beaks would attack again. 'We have to do something,' I told Neferkitty one evening. That morning, I had seen the squirrels keening in a sad huddle, mourning the loss of yet another of their family.

Neferkitty had a gaunt look to her, by then. She'd been a handsome, well-muscled queen, but the last few months had taken it out on her—she'd melted down to bone and muscle. It was only later that I discovered she'd been feeding the kittens and nursing mothers from her kills, barely eating enough herself to keep tail and whiskers together. But her mind was as sharp as ever.

'I have a plan,' she said. 'It's desperate, but it'll have to do.' She told me the details and I agreed; it was desperate, but what other choice did we have? We would give Bitterbite and Bakbuk one chance—ask them to get half the crows to leave, perhaps to find homes a little further off, at Humayun's Tomb with the peacocks and the bulbuls.

Or perhaps they could go even further out, to the Golf Course with its spacious, green grounds. If they refused, we'd attack that night itself. The dogs were with us. They had suffered equally from the invasion of the crows, and when we approached them to ask for truce, their leader Tommy went further and said they'd stand by us and fight if need be. But there were only a few strays, and ours was still a woefully thin force.

'It would help if we had the cheels on our side, Miao,' she said. 'Any news of Stoop?'

There was none; and when I spoke to Conquer that night, your father was civil but distant. 'Not our fight, Miao,' he said. 'The cheels have moved on. Besides, I haven't seen Stoop myself in many moons. She's all right—my pinions would fluff and tell me if she was in serious danger—but that's all I know.' I pleaded with him until his tail feathers began to ruffle in annoyance, and then I had to back off.

It would have made a difference to have Conquer and his squadrons on our side. Without the cheels, the other birds refused to get involved.

'Look at us,' said Spackle Sparrow and Grackle Sparrow. 'We're too small, Miao, the crows would make keema of us in no time.'

The pigeons had long since fled; Bismillah, the bulbul, said he'd do what he could, but he couldn't put his brood in further danger. And Petuk and Potla, the vultures, had left for a long holiday, preferring the Yamuna river with all its pollutions to the overcrowded environs of Nizamuddin.

Neferkitty and I went to meet Bitterbite and Bakbuk. It was an unpleasant task; they were squabbling over one of their kills, though we couldn't tell what animal it was. Just as well; sometimes it was best not to know. Bakbuk lifted his head; his beak was bloody, his eye angry.

'You dare interrupt my meal, cats?'

'Mine!' cawed Bitterbite furiously. 'Mineminemine! I found it first, so I did.'

Bakbuk stabbed at her, tearing a feather slightly. Then he turned back to us. 'Well?'

Neferkitty's feathery tail twitched warily as she laid out our terms.

All were welcome in Nizamuddin, but he would agree there were too many crows. Food for all—the crows as well as the other animals—was running short; the Bigfeet were getting restless and would soon take steps, as they had with the garbage heaps in the market. We didn't want a fight, and there were many other parks and neighbourhoods; if half the crows would agree to leave, we could continue to live in peace. Would Bakbuk agree? Before Bakbuk could say anything, before I could do anything, Bitterbite flew at Neferkitty, slashing fiercely at her face. Neferkitty screamed as the crow's sharp talons shredded her ear. 'Truce-breaker!'

I cried in shock, leaping out of Bakbuk's way. 'We came here under truce terms!'

Neferkitty, despite her bleeding ear, was now swatting at Bitterbite, but I could see the rest of the murder swarming into formation.

'Neferkitty, follow me!' I howled, and we both fought our way out of there. If the dogs hadn't helped us, we wouldn't have made it.

Bakbuk's hoarse, mocking caws followed us: 'Come to us next time and we'll tear you to shreds, you furbags! Nothing will make us leave, you hear? Our trees. Our park. Our kills. Ours!' The sky was black with crows, cawing and shrieking their defiance.

We rejoined our clan in the small park at the back. None of us had much to say; we didn't need to link to know that we were all apprehensive of the night to come. Instead of even considering the situation or offering some sort of solution, the crows were now on guard, and there were so many of them.

'Neferkitty,' I said after a while. 'Should we attack as planned, or is there no hope?'

'I've been thinking the same thing,' said Neferkitty, her black fur gaping here and there with red where the blood still streamed from her cuts. 'It seems desperate, doesn't it? Perhaps it's us who should leave.'

I'd thought about that too, but the idea of leaving Nizamuddin, turning our backs on the neem trees and the gulmohar trees, abandoning the rooftops we'd played our stalking games on as kittens…it was too much, and how would we shift all the cats?

Where would we go? The crows could take flight, map neighbourhoods, find trees; it would take one cat scout many moons to locate a suitable territory.

Where would we find a place that had enough scavenging for so many of us, that was free of other cat clowders, that didn't have too many predators, that was close enough to Nizamuddin? And even if we did…in the vast shared memory of Delhi's cat clans, I could see not even the faintest pawmark that indicated a successful migration. Cats were not birds; we grew up and lived in the same territories as our mothers and fathers, and that was that. I said as much to Neferkitty.

'It sounds crazy, I know,' she said. 'But Miao, we can't go on much longer. With the crows here, we'll starve this winter; we're all weakening, and who knows if we'll be able to protect the next litter of kittens? We have to think of the unthinkable.'

We would have talked further, but there was a great beat of wings, and then we heard the high, pitiful screaming of one of the young stray pups, and the sound of the caws rose until we were nearly deafened. Nizamuddin was under attack.

You have to imagine it for yourself. All of us, cats and dogs, squirrels and mice, hedge pigeons, mynahs...scattered in disarray, while great black clouds of crows poured out like smoke descending from the trees. The noise! The rustling of their wings, the crescendo of caws—it was deafening and confusing, some of the smaller animals could do nothing but run up and down, making targets of themselves, the poor things. The squirrels ran back and forth along the branches, getting picked off two at a time; the mice scurried in desperate circles on the ground. It was terrible.

That first hour was dire. Neferkitty got out there, of course, and did the best she could, along with the fighting toms. The dogs helped, but soon we were bombarded by clusters of crows. The only thing that saved us was that the crows weren't proper fighters. They were from different families wherever they came from and I suppose they hadn't really expected much of a fight. They made a fearsome racket, but they weren't attacking in formation—any old group would take off any time it felt like it, and they banged into each other, in the air and on the ground. They squabbled too, and stabbed each other whenthey grew cross, and that saved many of us. Bakbuk got so annoyed with his best fighters for diving before he did that he snapped at three of them, wounding them so badly they had to retreat.

Even so, they had the advantage of numbers—however badly they fought, each injured crow was replaced immediately by another ten, and they covered the grass with the black of their wings. Neferkitty kept her head. She had crept into the trees, and she moved fast from branch to branch, from neem to gulmohar to amaltas, attacking them from behind, attacking their leaders just as they were poised for take-off, ducking back into the leaves if they tried to turn on her.

The pups stood with us, the Nizamuddin strays, barking their heads off, bounding into the thick of the press, not letting the crows land.

Neferkitty was bleeding heavily—some of the wounds of the

morning had opened up again. But the owls had woken up and rallied around her. Hootem and Hutom made darts from the safety of their hole in the ancient laburnum tree, getting in some good shots and buying Neferkitty a little breathing space. But the beat of the black wings never stopped; it seemed the trees were spewing out crows nonstop, one after another.

Bitterbite was in between us and Neferkitty, with a proper murder of crows, six of them who had clearly seen fighting before. I measured the distance between us and shuddered—the thought of trying to get to her, or her trying to get to us, through a thicket of sharp beaks and blood-hungry claws, was not pretty. It was desperate; we were badly outnumbered, and the air was thick with cawing.

There was a hard thud and I felt something bounce off my back. I whipped around, my whiskers quivering, and found myself staring at a tiny, terrified, chittering squirrel, who had rolled off my back and was tugging its furry tail around itself in fear. 'Iiiiiiiiiiiiiif yyyyyyyyyoouuuuuu plllllllleeeeeeaaaassseee,' it said through chattering teeth, 'a friend sent me. My name is Aaaaoooo ooww owww.' I was too shocked to even take a swipe at it, but before I got my brains in order, there was a second shock. Flying so low that her plumage skimmed the ground, Stoop shot over us, braking in mid-air to hover, hummingbird-fashion. 'Miao, meet Ao; this is Jao,' she said, depositing another small heap of tumbled fur on the ground. 'Friends of mine; keep them safe for me, you hear? No time to explain. We'll touch talons later.' And then she had pulled out of her brief hover and shot away, a lethally fast, soaring streak aimed like an arrow at Bitterbite.

The crow never saw what hit her, Tooth, your mother was that fast. There was a ripping sound, a desperate squawk—that was all, and then we saw a bundle of black feathers falling out of the sky.

Bitterbite was gone, and before the crows in her murder could react, Stoop had done a three-point roll and come back at them with her talons extended. Two more followed Bitterbite out of the sky, plunging down to the ground. A third screeched in pain and flapped slowly over to a nearby branch to rest; the fourth tried to engage Stoop in battle and had his wing torn off; Bakbuk flapped his wings in fear and fled. Bakbuk was the kind of crow whose caws were louder than his courage; he didn't like getting his feathers bloody.

But as Stoop rose above the black mass, their caws now deafening, we could all see that something was wrong. She flew at an angle, dipping her right wing slightly, and seemed to be in pain. The crows saw it too. The birds that had ducked and weaved out of her way started to gather again, massing behind her even as she tried to gain some height. It's odd—they didn't attack her in a group, but every so often, one of them would dart out from its murder and fly at her, staying just out of range of her talons.

Tooth looked into Miao's eyes and then away. 'Counting coup,' he said, his eyes yellow and sad. 'It's a classic crow manouevre when they're faced with a predator bird on its own. Cornered, a cheel can take on a murder—even injured, we're—well, let me demonstrate.'

Tooth's talons slashed viciously at Miao's face. She felt the rush of air on her whiskers, felt the claw miss her nose by a millimetre—andthen the cheel was offering her a wet leaf, impaled on one of his deadly, curving nails. 'It was stuck on your cheek,' he said, 'kind of annoying to look at.'

Miao had too much self-control to mew, but she quickly washed a paw. 'I see what you mean about speed,' she said.

'Crows are cowards,' Tooth continued. 'They don't like getting hurt. So instead, they take turns coming up close to the predator, close enough to disturb our flight patterns and paths, but pulling back before they get hurt. If they come in one after another, weaving and ducking around a predator, especially a wounded one, they'll tire the predator out, cause confusion, get the raptor to use up all its energy in useless attacks. And then, once the predator's weakened, that's when the whole murder will attack…' He turned away and ruffled the ends of his feathers. 'So that's how Stoop died.'

Miao hesitated, and then gingerly, not knowing if Tooth would be angered, she put her head up and very quickly, brushed her head against the hawk's feathery face. Tooth jerked his head back, his eyes flaring bright red for a second, and then stilled.

'No, Tooth,' she said gently. 'That wasn't how your mother died.'

Stoop's wings drooped, continued Miao. She appeared to be losing height, but awkward as she was, she kept ahead of the crows, using her right talon to fend off attackers.

'Don't worry, Miao ji,' said a squeaky voice near my paw. 'Stoop knows what she's doing.'

'Does she?' I said sharply—I wasn't used to talking to squirrels.

'Flying by the side of your foes when you're badly injured doesn't seem like much of a plan to me, squirrel.' Ao kept her squinty eyes on me. 'Been watching Stoop for many days, Jao and I have. Stoop often flew near us but never hurt us, never even threatened us. It was different with the crows. First, the crows went after my mum. Then the crows went after my dad. Thenthere were just the two of us. We didn't know what to do. We sat at the top of the trees, scared to come down to the ground and feed, scared to look for shelter. Every time we came down the tree trunk, the crows attacked. Then one evening, there was Stoop, resting on the high branch above our heads.'

The squirrel took a deep breath, her fluffy tail quivering nervously.

'Jao took his courage in both paws and said, "Cheel, cheel, may we speak?" She whipped around, her red eyes glaring at us, but in curiosity, not challenge. I was scared. But Jao said, "Cheel, maybe you'll kill us, maybe you won't, but those crows, they're going to kill us anyway. That's the truth. So we're asking for help. Cheel, you're a predator, one of the big ones. We're just squirrels, us little ones.

But perhaps, sometimes, the big ones look out for the little ones?"'

Jao pulled his head out of his bushy tail and nodded in confirmation. Ao touched her tail to his, gently, and went on. 'Stoop stared at us for a long, long time. She said nothing, just took us in with her tired red eyes. So I spoke up next, seeing that Jao had been so brave. I told her about our mum, our dad, what the crows did to so many of the little ones. And as I was speaking, suddenly, Stoop put her beak out and picked me up by the middle. She brought me close to her great sharp talons, and I thought, this is it: a cheel will get me instead of the crows. I hoped she would kill me fast. But instead, she just looked me over, closely. And then she put me down, and said, almost to herself, "This has gone on too long." It was the next day that she flew in, landing on our branch, and told us: "Get on my back".'

Jao nodded, holding his paws together as he took up the tale.

'We were scared, my teeth chattered and I could hear Ao squeaking in fright, but we got on and we stayed on, holding hard to Stoop's feathers. She took us first to the roof—over there, that house, can you see it?—and then she told us what she planned to do. You know the rest; she's brought us to you, and now she's off putting her plan into action. Stoop knows exactly what she's doing. It's all under control.' I looked up at the sky. The crows were close to the perimeter of Nizamuddin now, near the dargah, and three of them were tagging the small black dot that was Stoop's form in the sky. It seemed as though she was towing a flotilla of crows behind her; the trees down in our park were bare and empty. They had to duck every so often to avoid the thick tangle of electric lines, and the brightly coloured kites the Bigfeet kids were flying from the roofs. As we watched, the trio slashed at Stoop, in arrow formation; she wheeled sideways, and stabbed back at them, but again, she was dropping, and then the trio closed in on her, and she went into a steep dive, the crows cawing in celebration as they followed.

Jao squeaked. 'Over there,' he said. 'Do you see?'

Stoop did a triple roll and shot, unbelievably, upwards, slicing through the black wave of crows like a claw going through butter. There was no sign of a damaged wing now, no sign of distress as she arced towards the sky.

Too late, the crows saw the still dots hovering motionless at the corners of the park. Cheels from the next colony, dozens of them, scattered at intervals across the horizon in tight knots of ten or so; others rose up now from the surrounding buildings, from the edges of the roofs and the crowns of the telephone poles and trees that were scattered through the dargah. Led by Conquer, they formed a kind of net around the confused cloud of crows, hemming them in, almost herding them, the way dogs will sometimes herd their pups. And now, the crows could see that Stoop had led them into a trap—straight towards the tangle of power lines that crisscrossed the perimeter of the dargah.

Without Bitterbite and Bakbuk to guide them, the crows were in disarray. Some flew into the powerlines, and with more and more birds colliding into each other, they were soon in a tremendous tangle—and then there was a spark and a horrible smell, and first one and then another of the powerlines went up in flames, taking more crows with them. Three of the best crow fighters tried to take on Conquerhimself, but the feathers flew as the massive cheel fought back, and soon he rose triumphant, if somewhat worse for wear, above the vanquished crows. A few murders veered to the right and the left, but the cheels closed formation on them and the air was thick with torn wings and hoarse cries as the crows got the worst of the battle. Some—a small cluster towards the back of the murder—managed to get away, screeching their dismay and surrender as they plunged for the safety of the trees, clearly on the run. We never saw them again. It was over in a matter of minutes, and I saw Neferkitty and some of the toms slump to the ground, grateful for the rest. Jao and Ao chittered behind us in celebration. 'Incredible,' wuffed Tommy—he and the stray dogs had watched the rout in wonder. I knew what he meant; it had all happened so fast, and now the cheel squadrons were reforming into a large, neat arrowhead. It was a stately, soaring group of cheels that came to roost in the rooftops of Nizamuddin—this very roof, Tooth.

Stoop arced overhead as Conquer watched her proudly. 'Little ones,' she called, streaking down so low between the trees that she almost brushed our heads, 'I kept my promise, little ones! What a day, kya, Miao? Did you like the show?'

And then she was off again, soaring, rolling and diving, a beautiful black streak across the sky, hitchhiking the winds and gliding along. Up on the roof, I saw her Wing Commander, Slash, spread his feathers out in sudden alarm. He gave a loud startled call. 'Stoop! Watch out!'

She was doing her aerobatics between the edges of the roofs of the dargah and the long black power cables, and she was, not for the first time, too close, far too close. She heard Slash's alarm call, flicked her tail feathers into a closed fan and dived smoothly downwards, easily avoiding the ominous dark line of the cables, streaking far above its deadly width, towards us. I saw Slash shift his claws back on his perch, riffing his feathers back into shape in relief.

She looked so beautiful in that moment, Tooth. Your mother had a knack of cutting through the air cleanly, her wings held back justan inch more than the other cheels. The sun glinted off the brown feathers on her back, turning them gold. And then: 'Slash! Have you ever seen an upwards triple roll?' she called as she plummeted all the way back down, hovering in the air like a hummingbird rather than a cheel, near a first-floor parapet. Slash tensed: 'Stoop! No, it's too dangerous!' he said, and his voice shrilled with alarm. 'Come back!' called Ao. 'Come down!' squeaked Jao.

But she had already risen into the air, spinning like a golden top, doing a perfect roll upwards into the clear blue sky, then a second, skating easily higher on a sudden tug from a sharp breeze, and then the third, spectacular, looping roll. There she was, a golden-brown streak of light, and we saw her rise higher, higher, upside down now.

And then Slash called out again, his hoarse voice urgent and harsh, as a smoking power cable, damaged from the battle, erupted in a shower of sparks.

We couldn't tell her golden feathers from the flames.

For a long while, there was no conversation—only silence and the rain. Miao said nothing, just sat next to the cheel, both of them gazing out and down into the park, and if they saw a slim, graceful golden-brown phantom skimming the trees and the rooftops, neither of them said so.

Finally, Tooth turned back to Miao. 'I'll have to speak to Conquer and to Claw, but this is what we can offer. We won't start your fight for you, Miao. We won't attack first. We won't take orders from any cat but you or Katar. But when you need our help, we'll be there.'

Miao let her whiskers relax, wanting to give Tooth another headrub, but knowing from the stiffness in his maxillary feathers and the way his talons tightly gripped the edge of the roof that the cheel wouldn't welcome a touch at this moment. 'Thank you, Tooth,' she said and began to make her descent. As she went down the stairs in brief hops, Tooth called out to her. 'Miao?' he said. Yes, Tooth?'

'Just tell the little ones in Nizamuddin, the mice and the chuchunders and the sparrows...tell the little ones it'll be all right.'

And then the raptor turned his head back to the rain, which was falling in a steady torrent.

POONACHI[*]

PERUMAL MURUGAN

Translated from the Tamil by N. Kalyan Raman

The old man climbed the hillock and stepped into the field. He had plucked some grass and filled a basket with it. After laying the kid on the bed of grass, he lifted the basket and placed it on his head, and started walking. Arriving as a smoky haze, darkness had begun to settle slowly across the crimson sky in the west. It was time to head homeward. Someone like that giant, with his long strides, would probably have got there in no time.

The old man's thatched shed was at a walking distance from the field. He had to pass the field, take the mud track, then cross the lake shore and trudge along the very long foot trail that wound through the stretch of semi-arid fields in order to reach home.

By the time he got on the foot trail, his shadow had begun to fade. He took long strides, in a hurry to reach home before it was too dark to see ahead. There were shorn fields all across the stretch. Here and there, he saw a few men who were taking their goats back home after grazing them on the new grass. But for this goat kid, he would have been home by now with the basket of grass.

As he walked on, he suddenly heard the sound of the kid crying, like a steady hum. The worm of a kid had not only eaten up his time, she was now crying; it provoked him to abuse her. Then he saw a bunch of goatherds come running towards him from all four directions, yelling, 'Dhooyi, dhooyi.' The old man stopped in his tracks, sensing

[*]Extracted from *Poonachi: Or the Story of a Black Goat.*

that something was amiss. A gust of wind seemed to be pushing the basket off his head. He held on to it tightly. A man rushed forward, caught the old man by the arm and steadied him. Otherwise, he would have fallen face down in the dirt. He lifted the basket off the old man's head and kept it on the ground. After recovering his wits, the old man asked breathlessly, 'What's happening?'

'Look over there,' the man said, pointing to the west. Flapping its wings, a large bird was flying away towards the hill where it was already dark.

'What do you have in the basket that a large bird would hunt?' Two or three men approached him with the question. 'Is it a rat that you caught in the field?'

Meanwhile, the kid stood up slowly inside the basket and moaned: 'Mmmm.' Still shaken, the old man was unable to speak.

'You had this big black worm in the basket. That's why the eagle struck,' laughed one man as he picked up the kid.

'This is a goat kid, 'pa,' said another.

The kid wriggled like a worm in the hands of the man who had picked it up. All the goatherds looked at it in wonder. 'Is she really a goat kid?'

They took her in their hands and examined her. The old man was embarrassed. If the goatherds had not spotted the eagle swooping down on the basket, it would have snatched the kid in its talons and eaten her by now.

'Look at the kid. This moment of peril must have been in her destiny,' the old man thought to himself. Then he addressed the goatherds: 'Like providence, you people turned up at the right time to help me. On top of losing the kid, I might have taken a fall with the basket and broken a limb. What would I have done then? There's an old woman at home. She feeds me every day because I do a little work and earn something. If I am laid up in bed with a broken limb, would she look after me?'

A goatherd in a loincloth held the kid in his hand and said, 'Her belly is empty,' pa. Look at her. She is so hungry she can't even open her eyes.' He called out, 'Bu-ck-oo, bu-ck-oo' and his goats came running to him. He picked a nanny goat and held the kid under her udder. The kid was too weak to reach for the udder, so he crammed the nanny goat's teat into her mouth. It was perhaps the first time the kid was trying to hold a teat in her mouth. After a bit of a struggle, she managed to hold it firmly and sucked on it. When the first drops of milk touched her tongue, she discovered a new taste and began to suckle eagerly.

'The kid is quite smart,' said the man who had arranged to feed her. After a few sucks had drenched her belly, her jaw began to ache and the kid let go of the teat. 'Go on, drink a little more. It'll make sure that you pass the night without hunger pangs,' the young man said and made her suckle some more. Then he picked her up and handed her over to the old man. 'She looks like a worm, but with her attitude, she is already an adult,' he said.

The men set out behind their herds. After placing the kid safely inside the basket and covering her with grass, the old man started walking on the trail. 'I don't know how many more hazards this creature will have to face. Will she overcome all of them or go under? Who knows what is fated for her?' he mused.

The old woman didn't like the look or sound of the kid. She scowled at her husband. 'Where did you pick up this kitten from? Why do we need her?' When the old man told her she was a goat kid, she picked her up and exclaimed in amazement: 'Yes, she *is* a goat kid.'

All night, they went over the story of how the kid had come into their hands. They already owned two goats. One of them had littered just a month ago. Three kids: two male and one female. All three jumped and played around in their front yard. The other goat was pregnant and would deliver about a month from now. 'They had sold the kids from her previous litter to the butcher only ten days ago. They also owned a buffalo calf, a heifer. If she grazed for another year, she would be old enough to mate, and they could sell her.

The couple spent their days raising a few crops in the half acre of land adjoining their thatched shed, grazing their goats and tending the buffalo calf. It fell to the old man to take the goats to the fields for grazing and fetch fodder for the goats and the calf. Using that as an excuse, he liked to wander across the fields and villages, bantering with people at large and enjoying a few laughs. His wife rarely went out anywhere. Since their needs were very few, she visited the market fair once a month to buy groceries. They also visited their daughter's home once a year for the annual festival at the village temple, which involved being away for a fortnight. She was their only daughter, and they had no other wish than to pass the remainder of their lives as serenely as they had done all these years.

That same night the old lady gave the goat kid that resembled a kitten a nickname: Poonachi. She once had a cat by the same name. In memory of that beloved cat, this goat kid too was named Poonachi. She once had a cat by the same name. In memory of that beloved cat, this goat too was named Poonachi. They had acquired her without spending a penny. Now they had to look after her somehow. Her husband had told her a vague story about meeting a demon who looked like Bakasuran and receiving the kid from him as a gift. She wondered if he could have stolen it from a goatherd. Someone might come looking for it tomorrow. Maybe her husband had told her the story only to cover up his crime?

The old woman was not used to lighting lamps at night. The couple ate their evening meal and went to bed when it was still dusk. That night, though, she took a large earthen lamp and filled it with castor oil extracted the year before. There was no cotton for a wick. She tore off a strip from a discarded loincloth of her husband's and fashioned it into a wick.

She looked at the kid under the lamplight in that shed as though she were seeing her own child after a long time. There was no bald spot or bruise anywhere on her body. The kid was all black. As she stared at the lamp, her wide open eyes were starkly visible. There was a trace of fatigue on her face. The old woman thought the kid looked haggard because she had not been fed properly. She must be just a couple of days old. A determination that she must somehow raise this kid to adulthood took root in her heart.

She called the old man to come and see the kid. She looked like a black lump glittering in the lamplight in that pitch-black night.

He pulled fondly at her flapping ears and said, 'Aren't you lucky to come and live here?'

It had been a long time since there was such pleasant chit-chat between the couple. Because of the kid's sudden entry into their lives, they ended up talking a while about old days.

A TALE OF ANIMALS*

MOTI LAL KEMMU

Translated from the Hindi by
Siddhartha Gigoo and Tej K. Zadoo

Curfew was imposed in Vananchal and the animals fell silent. After two days, when the curfew was relaxed for a few hours, posters were found pasted on trees warning the hangul and other deer to leave Vananchal forever. The wolves had taken on the responsibility of terrorising and killing some hangul and deer.

Upon seeing the deteriorating state of affairs, the violent atmosphere, the bloodshed, and the collapse of law and order in Vananchal, the authorities replaced the governor of the forest. New problems arose. Unknown animals started setting everything on fire. The sacked governor made a fiery speech and held the central government responsible for the mess. He made a startling revelation that a huge quantity of arms and ammunition had been smuggled from across the border to fuel the mayhem. Jackals were actively involved in killing others. The armed forces deployed on the border were also held responsible by the former governor for the worsening situation.

The new governor clearly stated that steps would be taken to eliminate those spreading terror in Vananchal. His speech, which was full of warnings, was broadcast on the radio.

After two days, when the curfew was lifted for some hours, a jackal attacked some deer while they were on their way to a river to quench their thirst. When the greviously wounded deer collapsed

*Extracted from *Pashugatha*.

to the ground, the jackal shouted: 'This is your fate, you informants. To die. Leave Vananchal immediately or else face the consequences. This place is ours.'

Such killings of innocent animals forced the new governor to put the whole of Vananchal under curfew for an indefinite period. In spite of the curfew one could sense the frantic movement of animals in the nooks and corners of the forest. Whenever the curfew was relaxed, the jackals would protest against the high-handedness of the administration. At first, the newspapers carried the pictures of deer which had been killed by the jackals. Soon, the tone of the editorials and reports changed. One could sense that the newspapers were under threat too. The deer and hangul were warned and asked to leave Vananchal. The carcass of a prominent deer, a leader, was found by police personnel and then cremated.

In the area inhabited by the jackals there was widespread resentment and anger against the imposition of curfew. There were strict restrictions on their movements. However, the jackals hit upon alternative ways to circumvent any restrictions. They got the wolves, bears and foxes together, and came out in hordes to announce their intent. Voices were heard all over Vananchal. 'Vananchal will be free.' When the authorities arrested Gidadjoo, the leader of the jackals, the jackals got angry and set fire to the trees. Some jackals took revenge by killing some more deer.

In this chaos, nobody knew how many deer and hangul had been killed and how many fled Vananchal.

An old jackal lived alongside the deer and hangul. The jackal visited the deer at night and asked them to flee Vananchal because they were not safe there any more. 'Save your lives,' said the old jackal to the deer. 'Don't trust us. The days of living in harmony and peaceful co-existence are gone. Our leaders are dangerous. You will be killed if you stay here. Your fodder will be burnt. Your shelters will be destroyed. Remember, you are the minority. You will be wiped out in no time. If you want to save your lives, run away from here. Leave Vananchal to the jackals. No one will save you. The authorities have become corrupt. They will side with the jackals...'

On hearing the words of the old jackal, a young deer addressed the others, 'We can run away. But can we tolerate the pain and pangs of leaving our Vananchal? This forest is ours. We have been living here for centuries, much before the jackals came into the picture. The wolves and jackals want our ouster.'

'Don't be emotional,' said a skinny deer. 'If we want to save ourselves we must run away from Vananchal. This place has already been snatched from us. It has been taken over by hungry jackals from the forest nearby. We are too puny to put up a fight. Don't you see we are being hunted down one by one? Those who left didn't talk to others about it. They did not even confide in others. They just bundled their belongings and ran away quietly...'

'If we survive, we can come back,' said the deer in a chorus. 'But for now, we must not wait...'

While the hangul and deer were debating whether to flee Vananchal or not, a sound blared out. Shoon, shoon, shoon... Everyone was startled and afraid. The deer and hangul fell silent. After some time when the hangul and deer mustered the courage to check what was going on, they found the old jackal lying in a pool of blood. He was trembling as the life oozed out of him. 'They shot me...the wild beasts came and did this to me,' the dying jackal cried, 'see what they have done...O God...'

'The old jackal has been killed,' an old deer whispered in fear, 'This is the final warning...'

A young deer read the message that had been carved into the bark of a tree next to where the old jackal now lay dead: 'We will kill all informers. The old jackal was an informer. We are fighting for freedom and the old jackal was supporting the hangul and deer.'

The young deer whispered to the others, 'If this is the fate of a jackal, what will be ours?'

Sometime later, a speeding police vehicle stopped abruptly near the deer-hangul lane. Three policemen took the body of a young hangul out of the jeep and placed it on the ground. Soon after, they left. The deer and hangul watched in horror. Even the hangul working for the Government weren't safe.

The same night, when the deer and hangul fearfully huddled in their shelter, unable to sleep, loud voices were heard all across Vananchal:

He will come and get us freedom.
He who will be called Sarhadi, he will sacrifice his life.
High-handedness of the authorities will not be allowed.
This government is a government of slaves.
We need a free government, our own government.
We have nurtured Vananchal with our blood.
This Vananchal is ours.
Today or tomorrow, we will get our freedom.
You deer and hangul, leave our Vananchal
While there still is time, leave Vananchal.

For the whole night, the voices blared out, spreading terror and fear. Herds of deer and hangul started to leave Vananchal for alien forests. The next morning, the forest was ablaze. The jackals and wolves occupied the shelters of the deer and hangul.

Years later, when there were no deer and hangul left in Vananchal, the jackals and wolves asked the same question over and over again: 'Why did the deer and hangul run away from here?'

ELEPHANT AT SEA

KANISHK THAROOR

In the late summer of 1979, the Second Secretary of the Indian embassy to Morocco received a cable that undid his considerable years of training and left him floundering. The message read simply: 'Elephant en route.' Was it some sort of code? Further investigation only deepened his confusion. The cable had come from the customs office in Cochin, a port in the south of India. No, the customs officials reported back to him, it wasn't code. It was an elephant—an elephant, that along with its mahout, was now very much headed by ship to Casablanca. The Second Secretary probed: why send an elephant? Here at the customs office, the reply came, we handle only the movement of goods; for the movement of reasons, please refer your inquiry to the Ministry of External Affairs.

The Second Secretary telegrammed his colleagues in the ministry in Delhi. With telegrams to the ministry, it was important, first, to be terse so that you were considered economical and, second, to be sharp so that in the midst of reams of communication from outposts around the world, your message would be noticed. WHY SHIP ELEPHANT STOP EMBASSY ALREADY HAS CARS STOP. No one in the ministry seemed to know anything about the elephant. A flummoxed telegram returned to the embassy. WHAT ELEPHANT STOP IS THIS CODE STOP. Embarrassed, the Second Secretary finally consulted the ambassador, who knew through long experience that it was pointless to question the whims of the capital. Marvellous, the ambassador said smoothing his moustache, an elephant, just what we need, and they couldn't even send it to us, no, they're sending it to Casablanca. You'll have to arrange for the thing to be met and picked up. He sprayed himself with cologne and mused: If an elephant can even be picked up.

That night the Second Secretary lay awake in bed, resenting the sheets, resenting the pillow, resenting the indifference of his work, resenting Morocco, resenting Arabic for its impossible, secret throatiness, and resenting, with what little bitterness was left to him, the unknown buffoon who would make diplomacy out of elephants.

The buffoon was not, as he imagined, some self-satisfied civil servant in South Block, but the princess of Morocco. Explanation arrived via telex from a friend in the ministry who owed him a few favours and so mustered the initiative to ask around.

The story of the elephant had begun six years earlier in the same Indian embassy in Rabat. At one of those habitual functions whose purpose seems so obvious in the preparation but disappears in the operation, the little Moroccan princess had come to the embassy and frozen before a picture of an elephant. It was among the many stock images—all approved by the ministry of tourism—that lined the lobby of the embassy: dawn over the Himalayan ranges; houseboats on the backwaters; the Taj Mahal rosy in its cushion of smog; a bright tractor devastating a field of wheat. The princess only had eyes for the elephant. Her wordless arm extended towards the picture, pointing. C'est un éléphant, said the embassy official tasked with escorting the princess. She remained transfixed. Vous aimez les éléphants? the unlucky man suggested. It seemed the princess did love elephants because she wouldn't move. The official, who had in previous posts offered counsel on trade policy with Indonesia and arms deals with the Soviet Union, looked around for help before lowering himself to her level. Mademoiselle, vous voulez un éléphant? he asked with the desperation stoked in him by all children—never mind the princess of Morocco. She turned, smiled, and gave him the smallest gift of a nod. It was enough. The official eventually spoke to the then ambassador who put in the request to Delhi, recommending the delivery of an elephant to satisfy the princess and to strengthen a bilateral friendship. The request passed through the appropriate channels at the usual speeds. Six years later, the creature was irrevocably on its way.

The Second Secretary received updates about the elephant's

progress from various consular staff. In Yemen, it posed for photographs in front of the oldest coffee house in Aden. It bumped a football back and forth with boys on the beach in Alexandria. In Algiers, veterans of the war against the French held a reception in its honour; the Indian elephant was, in their words, a symbol of the ancient wisdom of a civilization that had inspired the global struggle against western imperialism. After it passed through Gibraltar, the Second Secretary got an excited telegram from the British naval high command. BRILLIANT STOP TOP PACHYDERM STOP.

The Moroccans were less enthused. What are we to do with it? they said. Casablanca's zoo has enough African elephants and there's no space for an Indian one. The Second Secretary protested. It's for the princess, he reminded them, she asked for it. Well, she may have, the Moroccans said, but she's away studying sociology in Paris now and has no interest in elephants. So you might have to take the thing back.

Only the Indian ambassador's persistence at a cocktail party won their grudging cooperation. It was agreed that the elephant would be specially housed in a portion of the royal gardens in Rabat. How it would get there was another matter altogether. The Moroccans insisted they had no trucks big enough to carry the creature between the two cities. This was a time of war and their heaviest military vehicles were all rumbling around the south. Worse, thanks to the mischief of Polisario terrorists, the single rail line between Casablanca and the capital was broken. But these inconveniences, the Moroccans claimed, shouldn't be a problem. After all, the elephant is its own means of transportation.

The Second Secretary was sent to Casablanca to escort the elephant back to Rabat. It took some time to find an appropriate launch in which to ferry the creature to port. When it finally disembarked, the small police band awaiting its arrival had grown sour in the heat. They rushed through the welcoming ditty and swiftly packed away their trombones. The reporters also sped through their work. They found the mahout altogether too clothed. As he perched on the elephant's back, they had him remove his shirt and roll up his trousers to look more convincing for the cameras, all knobby knees and gleaming skin. Instead of asking the mahout questions about the elephant, they surrounded the Second Secretary—he was wearing a suit. We are proud to share the joy of elephants with the people of Morocco, he said. The haathi belongs not to one nation, but to all.

What little the Second Secretary knew about elephants came from an urban childhood of zoos and encyclopaedias. As a measure of their robust memories, elephants hold grudges and harbour very finely developed notions of revenge. Elephants have sensitive feet capable of feeling through the earth, from long distances away, the approach of other elephants, or of rainstorms, or of bulldozers. Studies have shown that they can recognize their own reflections, suggesting that, however rudimentary, there may exist among elephants an amorphous theory of mind.

In sum, these scraps formed an altogether surreal idea of the elephant, one incommensurate with the full being in front of him, dappled with cooling splashes of mud, blinking restlessly and curling its trunk around the legs of its mahout. The mahout supplied more practical information. In its present ship-weary condition, the elephant could walk at most forty kilometres at a single stretch, probably no more than twenty-five. How far is it to the capital? he asked. He spoke no Hindi and the Second Secretary spoke no Malayalam, so they talked in a manner of English. A little more than ninety kilometres to Rabat, the Second Secretary said. Hoisting himself on to the elephant, the mahout surveyed the road leading out from the docks through the flat outskirts of Casablanca. For all the immensity of this unknown continent, the world always seemed more manageable from the back of an elephant. He smiled at the Second Secretary. Ninety of their Moroccan kilometres or ninety of ours? What are you talking about, the Second Secretary said, there's no difference. The mahout shook his head. You and I may not be able to tell the difference, but the elephant can.

In consultation with the two Moroccan gendarmes assigned to them, they agreed to break journey several times en route to Rabat. The convoy set out from Casablanca in the middle of the afternoon. The gendarmes led in their battered white car, its red lettering chipped and peeling. The Second Secretary brought up the rear in the embassy's sedan. In the middle, the mahout set a gentle tempo. The elephant wore an anklet that, wrapped around a man, would have had all the thickness of chains. Its every step tinkled with the jewellery of another land.

Perhaps because it was on its way to await the uncertain pleasure of a princess, or perhaps because it had already travelled so far, the elephant chose not to exert itself. But it quickened its pace whenever the coastal road veered west towards the Atlantic. The change would have been imperceptible to observers—and there were many on the busy highway—but the mahout felt it in his thighs. Each time the cobalt ocean wheeled into view, the creature's muscles seemed to quiver with new desire. It was an urge all the more palpable in its restraint; elephants are polite creatures of typically conservative temperament. Yet it was enough of a rumble and churn for the mahout to sense that his mount was already missing the sea.

At dusk, the elephant drank from a pond in the golf course of Mohammedia, a pleasant enough beach town that brushed up against Morocco's only oil refinery. The last of the day's players lofted their balls in long arcs overhead before descending on the fairway and finding the creature asleep in a bunker. It lay on its side, flanked by the apologetic guards, its heavy breathing raising little tempests of sand. Nobody protested. Golf can only be improved by the intrusion of an elephant, even a snoring one.

The Second Secretary was given accommodation in the clubhouse, in a room glowing with trophies and the lidless glare of the nearby refinery. He smoked and dipped at a plate of zaalouk. The mahout came in but declined the invitation to share in the dish. He had already eaten with the policemen. The Second Secretary gestured to a couch for the mahout to sleep on. The man looked restless. No, I'll stay with the elephant, he said, this is our first night back on land after weeks... It will rest poorly without me, and I without it. The Second Secretary shrugged and returned to his puréed eggplant, only to be surprised by the touch of the mahout's hand on his shoulder. In the parallel universe of their own country, such contact would be almost unimaginable, a movement far too intimate to cross the wide gulf of rank. Indians turn into more equal beings when not at home.

Tell me truthfully, the mahout leaned forward, are there no other elephants in Rabat? The Second Secretary sighed. I've told you already, it will have to be kept by itself. The royal gardeners can only manage one elephant. It will have all its creature comforts...don't worry. The mahout listened, see-sawing his head from side to side. This was the strongest and happiest elephant he had ever known, but he feared that it would struggle with its solitude. Like humans, elephants yearn for other elephants. It will be lonely, he said, it will need distractions. Annoyed, the Second Secretary promised they would make sure that it was the most distracted elephant in Africa. He unlaced his shoes and stretched out to sleep.

A few hours later, with the red and orange light of the refinery's towers angling upon his face, he awoke to find the mahout sitting cross-legged in front of him. I'm sorry to disturb you, the mahout said, but promise me something: that you won't let them use it in the circus. In the circus? The Second Secretary said. The mahout climbed to his feet and paced about the room. In the circus, yes... I have heard about the way the firangs treat elephants, like dolls, like puppets, like cartoons. He grew more animated still. They make them dance, they make them ride cycles, they make them stand on their heads... Sometimes, they think it is amusing to have the animals sit down to tea as if elephants were old women...this can't be its fate. The Second Secretary sat up. We won't let that happen, he said. Besides, you have nothing to worry about; these people aren't firangs, they're Moroccans, they're so much like us...just go to sleep.

But mahouts sleep as fitfully as elephants, and when the Second Secretary rose at dawn to perform his ablutions, he found the man at the door of the clubhouse, standing in a pose of total stillness, at war with the anxious writhing of his eyebrows. The mahout burst into speech at the sight of the secretary. These royal gardens, are they near the water? The water? The Second Secretary blinked. Yes, the water, the ocean. I have no idea, the Second Secretary replied. The mahout held the Second Secretary's hand in both of his. The elephant...for it to be happy, it must be near the sea.

As he shaved, the Second Secretary muttered to himself about the mahout. All the man has to do is deliver the elephant to Rabat and then the government will give him a tidy cheque and send him home by plane. How many mahouts ever see the inside of a plane? He'll never again get to be in a plane. He can tell his parents, his wife, his children, if he has any, his grandchildren in the future, that he was in a plane. And they'll tell all their friends and enemies and the mahout will be famous forever throughout his village. Yet this madman keeps me awake all night with his ridiculous demands for an elephant nobody actually wants. If he fusses any more, we'll return him by boat. What glory is there in a boat?

What the Second Secretary did not know—and what the mahout found impossible to explain—was that, for the elephant at least, travel by boat was utterly glorious. Before they left India, the mahout had worried about the creature's well-being. How would it cope in steerage for all those cramped weeks? Would it endure the din of the ship's innards, the engines and pipes pumping at all times, soot-faced engineers swinging like monkeys from the levers? Surely, the clamour of a mechanical universe would depress a creature that loved nothing more at the end of the day than lowering itself into mud. The only consolation the mahout could find was that he too was terrified of the ship. There was a solidarity to be had between two beings who had never travelled further than Kozhikode, two beings for whom the rusting expanse of an ocean-going ship was only ever something to behold, not enter. In its salty dark, the mahout imagined, they would comfort each other, leaning close, pressing head to trunk.

It was not to be. While the mahout lurched from deck to deck vomiting, the elephant thrilled to life at sea. It trumpeted every time the captain sounded the great foghorn. The ship's sailors fawned over the creature, playing it music, showering it with nuts and chocolate. There were pleasures to be had even in its hold in the cargo bay, which rattled with the vigour of the ship's machinery. One morning, the mahout discovered the elephant rumbling. Serenely, it produced a low and eerie noise that seemed to come from its most interior parts. The mahout rushed to its side and held it as best as he could, trying to calm the animal. A moment's listening dispelled his fears; in perfect pitch, the elephant was merely mimicking the sound of the engines, as if through imitation it could bridge the divide between thought and matter and speak with the grey monstrosity of the ship.

On deck, the elephant stormed from side to side, relishing the heave of the ship, the rise and prostration of the bow as it carved its mass through the blue. The mahout studied the joy of the elephant with awe. He thought the elephant would grow bored—as he swiftly did—of the sea, but the wonder never wore off. As the wind sprayed it with foam, the creature seemed to admire the uninterrupted ocean in a kind of a rapture, a dervish-like ecstasy. It once occurred to the mahout that this might be the closest he would ever get to touching the divine: the elephant forgetting its elephantness in the vista of the sea, the veils of moksha parted, the creature poking its trunk into the beyond and feeling its way towards cosmic oneness. Then the motion of the vessel shook the mahout's insides loose. He staggered to the rim of the stern and emptied himself into the deep.

The sailors also felt the magic of the elephant's presence. Once, in the Indian Ocean, a solitary whale bobbed into view. This was hardly an unusual sight for the tanker's crew but they watched as the whale crested the surface and snorted through its blowhole. They hoped at that moment for a response from the elephant, a trumpet, a bellow, a spout of water from its trunk, some little signal of recognition. After all, what was the whale but the elephant of the sea? These two creatures were kin in bulk and grace, breathing the most air through the largest lungs in a world rightfully made for them. There could be no better omen than that shared understanding. For men who commit their bodies to the ocean, who surrender childhoods on paddy fields and factory floors for the education of currents and gales on the shipways, the communion of these beasts would be a vindication of their lives. But the sailors were disappointed. Standing on the starboard side, the elephant had not seen the whale at all, or if it had, it chose to ignore it, keeping its eyes fixed instead in contemplation of the water.

On the golf course, the mahout found the elephant by the pond, its trunk lingering at its feet. He massaged the hard knot of muscle on its lower back, the corbelled arch that lifted the creature's mass from the earth. As he readied the elephant for the onward march, he wondered whether a journey across the seas had the ability to change us. When the elephant regarded its reflection in the still water, did it see a being transformed? Could it? Maybe it was presumptuous of the mahout to think so grandly of the elephant's capacities, its self-awareness, its very sense of the possibility of a self. Perhaps this sad-eyed creature merely looked at the pond and thought: What a miserable excuse for a sea.

The convoy reached Skhirat in the early evening. On the way, the mahout had suggested to Adil, one of the Moroccan gendarmes (he had learned their names; the other was Marouane), that he come sit on the back of the elephant. Adil stripped off his uniform jacket, approached the elephant from the front, hesitated, crept around the side and kept creeping till he made a full circle, and looked imploringly up at the mahout. The mahout laughed. He scratched the back of the elephant's head and pressed one knee against its neck. It dipped to the ground. Adil tried to look the creature in the eye for reassurance, but it stared beyond him up the road, its ears flapping like fans. He grasped the mahout's forearm and heaved himself up, gripping the hairy hide with both hands as the elephant rose to its feet and lurched on.

Elephants respond to confidence, the mahout said, to certainty. You do not need to charm them so much as direct them... Like us, they are logical creatures, and like us, they understand that the order of the universe dictates to them a certain place, a certain rank, a certain dependence on the demands of others. The mahout spoke in Malayalam, but Adil listened to the tumbling words anyway, trying his best not to look at the road swaying beneath him. The truth is, the mahout continued, that driving an elephant does not require intuition or special intelligence, only a willingness to command...more than that, a belief in your command.

Command was in his blood. The mahout was raised to ride elephants, as was his father, and his father's father, and as far as he knew all the males of their line snaking back to some letterless past when man first wrestled the beast into obedience. No better life had presented itself to him than that of ordering elephants. He was aware that many in his village were jealous of his trade, the princely work that saved him from the drudgery of the fields. When the news arrived that he would be sent with the elephant to Morocco, his family lit many candles to fend off the evil eye. You'll come back a big man, they said, and nobody wishes well for big men. What nonsense, he laughed them off, I'll come back just the same…this isn't my journey, it's the journey of the elephant, I'm only an appendage of flesh. Adil squirmed behind him and cars passed, honking. How true, the mahout thought, I am commanded to command. I am an instrument of command. I am an instrument.

From the trailing sedan, the Second Secretary watched the spectacle of the Moroccan gendarme clinging to the elephant. He was surprised to feel a degree of envy. No invitation to mount the elephant had been extended to him. If anyone should first get a turn on the elephant, he thought, it should be me, not that fellow. He filed this grievance away as yet more proof of the strangeness of the mahout and as further evidence, if he needed any more, of the unending injustice that was the daily life of a Second Secretary.

At Skhirat, Adil slumped nauseous from the back of the elephant, attempted a few steps, and tumbled to his knees. The children of the village roared at his collapse and flocked about the elephant. Marouane, the other gendarme, dispersed them as best he could, but they remained bubbling in the corners of the village square, pantomiming the elephant and its minders. Skhirat's mayor, who was also its lead cleric, came to shake hands with the visitors and admire the elephant. In normal circumstances, the village was used to strangers passing through; it was a stop on the Casablanca-Rabat rail line. But since the interruption of rail service, the place had grown dustier and quieter. Its people were happy to produce a welcome fit for any occasion. They brought trellised tables into the square. Pitchers of fresh juices, cups of tea, and miraculous tagines came steaming from nearby houses. All the village's luminaries—its post office clerk, its librarian, its accountant, its letter-writer, its chief constable (its only constable), its doctor, its farm veterinarian (who kept his distance from the elephant, eyeing the creature with trepidation), and so on—assembled to have a meal with the Second Secretary, who was made to repeat, over and over again, in slow French, the basic facts of his life and of his world. The children cheered as the elephant munched carrots dipped in harissa. The gathering continued till late in the evening. When the day's last azaan interrupted proceedings, the elephant raised its trunk towards the minaret and bellowed in its own fashion the call to prayer. All the men of the village made their way to the mosque except for the librarian, who patted the Second Secretary on the back and smuggled him home to share a bottle of arak.

During the night, the Second Secretary snored drunk on the librarian's sofa. Adil slept on a bench. The mahout tucked his chin into his knees and dozed against the slumbering bulk of the elephant. Marouane stood awake, vigilant for any mischievous children lurking at the edges of the square. Nothing happened until an hour before the morning azaan. A shape formed in the provincial gloom and drifted towards the elephant. It was the cleric-mayor. Peace be upon you, Marouane said. And you, the cleric-mayor returned. He rolled up the sleeves of his robe and worked his way around the horizontal elephant. I just want to check, he said half to himself, I just want to check. Marouane watched him dubiously. Check what? The cleric-mayor had already knelt by the elephant's loins. He startled. Well, I'm just curious if the creature is Muslim. In three strides, Marouane had grabbed him by the collar, dragged him away, and dropped him to the ground. You fool, he looked down on the older man, you bumpkin... Be decent and keep your crazy ideas to yourself. Does a donkey have religion? Can a donkey be Muslim? How can this animal be Muslim? The cleric-mayor straightened up and jabbed a finger into Marouane's uniform. Boy, he snarled, have some respect...that peaceful creature is more of a man than any of your kind will ever be.

The commotion woke the elephant and the mahout. Alarmed by the animal's surging to its feet, the cleric-mayor made apologetic noises and ghosted away. The mahout saw Marouane's agitation. He pointed at Adil sleeping on the bench, urging the gendarme to follow his colleague's example. Marouane nodded and tried to get to sleep. The elephant snorted. It stamped. It wrapped its trunk around the mahout's waist, hugging the man close. Whatever beliefs it did possess, it certainly disliked being roused from its dreams.

The mahout stood for a little while, stroking the elephant's trunk until it subsided once more to its knees, then rolled on to its side. They were alone in the village square. At this time before dawn in the mahout's own village, the roosters would be outdoing one another, the potholed roads would already be clanging with traffic, his family in their multitude would be scratching and groaning and clucking in the shared sleeping space. Morocco had so much room, so much silence. The mahout watched Skhirat take shape in the leavening dark. There was an enviable modesty to the even spread of low buildings, the humble bakery warming its ovens at the edge of the square, the grace of the mosque's silhouetted minaret, the peace of all its obscurity. He knew that this was a tiny country pinned between desert and sea. He knew that his own country was large by any estimation. And yet the calm of this small place felt infinite.

The elephant nuzzled his hand and murmured in its sleep. He buried his face in its ear. He whispered: Sleep well, my beauty, sleep well, my prince. If you dream, don't dream of home and don't dream of me. Dream of the sea. You and I are now so alone in this world... Dream of the sea, my life, dream of the sea. The elephant slept, but its trunk remained wrapped around the body of the mahout. It refused to release him. Only as light began to escape down from the eastern mountains did the elephant loosen its grip and let the mahout go.

Dawn came with the first azaan. Adil shook awake, as did Marouane. The village crawled into its quiet, habitual motion, making the small adjustment for the sleeping elephant at its centre. The Second Secretary staggered to his sedan for his toiletries. By the time he finished brushing his teeth next to the well, both the gendarmes stood before him, delivering the news as best they could that the mahout had disappeared.

The Second Secretary was incredulous. Disappeared? Impossible. Skhirat was mobilized to find the mahout. Children swarmed over the rooftops. Scooters buzzed down the road in both directions. Farmers turned over their cauliflowers. The chief constable furiously blew his whistle. There was no trace of the man. At the post office, the Second Secretary sent a message to the embassy. MAHOUT ABSCONDED STOP PLEASE ADVISE STOP. The Indian ambassador rang the post office. He's vanished, has he? The Second Secretary said he had. That's a real pity, the ambassador lamented, but what to do. It's pure physics... You propel an object a certain distance and you just can't expect it to come to rest, it will keep going forward. You take a man this far from his benighted village and he'll lose all interest in going back… so it goes. But, sir, the Second Secretary interjected, what do we do about the elephant? I don't know, the ambassador said, Rabat isn't all that far. Yes, the Second Secretary agreed, but how do we move the elephant? Why are you asking me? The ambassador snapped. If I were a mahout, I wouldn't be having this bloody conversation with you, would I? Just do whatever it is you need to do.

The Second Secretary sat on the hood of his sedan, staring at the elephant. It looked back at him, long-lashed and indifferent. He imagined the various means at his disposal that would convince this mass of flesh to proceed down the last stretch of highway to the capital. Perhaps he could lay down a trail of carrots all the way to Rabat. Or maybe if all the children pushed hard enough together, they could inch the elephant up the road. Or better yet, why not just leave the elephant here for the people of Skhirat? Why not be generous and gift them the problem?

Pitying the glum resignation of the Second Secretary, Adil was stirred to provide the solution himself. He came forward to the elephant and placed his hand behind its head, speaking to the creature in Arabic. It bent down. Gingerly, he clambered on top. The elephant returned to its feet. Adil's prodding steered it on to the road. For the first time in two days, the Second Secretary smiled. Allons-y! he cried. Allons-y!

It was imperative to get going before Adil's luck ran out and the elephant decided to stop cooperating. The convoy reassembled and bid a hasty goodbye to Skhirat. All the villagers waved, except for the cleric-mayor. From the window of the mosque, he had seen the mahout slink away in the early hours, seen the alien gleam in his eyes, the rootless abandon of the wanderer. It was a sad spirit, one the cleric-mayor could not comprehend and dared not interfere with; who was he—who had never seriously left his village nor contemplated doing so—to judge the actions of a stranger come to a strange place? So he kept his peace. God be with you, the cleric-mayor said to the departing rump of the elephant, God be with you.

They had reached the outskirts of Rabat when the handlers from the royal gardens finally emerged and relieved them of the elephant. For the cameras, the ambassador posed in front of the creature with Adil, the hero who saved the day and strengthened the bonds between the people of India and Morocco. It was reported to the newspapers that the mahout had been incubating a mysterious tropical disease that had killed him en route to Rabat. The ambassador asked the Second Secretary to ensure that Adil's wife received a very tasteful flower arrangement. The Second Secretary did as he was told.

When the princess returned during her holidays, she was enchanted by the elephant. She would lie next to it and read aloud her books of philosophy and critical theory. She introduced it to champagne. The princess was so enamoured of the creature that she insisted it accompany her on a trip to the beach. The elephant hurried over the dunes at the sight of the ocean, the clarion call of its trunk warning the waves. Everybody laughed as it played in the surf. It seemed to enjoy being knocked over in the shallows, finding its feet, retreating to the beach, and then wheeling its bulk around for another charge against the sea. It all seemed a pleasure, but the elephant was sad that no matter how earnestly it plunged into the water, the tide always drove it back to shore.

SNAKE

SUJATHA

Translated from the Tamil by Malini Seshadri

At Nanu Vadhyar's house next door they had recently bought a pile of tamarind firewood. It must have come from there, this snake. After a lengthy price negotiation in the morning, punctuated with protests of, 'What, Saami, you're leaving me with nothing to eat...look at the wood, see how fine it is...' the cartman finally unyoked the bull and tilted the cart to unload the firewood. I knew it would lie right there in front of their house for at least the next week, drying in the sun. But no one told me there was a snake inside that pile of wood.

In the evening Sivaraman came riding along in great style on his bicycle. He would pretend these visits of his were to see me, but, in fact, his purpose was to 'eye' my sister, Vatsala. In his laundered shirt and dhoti, wearing Cuticura powder, and with a broad streak of sandal paste on his forehead, he was convinced that all the young girls would swoon at the sight of him. We didn't want to puncture his delusional vanity, and so, Vatsala and I always waited till he had left before trading comments about him and laughing.

With its green body, metallic handles, elaborate, colourful decoration on the wheel hubs, and glittering carrier, Siva's Raleigh cycle looked rather like an ornate Vaiyali horse at a temple festival. When he got off the cycle in the front of our house, Vatsala called out 'Hello Siva.' As though under a spell, he came over and sat next to me on the thinnai, while Vatsala stood in the doorway. In a voice pitched loud enough to carry to Vatsala, Siva embarked on a litany of self-praise. He declared that he would go to Madras to watch the cricket test match; that his uncle was in the Middle East; and another uncle worked in Narayan Company. 'So if you want to catch any of the latest movies, just tell me,' he announced.

When Amma called Vatsala into the house, it was as if a light had been switched off in Siva. That's when I spotted the snake. Well, at first I didn't recognize it as a snake, it looked like some kind of extra decoration on Siva's bicycle wheel. A sort of mossy green to complement the darker green of the bicycle, it was curled around the slanting support bar. 'Siva, what is that new decoration you've added to your bike?' I asked.

'Where, da?'

'Look, on the slanting bar in front,' I said. Even before I had finished speaking, it moved. The realization dawned on me that this was no decoration. It was a snake. I could feel my hairs bristle. 'Pa… pa...pa' I stuttered, like Janaka trying to teach the musical scale.

'What?' Sivaraman was still mystified.

'Look there, on your cycle wheel. Pa...pa...paambu.' I managed to say it at last. Paambu. Snake.

Siva couldn't spot it straight away. 'Where, da, where?' he kept asking, glancing the other way towards the Peshkar's house.

'On the cycle...pa...pa...big pa...' I was back to stuttering. Couldn't say paambu. In fact, it took me a while to say, 'Look!' Meanwhile, Sivaraman had also spotted the snake. He was in a quandary about his next course of action, when Vatsala emerged from the house. The need to display valour came to the fore in Sivaraman's mind. 'Vatsala, is there a cricket bat?' he asked.

'Why?' Vatsala wanted to know.

'Pa...pa...pa…' I chimed in.

Sivaraman said: 'Don't be scared, Ranga. You too, Vatsala, no need to panic. A snake has got on to my bicycle.'

Instead of being alarmed as we had expected, Vatsala asked 'Where is it?' She went up closer to inspect it. 'Yes, it is a snake,' she declared definitively.

'Endi, Moodevi, don't go near it, di. It may bite you or something...' I told her.

'Vatsala, you shouldn't go near it,' cautioned Sivaraman. 'Why don't you go and fetch something to kill it with.'

Since my younger sister had walked up close to take a look at the snake, I ventured a further inch and inspected it myself. It was all tangled and twisted like the Sri Lanka issue. While lying there in the middle of the firewood heap in front of Vadhyar's house, who knows what went through its snake mind? Maybe it had decided that the evening hour would be a good time to take a stroll in the open air. And then it couldn't find its way back. And so it climbed onto the bicycle. Bad luck...

'What are you going to do?' asked Vatsala.

'What a question, Vatsala! Of course we're going to beat it to death,' replied Sivaraman.

'Oh, poor thing, da.'

'What do you mean 'poor thing'? If it starts spitting poison then you'll be sorry. Go inside, di. Do as I say. Go and fetch the cricket bat. Don't tell your mother about this, or she'll bring the whole town here.'

As Sivaraman and I were standing there contemplating the snake, the milk depot worker Govindan happened to pass that way. 'What's the matter, Saami?' he enquired.

'Nothing, Govinda, just a snake.'

'Where?' he wanted to know.

'Look here, on the cycle.' By this time the creature had tangled itself up even more; there was a longish interval between the movement of its head and the subsequent movement of its tail.

Govindan threw a stone at the snake. The missile missed its mark, smashed into Naanu Vadhyar's house and shattered to bits.

'Who's throwing bricks?' demanded Vadhyar, emerging from his house.

'There's a snake, sir,' we told him.

He retreated hastily and shut the door. After that no one from the household (wife and four daughters) came out at all. Meanwhile, Vatsala emerged from the house and handed my much-bandaged cricket bat to Sivaraman. He inspected the item and then approached the cycle gingerly.

It soon became very evident that Sivaraman had absolutely no experience of killing snakes. He swung wildly at it as though he wanted to split it in two. The bat missed the snake but landed hard on the bicycle seat. The seat was dislodged and fell to the floor.

The snake had now been alerted to its perilous situation. It speedily untangled itself, slithered to the ground, and wriggled away in an instant into the three-feet-long municipal pipe nearby.

This drain in which the creature had found refuge was just outside our front door where, as a concession to us, the municipality had connected a three-foot-long pipe. Govindan chided Sivaraman, 'Thambi, is that the way to swing the bat? See, now the snake has escaped.'

Sivaraman's attention was on Vatsala as he responded to Govindan. 'Hold on, Govinda...it can't get away. Just don't confuse me, all of you.'

Just then, Thatha shuffled out from inside the house. So further proceedings in the matter of the snake had perforce to be suspended. Thatha was seventy-seven years old. After his retirement, a kind of senility had set in. Then, Paati died, and nowadays, Thatha was often confused about people, places and events. Often, he would not be sure whether he was in Srirangam or still in service in Delhi.

Sometimes he would get my name right... 'What, Ranga,' he'd say. But at other times he would call out to my mother, saying, 'There's someone inside...Oh, it's the butter man who has come.' Of late, he imagined that every day was the day of the Panguni Uthiram festival, and that the procession with temple cars would come down the street. Every evening he would set up the string cot outside the house and sit there waiting for the procession to arrive.

Thatha was now preparing to set up his cot right on top of where the snake had taken refuge in the drain. If the whole story were to be explained to him...about the firewood bought by the neighbour, about how the wood pile had harboured a snake, and about the circumstances leading to the snake's journey into the drain...we would have been at it till dawn! So we decided to just lift the whole cot, Thatha and all, and reposition it on the opposite side. But Thatha noticed that the cot had mysteriously risen upwards and was moving seemingly on its own. 'I'm not yet dead, da,' said Thatha. 'Just sit quietly here, Thatha,' Govindan told him. To which Thatha responded, 'Has the Panguni festival temple car come by yet?'

We, the valorous trio, left Thatha in the care of Vatsala and set about the task of finishing off the snake. Just then who should arrive but 'Pathanna' (Ten Annas) Padmanabha Iyengar. His policy was to 'help' everyone, come what may. He would never take no for an answer. 'Ennada, what's it? A snake?' he asked. 'Yes, maama. Before we could land a blow on it, it wriggled into the drain. We were just debating how to get it out.'

'Is it a 'nalla paambu' (good snake)?' asked Maama. We had no clue what he meant. A 'good' snake?

'Why are you all gaping at me?' admonished Maama, 'If it is a nalla paambu I wouldn't kill it. Because I'd have to do a Shanthihomam afterwards.'

'Well, we don't know whether the snake is a nalla one. We haven't yet asked it that question.

'Ennada, trying to make fun of me or what?'

'No, no, Maama. It was sort of brownish and slimy looking. That's all we know.'

Vatsala chimed in, 'Maama, it didn't look like a nalla paambu at all. I had a good look at it. It looked like some harmless variety. I'd say there's no need to kill it.'

'Shut up, you stupid girl! Look after Thatha properly, that's all you need to do. Don't interfere in men's affairs,' I said to my sister. She made a face at me.

Thatha asked, 'Is the Panguni temple car going to come now?'

Govindan was poking the drain in an exploratory fashion with the long, reed-like rib of a palm leaf. He was going about it in a very gingerly manner, standing well away from the drain and holding the flimsy reed at arm's length as though about to light a firework.

'What is this, Govinda, is this the thinnest stick you could find?' I asked mockingly.

'If I use a thick one...well, I am alone at this end...'

'But that doesn't mean you have to use a delicate reed as though you are going to pick your ear.'

'Well, your highness, you're welcome to try,' retorted Siva.

'Look, you fellows, this kind of thing won't work to make it come out. Patta, go to the DPG store and buy some incense powder. I will get the snake out in no time.' Since quite a few people had gathered at the scene by this time, suggestions and instructions were flying around from all directions and it was difficult to tell straight away who was dispensing this particular piece of advice.

'No need for incense and all that. There's a snake charmer at the donkey stable. He will lure out the snake just by playing his pipe.'

'I hope each of you has kept your own snake safe.'

'De! Want me to give you a slap across the face?'

'When will the Panguni temple car arrive?'

Sivaraman spoke firmly: 'Ranga, you have no experience with this. Go and stand near the thinnai. We will kill the snake. If all you spectators will kindly stand aside and give some space for the snake-killer team, it would be appreciated.'

Padmanabha Iyengar had gone back to his house to fetch a ladle with glowing embers. He arrived at the scene of action, blowing gently on the embers to keep the flame alive. In addition, he was also carrying an umbrella. Patta sped back on Sivaraman's bicycle, having successfully accomplished his mission of going and buying incense from the designated shop. The moment the incense was tossed on the glowing embers, a billowing cloud of fumes arose; Padmanabha Iyengar, holding the smoking ladle like some ancient practitioner of the magic arts, was waving the fumes encouragingly in the direction of the drain with the help of a folded-up copy of the *Dinamani* newspaper; on one side stood Govindan, Patta and Sivaraman, holding a variety of implements to be used as weapons. The whole street was represented in the crowd that stood at a distance of about ten feet, offering advice and suggestions.

That snake must have been in the throes of some dilemma we knew nothing about. Anyway, it did not emerge. By then, the smoke had become a smoke-screen, like the dream sequence in the movie *Awaara*. It was difficult to make out who was whom...was that Thatha...

or was it Patta...?

And why was Padmanabha Iyengar holding up an open umbrella? 'With this much smoke, even a crocodile would have come out by now,' he declared. De, Ranga, did you actually see it go in there?'

'Didn't you see it, Govinda?'

'Actually, there was no snake to see by the time I arrived. Maybe these fellows are making up a snake story,' suggested Govindan.

'Che, che...Saami, I swear I saw it going into the drain,' I assured them. Five thirty in the evening...the Lalgudi passenger train must have just arrived. The office-goers were returning home. Among them was KV. The moment he arrived, he took over leadership of the ongoing catch-the-snake project. He laid his tiffin box on the thinnai. He lifted and tied up his dhoti to reveal the edges of his khaki knickers. 'Where's the snake, da?'

'Here, inside this drain.'

'It's a harmless snake, KV,' said Vatsala. 'There's no need to kill it.'

'Whatever kind of snake it is, it's best to kill it. All of you spectators...stand away or climb on to the thinnai. Ranga, I need a thick stick...bring the one from the clothes line. The drain has to be poked with some force. Your kind of namby-pamby approach is no good. Oy, why are you messing about waving smoke like some sadhu or something? Whom are you trying to propitiate? Go and fetch a stick, da, Ranga. Can't make out the people in the middle of all this smoke...what a silly thing to do...'

When I went into the house to fetch the stick to which the clothes line was tied, my mother asked, 'What's going on, da?' I ran out without answering her.

KV was a fearless fellow. He plunged the entire length of the stick into the drain and prodded vigorously. The blood froze in my veins. I envisioned the creature bursting out BOOOSSSS...from its hiding place and rearing up menacingly to elbow height, with hood spread.

Nothing happened. KV continued to prod the drain as though to break up a major clog in it. Finally he declared, 'There's not even a tiny earthworm in there. Someone has been pulling a fast one on us.'

'No, no, KV. It was on the cycle bar. Sivaraman tried to hit it. It escaped and wriggled into the drain.'

'Sivaraman? Tried to kill a snake? Enda, have you ever even squashed a caterpillar?'

'You're talking big...let's see you do it,' challenged Sivaraman.

'Show it to me and I'll kill it,' declared KV, as he quickly pulled the stick out of the drain and twirled it menacingly in front of Sivaraman. The latter, in momentary shock, took a step backward. KV laughed uproariously. 'And you say this is the fellow who was trying to beat a snake to death?'

KV turned to Padmanabha Iyengar and said, 'Oy, go and light a petromax lamp and bring it back here. It looks like this task will go on into the night.' But just then, KV spotted the snake. It must have emerged from the drain under cover of the convenient smoke screen. Otherwise how did it end up wrapped around the leg of Thatha's string cot? What possible business could it have there?

'Vatsala, don't move. Stand still. Look, it's on the leg of the cot.'

'What, KV?'

'Don't even breathe, don't move a muscle. We will make a bajji of the creature right there.'

'When will the Panguni temple car come?' Thatha wanted to know.

I had expected Vatsala to shriek, leap up in fright and run away. Instead she picked up a stick that lay nearby, and gently manoeuvred the snake from the leg of the cot on to it. Now the snake was dangling at the end of the stick she was holding, half its length hanging to one side and half to the other. Its underside was visible for the first time. It was pale coloured. It looked frightened, and it was darting its tongue, pleech-pleech, in and out of its mouth. It wasn't showing any other signs of aggressiveness.

Vatsala walked over to Sivaraman with the stick bearing the dangling snake. She laughed as she challenged him, 'Here's the snake. Come on, hit it.' Sivaraman, so terrified that he was unaware of his dhoti having slid off, ran away and climbed onto the thinnai in front of Nanu Vadhyar's house. KV was the only one who stood his ground.

'This isn't a game,' he told her sternly. 'Throw the snake down now.' Vatsala swivelled and exhibited the snake in every direction. In each direction in turn, people cowered away as they sighted the snake. Meanwhile, Amma had come out of the house. 'Hey, you monkey,' she called out to Vatsala, 'drop it before it bites you.'

'No, Amma, this looks like a harmless snake. Ranga, fetch a basket. We will get the snake into the basket and go and release it in the forest. There's no need to kill it.'

Just then the snake lost its balance on the stick. It fell to the floor and wriggled away towards the drain. KV snatched up the cricket bat and slammed it hard on the snake.

Vatsala was screaming, 'No, no, please don't KV, please... Don't kill it. What harm has it done? Don't, don't...' KV ignored her wails and pleas; he smashed the bat on the snake again and again. The front of the snake now looked like eggplant paste. The tail, as though clinging on to a cherished memory, waved elegantly and gently a couple of times and then stopped moving. KV went on to hammer that too. He was laughing as he picked up the squashed snake on the stick. They took it to the corner adjoining the temple car shed and consigned it to the flames.

Vatsala was sobbing aloud as she kept repeating, 'Poor thing. What harm did it do to you all? Why did you kill it?' She sobbed for a long time; I was mystified by this reaction from her.

After that, Sivaraman stopped coming by to see Vatsala. And I began to understand my sister better.

AND THEN LAUGHED THE HYENA

SYED MUHAMMAD ASHRAF

Translated from the Urdu by M. Asaduddin

The early hours of the morning. A cold wind was gusting against the darkened windows. Inside, the room was stuffy. The dim glow from a light bulb cast blue shadows everywhere, making the atmosphere mysterious and threatening. Apart from Munnu Bhaiya, everyone else lay awake. Even though everyone was aware of this, nobody spoke about it because of an unknown fear that gripped them. They felt very alone despite the presence of others.

Their hearts were drumming in their chests as though some creature was crawling over them.

Just then, Badi Appi asked in a breathless voice.

'Is it necessary to take Munnu Bhaiya to the zoo to show him a hyena?'

Everyone listening shivered. Badi Appi's voice died away in the bluish gloom. In the silence, you could almost hear the pounding of the hearts of the family who were her audience.

Ammi turned on her side and looked in Badi Appi's direction. She felt that the stuffiness in the room had intensified. The wind outside was blowing harder. She fixed her gaze on Badi Appi's frightened eyes and said in a strange, unnatural tone:

'So what are you suggesting I do? Take him to the jungle…'

'Oh, no. Who's talking about the jungle? Are you awake? Did you hear what I said?' Badi Appi asked tearfully.

'Go to sleep, girl. You must only be half awake to ask such a question. Go to sleep. It's very late.'

Papa, Bhaijan and Chhoti Appi who were silent and awake knew that Appi had not asked that question in her sleep. Ammi herself knew that such questions are only asked when one is wide awake. But no one was going to give Badi Appi's question the seriousness it deserved for fear that Ammi might come up with the right answer. None of them wanted to hear the right answer. Badi Appi herself, having asked the question, prayed fervently for Ammi to stay silent.

Outside, the wind blew fiercely. Everyone seemed to hear a frightening noise, chat-chat…chat-chat…chat-chat…

Hearing the noise their hearts began to beat even harder. They felt the presence of a shadow in the half-dark room. It became difficult to breathe; they cringed under their blankets and fervently hoped that dawn would break soon. Ammi turned and clasped Munnu Bhaiya to her chest in an effort to lessen her own fear. She felt that all this was happening because of Munnu Bhaiya.

For the past ten to fifteen days a hyena had created panic in the villages beyond the railway lines. Every second or third day would bring with it news of some incident involving the animal. When Munnu Bhaiya was told that hyenas like the flesh of small children, he was stricken with terror. He had never seen a live hyena or even its picture. He had just heard its name since childhood. Whenever he heard its name he also heard that it was responsible for the death of children. That is why he was terrified.

That evening he again heard that the hyena had carried off a child from the area beyond the railway lines. His face had turned ashen when he had heard the news, he didn't go out of the house in the evening. Scared, he kept silently pacing up and down. At night, Akhtar Bhai, Bhaijan's friend, tried to calm him down by saying that he would talk to the hyena and ask him not to come to the area. Munnu Bhaiya, who was only eleven or twelve years old, did not have the courage to ask whether a hyena could talk like human beings. He grew even more afraid when he heard that hyenas could. He felt that a hyena was a unique creature, although he had no idea what it looked like. His friends had told him that a hyena was as tall as a high brick wall, and that was how he could cross over walls to carry away children.

Papa and Ammi had told him that a hyena was about the size of a dog but ferocious and wild. Bhaijan, Badi Appi and Chhoti Appi did not say much about the size of hyenas because they had never seen one.

Before going to bed Munnu Bhaiya secretly put a cricket bat and matchbox under the mattress. He had studied in the fourth standard that wild animals are afraid of fire.

Throughout the evening the hyena appeared in his imagination in different shapes and sizes. When he was going to bed these shapes and sizes took on frightening proportions.

Bhaijan got up and checked the bolts of all the doors, closed the windows and called out to the neighbours to warn them. He reassured us saying that there was no need to worry as the hyena would be captured or killed in a day or two. Nevertheless, there was panic in the neighbourhood. People locked themselves into their houses and made sure to keep an eye on their children at all times. The panic was at its height in the houses that were situated near the railway lines. Munnu Bhaiya's house was close to the railway lines.

Munnu Bhaiya, scared, huddled close to Ammi. Papa, once again, went over to the door and checked the bolt and then lay down.

Outside, a hard wind blew through the cold December night. Suddenly, Munnu Bhaiya screamed and the entire house woke up. After that, no one was able to go back to sleep.

'What's it, Munnu Bhaiya…? Why did you scream?' Ammi asked nervously.

'Ammi Ammi…' Munnu Bhaiya hid his face in her body.

'Tell me, beta. Tell me quickly, what happened?' Papa asked.

'Ammi, the hyena…he was standing by me, he bent down and sniffed me.'

'No, Munnu Bhaiya, you must've seen a dream.'

Papa, Bhaijan, Badi Appi and Chhoti Appi gathered around Ammi's bed. It seemed that all the blood had drained from Munnu Bhaiya's face. His eyes were bulging with fear and his lips were dry.

'No, Ammi… I saw him, tall as a brick wall. He bent his long neck, sniffed me and thrust his long horns into my body.'

Everyone gazed at him, excitedly.

Papa said, 'Munnu beta, a hyena is not tall like a brick wall but like a dog in size, and it doesn't have horns. You've just had a terrible dream. Say the kalma prayer before going to sleep.'

'I did, papa. I said the Al-Hamd prayer, too.' Munnu Bhaiya put his head in Ammi's lap and began to cry.

Everyone felt ill at ease. They didn't know how to tell him that it was not the hyena that had frightened him but his fear of it, his imagining of it as a figure of terror.

At that moment Ammi said, 'Munnu beta, let me tell you what a hyena looks like so you are no longer afraid of it.'

Everyone dispersed to their beds, and said hoon or haan in response to what Ammi was saying. This was intended to let Munnu Bhaiya know that everyone was awake and listening to what was being said. The doors and windows rattled in the gusts of wind, adding to the scary atmosphere that had filled the room. They shivered in their beds. Munnu Bhaiya's muffled sobbing heightened their fear. In the mysterious blue light that fell on their frightened faces, Ammi began to talk of the hyena:

'Munnu Bhaiya, a hyena...are you listening to me? A hyena is an animal that looks like a dog. But in a pack of dogs you can identify it easily. It is a mean and violent animal... You can't call it courageous.'

Bhaijan indicated that he understood all this with a long-drawn-out exclamation—hoon. Everyone was listening to Ammi with rapt attention.

'It always attacks innocent young children. It follows people stealthily. Hearing footsteps if you look back, you'd think that a faithful dog is following you...slowly, with his head lowered. But the moment he gets an opportunity...you look away and he pounces on you.'

Having proceeded this far, Ammi herself realized that her voice was beginning to sound strange. Munnu Bhaiya could feel the silent presence of the others, awake and listening.

'Ammi, is there any way to escape his clutches?' Munnu Bhaiya murmured.

'You have to take the right precautions if you want to escape. You shouldn't stay out late. Whenever you are passing a patch of jungle or shrubbery, always carry a sharp weapon. Most of all…if it's dark or foggy, never make the assumption that an animal which looks like a dog is a dog.'

Lying tense and watchful in their beds everyone listened and reflected on what Ammi had just said.

'When night begins to fall, be suspicious of any animal that appears to be a dog… You want to fight it with a cricket bat and a matchbox?… How stupid! Once an innocent child thought he could do exactly that. But when the hyena came, he froze, he couldn't do anything. The hyena pounced on him, locked his jaws on the child's throat, and drank his blood… Then he opened up his stomach, pulled out his entrails,…and tore off large mouthfuls of his flesh and swallowed it.'

'Ammi, Ammi…' Munnu Bhaiya cried out in terror and held his mother tightly.

'Don't be scared. I want to alert you to all the dangers, so you aren't taken by surprise.' Ammi said, seriously.

Outside, a thick mist had descended. The wind roared, it seemed to be having a conversation with the darkness. Inside the stuffy room everyone lay listening to Ammi.

'*Beta, I'm giving you so much detail about the hyena so you are able to take every precaution necessary. It's not courageous like the tiger which attacks from the front. It's a vile animal which pounces on you from behind. He knows that people mistake him for a dog and allow him to come close. Then he waits for an opportunity and when you aren't alert…the moment you become careless…*'

There wasn't a sound in the room, it was so tense. Again you could fancy you could hear the pounding of people's hearts.

'There's just one way you can identify it. When it walks, its claws make a clicking chat-chat sound. But people, sunk in their own thoughts, often do not hear it. That's why it's important that when you see an animal looking like a dog following you and pretending to be as innocent and loyal, then…stop in your tracks and listen carefully whether you can hear the chat-chat sound. But, my dear son, people cannot hear it unless they pay attention.'

Papa, Bhaijan, Badi Appi, Chhoti Appi—all of them felt as if their breathing would stop. All of them thought they could hear the chat-chat sound outside the house.

'Ammi, will you show me a hyena?' Munnu Bhaiya asked. Exhausted by all the tension, and the lateness of the hour, he was falling asleep.

'Of course, this time when we go to Lucknow, you can see it in the zoo. Now go to sleep. It's quite late.'

Ammi fell silent. Munnu Bhaiya was asleep. But Ammi's voice still reverberated in everyone's ears:

'When it's windy or dark, it looks exactly like a dog...pretends to be trustworthy but is very tricky...slinks up to you before you know it and the moment it gets an opportunity...pounces on you. It's very mean and cunning...never makes a frontal attack.'

All those who were awake in that darkened room, faintly lit with the mysterious blue light, were wondering why they had forgotten to utter hoon-haan when Ammi was speaking. They were still wondering about it when it seemed that the light in the room had brightened. Then, an idea struck Badi Appi. She suddenly seemed to get why everyone in the house was so frightened. She realized that everyone except Munnu Bhaiya was awake although they gave no indication that they weren't asleep. The blue light made the room mysterious. The windows rattled in the wind.

Badi Appi asked hesitantly.

'Ammi, is it necessary to take Munnu Bhaiya to the zoo to show him a hyena?'

Everyone else had the same question on their minds.

Why were they thinking that?

They felt that it was only natural that such a question would occur to them. Ammi asked Badi Appi to go to sleep...and then everyone heard the chat-chat sound resound in their heads. It wasn't coming from outside but from within their subconscious.

The long night finally came to an end and their daily routine began. But even as they went about their tasks they realized that the events of the night were still occupying their minds. No matter what it was they were doing, they could feel a mysterious...chat-chat... chat-chat...rising from somewhere—as though a hyena were close by. When Papa and Bhaijan went to work they heard the same sound at various places. The events of the night came to them. When they heard this sound while they were working, they would stop whatever they were doing and look around, scared. But it would be nothing, just a friend standing there. They would try and shrug it off, put the sound out of their heads.

He follows you like a trustworthy dog... The moment he gets the opportunity...pounces on you...doesn't make a frontal attack...vile and deceptive animal...

Badi Appi and Chhoti Appi went to their school. After class, when their friends were chatting and laughing, they heard the mysterious and frightening sound. Chat-chat...chat chat. Agitated, they looked at each other but didn't say anything. What could they say?

In the evening when everybody came home, although everything seemed normal, all of them felt bonded together in a strange sort of way. The way to describe it would be the sort of connection that develops between patients in a hospital ward. A sense of dependence and helplessness binds them. But none of them gave any indication to the others of what they had been feeling all day.

All of them concealed the roiling tension within, pretended everything was normal. But every couple of minutes they seemed to hear the chat-chat sound reverberating in their heads.

Khaja Sahib, Papa's friend, was leaving the house after advising him on a very important business matter. It was dark outside the drawing room. Papa felt that the chat-chat sound was coming from Khaja Sahib's feet as he walked. When Khaja Sahib turned back and told Papa that he would gain immensely if he followed his advice, Papa felt that Khaja Sahib's eyes had turned red and ferocious just like...just like....

Papa threw himself on the bed as soon as his friend left.

A short time later Bhaijan's friend, Akhtar Bhai, arrived. Munnu Bhaiya discussed with him at length how much a big knife would cost. Then Bhaijan asked Munnu Bhaiya to go to the inner room and Akhtar Bhai and he began discussing something.

Chhoti Appi, who was passing, carrying water, paused when she heard what they were saying. Suddenly Bhaijan whispered into Akhtar Bhai's ear, 'You'll profit greatly if you begin this work. I'll assist you wholeheartedly. Friends must help one another. Don't you agree?'

It was a good thing Akhtar Bhai couldn't see Bhaijan's face because had he done so he would have seen that Bhaijan's eyes had become fierce and sharp teeth jutted from his jaw.

When Akhtar Bhai left, Bhaijan saw him out. As he was returning to the house, Chhoti Appi cried out,

'Hyena…the hyena!'

'Where is it?' Bhaijan cried as he entered the house. He stared at her.

'I don't know… Were you coming in from the drawing room? I just heard the sound, chat-chat. Were your feet making that sound?'

'I've no idea', answered Bhaijan. His mind seemed somewhere else.

'I don't know what's happening…he said. God knows, today I've heard this sound coming from the feet of several friends. Just now, when Akhtar left, I heard… Don't know whether I'm imagining it… or probably…'

'Bhaijan…do you also…do you…' Chhoti Appi sounded scared.

'Shut up…please shut up. Don't talk about it.'

Papa and Bhaijan checked the doors several times at Munnu Bhaiya's insistence. And when they lay down to sleep all of them had something to think about. All except Munnu Bhaiya. They thought about their world, about their friends…about thousands of people they knew…and then…they thought about themselves.

Outside, the cold wind picked up. The people in the house were lost in an unpleasant reverie. They began thinking about things in the remote past that had been buried deep down, hidden. They felt something was crawling down their gullets. In their trance-like state they saw a jungle spreading deep into the gloom, in which many doglike creatures were roaming. Munnu Bhaiya, who was asleep, turned on his side violently, and the sound drew everyone back to the room.

Their hearts began to flutter. It seemed to them that the clock hanging from the wall had just come alive...tick tick...tick tick...

The ticking of the clock, the hissing of the wind and the beating of their hearts blended together to form the frightening sound—chat-chat. Everyone felt that just as there was a jungle outside the windows so also was there one inside. Lying in the jungle enclosed by walls, everyone remembered the previous night...follows silently like a dog... Ammi had remarked.

Everyone kept thinking...reflected on their own lives...kept on reflecting.... Everyone was awake and they knew that the others, too, were awake.

The whistle of the night watchmen could be heard from a distance. The terrifying darkness of the night slithered outside the window...

In the morning, when Papa got up before everyone else, a strange thing happened. He felt as though his feet were making the sound, chat-chat. Startled, he stopped in his tracks. As he took a step forward he heard the same noise. He stopped and looked at Ammi who was standing and looking down at her own feet.

'You, too...' Papa said...

'Yes.' Ammi replied in a tearful voice.

Both of them stared at each other. After a little while Badi Appi came over to Ammi and said in a hesitant, scared voice that she was hearing the chat-chat sound coming from her feet. Ammi looked at Papa helplessly and tried to comfort Badi Appi:

'Beti, don't worry, it's a delusion. Because of Munnu Bhaiya, since yesterday we have been able to think of nothing but the hyena. But there's no truth to it. Really.'

'Are you sure, Ammi?' Chhoti Appi, who was standing near Ammi, asked.

'Yes, beti. There's no truth to this... Not at all...' Papa said.

Chhoti Appi had just opened her mouth to say something when Bhaijan got up from his bed, took one or two steps forward and then stopped. He was looking at his feet in such a way that it seemed he was listening for something. Then he walked a few steps more and stopped again and paused to listen. Everyone looked at him, then looked at each other. Everything grew quiet.

Just then, the family servant came running. Panting for breath, he said that a hyena had been caught in the neighbouring village the previous night… The villagers were planning to take him to the town. They would pass our house in a little while.

If he had expected his announcement to come as a surprise or create a ruckus he was disappointed. None of us seemed in the least bit surprised by his news. Disappointed, he left.

The family just kept standing there silently. It was as though they were waiting for something to happen even though they were scared. Finally, when Munnu Bhaiya woke up, their wait was over. Munnu Bhaiya jumped up and asked in a groggy but restless voice,

'Why are you all standing around like this? Has the hyena come?'

'No, beta. The hyena has been caught. Now you needn't be afraid of it.'

Saying this Papa took Munnu Bhaiya to the inner room. He gave him some toffees and asked him,

Bhaiya, when you walk, do you hear the sound chat-chat coming from your feet?

Munnu Bhaiya seemed stunned by the question.

'Beta, tell me quickly… Do you hear the sound coming from your feet?'

'No, Papa. Why do you ask? Am I a hyena?' Munnu Bhaiya said.

Right at that moment they heard a noise outside. Everyone rushed to the window. A hyena was walking down the path, surrounded by hundreds of villagers. A muzzle was clamped over his powerful jaws, and there were chains on his feet. His eyes were red and he was trying to rip the muzzle off. Wounds striped his hide and his front paws were soaked in blood.

Papa, Ammi, Bhaijan, Badi Appi, Chhoti Appi—all looked at their own hands stealthily and kept on looking at them for a long while—it wasn't clear why. Now the hyena was passing by the window. The chat-chat sound of his feet could be heard clearly. Behind him were the villagers, armed with lathis and spears. Suddenly the beast stopped right outside our window. The chat-chat sound stopped. The people following him stopped. The dust slowly settled. The members of the family found it difficult to breathe as they peeped out of the window. Munnu Bhaiya clutched Ammi's feet. The crowd outside fell silent. The hyena looked at the window for a long moment. Then he broke into frenzied, maniacal laughter. His captors thought the sound meant he was making a determined effort to get rid of the muzzle. A villager struck him hard with a stick from behind and said in a voice filled with hate... '*Bastard, he steals up to people pretending to be a dog and then pounces the moment he gets a chance...*'

The savage blow brought tears to the hyena's eyes... He took a long, hard look at the villager... Then his moist eyes took in the members of the family, one by one. That terrifying laugh burst forth once more and he moved on, surrounded by the crowd, the chat-chat sound marking their passage.

Papa stood at the window looking out. The crowd accompanying the hyena had not yet disappeared entirely. The dust kicked up by them still filled the air. Through it, he could see Munnu Bhaiya talking to his friends as they set off for school.

Papa felt that Munnu Bhaiya had suddenly stopped and was looking at his feet. It was as though he was trying to listen for something. Papa closed his eyes and prayed to God that the chat-chat sound might never rise from the feet of Munnu Bhaiya and those of his friends.

When Munnu Bhaiya and his friends disappeared from view, Papa clutched the iron bars of the window and gazed out at the world that spread beyond the railway lines, silently reflecting on everything that had taken place. When he finally turned around, he saw the members of the family sitting silently. They looked sad and disappointed with themselves. It was as though they had heard about the outbreak of an epidemic. They looked at each other shamefacedly. Ammi sighed deeply. Then everyone stood up and went about their work...

ACKNOWLEDGEMENTS

Grateful acknowledgement is made to the following copyright holders for permission to reprint copyrighted material in this volume.

'Mahesh' by Sarat Chandra Chattopadhyay translated by Arunava Sinha is extracted from *The Greatest Bengali Stories Ever Told*, selected and translated by Arunava Sinha (Aleph, 2016); reprinted with permission of the translator.

'A Tale of Two Bullocks' by Premchand. Translated by Rohit Manchanda. Reprinted by permission of the translator.

'Jumman' by Shripad Narayan Pendse. Copyright © Aniruddha Shripad Pendse. Translated by Shanta Gokhale. Reprinted by permission of Aniruddha Shripad Pendse and the translator.

'The Flood' by Thakazhi Sivasankara Pillai. Copyright © Balakrishnan Nair. Translated by O. V. Usha. Reprinted by permission of Balakrishnan Nair and the translator.

'The Mark of Vishnu' by Khushwant Singh. Copyright © Mala Dayal. Reprinted by permission of Mala Dayal.

'Bulbuls' by Habib Kamran. Copyright © Azad Ahmad and Aneesa Batul. Translated by Neerja Mattoo. Reprinted by permission of the author's estate and the translator.

'A Horse and Two Goats' by R. K. Narayan. Copyright © Bhuvaneshwari Srinivasamurthy. Reprinted in arrangement with Indian Thought Publications.

'The Copper-tailed Skink' by Manjula Padmanabhan. Copyright © Manjula Padmanabhan. Reprinted by permission of the author.

'The Last Tiger' by Ruskin Bond. Copyright © Ruskin Bond. Reprinted by permission of the author.

'The Owlet Who Craved the Sun' by Achyutananda Pati.

Copyright © Achyutananda Pati. Translated by Shaswat Panda. Reprinted by permission of the author and translator.

'The Crocodile and the Monkey' by Vikram Seth. Copyright © Vikram Seth. Reprinted by permission of the author.

'Labour' by R. R. Borade. Copyright © R. R. Borade. Translated by Anjali Nerlekar. Reprinted by permission of the author and translator.

'The Reflections of a Hen in her last Hour' by Paul Zacharia. Copyright © Paul Zacharia. Translated by A. J. Thomas. Reprinted by permission of the author and translator.

'The Summer of the Crows' is extracted from *The Wildings* by Nilanjana Roy (Aleph, 2012). Copyright © Nilanjana Roy. Reprinted by permission of the author.

'Poonachi' is extracted from *Poonachi: Or the Story of a Black Goat* by Perumal Murugan (Context, an imprint of Westland Publications Private Limited, 2018). Copyright © Perumal Murugan. Translated by N. Kalyan Raman. Reprinted under a license arrangement originating with Westland Publications Private Limited.

'A Tale of Animals' by Moti Lal Kemmu is extracted from *Pashugatha*. Copyright © The Estate of Moti Lal Kemmu. Translated by Siddhartha Gigoo and Tej K. Zadoo. Reprinted by permission of the author's estate and translators.

'Elephant at Sea' by Kanishk Tharoor. Copyright © Kanishk Tharoor. Reprinted by permission of the author.

'Snake' by Sujatha. Copyright © The Estate of S. Rangarajan. Translated by Malini Seshadri. Reprinted by permission of Sujatha Rangarajan and translator.

'And Then Laughed the Hyena' by Syed Muhammad Ashraf. Copyright © Syed Muhammad Ashraf. Translated by M. Asaduddin. Reprinted by permission of the author and translator.

We regret any errors or omissions in the above list of acknowledgements and would like to be notified of any corrections that should be incorporated in future editions of this book.

NOTES TO THE STORIES

Sumana Roy: An Animal on Animals

p. ix Indian writers about animals: I have defined 'animal' as any member of the taxonomic kingdom 'Animalia'.

p. xiii George Orwell's 'Shooting the Elephant': Purists might be a bit startled to find 'Shooting the Elephant' classified as fiction but there are some knowledgeable observers of Orwell's work (including his biographer, Bernard Crick) who doubted whether Orwell had actually shot an elephant. Others, among them his wife, Sonia Brownell, believe he did shoot an elephant, thereby classifying his essay as non-fiction. In this collection, we have chosen to abide by Crick's take on the matter—*The Guardian* (18 March 2017) reported that the biographer felt that 'he (Orwell) was merely influenced by a fashionable genre that blurred the line between fiction and autobiography'.

Rudyard Kipling: Rikki-Tikki-Tavi

Although Rudyard Kipling's political views have been widely discredited for being racist and imperialist, some of his greatest creative work is relatively free of such biases. 'Rikki-Tikki-Tavi', one of his best-loved stories, is excerpted from his 1894 anthology, *The Jungle Book*, which follows the adventures of a young Indian mongoose and the lengths he must go to in order to protect his adoptive human family. Kipling and Orwell are included in this collection of Indian stories about animals because both of them were born in India and the stories in this collection are set in British India.

Sarat Chandra Chattopadhyay: Mahesh

Sarat Chandra is one of the finest writers of fiction in the Bengali language. 'Mahesh' was first published in 1926.

Premchand: A Tale of Two Bullocks

Originally titled 'Do Bailon ki Katha' in Hindi, this story was published in 1931 and since then, has appeared in a number of collections including the comprehensive eight-volume book of Premchand's stories, *Mansarovar*.

p. 31 the phrase 'the calf's uncle': Strictly, in Hindi, 'the heifer's uncle', an idiom meaning dolt, fool, etc.

p. 33 a bit of oil-cake, bey?: bey resists translation. It is a term of address that signifies contempt, on the lines of the archaic 'sirrah'.

Shripad Narayan Pendse: Jumman

'Jumman' first appeared in the short story collection *Jumman*, published by Mouj Prakashan in 1956.

George Orwell: Shooting an Elephant

This story was first published in the literary magazine *New Writing* in 1936.

Thakazhi S. Pillai: The Flood

Titled 'Vellappokkathil' (In the Flood) in Malayalam, the setting for the story is Thakazhi's Kuttanad, which is periodically ravaged by floods.

Khushwant Singh: The Mark of Vishnu

This story was first published in 1950 in *The Mark of Vishnu and Other Stories.*

Habib Kamran: Bulbuls

'Bulbul' appeared in a volume of stories titled *Aevil Baana,* published by the author in 1994.

R. K. Narayan: A Horse and Two Goats

Although R. K. Narayan's most famous piece of fiction featuring an animal is the novel *A Tiger for Malgudi*, we picked this story in which animals are rather more peripheral for its brilliance as a short story. It was first published in *The Hindu* in 1960.

Manjula Padmanabhan: The Copper-tailed Skink

'The Copper-tailed Skink' explores the exploits of an English scientist in India struggling with the local culture and traditions. It was a part of the author's collection of short stories *Hot Soup, Cold Soup: Twelve Short Stories* (1996).

Ruskin Bond: The Last Tiger

This stand-alone novella was first published in 1971. Since then, it has been widely anthologized, including in *Unhurried Tales* (Aleph, 2017). The author has called the story one of his favourites.

Achyutananda Pati: The Owlet Who Craved the Sun

This short story was originally entitled 'Asubha Putra ra Kahani' in Odia and first appeared in an eponymous collection of short stories. The story explores the tragic consequences of idealism.

Vikram Seth: The Crocodile and the Monkey

This is the first tale from *Beastly Tales from Here and There* (1992)—a collection of animal fables in poetry. The author tells us how this tale took shape: 'Because it was very hot in my house one day and I could not concentrate on my work, I decided to write a summer story involving mangoes and a river. By the time I had finished writing "The Crocodile and the Monkey"...another story and other animals had begun stirring in my mind. And so it went on until all ten of these beastly tales had been born—or reborn.'

R. R. Borade: Labour

This story was originally published in the anthology of short stories by R. R. Borade titled *Vaalvan* in 1970. The translator would like to thank Mr Chandrakant Patil for help with the translation.

Paul Zacharia: The Reflections of a Hen in Her Last Hour

The original Malayalam story entitled 'Oru Pidakkozhiyude Aasannamaranachintakal' was first published on 12 April 1981 in *Kalakaumudi Weekly*. The writer has noted that 'it is believed that a jackal will come and sit down under a tree on which a hen is perched and fix its gaze on it. In our land, the saying goes that if the hen's eye catches the jackal's eye, the hen will swoon and fall down into the jaws of the waiting jackal.'

Nilanjana Roy: The Summer of the Crows

This extract is from Roy's acclaimed novel, *The Wildings* (Aleph, 2012) for which she won the Shakti Bhatt First Book Prize in 2013 and was nominated for the Commonwealth Book Prize 2013. The novel follows the exploits of a small band of cats living in the labyrinthine alleys and ruins of Nizamuddin.

Perumal Murugan: Poonachi

This extract is from the English translation of Perumal Murugan's recent bestselling novel, *Poonachi* (2018). Like many stories about animals, the author uses his protagonist as a means to comment on inequalities based on class and colour in Indian society. The novel also criticizes the prevailing intolerance in the country. The author says in his preface that 'I am fearful of writing about humans; even more fearful of writing about gods... Goats are problem-free, harmless and above all, energetic. Therefore, I've chosen to write about goats.'

Moti Lal Kemmu: A Tale of Animals

First published in 2002, this story was a part of the late author's self-published Hindi novella entitled *Pashugatha*. The story is an Orwellian allegory on contemporary Kashmir, in which animals become a central part of the politics and violence brewing in the region.

Kanishk Tharoor: Elephant at Sea

This story is based on a tale told to the author when he was a child by a diplomat friend of his parents. He has always believed the story was true although he hasn't been able to confirm its veracity.

Sujatha: Snake

Originally entitled 'Paambu' in Tamil, this story was first published in

Srirangathu Kathaikal in 2003, a collection of fourteen stories set in the author's native town, Srirangam.

Syed Muhammad Ashraf: And Then Laughed the Hyena
This story is one of three tales on the hyena by Syed Muhammad Ashraf—'And Then Laughed the Hyena', 'The Hyena Cried' and 'The Hyena Fell Silent'—where the shadow of the hyena is omnipresent in the narrative, until man and animal become one and it is difficult to tell who is more dangerous.

NOTES ON THE AUTHORS

Syed Muhammad Ashraf (born 1957) is an Urdu novelist and a short story writer of great distinction. He has published two novels and several collections of short stories. Several of his stories have been translated into English and other Indian and world languages. He received a Sahitya Akademi Award in 2006 for his collection *Waiting for the Morning Breeze.*

Ruskin Bond (born 1934) wrote his first novel, *The Room on the Roof,* when he was seventeen, for which he won the John Llewellyn Rhys Memorial Prize in 1957. Since then he has written several novels (including *Tales of Fosterganj*, *A Flight of Pigeons* and *Delhi Is Not Far*), essays, poems and children's books. He has also written over 500 short stories and articles that have appeared in a number of magazines and anthologies (notably *A Gathering of Friends*, *Small Towns, Big Stories*, *Unhurried Tales*, and *Upon an Old Wall Dreaming*). He received the Sahitya Akademi Award in 1993 and the Padma Shri in 1999.

R. R. Borade (born 1940) started his career as a writer through a story published in the Marathi newspaper *Sakal*. He has written over fifteen novels, seven short story collections and thirteen plays and has been the recipient of numerous awards for his work: the Bhairu Ratan Award (1989); the Marathwada Gaurav Award (2001); the Jayawant Dalwi Award (2003); and the Sadashiv Kulli Memorial Award (2011).

Sarat Chandra Chattopadhyay (1876–1938) was a famous Bengali short story writer and novelist of the late nineteenth and early twentieth centuries. His notable works include *Devdas*, *Srikanta*, *Choritrohin*, etc.

His powerful portrayals of human and economic distress, colonialism and middle-class life continue to be widely read, translated and adapted into films.

Habib Kamran (1927–2007) worked in the School Education Department of Jammu and Kashmir Government as a teacher/administrator. He started his literary career as a novelist, but did not publish anything in his lifetime except a collection of Kashmiri short stories, *Aevil Baana*. His short stories have been published in anthologies and literary journals in the original Kashmiri as well as in English translation.

Moti Lal Kemmu (1933–2018) wrote twelve plays in Kashmiri, one in Hindi, a novel in Hindi and a book in Kashmiri on folk theatre and the culture of Kashmir. He received the Sahitya Akademi Award in 1982, Sangeet Natak Akademi Award in 1997, and the Padma Shree in 2012.

Rudyard Kipling (1865–1936) was born in Bombay, India. He wrote *The Jungle Book* in 1894. His other works include *The Second Jungle Book*, *Just So Stories* and *Kim*. He won the Nobel Prize for Literature in 1907, the youngest writer to be awarded the honour.

Perumal Murugan (born 1966) is the author of seven novels, four collections of short stories and four anthologies of poetry in Tamil. His most recent novel, *Poonachi* (2018), was nominated for numerous awards including the Hindu Prize for Fiction, 2018 and the JCB Prize for Literature. He was a professor of Tamil at the Government Arts College in Namakkal before taking to writing full-time.

R. K. Narayan (1906–2001) is one of the most prominent Indian novelists of the twentieth century. Born in 1906, Narayan was a recipient of the Sahitya Akademi Award in 1958, the A.C. Benson Medal by the (British) Royal Society of Literature in 1982 and the Padma Vibhushan—India's second-highest civilian honour—in 2001.

His numerous works include *Swami and Friends, The Man-Eater of Malgudi, The Vendor of Sweets, The Guide, A Horse and Two Goats, Waiting for the Mahatma* and *Gods, Demons and Others.*

George Orwell (1903–1950) was the pseudonym of Eric Arthur Blair, born in Motihari (Bihar) in British India. He was a prominent English novelist, essayist, journalist and critic, famous for his dystopian novels on totalitarian regimes, *Animal Farm* (1945) and *Nineteen Eighty-Four* (1949).

Manjula Padmanabhan (born 1953) is a writer and artist. Her comic strips appeared weekly in the *Sunday Observer* (1982-86) and daily in the *Pioneer* (1991-97). Her books include *Hot Death, Cold Soup* (1996), *Getting There* (1999) *This is Suki!* (2000), and *Kleptomania* (2004). *Harvest*, her fifth play, won the 1997 Onassis Award for Theatre. Manjula has illustrated twenty-four books for children including her own novels for children.

Achyutananda Pati (born 1927) is a renowned writer of fiction and short stories in Odia. His writings are popular and have been included in school and college curricula. He is a recipient of numerous honours and awards, among which are the Odisha Sahitya Akademi Award in 1983, the Atibadi Jagannath Das Puruskar in 2015 and the Sarala Award (the highest literary award in Odisha) in 2013.

Shripad Narayan Pendse (1913-2007), popularly known as Shri Na Pendse, was a celebrated Marathi novelist. His novel, *Rathachakra*, received the Sahitya Akademi Award in 1963. As part of the UNESCO Collection of Representative Works, in collaboration with the Sahitya Akademi, his novel, *Garambicha Bapu*, was translated into English as *Wild Bapu of Garambi* in 1969. His short story collection, entitled *Jumman*, was published in 1956, and his autobiography, *Shri Na Pendse-Manus Ani Lekhak*, in 1974.

Thakazhi Sivasankara Pillai (1912–1999) was a Malayalam novelist and short-story writer, popularly known as Thakazhi, after his place of birth. He wrote several novels and over 600 short stories. His most famous works are the novels *Chemmeen* (1956) and *Kayar* (1978), for which he won India's highest literary award, the Jnanpith in 1984.

Munshi Premchand (1880–1936) was a pioneer of modern Hindi and Urdu fiction. He wrote nearly 300 stories and novels. Among his best known novels are *Sevasadan*, *Rangmanch*, *Gaban*, *Nirmala* and *Godan*. Much of Premchand's best work is to be found in his 250 or so short stories, collected in Hindi under the title *Mansarovar*.

Nilanjana Roy (born 1971) spent most of her adult life writing about humans before realizing that animals were much more fun. She was the recipient of the Shakti Bhatt First Book prize 2013 for her bestselling debut novel, *The Wildings*. She also published a sequel to the book entitled *The Hundred Names of Darkness* in 2013.

Vikram Seth (born 1952) is the acclaimed author of three novels, *The Golden Gate*, *An Equal Music* and *A Suitable Boy*, one of the most beloved and widely read books of recent times. He has also published several books of poetry, an opera libretto, a book of other libretti, and two highly regarded works of non-fiction, *From Heaven Lake* and *Two Lives*. He is presently at work on *A Suitable Girl*.

Khushwant Singh (1915–2014) was, arguably, India's best-known and most widely read author, columnist and journalist. He was the founder-editor of *Yojana*, and editor of the *Illustrated Weekly of India*, *National Herald* and *Hindustan Times*. He wrote several books, including the novels *Train to Pakistan*, *I Shall Not Hear the Nightingale* and *Delhi*; his autobiography, *Truth, Love & a Little Malice*; and the two-volume *A History of the Sikhs*. He also translated from the Hindi, Urdu and Punjabi. Khushwant Singh was a member of the Rajya Sabha from 1980 to 1986. In 2007, he was awarded India's second highest civilian honour, the Padma Vibhushan.

Kanishk Tharoor (born 1984) is a writer based in New York City. His work has appeared in several international and Indian publications; his short fiction was nominated for a National Magazine Award in 2009. He studied at Yale, where he graduated magna cum laude and Phi Beta Kappa with BAs in History and Literature, and at Columbia, where he was a FLAS fellow in Persian and South Asian studies.

Sujatha (1935–2008) was the pseudonym of the Tamil writer, S. Rangarajan. Rangarajan was a polymath, well-versed in writing fiction and screenplays in several genres including crime fiction and science fiction. He is the author of over 100 novels, 250 short stories, ten books on science, ten stage plays, and a book of poems. He received an award from the Government of India's National Council for Science and Technology in 1993. Rangarajan used his wife's name, Sujatha, as his pen name. Several famous movies such as *Enthiran* and *Dil Se* are based on his screenplays.

Paul Zacharia (born 1945) is an eminent Malayalam fiction writer and essayist. He was awarded the Sahitya Akademi Award in 2004 for his short-story collection, *Zachariyayute Kathakal*, and is a distinguished fellow of the Kerala Sahitya Akademi. His works that have been translated into English include *Bhaskara Pattelar and Other Stories*, *Reflections of a Hen in Her Last Hour and Other Stories* and *Paul Zacharia: Two Novellas*. He is also the author of *A Secret History of Compassion*, a novel in English.

NOTES ON THE TRANSLATORS

M. Asaduddin (born 1958) is an author, critic and translator in several languages, and writes on syncretic cultural traditions in India, literature and language politics. Among his fourteen books are: *Image and Representation: Stories of Muslim Lives in India* (with Mushirul Hasan, OUP, 2000), *Filming Fiction: Tagore, Premchand and Ray* (OUP, 2012) and *Premchand in World Languages: Translation, Reception and Cinematic Representations* (Routledge, 2016). He is a regular speaker at literary and cultural festivals in India and abroad and has received the following awards: Katha Award (1991 and 1992), Dr A. K. Ramanujan Award (1993), Sahitya Akademi Award (2004) and the Crossword Book Award (2013).

Siddhartha Gigoo (born 1974) is the author of *The Garden of Solitude*, *A Fistful of Earth and Other Stories* (longlisted for the Frank O'Connor International Short Story Award 2015) and *Mehr*. He is the recipient of the Commonwealth Short Story Prize for Asia, 2015. His two short films, *The Last Day* and *Goodbye, Mayfly*, have won several awards at international film festivals. He also co-edited *A Long Dream of Home (The Persecution, Exodus and Exile of Kashmiri Pandits)* and *Once We Had Everything (Literature in Exile)*. He was longlisted for the Royal Society of Literature's V. S. Pritchett Short Story Prize, 2018.

Shanta Gokhale (born 1939) is a novelist, editor, translator, playwright, columnist and performing arts critic. Her two novels in Marathi, *Rita Welinkar* and *Tya Varshi*, won the Maharashtra State Award for the best novel of the year in 1992 and 2005, respectively. She translated her novels into English as *Rita Welinkar* and *Crowfall*. She has also translated many works of Marathi drama into English, most notably the plays of Vijay Tendulkar, G. P. Deshpande and Mahesh Elkunchwar. Her translations of Marathi literature and involvement with Marathi theatre have greatly helped to introduce the Marathi literary world to the non-Marathi reader. She was awarded the Sangeet Natak Akademi Award in 2016 for her overall contribution to the performing arts.

Rohit Manchanda (born 1964) has written two award-winning novels, *In the Light of the Black Sun* and *A Place in Mind*. He has also authored a history of IIT Bombay, the institute where he lives and works.

Neerja Mattoo (born 1938) taught English in the Government College for Women, Srinagar, from which she retired as principal. She was awarded a British Council Visitorship to the University of Oxford and the HRD Ministry's Senior Fellowship in Literature to work on Kashmiri women poets. She has published three books of translations of Kashmiri short stories into English—*The Stranger Beside Me*, *Contemporary Kashmiri Short Stories* and *Kath: Stories From Kashmir*. She has also published a well known cookbook, *Sal: A Feast of Kashmiri Cuisine*.

Anjali Nerlekar (born 1962) is an associate professor in the Department of African, Middle Eastern and South Asian Languages and Literatures (AMESALL) at Rutgers University, with research interests in global modernisms, Indian print cultures, Marathi literature, Indo-Caribbean literature, spatial and cartographic studies, and translation studies. She is the author of *Bombay Modern: Arun Kolatkar and Bilingual Literary Culture*. She has also created an ongoing collection of documents and manuscripts related to English and Marathi Bombay poetry entitled *The Bombay Poets' Archive*.

Shaswat Panda (born 1991) teaches English literature at North Orissa University, Keonjhar Campus, in Odisha. He is a researcher and translator.

N. Kalyan Raman is a translator of contemporary Tamil fiction and poetry. He has so far published twelve volumes of Tamil fiction in translation. He received the annual Iyal Award for translation from the Tamil Literary Garden of Toronto, Canada, for *Farewell, Mahatma* in 2015, his translation of a collection of short stories by Devibharathi. In February 2017, he received the Pudumaipithan Award for his contribution to Tamil literature. Most recently, he was shortlisted for the Hindu Prize for Fiction, 2018, and the JCB Prize for Literature, 2018, for his translation of Perumal Murugan's *Poonachi* and for the Crossword Book Awards, 2018 for his translation of a collection of short stories by Perumal Murugan, *The Goat Thief*. Kalyan Raman lives and works in Chennai.

Malini Seshadri (born 1946) is a Chennai-based writer, editor and translator of Tamil works.

Arunava Sinha (born 1962) translates classic, modern and contemporary Bengali fiction and non-fiction into English. Nearly fifty of his translations have been published so far. He selected and translated *The Greatest Bengali Stories Ever Told*. Twice the winner of the Crossword Translation Award, for Sankar's *Chowringhee* (2007) and Anita Agnihotri's *Seventeen* (2011), he has also won the Muse India award for his translation of *When the Time is Right* by Buddhadeva Bose (2012) and been shortlisted for The Independent Foreign Fiction prize (2009) for his translation of *Chowringhee*. Besides India, his translations have been published in the UK, US, Europe and Asia through further translation. He grew up in Kolkata and lives in New Delhi.

A. J. Thomas (born 1952) is an Indian English poet, fiction writer, translator and editor. He is an acclaimed translator of poetry, fiction, drama and non-fiction prose from his mother tongue Malayalam, with more than 20 titles to his credit including: *Keshavan's Lamentations* (2006), *Reflections of a Hen in Her Last Hour and Other Stories* (1998) and *Like A Psalm...*(2017). He has been the recipient of the Katha Award for translation in 1993, the AKMG Prize in 1997 and the Vodafone Crossword Award in 2007.

O. V. Usha (born 1948) has worked as an editor with Tata McGraw-Hill and Vikas, in Delhi. She is a well-known Malayalam writer and has published four collections of poems, a novel, a collection of short stories and five collections of non-fiction. She lives in Santhigiri Ashram, Trivandrum.

Tej K. Zadoo (born 1947) is a retired professor of Physics, and has translated the Shaiva texts *Parapraveshika* into English and *Pratibhignya Hridyam* into Hindi. His research papers have appeared in several scientific journals.